The Lost Horse

by Lee Lowry

iUniverse®

THE LOST HORSE

Artwork by Amy Lowry
Graphic design by Jenny Sandrof, Blue Heron Design Group
Poems adapted from works by Allen Rozelle, with kind permission of the poet

For more information about this and other books by Lee Lowry, contact the author's website: www.leelowryauthor.com

iUniverse books may be ordered through booksellers or by contacting:

iUniverse
1663 Liberty Drive
Bloomington, IN 47403
www.iuniverse.com
1-800-Authors (1-800-288-4677)

ISBN: 978-1-4917-9836-2 (sc)
ISBN: 978-1-4917-9838-6 (hc)
ISBN: 978-1-4917-9837-9 (e)

Library of Congress Control Number: 2016908432

Print information available on the last page.
iUniverse rev. date: 06/17/2016

For Gordon and Nancy

Prologue

September, 2000

The school's music director sang *Ave Maria* for the assembled mourners and finished the hymn in tears. David Perry's eyes streamed as well as he took back the microphone. "Thank you, Alice," he said as they hugged. "That was so beautiful. It was so Sandie."

He looked out at the gathering of friends, students and fellow teachers who had come to honor the memory of his late wife. "With all my heart, I thank you for coming. I want to close this service by telling a Taoist story called *The Lost Horse*:

> "Once upon a time, along the northern border of China, there lived a man skilled in foretelling the future, and his son. One day their mare ran off over the border. The son went to his father, bewailing the family disaster. His father suggested that it was perhaps a blessing.
>
> "A week later the mare returned, bringing with her a magnificent black stallion. The son rushed to his father with the news of their good fortune. The father suggested that it was perhaps a catastrophe.
>
> "The son soon learned to ride the powerful stallion. One day the horse threw him, and he broke his hip. He dragged himself to his father, bemoaning his fate. His father looked at him compassionately and asked how he could be sure it wasn't a blessing.
>
> "Several months later, barbarians attacked the border towns. Imperial officers were sent into all the villages to conscript the able-bodied men. The son, who was lame, was not taken into the army. In the war that followed, nine out of every ten Chinese soldiers were killed.
>
> "And so disasters turn into blessings and blessings into disasters. The wheel of life is always in motion."

July, 2003

Which Way?

Right, been down this road before.
Still can't read the signs, for fear
Of missing a turn, hitting the brakes
And being sideswiped or rammed from the rear.

Inner wipers work most of the time
Though sudden storm bursts blur my sight.
Have to concentrate, stay in the lane,
Avoid the cops, keep to my right.

Not wanting to go there doesn't help.
Fearing the final destination can't prevent
The mindless errands on the way
Just in case a sudden detour is Life's intent.

How long have I been on this road?
How far have we gone?
Would I could stop and check a map,
But I'm scared I'd find myself alone.

Chapter 1

Of all the medical appointments she had lined up in Boston, Jenny Longworth expected her annual GYN checkup to be the simplest. Having reached her late fifties, Jenny took a no-nonsense approach to aging and dismissed her recent problems as a normal post-menopausal nuisance. A solid New Englander, she was disinclined to worry about things unless given a good reason to do so.

Despite her new status as a resident of Switzerland, Jenny declined to give up the health care providers she had counted on throughout her prior life in the US.

Jenny's husband, David Perry, taught seventh and eighth grade at Geneva's prestigious Académie Internationale. He still had a week to go before school was out, so Jenny arranged to fly to Boston ahead of him, allowing time to get her medical appointments out of the way – the GYN visit, an eye exam, a dental cleaning, and a follow-up scan for the thyroid cancer that had been successfully treated six years earlier.

Though they had known each other for decades, Jenny and David had been married for just eighteen months. They had dated in college and briefly shared a post-graduation adventure in Paris, but fate steered them in different directions, with David settling permanently in Europe and Jenny returning to Boston. Despite the geographic distance, they remained close. Over time, their friendship expanded to include David's French wife, Sandie, and the couple's two children, Marc and Delphine.

When Sandie succumbed to breast cancer at the age of fifty-two, Jenny flew to David's side to offer her strength and her sympathy. Their long-ago romance was unexpectedly rekindled, and David ultimately asked Jenny to come live with him in Geneva. Saying yes, she had an odd sense of her world coming full circle. *We did the right thing all those years ago, following our separate paths, but here we are, back together again. And this time, I'm staying with him no matter what,* she promised herself.

"Jenny and I have known each other since the memory of man runneth not to the contrary," David wrote when he announced their marriage to far-away friends. "The kids and I were in desperate need of support during Sandie's illness and after her death, and Jenny was there for us in innumerable ways. She and I have a well-seasoned affection for one another. We just sort of followed our intuition, and there you have it."

Jenny had smiled at David's description. *David is many things,* she considered. *Bright. Gracious. Articulate. Capable of charming guests at a Country Club dinner, and equally at home at a roadside ribs stand, fingers dripping with barbecue sauce. But there is one talent he definitely lacks: romantic language.*

David's discomfort with what he dismissed as "mush" had not substantially altered since their marriage. Rather than complain, however, Jenny found ways to circumvent his reticence. Before leaving for Boston, she sent an e-mail that he wouldn't see until she was in the air.

From: JWLongworth
To: DavidP
Date: June 22, 2003
Subject: I love you

The best thing about my preceding you to the States is that it gives me an excuse to send you gooey love letters. After living with you for almost two years, you'd think I would no longer feel like a newlywed, but the love just deepens.

I have my book to distract me on the plane, but my thoughts will be with you.

See you next Saturday. J.

David's reply awaited her when she walked into the condo she had kept as a *pied-à-terre* in Shawmut, a leafy suburb just south of Boston.

De: David
A: Jenny
Envoyé: 23 juin, 2003
Objet: Re: I love you

GyAHHH! Too much sugar! Must have something to do with that god-awful iodine-free diet you're on for your scan.

Sun's up. Cats are out. Miss you already.

Love and kisses, me

From: JWLongworth
To: DavidP
Date: June 24, 2003
Subject: Re: Re: I love you

Of course it's heavy on sugar! You would never let me get through the first sentence if I attempted to say such things in person, so I always have to ambush you from afar.

Had the first of my shots in preparation for the thyroid scan. I wore a short-sleeved blouse in anticipation of the injection, only to discover that they preferred to deliver it into my tail.

I did my eye doctor and dental cleaning this afternoon. I also picked up a bright shiny red rental car!

Kisses, *moi*

De: David
A: Jenny
Envoyé: 25 juin, 2003
Objet: Wednesdayt

Bright red! Oh, you devil. I thought that sort of thing was banned in Boston.

Hotter than the hinges at the moment. I may have to commit the ultimate heresy of adding an ice cube to my wine.

Love, David

From: JWLongworth
To: DavidP
Date: June 26, 2003
Subject: Re: Wednesday

Hot here too, at several levels. Having swallowed a horse pill full of radioactive iodine, I am now glowing with nuclear charge. Tomorrow I have my GYN check-up, and then I'm done.

Love, *moi*

As soon as Jenny got word that her thyroid scan was clear, she e-mailed David. They had joked about Jenny's tedious pre-scan diet, but David had lost Sandie to cancer just three years before. Beneath the joshing was a deep fear that he might lose Jenny as well.

David flew to Boston the next day. Jenny's condo, originally a carriage barn, was a small freestanding unit, set on a former country estate abutting conservation land. When he walked in the door, David sniffed the air. "Yup, it smells like Jenny's house."

"Sorry it's so musty," Jenny apologized. "Ross checked in on it a couple of times, but basically, it's been closed up ever since Christmas. I've tried to air it out, but it's so hot I've had to keep the windows shut and run the air conditioner."

"It's not a bad smell," David clarified, "just a special one. It's all the old wood. You don't get this kind of scent in Geneva because everything's made of concrete. It reminds me of my grandparents' farmhouse outside Chattanooga."

To their relief, the heat wave broke the next morning, allowing them to sit on the sunny patio and enjoy the necklace of gardens with which Jenny had surrounded her unit.

"There's an exhibit I'd like to see at the Fogg Art Museum," David noted, looking up from the Boston Globe entertainment guide. "I know you're not much of a museum fan, but you're welcome to come along and keep me company."

"Between the heat and my medical appointments, I haven't put any time into gardening, and there are a ton of weeds that need tackling. Do you mind going alone?" she asked.

"Nope. That'll let me peruse at my own pace. I'll pick up something for dinner on the way home."

Not ten minutes after David left for Cambridge, Jenny's gynecologist called with the lab results for her endometrial biopsy. "The biopsy showed positive," he said, clearing his throat. "Adenocarcinoma of the endometrium. You have uterine cancer."

Jenny's stomach seized, and she could feel the adrenaline shooting through her veins. Her jaw tightened and a wave of dizziness swept over her. *Sit,* she ordered herself, summoning her innate pragmatism. It was a trait that had always served her well. *Be practical, Jenny! Deal with this logically. You've done this before, and you can do it again.*

She adjusted her voice to an objective, professional level. "What are the options? How do you suggest I proceed?" she asked, reaching for a note pad and pulling a pen out of the stash that sat in a brass holder next to the phone.

"It's early-stage and well-differentiated, which makes it easier to treat, but you should move quickly. I'm recommending an immediate hysterectomy."

"I'm ready whenever you are," she replied. "David and I have the whole month of July before we fly back to Geneva, so I have plenty of recovery time. We're supposed to go to California our last week in the States, but we can change that if need be."

"It won't be me doing the surgery," the doctor explained. "You need an oncologist and an abdominal surgeon. If the lymph nodes are involved, there will likely be extended post-operative treatment – radiation or chemo."

Jenny's mind rebelled at the thought – *no, no, no, please no chemo!* – but the words coming out of her mouth remained calm and controlled. "How long are we talking about if I need additional treatment?"

The doctor wouldn't be pinned down. "It depends on what they find. That's why I want you in the hands of a specialist."

My god, she realized. *This could involve months rather than weeks.* "Do you know how quickly they could schedule me? My husband has to be back in Geneva in August to prepare for the beginning of school. I'll explore the alternative of having the procedure done there, but I'd much rather do it here in Boston."

"I'll call back as soon as I have some concrete information," he promised.

After Jenny hung up, she considered her next step. There was nothing useful she could do until David was informed, but her mind was spinning. She went to her computer, looked up adenocarcinoma and read through several different sites. If it was caught at an early stage, the prognosis was good. She printed out the most comprehensive yet understandable medical treatise she could find and set it aside to give to David.

Now what? Maybe if you keep your hands occupied, your mind will slow down, she scolded. She considered the gardening she had committed to earlier. *Go dig in the dirt, Longworth. Think about the weeds, not the fact that you have cancer again.*

The physical activity was helpful, but not a total distraction. Her mind was trying to marshal incomplete facts and tumbling feelings into a semblance of order. As a professional CPA, Jenny often saw things in terms of checks and balances. She wanted to sort the situation into a tidy list of possibilities, probabilities, and preferences. *Keep this in perspective,* she counseled herself. *My thyroid cancer came close to killing me, but here I am.*

As she awaited David's return, Jenny rehearsed her announcement, seeking calm words and an even calmer tone. *This is going to scare him more than it scares me. I won my last battle with cancer. Sandie lost hers.*

At five o'clock the car pulled in. Jenny greeted David halfway down the walk and gave him a quick welcoming kiss. "How was the exhibit?" she asked.

"Good," he said. "I had the gallery pretty much to myself. How was your afternoon?"

"Interesting," she replied. "I have some news that might alter our vacation schedule."

"Is this something I need to hear right away, or can I put these things in the fridge first?" he asked, holding up a bag of groceries.

"Go put them away," she said, determined to keep stress at bay. "I'll take some glasses out to the patio. You can choose the wine." Jenny's tone was so matter-of-fact that David assumed her news was nothing more disruptive than a looming visit from an unexpected out-of-town guest.

When David joined Jenny on the little brick terrace, he poured them each a glass and settled into a chair.

"Okay, here's the situation," she began, recapping the conversation with her gynecologist. "He's going to line up a surgeon here and give me a probable time frame. The sooner I have the hysterectomy, the better. Unfortunately, if extended care is required, we may have to shift this whole process to Geneva. And there's the further question of whether my Swiss insurance will cover me in Boston. I told him we'd check on the Geneva possibility as an alternative."

David received the news in silence. He looked across the lawn to the garden Jenny had created at the woods' edge in memory of his first wife. A statue of Buddha stood serenely on a stump in seeming contemplation of a meandering dry streambed. A flat oval stone at the entrance was engraved, "Sandie's Garden." Some of her ashes had been sprinkled over the plantings.

Normally, David's most obvious wrinkles were laugh lines etched in a face weather-beaten from a childhood in the southern sun and a life-long aversion to hats. At that moment, however, it was his brow that was deeply furrowed. His face was drawn into a scowl, and his dark eyes were suddenly hard.

"Shit," was his only comment.

"Well, it *is* pretty ironic," Jenny observed. "After all the to-do with my thyroid scan, here I am with a clean bill of health on the endocrine side, and uterine cancer instead. Maybe you should annul our marriage and trade me in for a newer model, or at least one with a better warranty."

David gave a weak smile but made no attempt to joke back.

"My thought is that we should call Dr. Payot in Geneva to clue him in," Jenny continued. "Since he's your family doctor, I presume he's the one to start the Swiss ball rolling with a referral to a surgeon. And then maybe you should contact Sandie's oncologist, Dr. Blanchard? I may need him for long term follow-up no matter where I do the surgery."

There was a six-hour time difference between Boston and Geneva. It was already after midnight in Europe. "I'll call them in the morning," David agreed. That night, he set the alarm for 5:00 a.m., climbed into bed, and gave Jenny a hug. She nestled close and finally fell asleep.

After the alarm rang, Jenny went to the kitchen and started the kettle boiling. When she returned to the bedroom, David was sitting half naked on the bed. His sandy hair was disheveled, and, telephone in hand, he was squinting through his wire-rimmed glasses at their "Bible," an all-purpose directory containing their personal and professional contacts.

Once David reached Dr. Payot, the discussion was animated but brief.

"Payot thinks you should stay in Boston so you can be operated on by the gynecologist who's been treating you all these years," David reported afterward.

With all the information Jenny had thrown at him, David hadn't registered the fact that her GYN wouldn't perform the surgery.

"I'll be dealing with a new face no matter where I have the hysterectomy," she explained. "The big advantage to Boston is language. The big disadvantage is that I might need to stick around for a while, and you've got to go back for school. I'd rather we weren't separated."

"We won't be," David declared emphatically. "Shall I call Payot back?"

Jenny hesitated. "Let's see what Dr. Blanchard thinks before we call Dr. Payot again."

Dr. Blanchard had served as Sandie Perry's oncologist from the time she was diagnosed with breast cancer until her death nine years later. Jenny started to look up his phone number, then realized David was already dialing it. He knew it by heart. The conversation was in French, but David spoke slowly and clearly, allowing Jenny to follow his remarks. "So," he summarized for Dr. Blanchard, "you recommend that Jenny do the procedure in Geneva because of the follow-up issues."

Jenny signaled to David that she understood, but she mouthed a question.

"My wife is not yet comfortable with her French," David said into the phone. "Do you understand English?" he asked. Jenny couldn't hear the response, but David looked at her and nodded his head. After another minute's exchange, he thanked Dr. Blanchard and hung up.

"He says we should go back to Geneva as quickly as possible," David announced, "and I agree. Blanchard wants us to fax him everything regarding your history and diagnosis. He'll contact Payot, start scheduling tests immediately, and book an admission date."

"I guess that settles it," Jenny sighed. "So be it."

At nine o'clock Jenny called her gynecologist to report their decision. They went in town to his office mid-morning, and she dashed in to collect a copy of her records while David waited in the car. "What shall we do about California?" she asked as they drove back to Shawmut.

"I'll call Marc and explain," David replied.

"I'm really sorry about this, David."

"It's not as if you planned it, Ducks."

It had been nearly a year since David had seen his son. A student at San Francisco State College, Marc had skipped the family gathering at Christmas and had chosen to stay in California for the summer. David eagerly anticipated their planned visit to San Francisco. It was a blow to have to cancel it.

David's daughter, Delphine, attended the American University in Paris, so they were able to visit regularly, but Marc was half a world away from Geneva. David missed him and was also concerned about him.

The father-son relationship wasn't an easy one. Marc's teenage years were turbulent. Even his mother, who had doted on him, had been at a loss to understand his moods. When Sandie died, Marc reacted with erratic behavior, scatter-shot anger, and emotional withdrawal. After much delay and several false starts, he finally entered college as a twenty-two year old freshman. Both David and Jenny hoped the experience would help him focus and settle, but the outcome remained to be seen.

"Maybe he'd be willing to come to Geneva for a few weeks. We can cover his ticket. We could ask Dellie to come back from Paris, and make it a kind of family reunion. Marc hasn't seen his sister since last summer."

"We'll see," said David tersely. He was clearly pre-occupied with the medical issues they faced.

Jenny faxed her medical history to Dr. Blanchard the minute they got back to the house. Crossing off items on her "to-do" list gave her a feeling of control. She then called the airlines to cancel the San Francisco trip and reschedule their flight to Geneva.

"The agent was really nice. I explained the situation, and she was totally helpful. They won't even charge us for changing the date. The only problem is that it's maximum tourist season. The first seats available are on July 10, so we have a ten day wait."

"Can't they bump someone for a medical emergency?"

"This is urgent, but not a real emergency. If it were a real emergency, we'd be on our way into town right this minute. Boston doesn't exactly lack for hospitals. And anyway, I'm grateful that we'll have some time before we leave. I spent my solo week doing appointments and errands. I put off all my social calls until your arrival. I haven't even laid eyes on Ross yet, and there are people I really want to see before we turn tail and go back to Europe."

"All right. You set up the social calendar. I'll telephone Marc."

David called San Francisco and got Marc's answering service. "Marc, it's Dad. There's been a change of plans regarding our California trip. Call me when you get in. We'll be awake until ten or so."

"I need to alert Bibi as well," Jenny said after David hung up. "She's not going to be happy about this."

Bibi Birnbaum had been a close friend of Jenny's for three decades, sharing adventures when Bibi lived in Boston and sustaining their friendship with regular communication after Bibi's move to Sausalito. With Jenny now living in Europe, the geographic distance made in-person visits a challenge, but Jenny knew she could count on Bibi's emotional support no matter how many miles lay between them.

"Hey there, Miss Jet Set!" Bibi exclaimed when she answered the phone. "I was just thinking about you! I've been making a list of restaurants I want you and David to try when you get here."

"Let's hope they stay in business for a long time," Jenny said, "because we have to cancel our trip to California. My GYN wants me to have a hysterectomy as soon as possible. We have to head back to Geneva."

Bibi cut straight to the chase. "What's with the hysterectomy?" she demanded.

"Early-stage endometrial cancer," Jenny replied succinctly. "I went in for a routine check-up last week. They did an endometrial biopsy, and zap! There it was. A small adenocarcinoma, apparently well-differentiated, which means it should be easy to take care of."

"Easy for real? Or are you just doing your stiff-upper-lip routine?"

"At this point, it's for real. The diagnosis was so unexpected that it threw me for a loop at first, but in fact, a hysterectomy is a straightforward procedure. I'm not afraid of it per se, though the idea that I might need some chemo at the end gives me the willies. You know how I feel about nausea."

"Well, if it's as early-stage as the doc says, hopefully you can avoid chemo. I trust they're taking everything out?"

"Yes, including a good-sized benign fibroid I've been carrying around for years. Maybe I'll even have a flat stomach when this is over."

"Longworth, you're the only woman I know who could take a cancer diagnosis and talk about it as if it were a weight loss program."

"Well, there *are* benefits," Jenny opined. "If nothing else, I'll have more bladder room."

"Yeah, yeah, enough with the jokes. How's David taking it?"

"He's toughing it out on the surface, but he's scared. His efforts at verbalizing come out either as poetry or profanity. There's not much in between. He'll be fine so long as I survive. But if I don't, well, that's my real worry. Do you remember the story I told you about Sandie's last days? How she sensed that David wouldn't be able to cope on his own, and trusted that I would step in to help? But who could I count on to take care of David if I die? I don't have a 'Jenny' waiting in the wings."

"The simplest solution would be for you to sail through this and come out the other end healthy as a horse."

"That's certainly my intention, though I don't think 'healthy as a horse' is an expression the Swiss medical folks are familiar with."

"David must know an equivalent expression in French. Even so, everyone at the hospital has gotta speak some English."

"Bibi, it is a common American illusion that everyone in Europe speaks some English. Switzerland has four national languages, but English is not one of them."

"French, German, Italian – what's the fourth?" Bibi asked.

"Romanche. It's a holdover from the Roman occupation two thousand years ago. They still speak it in some isolated valley in the eastern half of the country. Anyway, at least Dr. Blanchard, the oncologist, speaks English, and David trusts him. He was Sandie's doctor for nine years."

"Have you met him?"

"Not yet, but I expect the medical gauntlet will start as soon as we get there. We're flying back on the tenth. I'm really disappointed that we won't see you this trip. Of course, you could always come visit us in Switzerland," Jenny suggested hopefully. "They have fabulous chocolate, and you could entertain me during my convalescence."

"I'll think on it. Meanwhile, keep me posted. I'm just a phone call away whenever you need me. Be well."

David took over the phone again and called Graham Wells, his former college roommate and closest friend in the US. Graham had been an important source of support when David was struggling with Sandie's illness and death. He was one of the few people with whom David was completely open about his feelings.

Jenny was at her computer in the loft when David called up to her ten minutes later. "Graham wants to say hi," he said. "You wanna take it up there?"

"Got it. Thanks," she replied.

"How are you doing?" Graham asked when Jenny picked up the phone.

"Better than David, I expect. I don't think this is anywhere near as serious as my thyroid cancer was. I'm not going to count my chickens, but there's not much point in getting all exercised until a surgeon gets in there and sees what the story is. Meanwhile, I'm really sorry that our west coast trip is off."

Graham and his wife Barbara lived a bi-coastal existence. David and Jenny had visited with them briefly in Boston over Christmas, and had been looking forward to spending time with them in California.

"Needless to say, we're sorry too. I'm not sure what we can do from here, but if we can help in any way, please let us know," Graham offered.

"The biggest help will be if you stay in frequent touch with David. I think it will be hard for him to separate what I'm going through from what happened with Sandie."

"Consider it done. And keep us apprised. Barbara sends her love. We'll both be thinking of you."

Jenny brought her calendar downstairs. "I want to squeeze in a run to Maine to give my siblings the news in person. We already have Friday night booked with Rachel Aronson in Gloucester. Camden is only three hours further north. I'll contact Caroline and Lem to see if we can piggyback the visits and go on up to Maine Saturday afternoon. If that works, I'll reschedule our Sunday dinner with Ross and Kevin for early next week."

The callback from Marc didn't come until late the following morning. The conversation was in French, but Jenny was able to follow David's explanation of their change of plans. Having lived in Europe most of his adult life, David's French was close to native level, but he pronounced his consonants more succinctly than the French and eschewed their heavily nasal speech patterns. Jenny also knew in advance what the subject matter was.

"He got in too late to call us last night," David remarked when he put down the phone. "He has a summer job, so it may be tricky for him to come home. He said he'd talk with his boss and see what's possible. He hopes you're feeling okay."

Jenny recalled how moody and difficult Marc had been before he left Geneva for San Francisco. *Even if some of that was jitters about going back to school after a three-year hiatus, Marc has a lot of insecurities and can get very defensive. It's hard to have an easy relationship with someone who doesn't have an easy relationship with himself.*

Jenny harbored reservations about how helpful Marc's presence would be, but she knew it would mean a lot to David. *David needs the support, and Marc deserves the chance to give it. Help make this happen, Jenny,* she told herself.

> *From: JWLongworth*
> *To: Marc*
> *cc: Delphine*
> *Date: July 3, 2003*
> *Subject: Geneva visit*
>
> I'm sorry we can't go to California, and I do hope you'll find a way to make the trip to Geneva.
>
> As David told you, my cancer is at an early stage. I feel fine, physically and emotionally, and I have no anxiety about the hysterectomy. Your father, however, is understandably uneasy because of the experience with your mother. It would be very helpful if you could come to Geneva – even if only for a week or so – to provide him with some moral support and distraction.
>
> I am sending a copy of this e-mail to your sister so she'll be aware of the situation. Actually, no, let me make this direct: Dellie, we're cutting our US stay short and will return to Geneva on July 10 (arriving July 11). I know you plan to be home in August. It would be wonderful if you could spend some time with us in July as well.
>
> We will cover travel costs. I hope to see you both soon.
>
> Love, Jenny
>
> PS - I am not sending a copy of this to David, because he would yell at me for being an interfering busybody.

Friday morning, Jenny packed overnight bags for each of them. "Let's head north right after lunch," Jenny urged. "Friday late-afternoon traffic is routinely awful. I'd rather have more time on Rachel's deck and less time stuck on I-95."

The scent of salty air as they neared Rachel's summer home in Gloucester was delicious. "It's so good to see you two again," Rachel said as they exchanged hugs in her driveway. "You're both looking healthy and happy!"

Might as well go straight to the point, Jenny decided. "Happy," she replied, "but not totally healthy. My gynecologist went poking around in my uterus and found an adenocarcinoma."

"Oh, my god!" Rachel exclaimed. "What stage?" Rachel was a healthcare professional who had nursed her own husband during his fight with pancreatic cancer, only to watch him succumb three months before Sandie. She didn't beat around the bush.

"It gives every appearance of being early-stage," Jenny answered. "We're heading back to Geneva next Thursday. I'm having a hysterectomy as soon as the Swiss doctors can schedule it."

Rachel knew Jenny as someone who could tackle almost any crisis with equanimity. It was to David that Rachel directed a look filled with sympathy and concern, which Jenny noted with appreciation. *Rachel's candor about her own grief was immensely valuable when I was struggling to help David cope with Sandie's death,* Jenny recalled. She trusted that Rachel would again be a superb resource, this time for David as he watched another cancer drama unfold.

"Rachel, we've been in traffic for an hour and a half," Jenny interjected. "May I use your ladies' room while David fills you in on the details?"

"You remember where it is, yes? We'll go out on the deck."

When Jenny returned, David and Rachel were engaged in earnest conversation. With total self-centeredness, Jenny assumed they were discussing her medical situation, but she quickly realized they were comparing notes regarding their on-going grieving process. Confident that her presence would not inhibit the conversation, Jenny quietly took a chair next to David.

"Yes, David, you're right," Rachel was saying. "When I'm with people who are reflecting or reminiscing about Josh, I'm so eager to talk about him that my emotional control is set on high. I suspect I present a fairly sprightly façade. But the tears still come, both at predictable and unpredictable times. The predictable, for example, was when I woke up on the morning of my birthday. Well, you know. The unpredictable tends to be during events Josh should be sharing, like my granddaughter learning to ride a bike or my grandson starting school."

David considered her words. "For me, the pain doesn't come from other people talking about Sandie. The hurt comes from inside me and only me. It's interesting to try to understand the movement. Maybe that's a way of dealing with the loss. Perhaps my wanting to talk about it with a soul-sister is another way," he added.

After an hour of conversation, Rachel said she needed to do a quick run to the store. David offered to go with her. "You two go shop," Jenny suggested, "but if you don't mind, I'll stay here and walk the beach." Jenny wanted to allow them more time to share their personal issues, but there was a selfish consideration as well. *Given a choice between the beach and a grocery store, I'll go for the beach every time!*

Strolling the long sliver of sand fronting Ipswich Bay, Jenny picked up softly clouded pieces of sea glass washed up by the tide. On her return walk, she debated tossing them back into the foamy water, but instead opted to save them for David. *He can add them to Sandie's shell collection in Geneva,* she decided. *Bibi thinks I shouldn't do anything to perpetuate Sandie's collections, but the reality is, David's still working on closure. I'd rather participate in that process than turn my back on it.*

Although Sandie had been dead for almost three years, her accumulated collections were still prominently displayed throughout the home David now shared with Jenny. Sandie had grown up in near poverty in post-war Paris, and Jenny inferred that Sandie's colorful sets of miniatures, pillboxes and whatnots reflected a hunger for pretty possessions that were beyond her reach during childhood. The collections were not to Jenny's taste, but at David's request, they remained in place, important symbols for David's children that their mother was still remembered and honored.

The only possessions Jenny had brought from Boston, apart from her clothes, were her journals and photograph albums – a life captured on paper. David had been part of that life since they first met in college. *A long and winding path,* Jenny reflected. *Still, "all's well that ends well."*

Jenny stood for a moment watching the tide's increasing encroachment. The Shakespearean reference summoned a sudden flashback to her former English Lit professor, reading one of the Bard's sonnets: "Like as the waves make toward the pebbled shore, so do our minutes hasten to their end...."

Be positive, Longworth, she advised herself sternly. *Stage I endometrial cancer is almost never fatal. You have promises to keep and miles to go....*

The following day, David and Jenny took off for Maine. They were warmly greeted by Jenny's sister Caroline and her husband Charlie when they arrived in Camden. Jenny's brother Lem and his wife came over from Rockport half an hour later. Once they were all assembled, Jenny told them her doctor's findings. Jenny's siblings were concerned about her diagnosis, but no one treated the announcement as worthy of a crisis response.

"You-all are being awfully calm about this," David told Caroline when the two of them were alone in the kitchen. "I know you New Englanders are a stoic lot, but Jenny has got to be worried about this."

"Jenny doesn't worry," Caroline replied flatly. "She's the family logician. Jenny makes plans. Jenny organizes things. She'll look at a situation, list the possible outcomes, and then rank them in terms of probability. I kid you not. She's too practical to worry. Too cerebral. That's why Lem calls her Spock."

"You don't think it's a cover?" David wondered.

"Well, everyone protects himself, but Jenny's rarely inclined to presume the worst in any situation. She'll have a plan for it, but she'll discount the likelihood of it happening. Remember that her thyroid cancer six years ago – or was it seven? – actually metastasized. Yet she came through with relatively little damage. I should add that she didn't tell us about it until well over a year after the operation."

"But she's telling you this time. She must think this is more serious."

"I doubt it. I'm guessing it's because we really yelled at her last time, and told her *never* to do that to us again."

The family's low-key reaction was reassuring to David. Their visit was spent picking wild blueberries in the scrubby hills behind Caroline's farmhouse and going out on Lem's sailboat, rather than sitting around discussing medical concerns. Aside from "We'll be thinking of you," and "Keep us informed," the cancer issue was not mentioned again.

Once back in Shawmut, David and Jenny began their countdown for the return to Europe. Jenny's longtime confidant and attorney, Ross Barrett, came down to Shawmut for dinner on Tuesday evening with his companion, Kevin McGarry. Like Jenny's friend Rachel, Ross was no stranger to grief. During the height of the AIDS epidemic, he lost his partner of ten years, Ramon Delgado, to the virus. Ramon had been one of David and Jenny's college classmates. It was a loss they felt as well, and one that galvanized Jenny to connect with Ramon's more recent social circle. Her resultant friendship with Ross was the shining silver lining of the dark cloud caused by Ramon's death.

Once apprised of the medical situation, Ross understood David's anxiety and did his best to be supportive. "You'll have to use a firm hand with her, David," he suggested, keeping his tone calm. "If memory serves, Jewel only missed one week of work through the whole episode with her thyroid cancer. She's headstrong and inclined to boss the doctors around. With charm, of course, but she's a force to be reckoned with."

Jenny always liked it when Ross called her Jewel. Ramon had created the nickname in their student days, drawing on Jenny's initials, JWL. Ross had picked it up from Ramon, and rarely referred to Jenny any other way.

"This, I know," David rejoined. "She's a goddamn busybody, but since her French isn't fluent yet, she's going to have trouble revamping Swiss hospital protocol on her own steam."

The mood remained light during dinner, and there was only a hint of worry on Ross's part as they said goodnight. "If you need me to take care of anything about the condo, just let me know," he said, giving Jenny a big hug. "Anything, Jewel," he repeated.

Anything. Ross was the executor of Jenny's Will. *Best case, he won't have to do anything; worst case, he'll have to do everything,* she realized. *I'm glad I kept my maiden name. At least I don't have to worry about whether I've got the right name on my legal documents. I'd better double-check to make sure everything else is in order.*

Three days later, they were in the air, headed to Europe. Delphine was at the airport to meet them when they touched down in Geneva. She had rearranged her vacation plans in response to Jenny's request and would now be in Geneva until her classes resumed in September.

"Great service, Dellie!" Jenny exclaimed as Delphine gave her a welcoming hug. "I thought we'd have to take a cab." Delphine and her father conducted an animated conversation for the first several minutes of the drive home. It was in rapid French so Jenny contented herself simply observing the exchange. As always, she was reminded of how strongly Delphine resembled Sandie, not just in looks, but also in her mannerisms and gestures. The only imprint from David's genes appeared in Delphine's well-defined cheekbones and strong forehead.

Jenny shed her travel clothes as soon as they got to the house and treated herself to a hot shower while David and his daughter did a grocery run. Disoriented by jet lag, they had a very early dinner and retired at seven o'clock. "This is a little tough for Delphine," David remarked as they got into bed. "She said it hit her like a ton of bricks when she heard about the diagnosis."

"We'll have to reassure her that my situation is very different from her mother's," Jenny replied. *Communicating optimism is going to be important for the children as well as for David,* she sensed.

Monday morning, David called Dr. Blanchard's office and got the medical schedule. A series of appointments had been lined up, the first of which was a scan the next day.

Geneva was still plagued by exceptionally hot weather. Since Monday remained an open day, David accepted an invitation from his closest Genevan friends, Michel and Josette Dupont, to take advantage of their swimming pool. Throughout David and Sandie's years in Geneva, the Perrys and the DuPonts had been colleagues at l'Académie Internationale. The two couples shared meals, travel and adventures for well over two decades. Michel and Josette had adored Sandie, and they sorely missed her. It was a tribute to their generous nature that they had gone out of their way to make Jenny feel welcome in their world.

Michel and Josette were in the pool when David and Jenny arrived, and they quickly joined them in the water. It was not until later, when they all sat down to lunch, that David signaled to Jenny with raised brows, and she nodded her agreement.

"We ran into a problem in Boston," David began. "In the course of some routine tests, Jenny's gynecologist discovered that she has uterine cancer." The DuPonts stopped eating and put down their forks as David described the events step by step.

I suspect this careful enumeration is one of David's ways of keeping things under control, Jenny speculated. *The slow recounting helps me too. At this pace, I can understand his French.*

"I called Dr. Blanchard's office to get his advice," David continued. "I used to know all the staff there, but the receptionist who answered the phone was new. I explained that Dr. Blanchard had treated Sandie for nine years, until her death. 'Now,' I told the woman, 'I need him to treat my second wife.' The receptionist gasped and said, '*Oh, mon dieu!*' before she recovered her composure and put the doctor on the line."

"So now Dr. Blanchard is in charge?" Josette asked. "When do you begin?"

"Tomorrow," David answered. "Blanchard has scheduled a battery of appointments. The first one is at l'Hôpital de la Tour."

The next morning, David delivered Jenny into the hands of the hospital's radiology department. "So far, so good," Jenny announced when she reappeared an hour later. "Their scan revealed a small, contained tumor with no apparent impact on any other organs. And

I had no trouble understanding their findings," she added, "because the senior radiologist speaks very good English."

David was clearly relieved to get out of the hospital, lighting a cigarette the instant they were through the door. As they approached the car, Jenny touched his arm. "It can't have been easy for you to come here this morning, David."

"It was easier than the last time," he replied.

The last time, Jenny thought glumly, *was when David came to sign the papers authorizing removal of Sandie's body to the mortuary.*

The weather report predicted another scorcher. The house, normally kept cool by thick concrete walls, was losing its capacity to offer refuge. They settled themselves on the shaded porch, David with the newspaper and Jenny with a new book. At the end of the first chapter, she lifted her head to comment about the story and caught David staring at her. He quickly shied away. Stretching out a leg, she rubbed his bare toes with her own and beamed him a cheerful smile. Her movement startled a zebra swallowtail butterfly that rose from the low hedge and fluttered off.

"I haven't seen one since my childhood!" Jenny exclaimed. "We should view it as a splendid omen!"

"Let's hope so," David breathed.

Not long afterwards, Dr. Blanchard called.

"Bloody hell!" David swore when he reported back to Jenny. "Blanchard is having trouble scheduling the operation at l'Hôpital de la Tour. The problem is August," he fumed. "Remember the difficulty we had booking a Saturday in February for our wedding at the *Mairie?*"

"I do," she smiled. "They didn't normally do weekend weddings in the winter because everyone in Geneva goes skiing then."

"Well, there's a similar problem with August. France and *Suisse Romande* – the French-speaking part of Switzerland – shut down in August. Everyone who's anyone goes on vacation. Even the hospitals are at skeletal staffing. Blanchard says the top abdominal surgeons at La Tour aren't available until September, and he doesn't want you to wait that long. He's trying to line up the head of surgery in Nyon. Meanwhile, he wants to see us on Monday after you get your blood work done."

"You're telling me the Swiss don't get sick in August?" Jenny remarked with raised eyebrows. "And where is Nyon?"

"Other side of the lake. It's about half way to Lausanne, nearly an hour away from our house in Morion. But time is of the essence, so I don't care about the commute."

The day of their appointment with Dr. Blanchard, the temperature was in the high 90's. Despite the heat, David stood in the sizzling parking lot and had a cigarette before they went in. The receptionist waved them into the waiting room where a window air conditioning unit struggled unsuccessfully to keep the thermostat reading below 80 degrees.

David occupied himself reading a magazine. Jenny contemplated the surroundings. The wallpaper was imitation sponge paint in a squash-orange color. There were modernistic chairs with fake suede, alternating in blue and yellow. *Waiting-room decor is clearly not their strong point,* she decided. On a corner table, a potted plant had shriveled to a few limp leaves. A vase containing a bedraggled bouquet sat on the floor. *You'd think someone would be more sensitive to the images that dying houseplants and wilted bouquets can conjure up among cancer patients and their caregivers,* she sniffed.

A petal fell from the bouquet. David glanced at it. "Yup, it'll happen," he commented darkly.

Fifteen minutes later, they were invited into Dr. Blanchard's office. His English was fluent, and his style was direct and non-patronizing. He carefully reviewed the paperwork, confirmed that the surgery would be done in Nyon, shook hands with David and Jenny, and ushered them out.

"That went well," Jenny said as they returned to the car. "My major reservation about undergoing surgery in Geneva is language, and thus far, it hasn't been a problem."

"It won't be a problem when you're under anesthesia either," David commented.

"True, but when I'm awake, I want to understand everything that's going on."

"That's what I call being a busybody," David said wryly.

"That's what I call being an informed patient," Jenny countered.

In the morning, when David was sitting outside with his coffee, Jenny came up behind him, put her hands on his shoulders and planted a kiss on his bald spot. Without turning, he reached up, took hold of her wrists, and pulled her close against him, holding her hands tightly against his chest. David did not normally express affection through physical channels. His anxiety was palpable.

For Sandie, three years on

Time's passed so fast

No noise did I notice
When the oak leaf snapped,
But the rustle it raised dropping,
Slapping other leaves, alerted me.
It fell no more than a second or two,
But enough to remind me
Gently of you
And the now three years
That you've been gone.
Time's passed so fast, so silently along
But has no more mass than the leaf's fall,
Yet carries so many scenes that call
For my attention unexpectedly
Day and night.
I've aged to expect it;
You haven't aged at all.
Three years ago
I said that would happen.
I was right.

D.P. - September 25, 2003

Chapter 2

Marc was due in from California two days prior to Jenny's hospital admission. Just hours before his scheduled arrival, he called, collect, from London. The conversation was in French, but from the look on David's face, Jenny immediately inferred there was a problem.

"Who did you talk with?" David asked. "What did they say?"

David listened in silence for a minute, then pulled out his wallet and read some numbers into the phone. He kept his voice even while he was on the line, but when he hung up, he sat down heavily and put his head in his hands. "*Incroyable!* Unbelievable!" he muttered.

"What is it? What's going on?" Jenny asked anxiously.

David issued a deep sigh. "Marc missed his Geneva connection. The San Francisco flight was late coming into Heathrow. He apparently lost his temper with the ground personnel, taking a strip off of British Air. As a result, they're refusing to carry him on their next flight from London to Geneva. I gave him my credit card number and told him to get a ticket on a different airline." He paused and shook his head. "I really thought he was getting more of a handle on himself," he said.

This airline cock-up does not bode well, Jenny worried. *Asking Marc to come home may have been a mistake.*

David spent the afternoon in a state of stress. "Let's go tackle the wisteria out back," Jenny suggested. "It desperately needs trimming, and hacking at unruly vines should be a good way to let off steam."

While David was up on the ladder, he overreached to get a drooping tendril, and the shears slipped from his fingers. Jenny was sweeping cuttings just below him. For a frightening split second, David thought the shears would land on her head. "Goddamn it to hell!" he yelled. He was so upset by the near miss that he had to come down and sit for a few minutes before he could continue.

Delphine arrived on the scene, and one glance at her father told her that he was in distress. "What happened?" she asked.

"David was having a tussle with the wisteria," Jenny replied, "and the wisteria won this round. Your brother has also been in a tussle of sorts. He got himself bumped from British Air because of bad behavior. He's trying to get a flight from Heathrow on another airline."

Delphine looked at Jenny in astonishment. She turned to her father. "Dad?"

David grimly recounted the story, tempering his language as best he could.

Delphine was the one who reacted with strong verbiage. "*Imbécile! Espèce d'idiot!* I can't believe he would do something so stupid with everything that's going on!" Delphine was deeply fond of her brother, and the two siblings could be very protective of one another, but Marc's behavior was as upsetting to Delphine as it was to David. She had little patience with it.

When Marc called again with a new arrival time of 10:00 p.m., Delphine told her father she would accompany him to the airport. "It's too late for Jenny to go," she insisted. "She's supposed to be resting up for her surgery. And if you go alone, you might just kill Marc when you see him. I'd rather you let *me* kill him," she added with an impish smile.

Jenny went to bed when the father-daughter team left for the airport. She heard them return around eleven, but she was too sleepy to get up. *I'll welcome Marc home in the morning,* she decided.

Jenny had an early appointment with the surgeon in Nyon, so they were out of the house right after breakfast. When they returned, Delphine had left to visit friends, but Marc was still asleep.

"He'll be jet-lagged for the next few days, and he never was much of an early riser," David commented.

The weather suddenly turned turbulent, and a hailstorm appeared out of nowhere. Little balls of ice bounced all over the yard, shredding flowers and frightening the cats, who streaked into the house to escape the noise and the pellets. For a few hours, it was blissfully cool, but then a dark scowling thunderstorm rolled in, with strong winds and rain that blew sideways. When it finally passed, the air was hot and steamy again. Throughout the upheaval, David was preoccupied with the question of how to begin a dialog with his son.

"He seems to have inherited my temper," he commented sadly.

"That may be, David, but if so, he's inherited it without the counter-balance of your humor and kindness. This anger thing is really troubling. Everyone else on that plane was late too. Marc isn't the only one who missed his connection."

"No, but I expect there are some heavy emotional issues tied to this trip. Geneva is no longer what he remembers growing up. Sandie's gone, Delphine is pretty much out of the nest, and Marc's childhood is over. Even our newly minted version of 'home' may seem in jeopardy, with you going in for cancer surgery."

"So you think, deep down, he feels homeless?"

"I think the past is gone, the present isn't the way he wants it to be, and the future is scary as hell. There's also some historical baggage that coming back to Geneva dredges up. I think he's angry, whether consciously or not, at the trials he put his mother through when he went to California the first time, after his graduation from l'Académie Internationale. He lost his return ticket and was too proud to ask for help, so he took odd jobs and pretty much dropped out of sight. It made Sandie frantic."

Jenny absorbed David's assessment in silence. Marc's former girlfriend, Valerie, had once offered a very different and much darker version of the "lost ticket" story. "It is not so nice a story as he tells to his father," she had confided to Jenny, practicing her expanding English. "Marc has left his art school only a few months after he arrives at San Francisco. It was required that he also leaves his dormitory. Afterwards, he has stayed in bad places, in shelters for the street people, and he has lived by selling drugs."

Jenny had immediately repeated Valerie's tale to David, but at the time, he discounted Valerie's comments. "Marc might have invented or inflated those tales to impress her," he suggested. "Besides which, they've been fighting like cats and dogs. I expect Valerie has it in for him right now."

Should I remind David about what Valerie once said? Jenny wondered. *No,* she concluded, measuring David's distress. *Whatever happened in the past, we have more than enough present problems to address.*

Marc finally emerged late afternoon. Jenny gave him a hug and a "Welcome home," but otherwise let David carry the ball. He didn't get very far.

"I need the car," Marc announced. "My bags are still in London, and the assholes are making me go all the way out to the airport to sign some stupid f***ing form authorizing British Air to send them *sans* passenger."

It would be nice if Marc could add please and thank you to his vocabulary, and subtract a few other words, Jenny observed silently. *I was naïve to think his coming would be a comfort to David.*

At dinner, however, Jenny revised her opinion somewhat. For the first time in a year, David had both his children at the table, and he clearly relished their presence. Delphine was in good spirits, looking forward to the start of her junior year at American University in Paris, and speaking with enthusiasm about the history of art classes she planned to take. "The apartment is working out really well too," she reported. "The first *arrondissement* is so central! I've gotten to know most of the local vendors, and that nice waitress we met still works at the corner wine bar. It's a really neat area."

"You're lucky your street hasn't been overrun with American globalization," Marc interjected. "I've found a place to buy good French cheese in San Francisco, but most of the food stores are American crap, except in the Chinese neighborhoods."

Jenny was tempted to respond, but remained silent. *Let David handle this,* she told herself. David's approach was to shift the focus of the discussion, but whatever the topic of conversation, Marc offered up only negative remarks. He didn't share his sister's enthusiasm for the upcoming academic year. He was cynical about his classes and his classmates, and through much of the dinner, he denigrated his host country. "To be an American you gotta be ignorant or nationally sadistic," he said snappishly. "It's the US of doublethink. Things are just as f***ed up as always. I've been reading *1984* by Orwell, and I can tell you that it's pretty relevant to this period of time. You oughta read it."

Jenny and David exchanged looks. Both had read the book in college, back when 1984 was still a date two decades in the future.

Marc went off on his bike after dinner, and Delphine retreated to her room to make phone calls.

"I'm far from a chauvinist," Jenny commented as she and David cleared the last of the dishes. "I'm well aware that there are a lot of things in the US that need fixing. But Marc pontificates with no perspective. 'Americans are all this – Americans are all that.' If there is anything Americans are all *not,* it's monolithic."

"He's still just shy of twenty-three," David shrugged. "I vaguely remember that when we were that age, we knew everything too."

"Okay, *touché,*" Jenny conceded, "but *we* were *right,*" she added, suppressing a smile.

David descended to read his e-mails while Jenny checked the hospital advisories telling her when to arrive and what to pack. They included a request that she bring her *Carte de Groupe Sanguin* – a blood type card.

"David, what constitutes an acceptable blood type card?" she called down the stairs.

"Oh, Jeezus! I should have thought of that. We'll have to get you one."

"Will they take an American version?" she asked.

"I should think so. Do you have it with you?"

"I don't have one. But I'll bet I can produce something that will pass muster."

Choosing a similar font, Jenny mimicked the layout of David's *Carte de Groupe Sanguin,* and printed an official-looking statement in English that she was O-Positive. She affixed it to the back of a patient-ID card from Boston with wide clear tape, making it look laminated, and showed it to David.

"I could tell them my blood type in two seconds, but if they insist on a plastic reference, who am I to argue?" Jenny said, defending her handiwork.

"Looks like a perfectly respectable *Groupe Sanguin* card to me," David agreed.

Jenny assembled the items suggested for her hospital stay and added several of her own, including an English-French dictionary, crosswords, CDs, and a headscarf.

Jenny didn't normally use headscarves. She wore her hair short, Peter Pan style. Although it was naturally wavy, it was also thin, with little body, so a headscarf tended to mash it down beyond recovery.

The scarf Jenny drew from the dresser had once been Sandie's. Most of Sandie's clothing had been given away, but Jenny saved one of Sandie's cotton bandanas to keep leaves and twigs out of her hair when she was pruning in the garden. Sandie had used it for a more serious purpose, to cover her scalp as her hair was falling out from the chemo treatments. As Jenny folded the scarf into a neat square, she recalled their last exchange, a month before Sandie died.

"The hair problem is solved," Sandie wrote, updating Jenny on her treatments. "It was falling so heavily and I was so depressed that I asked for a hairdresser to come to my room and shave it all. So I am wearing bandanas and I should have a wig ready next week."

Jenny had sent back a lighthearted response in an effort to cheer Sandie up. "Do you get to have more than one wig? It might be fun to have something outrageous, like one in shocking pink or day-glow orange!"

But there was no reply. Sandie was losing her mental faculties as well as her hair, and within a few short weeks, she would lose her life.

Jenny dragged her thoughts back to the present. *Whatever happens long term, I'm not about to lose my hair anytime soon! I just need something to conceal it. Without a daily shampoo, it's going to become flat and oily as my hospital stay progresses.*

Jenny saw nothing morbid in using Sandie's scarf. In years past, Jenny had often spent vacations with the Perry family, and had witnessed Sandie address her illness with optimism, resilience and courage. The two women had enjoyed a cordial relationship, enhanced toward the end by the special bond that grows between cancer patients.

Jenny had always admired and respected Sandie, but since her move to Geneva, she had uncovered layers of complexity that altered her earlier perceptions of David's first wife. Beloved as Sandie was by her husband and her friends, she was human, with flaws and failings, at the top of which was a secret affair with the Principal of the school where both she and David worked. David had long suspected it, but he kept his speculations to himself until after he and Jenny were married.

Highly skeptical at first, Jenny was the one who ultimately uncovered proof of the affair, and she was upset by the hurt it caused David. *And I wasn't exactly pleased at being so misled about what was going on in their marriage*, she recalled. As the details emerged, however, it became clear that Sandie viewed the affair as a way to hold the family together while still meeting her private needs. David had found the means to forgive Sandie's actions posthumously while continuing to appreciate the positive elements in their marriage, and Jenny followed suit.

Sandie and I have a unique relationship, Jenny mused as she tucked the scarf into her hospital bag. *We have a spectral sisterhood that can withstand an occasional spat – which is a good thing, given that she's an integral part of my life with David. Anyway, more relevant to the immediate issue, she was a warm and sunny person with a deep appreciation for each day she was given. That's the aura I want surrounding me. Her scarf will be my talisman. I want it near as I dance my second dance with cancer.*

Delphine appeared in her robe and slippers to see David and Jenny off to the hospital. They assumed Marc was still asleep, but discovered later that he hadn't returned home from his nighttime outing.

Throughout the admission process, David was at Jenny's side to offer moral support and lend his language skills as they dealt with receptionists and forms.

"Why on earth are they asking whether I'm celibate?" Jenny exclaimed, startled by such an odd question.

In any other setting, David would have laughed out loud, but he just shook his head. "They're not," he explained patiently. "*Célibataire* means single, not celibate. They're asking whether you're single or married. You want to check the box that says *Mariée*."

Jenny's homemade *Carte de Groupe Sanguin* was accepted as the real McCoy, and after a brief visit to the lab, she and David were sent up to Gynecology on the third floor. By pure chance, one of the nurses on rotation was Canadian and completely bilingual. "Hi," she said when Jenny registered. "You're the American patient, yes? My name is Doriane, and I'll be your intake nurse."

"Oh, thank heavens!" Jenny exclaimed. "I was on the verge of a panic attack about having to do this in French!"

Doriane escorted them to Jenny's hospital room and left David to help Jenny settle in. The room was coldly functional. The only appealing element was the view. Jenny was on the south side of the building with three large windows. In the foreground were the outskirts of Nyon – quaint houses with slanting roofs, window boxes and gnarled chimneys. Beyond them Jenny could see patches of Lake Leman, and then the low hills rising up to meet the mountains.

She unpacked and put a framed picture of David by the bed while he set up the CD player for her. David hated hospitals but was prepared to stay as long as Jenny needed him.

"I appreciate it, Love, but thanks to Doriane, I'm no longer worried about translation problems," Jenny advised. "The rest of today will involve a lot of sitting around and waiting. You should go on home. Marc's time in Geneva is short, and Dellie rearranged her school vacation plans to be with you. There's nothing to do here, and no need to come back until tomorrow."

David looked at her in mild amusement. "I'll do what I have to do," he said.

"What you have to do is to scoot, so the prep team can come in and begin performing their dastardly deeds," she told him.

David finally left when Doriane stopped by to process the intake interview, but he returned for an evening visit.

"I can't believe you drove all that way just to wish me good night in person!" Jenny exclaimed when he walked into her room. She looked for signs that he was moved by anxiety, but recognized it as a simple gesture of love. *I would have done the same thing if he were the one stuck in a hospital,* she realized.

"I had a talk with Marc," David mentioned after outlining the social activities he and the children planned for the next few days. "It turns out that he didn't really have a job this summer – at least, not a paying one. He got arrested during an anti-war protest and was sentenced to a hundred hours of community service. He just finished working it off before coming here."

"What was he arrested for?"

"Attacking a police officer."

"Dear god, David!"

"He says it's not true, that he was just trying to get the police to stop beating up someone who'd been knocked down."

"Marc's going to get himself in real trouble if he doesn't learn to control that temper."

"I agree. I wish I could help him figure out where it's coming from. He focuses on external issues, but he's got to identify the trouble inside him so he can begin to deal with it."

Jenny had nothing to add. She again questioned her judgment in thinking Marc's presence would be helpful to David.

"I should head back," David concluded. "You behave yourself and do whatever the doctor tells you to do."

"Yes, Sir," Jenny said, trying to look serious.

"See you tomorrow, Jewel. Nighty night."

"Love you," she called after him as he closed the door behind him.

Within minutes of David's departure, the chief surgeon, Dr. Dausset, stopped by for a final pre-operative review. Although he understood some English, he didn't speak it, but he was careful to choose the simplest of French words and phrases.

"Et voilà. Avez vous des questions, Madame?"

"Non," she replied, "No questions. But there is something important for you to know. The first wife of my husband died of cancer three years ago. Now he is afraid he may lose me also. Perhaps when you speak with him you can give him confidence in the outcome." Jenny had to look up "outcome" in her English-French dictionary. *Of course,* she thought when she found it: *résultat* – result.

Dr. Dausset nodded sympathetically. *"Je suis très optimiste, Madame."* After he departed, Jenny took a shower as directed and washed carefully with betadine solution. She emerged the color of a pumpkin, but the shower felt good because the room was hot. There was still some light in the sky, and in the dusk she could see many more mountain ridges than were visible during the day. Behind them, rising majestically, stood the Mont Blanc, covered with snow and crowned by a ring of clouds that masked the outlines of its highest peak.

De: David
A: Family & friends
Envoyé: 31 juillet, 2003
Objet: Jenny's hospitalization

Took the lady to the hospital this morning to get her settled in. When I left, she and her Canadian (English-speaking) nurse were moving headlong into serious gynecological theory. The lady was in good shape.

This evening, I found Jenny fully dressed lying on her bed reading a novel. She had seen the anesthesiologist and gotten all sorts of neat instructions about special scrubs and so on. Then a young assistant surgeon came in and introduced himself in English. Said he was there to ask some more questions to complete Jenny's hospital file. When I left, her eyes were sparkling as she moved into specific advice on exactly what might be the best way to proceed.

All is well. I'll send you another e-mail tomorrow. David

For Jenny, it was a night from hell. The outdoor temperature barely dipped into the 70's, and the indoor temperature was easily in the high 80's. There was no air conditioning. Despite the open window, the room was hot and stuffy. There were no screens. Moths fluttered in, attracted by the light on the emergency call button. From time to time the smell of cigarette smoke wafted in from the courtyard below.

In the middle of the night Jenny saw lightening flashes on the far side of the lake, but the hoped-for rain didn't come, nor did sleep. At 5:15 a.m., the village below began to wake up. Jenny gave up. She showered with the rest of the betadine and got into her hospital gown.

An aide came in and started giving instructions in French. Jenny understood most of them until the aide said she had to "put the *amaque*." Jenny's free-floating stress began to gather itself in a knot in her stomach. She could marshal logic and statistics to quell anxiety about the operation, but intellect couldn't dispel the irrational panic that threatened when she couldn't understand what the aide was saying. "*Amaque? Je ne comprends pas.* I don't understand. What is an *amaque?*" The aide tried sign language, but to no avail. Finally, Jenny retrieved her dictionary. "*Amaque,*" she repeated. "*C'est A-M-A-Q...?*"

"*Ah, non, Madame!*" the aide shook her head in frustration. "*C'est H-A-M-A-C.*" She needed to put a moveable sling – a hammock – beneath Jenny to facilitate transfer from the gurney to the operating table.

> *De: David*
> *A: Family & friends*
> *Envoyé: 1 août, 2003*
> *Objet: Jenny's Operation – AOK*
> Dr. Dausset just phoned to say that Jenny is awake. They are keeping her as groggy as possible so she won't ask too many questions or offer unsolicited opinions. Now we have to await the biopsy results, which should take a week to come back. He seemed pleased and sounded calm and professional. Marc, Delphine and I are relieved.
>
> I'll give her your wishes for a speedy recovery and a big kiss. David

When David came by in the early evening, he presented Jenny with a fragrant rose from the garden. He also brought her wedding ring. Surgical patients were instructed to leave jewelry at home, since there was no secure place to put it during an operation. Jenny abided by the rules going in, but told David she wanted her ring once the surgery was over. "Here you go, Ducks," he said, slipping it gently onto her finger as he kissed her on the forehead.

The following morning, the frustrations set in. Jenny was tethered by assorted tubes and wires. She couldn't move more than a few inches in any direction. Her elementary French had disappeared behind the haze of painkillers, leaving her reluctant to hit the call button for a nurse. Rescue finally came via an Ethiopian aide who spoke fluent English.

"I can't turn on the CD player," Jenny lamented, "or reach my book. I can't even get to my French dictionary!"

The aide had just finished rearranging the IV when David arrived. Jenny greeted him with a quick kiss, then launched into a description of her woeful morning. David remained respectfully silent until she finished. "Oh god, I'm being a nitpicking whiner, aren't I," she apologized, realizing how shrill she sounded.

"That's okay," David said. "Yesterday you weren't coherent. At least today you're making sense even if you're crabby."

By Sunday, Jenny was on the mend. She slept better during the night, thanks to the fan David brought her. With her new mobility, she could reach her books and crosswords, and sit up enough to appreciate the view. The day nurse helped Jenny with a washcloth bath, but her hair remained dank and matted. *Only one way to deal with that,* Jenny decided, pulling out Sandie's scarf.

Just before noon, David peeked his head around the corner, froze, and turned three shades of gray as he looked at her. His voice trembled. "What's with the scarf?"

What an idiot I am! Jenny realized, pulling it off. *It must remind him of Sandie when she lost her hair.*

"My hair gets flat and oily if I can't wash it every day," she apologized. "It looks really awful, so I figured I'd best cover it up."

"It doesn't look awful. Just a little mussed," he said, regaining his balance. "I brought you a get-well gift from my colleagues at school." He handed her a cute little beanbag bear sporting an Académie Internationale T-shirt.

"How are you feeling?" he asked.

"I'm feeling like getting out of here," she answered bluntly. "The doctor thinks he'll let me go home on Friday, but I'm shooting for Thursday."

They spilled out their news to one another, then each went quiet. Part of Jenny's strategy for an early release was to conserve energy so she could summon it to peak capacity whenever the doctor appeared. The children, the neighbors, and David's colleagues had all offered to visit, but Jenny declined. David understood this and didn't stay long.

When he was gone, Jenny picked up the little bear. She had encountered four similar beanbag animals when she first moved to Geneva – a lion, a pig, a donkey, and a nearly identical bear, all sitting on the headboard above what used to be Sandie's side of the bed. It had taken Jenny a week to diffidently suggest that David should perhaps store them someplace "safe," or give them to Marc and Delphine. He had complied immediately, but she sensed his conflict in moving them.

This must be so hard for him, she thought as she considered the little bear. *So many reminders of Sandie's last days – the fear – the helplessness. And the third anniversary of her death is just weeks away. What on earth will happen if I get a bad pathology report?*

Jenny had a book to read, but it was difficult to concentrate. Hot flashes came and went, and the stifling heat was ever-present. *Oh god, do I ever want out of this hospital! I feel stranded in a strange place with no sense of control.*

There was nothing to brighten her thoughts in the drab room, but eventually the view across the mountains drew her eye. *Just pretend you're outside somewhere, sitting on a hillside,* she scolded herself. As the hours passed, she watched the changing patterns of light over the fields of grain, followed the shadows slanting across the rooftops of the town, and studied the shifting colors of the mountains.

Monday was a beautiful day with a long-awaited cool breeze. The morning nurse removed the last of the needles from Jenny's arm. When David arrived, Jenny was mobile enough to go to him and give him a hug. She waved her arms to demonstrate that the last plug was out. "I am now officially unattached," she announced gleefully.

David looked her straight in the eye. "No, you're not," he said.

Jenny smiled. *I sometimes wish he would say, "I love you," instead of using double entendres, but however he says it, he makes me feel like Cinderella at the ball.*

De: David
A: Family & friends
Envoyé: 4 août, 2003
Objet: Jenny's convalescence - Escape plan

The lady is up and about. The doctors have removed all the drips except the glucose, so now Jenny gets up and moves around as often as possible. This is part of her strategy to get the hell out of the hospital as soon as possible. She makes public displays of athletic prowess whenever medical staff are in the room. ("Pass me the high-jump pole, would you, David? I feel a rush of energy coming on. See, Doc, no hands!") She plans to put the second part of her escape strategy (feminine coquettery) into operation on Tuesday morning. Her new goal: to be out on Wednesday. Obviously all is well. David

That night, Jenny slept straight through. It boded well for her plans to win an early discharge. As soon as the night nurse finished her 5:00 a.m. check, Jenny washed her hair and put on a touch of eye make-up. As requested, David had brought her a pair of earrings at the same time he brought the wedding ring. She fished them out of her toilet kit and put them on. It was impressive what clean hair and a little cosmetic artistry could accomplish in terms of projecting a healthy glow.

De: David
A: Family & friends
Envoyé: 5 août, 2003
Objet: Jenny's convalescence - a strategy fails!

Despite earrings, a powdered nose, clean hair and a plunging neckline, Jenny's attempt to scale the walls of her medical prison a day early has failed.

"Precocious," replied Dr. Dausset. "Thursday at the earliest. Friday would be preferred." No sooner had he shut the door than Jenny got her well-manicured talons into a nurse. "My stepson is going back to San Francisco in just a few days, and I've had so little time to spend with him." The nurse promised to speak to the doctor on Jenny's behalf. Will medical principle be thrown to

> the four winds? Will American cunning and hell-bent-for-home feminism shoulder aside European conservatism and male stodginess?
>
> Wait for the next installment! David

Reminded that she had, indeed, spent little time with her stepchildren, Jenny recanted on her visitor restrictions, but not without first securing David's promise that there would be no pressure on them to appear. "Has Marc settled down a bit?" she asked. "Being inside a hospital will surely bring back memories of going to see Sandie when she was dying. I don't want to add further stress to the situation."

"Not sure where Marc's head is. He's been out most of the time. But I'm confident he and Delphine can both handle a short visit."

David arrived Tuesday afternoon with Marc and Delphine at his side, each with a small bouquet of garden flowers in hand. Jenny had a flashback to her very first visit to Geneva, when Marc was around ten and Delphine close to seven. As Jenny joined David, Sandie and the children for lunch, Marc had asked his father for a pen and had started drawing on the back of a paper napkin. He produced a remarkably well-done sketch of a sunflower and handed it to Jenny with a smile. Delphine soon followed suit, drawing a fat hedgehog to honor their American guest.

I still have those napkins in a drawer in Shawmut, Jenny reminisced.

Coming back to the present, she offered thanks for the flowers. "You were great to come to Geneva and keep your father distracted during all this," she told them when David stepped out to have a cigarette,

"Yeah, well, he seems to be doing okay," Marc replied.

"The thing that's kept him busiest is all the cooking. He thinks we'll starve if he doesn't make a four-course dinner every night," Delphine offered.

Jenny smiled at Delphine's comment. "Cooking is one of the ways David expresses love," she said quietly.

The family visit lasted less than an hour. After David and the children left, a nurse arrived with a thermometer. Jenny had a scratchy throat, but she kept mum about it. *That's another reason to get out of here,* she thought. *Hospitals are full of sick people.*

David called that evening, "Any word on your release date?" he asked.

"Not yet," she moaned.

Twenty minutes later, Dr. Dausset popped his head in the door, clearly in a jovial mood. "Do you still want to go home?" he asked.

Jenny would have understood that question in any language in the world. She clapped her hands like a child. *"Oui, oui, oui!"* she replied.

"Then, if there are no complications, I will release you Wednesday evening," the doctor advised.

Jenny didn't know whether to credit the earrings, the eye makeup, the sympathetic nurse, or all three, but she was a happy lady. She called David back in a state of total glee. "Dr. Dausset's going to let me go tomorrow evening! I have to come back Friday for the stitch removal, but meanwhile, I am sprung!"

> *De: David*
> *A: Family & Friends*
> *Envoyé: 5 août, 2003*
> *Objet: Jenny's convalescence - the Great Compromise*
> The nurse must have interceded. Maybe she has a plunging neckline as well. Whatever the explanation, Dr. Dausset has seen Reason, and it is his ... or at least he thinks it is. What hath God (make that Goddess!) wrought? David

David had tutorials in the morning and the annual car inspection late afternoon, but he squeezed in lunch at the hospital. "See ya this evening, Kid," he said as he kissed her goodbye.

Jenny spent the afternoon trying to push the hands of the clock. She had never endured time that passed so slowly. When a nurse came in late afternoon to do a temperature check, Jenny held her breath.

"*Très bien, Madame.* Your temperature is normal."

The door opened again. Jenny's heart leapt in anticipation of seeing David's face, but it was just the dietician offering tea. David didn't arrive until 7:00 p.m., having braved rush hour traffic to secure Jenny's release. When they were finally home, David handed her a glass of wine, and they sat on the terrace enjoying the cool of the evening. "Good to have you home, Ducks," he said quietly.

They returned to the hospital on Friday as instructed. Despite David's aversion to the setting, he never once grumbled, burying his head in the newspaper until the nurse called them in to see the surgeon. In careful detail, Dr. Dausset reviewed the pathology data and the biopsy results. "The outcome is ideal," he announced. "There will be no need for radiation or chemotherapy. You are clean, Madame."

With a happy smile, Jenny turned to give David a kiss. "There, you see?" she said breezily. "I told you there was nothing to worry about!"

David sat mute, with tears in his eyes. Dr. Dausset was beaming.

De: David
A: Family & friends
Envoyé: 8 août, 2003
Objet: Jenny's convalescence - Final Report

Jenny's biopsy is negative, so everything is positive. The stitches are out, and she's as clean as a baby's bottom washed with a bar of Ivory soap.

Ouf! And love to all, David

"Marc, what time is your flight on Sunday?" David asked when Marc appeared in the kitchen for a lunchtime breakfast.

"I think it's at 9:15," Marc answered.

"Have you confirmed it?" Jenny queried. "Sometimes when you miss one leg of the itinerary, the computer automatically cancels the rest of the reservation. You should check to make sure they still have your seat."

Marc went into the living room to call the airline. After a minute, they heard a crash and a string of obscenities. Marc had hurled the phone down on the tile floor, breaking the casing. It took more than a few minutes for David to calm his son down and get the story from him. Marc demanded the car, but David wisely said no. Marc went out to the garage, got on his bike, and rode off.

"What happened?" Jenny asked when David returned to the kitchen.

"Not only was Marc's reservation cancelled. He's been blacklisted. Permanently. British Air won't serve him."

"What are you going to do?"

"Get him a ticket on a different airline. Hopefully someone still has a seat available on Sunday."

"No, I mean, what are you going to do about Marc. If the airline blacklisted him, there was more to that incident than a few cross words to the ticket agent."

"I can't live his life for him, Jenny."

If Marc doesn't defuse his anger, it's going to be a short life, Jenny worried, but she could think of nothing useful to say.

Marc didn't come home until the rest of the house had gone to bed. He was up early Saturday morning doing some packing, then he disappeared again. David wanted to do a special dinner in honor of Marc's last evening home, but it was not at all clear that Marc would attend. Late afternoon, Marc called.

"Will he be here for dinner?" Jenny asked after David hung up.

"Not sure," David replied. "I told him there would be plenty of food if he showed up, but I made no request about notice. I don't think he was in any condition to make reliable plans," David added. "He sounded stoned out of his mind."

"I remember Valerie saying that drugs were pretty much a constant before Marc left for San Francisco. He may have reconnected with a source here in Geneva," Jenny suggested carefully.

Back in the days when Marc and Valerie were dating, David had routinely defended his son against Valerie's accusations of drug-related behavior. Now he withheld comment. Jenny reluctantly let it go. *David has to take the lead on this,* she felt. *Even if I knew what to do – which I don't – I can't go charging ahead without David's participation and support.*

Sunday morning, with a new ticket in hand, Marc prepared to fly back to San Francisco. Delphine once again offered to accompany her father on the drive to the airport. Jenny was still under orders to limit car travel, so she said goodbye at the house. In contrast to his recent angry behavior, Marc seemed genuinely embarrassed by what had happened. He stood before Jenny, so awkward and uncomfortable that she felt a wave of sympathy for him. She gave him a hug and wished him a safe journey. As Delphine followed her father and brother out the door, Jenny caught her eye. "Thank you," she mouthed with a nod.

Delphine smiled back. "Men!" she huffed, rolling her eyes and adding a French pout for emphasis.

"Your sister's on the phone," David announced to Jenny the following afternoon.

"Hey, Caroline!"

"Hi, Jenny. How's the recovery going?"

"So far, so good. I'm doing my best to follow doctor's orders."

"Well, that gives you some leeway. If there's one you want to disregard, you can always say you misunderstood the French."

"David was present for all the order-giving at the end, so I can't get away with much. I just wish I'd had him with me all the time. The operation didn't worry me, but the language issue made me really nervous."

"In a Geneva hospital? I would have thought almost everyone would have some basic English."

"No, my surgeon spoke no English, and that was true for most of the staff. Two days after the procedure, a nurse told me to slide off the bed and take a few steps, but my left leg was completely numb. I couldn't think of the word for numb in French, so I tried to explain that I had no control over my leg, saying, *'Je n'ai pas de contrôle,'* but the nurse kept insisting that I get off the bed. I finally realized I was making the classic mistake my French teacher warns about: *les faux amis* – 'false friends' – identical words that mean one thing in English but something different in French."

Caroline chuckled. "And *contrôle* in French means a test or an inspection. The nurse must have thought you were arguing with her, saying you hadn't yet 'tested' your legs. So what happened?"

"In desperation I said, *'Je n'ai qu'un pied.'* 'I have only one foot.' It was the only phrase I could come up with. The nurse finally decided something was genuinely amiss and called in the anesthetist. He didn't speak English either, but he shut off the epidural, and *voilà*! Within a few hours, I had sensation in my leg again."

"I'm surprised they didn't have a translator on call. That was a potentially dangerous situation."

"Because my accent is good, people assume I both speak and understand French. Wrong, but it's a problem I run into a lot."

They talked for another ten minutes before signing off. In the days that followed, Jenny rested often, as per doctor's orders, but writing required no energy, and Jenny's ergonomic computer chair was designed for comfort.

From: JWLongworth
To: Bibi
Date: August 11, 2003
Subject: Thanks

I was going to prepare a major dissertation on my hospital stay, but the truth would pale against the colorful commentary David sent out.

You were good to be in touch with him during my incarceration. He joked his way through the week, but clearly there was a lot of underlying stress.

I'm home and settling in nicely. I'm not really allowed to do anything, but David is still on vacation, and he's taking very good care of me. The toughest side effect

> is the abdominal gas. I've used your tips about lying on my left side, but OUCH!
>
> Love, Jenny

When the phone rang that evening, David answered, then called to Jenny. "It's Bibi," he told her.

"Hey, Bibi! How's California?"

"Slowly falling into the sea, but otherwise fine. How are you doing? The gas problem is a real bummer. I remember how it could stop me in my tracks."

"Not fun, but I've been assured that this too shall pass, and everything else is going well. With Marc gone, peace has settled on the household."

"And what's up with that? Did you ever get to the bottom of the airplane altercation?"

"We had to deal with the results – the blacklisting – but what sets Marc off is anyone's guess. Given everything that was going on, I don't think David pushed Marc for a really detailed breakdown of what transpired. And frankly, I'm not convinced Marc is capable of analyzing what he does and why."

"If I were you, I'd get some help. Maybe he's bi-polar or has some other kind of disorder."

"But what kind of help can I get? I can do all kinds of research on-line, but Marc won't take advice from anybody, and his father holds to the theory that this will all blow over in time. I can't make Marc go see a professional, and I can hardly instruct David on questions of parenting."

"Maybe you could just yell at him."

"Yell at which – Marc or David?"

"Either. Both. I don't know. But at least let David know how you feel about it."

A further occasion to let loose that yell came earlier than Jenny expected. At the end of August, Delphine returned to Paris to begin her junior year at the American University. When David called to check on her, she sounded enthusiastic about her courses and happy with her life. He got no answer when he placed a similar call to Marc, so he left a short message with an update on Jenny's recovery and a query about Marc's course line-up for the fall semester.

From: Marc
To: Dad
Date: September 5, 2003
Subject: got your message...

hi there, i just got back from school and got your message. i cant call back because i broke my telephone to pieces, only the answering machine has survived it.

i have not got a fix class schedule because, ah, i dont even want to talk about it, stupid paper work and anglosaxone disorganization.

i am in the process of getting a new phone, will call u during the weekend.

hope all is well on your side of the planet, love marc

"What are you going to do?" Jenny asked as she read Marc's message over David's shoulder.

"Talk with him. Listen to him. It's September, so I expect he's thinking about Sandie. Three years ago he returned from his backpacking trip to find his mother lying in the hospital so far gone that she barely recognized him. I think he feels all alone in the world. He's lost."

"Lost? David, he's walking around as if he's the central victim in some major psychodrama. You wouldn't tolerate this in one of your students. Why do you tolerate it in Marc?"

David looked at her, face grim, but said nothing.

Jenny sensed she'd gone over the line, and she shifted her tone to a more positive register. *Bibi's advice to the contrary, caustic comments aren't going to ease David's paternal distress.*

"Marc reacts to stress with a violent response way above the norm. He must have been more than rude to get himself permanently banned from British Air flights. He breaks chairs. He smashes telephones. That level of aggression and rage surely has biological components. Maybe he needs some real help, professional help, getting his chemistry back in line."

"I don't disagree, but I can't drag him to a psychiatrist from half way around the world. I can only acknowledge his pain and provide a sympathetic ear while he sorts himself out. We'll be together at Christmas. Maybe the pathway will be clearer by then."

Maybe, Jenny thought.

That evening, David's brother Nate called from Chattanooga to check on Jenny's recovery. After chatting briefly with Nate, David turned to Jenny. "Our sister-in-law wants a word," he told her.

"We heard all about Marc's run-in with British Air," Margaret announced when Jenny took the phone. "That can't have been real fun for you in the middle of your surgery!"

During their last visit to Chattanooga, Margaret had urged that Jenny do more to assume Sandie's motherly role in the family. Given Marc and Delphine's initial resistance to their father's remarriage, Jenny was extremely reticent about taking over motherly duties – a stance that had disappointed her new sister-in-law. Now, however, Margaret seemed more sympathetic, and Jenny was grateful for her commiseration.

"Nate says Marc is exactly the way David was at a similar age," Margaret confided. "He remembers all sorts of arguments between David and their dad."

"That may be why David's so patient and forgiving with Marc," Jenny commented. "He remembers feeling alienated from his family. As David describes it, his father considered Harvard a 'Yankee breeding-ground for commies and outside agitators,' and was furious when David chose it over a southern college. They reportedly had knockdown drag-out fights about social issues and the Vietnam War, and didn't really reconcile their differences until David reached his thirties."

"I guess Europe did smooth out some of those rough edges of David's," Margaret chuckled, "and Sandie certainly tamed him. It's just real sad that she's not here to help Marc get past his problems. They were real close, him and Sandie. Marc needs a strong woman in his life to kind of set him straight!"

Ouch! Jenny thought. *I don't think Margaret meant that as a put-down, but she's not wrong. Sandie would have been a lot better at dealing with Marc than I am.* Jenny masked her discomfort by shifting the focus.

"I have to tell you," Jenny confessed, "that this experience has increased tenfold my respect for people like you who've raised polite, happy children."

"Why, you hang in there," Margaret counseled as they ended the conversation. "You're doing a good job with David. Nate keeps saying how happy David sounds and how big the change is from those awful days right after Sandie died. It's real obvious you're the one responsible."

There had been many factors in David's progress, Jenny knew, but she was reassured by Margaret's closing words. *I have a ways to go in the stepmother department, but at least I'm getting good marks as a wife!*

L'Académie Internationale resumed classes, and David quickly readjusted to a busy teaching schedule. Jenny was housebound, under orders to postpone a return to her French lessons. Despite regular communication with her US friends – or perhaps because of it – bouts of homesickness sometimes overtook her without warning. The passage of summer into fall was such a special time in New England, with its crisp air and glorious hues. Jenny's colorful garden in Geneva paled in comparison.

Raised with a stiff-upper-lip approach to life, Jenny normally emphasized the positive. *I'm so lucky, how can I complain? I have my health. I have the man I love. We live in a nice house, surrounded by nice neighbors.* Only to the mirror did she concede that life wasn't perfect. *I've been here two full years, and I still feel out of place,* she admitted to the frowning face reflected in the glass. *The culture remains foreign, and the language still defeats me.*

On September 25, Jenny awoke at 1:00 a.m. and couldn't get back to sleep. Insomnia was a frequent after-effect of her hysterectomy, but on this occasion, her changed hormonal status was not to blame. September 25 was the third anniversary of Sandie's death. The previous evening, David had composed a poem in observance of the occasion and had shared it with Jenny. She lay silently on her side of the bed, turning over David's reference to memories that captured his attention "unexpectedly day and night."

Finally, she got up quietly so as not to wake him, and tiptoed down the stairs. *Better to be part of the process than to be left standing awkwardly off to one side*, she decided. She took out two memorial candles, lit one, and set it beside Sandie's photograph in the living room. She left the second candle in the kitchen for David to use, and returned to bed. When she later came down for breakfast, David had made coffee and had her tea ready, but his candle remained unlit.

"That one's yours," she said, pointing it out in case he hadn't noticed it.

"Do we need one in the kitchen as well? I like having one next to the portrait. Why not let that be from both of us? A joint offering."

Before leaving for school, David e-mailed his poem to Marc and Delphine: "Light a candle for her," he told them. "My memories are sweet and gentle. Love, Dad."

Jenny's candle was still burning brightly when the phone rang late afternoon.

"Today's Sandie's yahrzeit, yes? How's David doing?" Bibi asked when Jenny answered.

"Hi, Bibi. Yes, today's the day. David's doing really well. He wrote a memorial poem and sent it to the kids. It wasn't what I'd call cheerful, but he described things reminding him "gently" of Sandie. That's a big improvement. Last year at this time, David was still subject to days and sometimes weeks of depression."

"And you? How are you doing?"

"Me? I'm fine. Had a check-up last week, and the doctor says everything is in good shape."

"I didn't mean your innards, Longworth. How's your head on yahrzeit number three?"

"Well, life has improved for me too. Twelve months ago, I was coming to the end of my first year as an ex-pat, struggling to fit in. I couldn't hold a candle to Sandie's French charm and social skills. I was afraid David might think he had made a mistake."

"But now, you say, David's doing really well. Does this mean Sandie is gradually fading from the scene, or is she still eating breakfast, lunch and dinner with the two of you?"

"Bibi, you're being harsh."

"Jenny, you're being evasive."

"Look, Sandie will always be a factor in my relationship with David. They were together nearly thirty years. All the life experience and character evolution that happened during those years was influenced by Sandie. She's part of him."

"In spite of her affair with her boss?"

"Bibi, let's not argue about this. David feels he's as responsible as Sandie was for the affair. She wanted something different from the marriage than he did, and she jumped the fence to get it. But she handled it with discretion. And he's forgiven her completely. It's a non-issue. Anyway, Sandie's 'presence' isn't going to change. What's changed is that the memories are no longer body blows. David's in way better shape than he was. The tears are rare, and his wine consumption has been back down to a normal European level for the better part of a year now. To my mind, that's proof positive that we're on a roll."

"Well, yeah, I'd have to agree that that's a good sign. So, back to the convalescence. Do you still have gas?"

"That's gotten better. My intestines are gradually adjusting. It's not painful anymore, just slightly embarrassing. David still fusses over me, but I think he's beginning to trust that I'm not exactly in imminent danger. In a strange way, this cancer episode has been a blessing in disguise. It helps David focus on the present rather than the past, and it reminds me to count my blessings."

"And how are the stepkids?"

"Dellie is happy in Paris and loves the American University. Marc remains a challenge. He's not thrilled with school, but then, he's not thrilled with much of anything."

"Is he dating anyone?"

"I don't know."

"Well, that's what it took for my Daniel. When he was Marc's age, he was no prize, but once he met Hannah, things got better. Like it says in Proverbs, a good woman is worth more than diamonds."

"Speaking of which, what are Daniel and family up to these days?" Jenny asked.

Bibi was finishing her report when Jenny heard the car pull in. "Gotta go, Bibi. David just got home."

"Do you meet him at the door in high heels and an apron like on *Leave it to Beaver?*" Bibi teased.

"You know I can't wear high heels with my bad hip. And David's the one who wears the apron in this house since he's the chef."

"You are one spoiled woman, Longworth."

When David walked in, he handed Jenny a bouquet of roses that a colleague had given him in Sandie's memory. "Several of the teachers made mention of the anniversary," he said. "Everyone at school loved Sandie."

"Was that hard for you?" Jenny asked.

"No. It's not as if they made me more aware of the date than I already was. And it's nice to be reminded of how much Sandie was appreciated."

Jenny felt a twinge of envy, but quickly overcame it. *Nice to be appreciated, but nicer still to be standing here with David.*

Shortly after David's arrival, their Iranian neighbor, Mehrak Pashoutan, came by and stayed for a glass of wine. Darkly handsome, with wiry black hair and near-black eyes, Mehrak observed a "when in Rome" philosophy, abstaining from alcohol in his own home, but sharing wine with non-Muslim friends as a gesture of appreciation for their hospitality. Mehrak offered a respectful acknowledgement of the anniversary of Sandie's death, yet there was no sadness evident in the exchange. The conversation that followed switched to English, but the subject matter was still beyond Jenny's range. Mehrak's enthusiasm for cooking rivaled David's. Most of their discussion concentrated on the best way to prepare *Coquilles St. Jacques.*

After Mehrak left, David called Delphine and then Marc.

"How are they doing?" Jenny asked when the conversations were over.

"They're working their way through it. Their lives would be very different if Sandie were still alive. I have you to travel this new road with me. The kids are walking new paths on their own. I'm here for them in my way, but ...." His voice trailed off.

Jenny felt a moment of guilt. *I wish I could say that I embrace all these ritual poems and flowers and candles. I understand how essential they are to healing, but sometimes I feel like hitting the overload button.*

Less than a week later, however, on October 1, Jenny insisted on observing a remembrance of her own. Three years before, one of Sandie's dearest and closest friends, Olga Gerasimova, had hosted a luncheon just days after Sandie's funeral. Jenny, a guest at the Perry house during the obsequies, accompanied David to the luncheon. David's behavior that day led Jenny to fear that David was so distraught that he might do harm to himself.

That fear moved her to reveal the extent of the love she had carried for him through all their years apart. "Do you not understand what you mean to me?" she had sputtered, tears streaming down her face as they stood in a field not far from the house. "That I love you as much as you loved Sandie? That if you died, I would suffer the same kind of pain you're suffering now?"

David had drawn her to him and for the next hour, their arms were entwined as they wandered along the wooded pathways. That night, they had clung to one another until the morning forced his departure for school and hers for Boston. Her determination to help him survive his pain and grief had led ultimately to their marriage.

The weather was rainy and gray when David got home from school. Jenny thought they might have to forego re-enactment of the tearful and revelatory walk, but the clouds suddenly lifted. "Are you sure you want to do this? It's a long walk, and it could be pretty muddy," David cautioned.

"Yes, I'm sure I want to do this. I accord the anniversary of Olga's luncheon even more significance than our wedding anniversary. The events surrounding that luncheon altered the course of our lives."

They managed an hour-long stroll despite Jenny's very slow pace. They didn't reminisce out loud, but that night, David used two separate pots to make pasta for their supper. One batch he cooked al dente, the way he liked it, and other he cooked longer, to accommodate Jenny's taste. In this simple gesture, Jenny felt David's love shine through, despite his resistance to honeyed phrases.

They sat out on the terrace afterward, watching the light fade. Jenny spoke, for the first time, of the significance of the day. "Three years ago," she said, "almost exactly to the minute, you were sitting out here suffering the tortures of the damned, and I was terrified you might remember how much morphine was still sitting in Sandie's medicine cabinet."

"Yup." He answered.

"Little did we know that our response to each other's agony would open the floodgates and lead us to a whole new life together," she commented. "Sometimes it feels like that night happened a hundred years ago, and sometimes it feels like it was only yesterday."

"Yup."

Blues Poem

~ For Jenny

January, 2004

Blues, pale as beach white
And dark as palm green,
Coat the rainy Florida
Evening sea scene.
Gulf images come to me:
Palmettos, clouds, sunset,
Yellows, greens, whites,
Through growing twilight gloom.
Fast-falling night has dispatched blues
To water down
The midday sunlight colors and subdue
My haste to squeeze
My terms to color views
By chance a blessing
Meant for anyone
Pulling back the curtain.
Words rush to follow pictures;
Of that I'm certain.

Chapter 3

As her energy returned, Jenny became increasingly restless. When she first arrived in Geneva, she had put her solo time to good use on the home front. Although Sandie's possessions and taste were considered sacrosanct by David and the children, Jenny had cautiously adjusted the furnishings to encompass her own way of using interior space. With these changes accomplished, however, the house now required little attention. Jenny's other domestic focus was their garden, but by mid-October, it had been put to bed for the winter.

Getting a job was not a possibility. Swiss immigration policy limited her to wifely duties. Her residency permit was based on "following your husband." Volunteer opportunities existed, but required a level of competency in French that she didn't yet have. Exploring Geneva on her own held no appeal. Her aversion to crowds and her agoraphobia left her extremely uncomfortable when alone in an unfamiliar city.

She resumed her French classes, but rarely stayed to have coffee with her fellow students because the nearby cafés were filled with cigarette smoke. Acquaintances were many, but friends were few. Most of the women Jenny had met were involved in some way with l'Académie Internationale and were at work during the day.

The one exception was Adelaide Swanton, who taught at the school for many years, but had recently retired. Originally from Argentina, with a British father and a German mother, Adelaide spoke French fluently, but she had no special allegiance to it and was quite happy to speak English. She was one of the few women in Geneva with whom Jenny could have a prolonged conversation.

Adelaide lived only twenty minutes away by foot. In good weather, the two women sometimes teamed up for walks through the domesticated countryside of small farms and vineyards that edged the village of Morion. Unfortunately, the heavy clouds that dominated Geneva's winter skies had already installed themselves, held in place by the ring of mountains that surrounded the city. Walking season was over.

Okay, Longworth. Enough is enough, she lectured herself. *You can sit and stew, or you can get off your tail and take responsibility for improving your outlook!*

"Adelaide, have you ever taken a yoga class?" Jenny asked over the phone.

"No. Why?"

"With all the inactivity after my hysterectomy, my muscles are turning to mush. I have friends back home who swear by yoga, so I thought I'd see what local possibilities exist."

"What a good idea!" Adelaide exclaimed. "I've heard yoga helps with joint problems. My knees have been bothering me for months, so maybe I should try it too. Let me know what you find out."

Through the International Women's Center that sponsored her French classes, Jenny found an American yoga teacher. When Jenny described her post-operative status and her sporadic hip problems, the woman counseled individual sessions. "It's difficult in a group setting to accommodate medical limitations and give you the attention you need to make the experience worthwhile," she explained. "I give private instruction on Tuesday and Thursday mornings, if that would work for you."

"I have a friend with knee problems. Could you take us as a duo?" When the instructor said yes, Jenny signed up.

"One thing to be aware of," Jenny and Adelaide were warned when they arrived for their introductory class, "is that new yoga students sometimes experience strong emotions as they unleash long-held tensions during the initial contemplative exercises."

Jenny dismissed this out of hand and was therefore astonished to find herself swept by waves of sadness while lying supine with instructions to empty her mind "like a sack of sand with a hole in it."

Why am I sad? What exactly am I thinking? Thwarting the exercise's intent, she lay on the mat and struggled to analyze her feelings. *I'm thinking ... I'm wishing ... I'm wishing I were home. Real home. Boston. I love David and I want to be with him, but I still don't feel comfortable here. Other people manage new lives and new languages. Why am I so bad at it?*

"Have you got time to stop by for lunch?" Jenny asked Adelaide when the hour was up. "We have leftover mushroom quiche, and David made a great potato and leek soup last night."

"David's soups are always a treat," Adelaide agreed. "I'd be delighted."

"What did you think of the class?" Adelaide asked as Jenny ladled steaming soup into bowls.

"I suspect I'm going to have difficulty mustering the proper reverence, but I'm sure the exercises will do me good."

"Why the difficulty with reverence?"

"Remember when she had us doing leg stretches?" Jenny asked. "At the point where she said, 'Imagine that your leg is pulling free, that the hip joint is leaving the socket,' all I could think was, *Oh, no, you don't want me to imagine that. The last time my hip joint left its socket was for real. Not fun. Don't want to imagine it happening again.*"

"I see what you mean," Adelaide nodded, suppressing a smile.

"And what about you?"

"I wasn't quite sure what to expect, but I enjoyed it."

"Did you feel anything during the contemplative exercises, when she warned us we might unleash some strong emotions?"

Adelaide was silent for a moment. "Actually, it was very odd. Out of the blue, I suddenly had a memory of my first husband, Eduardo. I left Argentina when I was young, during a very turbulent period.

I had friends who were thrown in jail and some who disappeared. Eduardo and I had very different political views. I had a chance to come to Geneva for an educational training program, and I took it. Once I was here, I was able to get a teaching permit as a native Spanish speaker. Eduardo wanted me to return to Argentina, but I felt I couldn't go home. The marriage ended. I was lucky that we hadn't yet started a family."

"Do you still have any contact with him?"

"No, and I haven't thought about him for years. Obviously there's some memory deeply buried in my psyche, but heaven only knows what it is. You were married before, weren't you? Do you ever think about your first husband?"

"Not if I can help it," Jenny laughed.

"Oh, dear. That bad?"

"No, actually. Seth was a nice guy. Unlike you and your first husband, Seth and I had identical political views. That's part of what drew us together. He was an MIT professor, handsome, socially conscious, politically active, and ambitious. I met him not long after I returned from my year in Europe with David. I was working hard to stop being in love with David, and Seth was just what I needed – someone solid, practical, and responsible. The marriage lasted fifteen years, but Seth couldn't resist a pretty face and a shapely pair of legs. He had multiple affairs, including some with his graduate students, and it finally became too blatant to overlook. The divorce was painful at the time, but now I see it as a 'Lost Horse' story."

"Lost horse story?"

"Do you remember the tale David told at Sandie's memorial ceremony? About the Chinese farmer whose mare ran away, then returned a week later with a stallion in tow? Things keep happening that the farmer's son views as either blessings or disasters, but he is looking at events too closely. What he thinks of as a disaster turns out to be a blessing, and vice versa."

"Yes, I remember now. In the end, the boy is injured when he's thrown from the horse, and therefore can't join in a battle where all the other boys are killed."

"Right. I sort of got thrown from my horse, but as a result I was free to go to David when Sandie died."

"I see you didn't succeed in your early efforts to 'stop being in love with David,'" Adelaide commented with a smile.

"No, I didn't. I met him during our junior year – I think I've told you that before – and I fell hard. He was sophisticated and epicurean – your classic Harvard intellectual – but he also had the gentlemanly manners, humor and down-home charm of his native Tennessee. The combination was devastating, on top of which he was incredibly cute. We were on-again off-again. In those days he wasn't about to be tied down. When he left after graduation to explore life in Europe, I threw caution to the winds and followed him. David had sufficient grounding in French to find work in Paris. I got a job in London, and we commuted back and forth across the English Channel. David loved Paris and wanted to stay there forever, but I got really homesick. The Women's Movement was picking up steam, and I wanted to go home to Boston, which, at the end of twelve months, I did. Still, my affection for him was unconditional, and here I am, back in Europe and wearing his ring."

"You two have a remarkable story," Adelaide observed.

"Do you ever get homesick for Argentina?" Jenny asked.

"Sometimes. When I'm there visiting, I'm not necessarily ready to leave when my ticket says its time to go. I have two sisters there still. But I came to Geneva as a young woman and remarried here. My children are here. My grandchildren are here. Several decades worth of friends are here."

"When I was doing the contemplative exercise, the one the teacher warned about, I suddenly felt very homesick," Jenny confessed. "I was lying there wishing we were in Boston instead of Geneva."

"I hope that was just the exercise, and that real homesickness is something you feel as rarely as I think about my first husband," Adelaide rejoined.

"It's more frequent than that," Jenny hedged, "but I left Boston by choice. No one held a gun to my head. I have to admit, though, that the language barrier is far more difficult than I anticipated. You have no idea how much I envy you your four languages! And thus far, I've found no replacement for much of what I gave up. But I will never leave David again for anywhere, anything or anyone. I'm not making that mistake a second time!"

"Well, if it helps, we've all seen enormous improvement in David's spirits and his outlook ever since you came. And on that note," she said, glancing at her watch, "I have to run. Thanks so much for lunch and this nice conversation," Adelaide said in parting.

"Yes, it's been fun," Jenny added. "Let's do this more often!"

Except for rare moments when the contemplation exercises touched a raw nerve, the subsequent yoga classes were enjoyable and, to Jenny's mind, entertaining. As she had warned Adelaide, Jenny was not of a reverent bent. In one session, at the very moment when Jenny was experiencing an intense hot flash, the teacher, unaware, counseled, "Imagine your breath reaching deep into your abdomen. Feel the gentle warmth spreading through you." It took everything Jenny had to keep from bursting out laughing. The warmth spreading through her was anything but gentle.

"I'm amazed the teacher hasn't kicked me out yet," Jenny told Bibi on the phone. "She must have figured out by now that I'm not convert material. This morning we were working on relaxation, and she told us, 'Search your body for any muscle that's tight, and gently let it go.' Given my post-operative difficulties with gas, you can appreciate that there was one muscle I definitely did *not* want to let go after working my abdominal muscles. I told David about these little trials, but he just accused me of being a smart-ass."

"I don't know what you can do about it in the classroom, but at home, you might consider getting a dog you could sweetly blame for any inadvertent pungency," Bibi suggested. "And what else are you doing besides making trouble for your yoga teacher?"

"Well, at the moment, I'm making trouble for David," Jenny answered. "We're at loggerheads over the format and the guest list for Thanksgiving. I want a formal sit-down dinner. David wants something really informal because he's thinking of inviting a couple with three small children, one of whom is just a year old. I'd be happy to have them over another day, with a meal more appropriate to children's tastes and a toddler's attention span, but no, David wants them for Thanksgiving. What makes it bizarre is that he doesn't really care about Thanksgiving per se. He and Sandie never observed it. He just loves hosting dinner parties, and he's very inclusive. Overly so, at times. If I didn't rein him in, he'd invite half of Geneva, and we'd have buffet tables out on the sidewalk."

"When it's my turn to host Thanksgiving," Bibi noted, "all the grandkids are at the table, but they're allowed to go watch cartoons after the turkey, which gives the grownups a break until we call them back for dessert."

"I know there are ways to do it, but for me, this is a once-a-year event, and I want to do a five-course meal. David is talking about really young children, which means the parents will be up and down as well. And our TV room is wide open. It's hard enough for me to follow French in a calm, quiet setting, much less with a background of chattering children and cartoon noise. Anyway, when I argued that a formal sit-down dinner was no place for a one-year-old, David dug in his heels. 'I don't *do* formal sit-down dinners in my house,' he said."

"Whoa, that sounds serious," Bibi commented. "Perhaps he's already invited this family and doesn't want to have to un-invite them."

"I don't know, but I figured something was going on that wasn't obvious. The fact that he said 'my' house was a red flag. Last night, we talked about it again. 'Sandie and I made a decision when the children were little,' he explained, 'that we wouldn't go anywhere they weren't welcome. We never got a sitter. And it always worked. This will work too. I've never given a bad party.' The trouble, Bibi, is that

David doesn't understand why I want to distinguish Thanksgiving from our usual dinner events."

Bibi chuckled. "As in, 'Why is this night different from all other nights?'"

"It's different because I want it to be *my* party. As you well know, when I came to Geneva, everything was already settled. The house was decorated, the routines were established, and the holidays were steeped in traditions no one wanted to change. I had to tiptoe through each day, being careful not to alter existing patterns. Thanksgiving, however, was a novelty in the Perry household. It was one of my few chances to implant my own traditions without offending anyone's sensibilities. Or so I thought."

"As I recall, you succeeded," Bibi offered. "I remember a long e-mail describing your first Thanksgiving over there as a culinary triumph."

"I succeeded in establishing an American menu – turkey, bread stuffing, pumpkin pie and so on. David tweaked it, but in good ways. He's the one who taught me to present the meal in courses, as the French do. I'll never go back to piling everything on the table at once. But our disagreement isn't about the menu. What I finally realized, listening to David last night, is that my guest plan is unwittingly in conflict with a Sandie rule."

"A *Sandie rule?*" Bibi queried.

"It was Sandie who raised a strong voice against ever leaving Marc and Dellie with babysitters. She relished the presence of toddlers no matter what the circumstances. They never had a Perry social event designated 'adults only,' and David doesn't want to amend that tradition."

"So how will you resolve it?" Bibi asked.

For a moment Jenny was silent. Bibi heard a sigh.

"If I'm honest about it, I have to concede that there's symbolism for me too. I want to feel as if I'm playing hostess in Boston. I want at least the majority of the guests to be English speaking. The family with the toddlers will tip the balance heavily to the francophone side, plus the additional noise will exacerbate the language problem."

"Does David understand this?"

"No, he really doesn't. I've told him, but my particular anxieties aren't within his experience. He can't believe that they're real."

"So what will you do?"

"Having just spent the last five minutes griping, I suspect it's time to wave a white flag. Tomorrow is David and Sandie's wedding anniversary, which makes it a tricky moment to do battle over a Sandie rule. If I ask myself, *What is the loving thing to do?*, the answer is pretty obvious. And you could be right. He's probably already invited these people. It would be awkward to suddenly withdraw the invitation."

"Longworth, sometimes I can't decide if you're bucking for Saint Jennifer or the world's biggest wimp. Or maybe both. Lemme know what happens."

That night, as soon as David went up to bed, Jenny readied a gift she had for him – a photograph of a youthful Sandie, newly restored and enlarged. The morning would bring what would have been David and Sandie's thirtieth anniversary. *I don't intend to mark the day in the future,* Jenny had concluded, *but David will certainly be thinking about it, and a thirtieth anniversary merits recognition. This way, I'm not just a bystander. I have a role.* She set the envelope containing the photograph on the kitchen counter for David to find at breakfast, with a note: "In remembrance of your first wedding and your first bride, with deepest love from your second. J." *And may this observance be rewarded by closure,* she breathed quietly.

When David opened his present the next morning, he seemed touched and genuinely pleased. Sandie had spent her entire marriage putting up with a poster-size photograph, prominently displayed in David's study, of a starry-eyed David and Jenny in their early twenties. "It seems only fair," Jenny commented, "that you and I now have a large portrait of Sandie to display. On top of which, to increase the chances of happily celebrating our own future anniversaries, I've decided to grant you a noisy, disorganized, toddler-friendly Thanksgiving. *But,*" she added sternly, "I'd really like a promise that it will be adults-only next year."

David looked at her, his eyes surprisingly serious behind his thick glasses. "Thanks, Jewel," he said quietly.

As an additional thank you, David offered to take Jenny to Paris for a quick weekend. Old British friends of his were planning to be in Paris briefly, and he wanted to see Delphine.

They took off right after school on Friday. The fog was thick in Geneva, but as soon as they crossed the mountains, they had clear skies. The drive was easy until they hit traffic in the outskirts of Paris. Knowing the city well, David decided on an approach that took them past Galleries Lafayette. The store was gloriously decorated in early anticipation of Christmas shopping, with lights festooned all over the building. The result was a cross between the stained glass windows at Chartres and a Middle Eastern palace out of a Disney movie. "That was always one of Sandie's favorite holiday treats," David remarked. "She loved to come down here and look at the animated window displays they have for Christmas."

"They're beautifully executed, so I can see the draw," Jenny remarked. "Still, my favorites are the exuberant displays in Boston's ethnic neighborhoods. Shawmut is old-fashioned and subdued, but the Italian North End at Christmas is so full of blinking lights and flashing colors that it's almost psychedelic!"

Their first social engagement the next day was an early lunch with Percy and Joanne Whittington. Percy had been the Director of the English-language program whose teaching staff David joined when he first went to Paris. The Whittingtons subsequently retired to a sleepy town on the south coast of Great Britain, but they made periodic trips back to France to see friends. "You owe us a bloody good excuse or a jolly good apology for not bringing your bride to England to show her off," boomed Percy when David introduced Jenny. "We were all gobsmacked when the news hit, but here you are, nearly two years married, and this is the first glimpse we get!" he declared, feigning annoyance.

"What Percy means," Joanne chimed in, beaming at Jenny, "is that we've been looking forward for some time to telling you in person how delighted we are for you both."

The conversation meandered, and included lots of reminiscing. Toward the end of the meal, Percy took out his cigarettes. David immediately intervened, citing Jenny's sensitivity, and the two men headed outside for a smoke.

"We really are so pleased to meet you at last," Joanne remarked. "David is one of our favorite people. When he joined Percy's teaching team in Paris, the two of them hit it off instantly. They're both bright, creative men, disinclined to be bound by arbitrary rules, and your husband's commitment to enjoying life is contagious. He and Percy were forever finding ways to instill fun, pleasure and good eating into their English seminars."

"I can imagine," Jenny smiled.

"Unfortunately, when David and Sandie moved to Geneva, all the joy went out of the job for Percy," Joanne confided. "I don't think he's found anything since that he liked as much as working with your husband. David is a very special person, and we're all quite relieved that you've come on board. It hasn't been an easy time for him." Joanne paused. "Of course, I suspect it's not been an easy time for you either, what with starting a new life in a new place. It must help to know you have Sandie's blessing. I heard from someone – I can't remember who now – that you and Sandie were good friends, and before she died, she practically ordered David to marry you."

Jenny had a flashback to the childhood game of "telephone," where you sat in a circle and one person started a story, whispering it to the next, and so on around the circle. By the time the tale came back to the starting point, it had changed, often to the point of being unrecognizable.

Jenny gave Joanne the more accurate version of the tale. "Sandie certainly didn't instruct David to marry me," she corrected. "She foresaw the union, but she shared her vision only with her close friend, Olga Gerasimova, who works at l'Académie Internationale. Olga waited until after the wedding to pass the story along to me. According to Olga, Sandie didn't say, 'I *think* that Jenny will come.' She said, 'I *know* that Jenny will come.' I didn't know. David didn't know. How did she?"

"Well," Joanne remarked, "I can see it all fits. You even look a lot like Sandie!"

"I'm always flattered when someone suggests a similarity," Jenny demurred, "but I have a hard time seeing the resemblance." *And even if we share certain features, I'll never come close to her Parisian style and elegance,* she sighed inwardly.

David and Percy returned to the table as small glasses of armagnac were being served. "Would love to sit here jawing all afternoon," David said, bringing the lunch to a close, "but I promised my daughter we'd meet her at 2:00."

Jenny was the first to spot Delphine, who was waiting for them at a café near the Luxembourg Gardens. *If anybody looks like Sandie, it's Dellie, not me,* Jenny observed. In Jenny's view, Delphine had inherited the best of both parents. She had her father's mischievous mien, strong cheekbones and winsome smile. The rest was pure Sandie, though Delphine was several inches taller than her mother had been.

"We just got back from Amsterdam," Delphine reported. "I *loved* the Rijksmuseum, and the Van Gogh and the Stedelijk were pretty cool too!"

The curriculum for third year Art History students included field trips. The American University of Paris didn't stint on student enrichment, so "field trip" meant visits to museums throughout the capitols of Europe. There had even been a four-day visit to Moscow. *He is certainly a proud papa,* Jenny observed as David listened to his daughter's tales.

After coffee, the three of them walked to the Luxembourg Gallery to see a Botticelli exhibit. On the way in, David stumbled on the stone steps. "Goddamn it!" he swore. Jenny instinctively reached out and grabbed his arm. She kept his hundred and ninety pound frame from tumbling over, but her shoulder was suddenly on fire.

"I might have pulled something," she said afterwards, not wanting to cancel the afternoon activities, "but I think I'll be okay."

They did some shopping afterwards, then strolled back toward Delphine's apartment. Crossing the Pont des Arts, they stopped mid-bridge to watch the waters of the Seine swirling beneath them, and David turned to his daughter. "It makes me think of the day we all came," he said, referring to the pilgrimage that he, Delphine and Marc had made to scatter Sandie's ashes.

"Me too," Delphine replied.

Jenny smiled sympathetically at Delphine, and Delphine smiled back. *She seems genuinely okay with my being here,* Jenny sensed. Fearful for her father's safety and sanity when Sandie died, Delphine had appreciated Jenny's swift intervention, but had initially opposed their marriage. Although Jenny kept her maiden name, Longworth, as her legal identity, Swiss custom dictated that she be referred to as Madame Perry. Delphine had been distraught at the notion that her mother's title would thereby be reassigned. Over time, Delphine had become more comfortable with Jenny's new role in the Perry family, but it had not been an easy process.

They began their homeward journey after Sunday lunch. "Is your shoulder going to be okay with that seatbelt?" David asked as they buckled themselves in.

"I'll be fine so long as you don't have to slam on the brakes," she answered, downplaying the discomfort.

They tended to be silent during car trips, except to remark on some passing sight, but out of the blue, David allowed as how he would never again get involved in Thanksgiving planning. "I'll help," he promised, "but in the future, I'm staying the hell out of the decision making."

Jenny understood this as an apology of sorts, and appreciated his gesture.

"It's odd that Thanksgiving is such a hot-button issue for us," she commented. "I know, for me, it's a link to Boston. It's also uniquely my contribution. There's no comparison with the past, no comparison with Sandie. I'm still struggling to make the house in Morion *my* house as well as your house. I'd like to feel as committed to Geneva as you do, to find ways to be more socially involved here. But noisy francophone events are not fun for me, even when they're under the guise of a Thanksgiving dinner. I don't think that's ever going to change."

"I hear you, Ducks, and I'm sorry I was so adamant. I accept that Thanksgiving is the only time you ask that a meal be done by your rules, not mine."

"I love you, David Perry."

"Hmpff," he grunted, pulling into a rest area so he could get out and have a cigarette.

Ironically, the couple with three children ended up declining their invitation. Delphine came home for the occasion, but Marc spent the holiday in San Francisco with a group of protesters on Alcatraz Island. "Thanksgiving is nothing more than a celebration of genocide and slavery," he declared. "When you observe Thanksgiving, you're just displaying contempt for Native Americans."

"Marc hasn't done his homework," Jenny commented. "Thanksgiving was proclaimed a national holiday by Abraham Lincoln in an attempt to unite the country after the terrible divisiveness of the Civil War. The greeting card companies feature cheerful Pilgrims dining with happy Wampanoags because that's a much nicer image than a battlefield at Gettysburg strewn with carnage."

"It's a pretty common misconception," David said.

"Even so," Jenny continued, "Marc's anger about historical injustice is a seething pot that often boils over. I get the feeling that there's something very personal about it," Jenny speculated.

"In what way?"

"Marc rails against injustices affecting people who don't have the same advantages he does, but he's very defensive about it, as if *he's* the injured party. He doesn't want to talk about rational, feasible ways to improve conditions and right wrongs. He just lashes out. There's no objectivity. His reactions are more about personal pain than empathy with the problems of others. If he were sixteen, I could chalk it up to adolescent angst, but he's twenty-three now. There should be some maturity beginning to emerge – some philosophical overlay."

"I wish I knew the answer," David sighed. "Marc's been a loner ever since middle school. His only friends were kids outside l'Académie Internationale. He hung out for a while with two boys who were in public school, but he would never bring them home. It used to drive his mother crazy."

"Do you know if he was bullied at school? Faculty child? Teacher's pet?"

"I'm not aware of any bullying, and he certainly wasn't any teacher's pet. Marc acted out a lot. He was something of a troublemaker, picking fights and disrupting classes. A lot of things happened that, I found out much later, were swept under the rug because everybody loved Sandie and nobody wanted to upset her."

"Maybe his status as a faculty child worked against him," Jenny speculated. "His attendance was gratis because you and Sandie worked at l'Académie Internationale, whereas most of the students there come from affluent families who can afford the pricey private school fees. I've heard you speak of twelve-year-olds with Rolex watches and chauffeurs picking them up in Bentleys. Maybe Marc felt outclassed. If he resented the economic disparity, one way to defend against it would be to reject that lifestyle and those values, which would ultimately mean rejecting his schoolmates."

"It didn't bother Delphine."

"No, but Dellie has a different personality, and she's female. Marc may have felt very competitive and very frustrated that he couldn't best anyone in his peer group economically."

"In any event, it's water over the dam. There's not much I can do here and now except hope that the Alcatraz celebration is reasonably sober and no one falls into San Francisco Bay. That water will kill you."

In the end, their Thanksgiving was small and simple, because Jenny's shoulder pain had worsened and rendered her right arm virtually useless. She couldn't lift a saltshaker much less a roasting pan.

The minute Thanksgiving was behind them, David took Jenny to see their family physician, Dr. Payot, who started Jenny down a path of x-rays, scans and MRIs. Knowing her discomfort with medical interviews in French, David scheduled Jenny's examinations for times when he could accompany her. At the end of the line, it was clear that the Jenny had ripped one tendon off the bone and inflicted a bad tear in a second one. Since Dr. Payot had little confidence in shoulder reconstruction, he prescribed intensive physical therapy and referred Jenny to a therapist. "I want to see how far Madame can progress before considering surgery," he counseled.

When David called to set up the first appointment, the therapist said she had only one opening left in December. Unfortunately, David had a full teaching schedule on that day. *Oh god!* Jenny thought. *I feel like a total ninny, but I can't see my way clear to finding the therapist's office by myself and negotiating the introductory interview in French.*

"I just – I don't – I'm sorry, David. Let's start the process after our Christmas trip to the States, and find a day when you can go with me, at least for the first session."

David seemed neither surprised nor disturbed that Jenny didn't want to do the initial visit alone. He booked Jenny for a mid-January appointment. That night, as they lay in bed, Jenny thanked him for being so patient with her agoraphobia.

He just shook his head. "Why should I complain about your not wanting to take an unfamiliar bus route to a part of town you've never seen, to a therapist you've never met, using a language you rarely use?"

I do love this man, she thought, as she snuggled into his arms.

Jenny called Adelaide and their yoga teacher, saying the doctor had advised her to discontinue classes in light of her shoulder injury. That afternoon, Adelaide stopped by to commiserate and deliver a gift of homemade empanadas. They sat and visited over tea. The enlarged photo of Sandie that Jenny had given David was lying in a clear plastic sleeve on the dining room table – a reminder for David that they needed to buy a frame for it.

"It's a wonderful photograph," Adelaide commented. "It brings to mind that poster-sized picture in your downstairs office – the one of you and David when you were so young."

"That's probably because it's the same photographer," Jenny responded.

"Oh, I think it's more than the same photographer," Adelaide said thoughtfully. "You and Sandie have a great deal in common, and you look enough alike to be sisters."

"People say that, but I don't think we look alike at all. Sandie was the same height as me, and had the same dark coloring, but her eyes were turned down at the corners; mine are level and closer together. And her nose had that perfect upturn at the end. Believe me, I'd give a lot to have a nose like that!"

"Perhaps it's a matter of bearing," Adelaide suggested. "Good posture, an aura of self-confidence, a certain intensity in your eye contact – you certainly have that in common. You're very logical, and so was Sandie. She managed finances well and was very organized – skills you also have. And then there's the way David behaves when he's with you."

"And how is that?" Jenny asked, curious as to Adelaide's assessment.

"David is extremely bright and very much an independent being. You seem to admire these traits in him, but they don't intimidate you. His occasional bursts of temper don't intimidate you either."

"That's because they're mostly directed toward his computer, or a pot that he's allowed to boil over on the stove," Jenny laughed.

Adelaide smiled. "Perhaps the simplest explanation is that David was happy when he was with Sandie, and he's happy now when he's with you. Perhaps it's his interaction with you, the teasing and the familiarity, that reminds people of Sandie."

Jenny's mind jumped unbidden into an awkward space. She paused, searching for an appropriate response. *Is Adelaide aware of Sandie's affair?* Jenny wondered. *Yes, David was happy with his marriage, but that wasn't always the case for Sandie. I'm willing to talk about it with friends who already know, but otherwise, I'd rather let sleeping dogs lie.*

"Perhaps," Jenny agreed, then steered the conversation away from Sandie and onto a discussion of their respective holiday plans.

Christmas loomed. Preparing left-handed for their holiday trip to the States was challenging, but Jenny managed. As was their custom, Jenny's departure preceded David's by a week so she could take care of administrative matters and see friends. David was predictably fidgety the morning of her departure. Jenny did her best to conceal her enthusiasm for the trip, knowing that being alone in Geneva, even for just a week, would remind David of the dark empty days that followed Sandie's death.

She didn't like leaving him, but she was excited about going home and eager to see how her condo was faring. Ostensibly, Jenny kept it for vacation purposes, but the knowledge that she could return as needed helped keep her homesickness in balance. Surrounded by gardens and woods, it offered a peaceful haven from the pressures of the outside world. *I really do love that place,* she acknowledged silently.

The minute she set foot in Boston, the feeling of freedom and independence was delicious and renewing. Sliding behind the wheel of her rental car, she set the radio to her favorite "golden oldies" station, drove through the airport tunnel and took the Southeast Expressway, knowing exactly which lane to use to avoid the slowdowns caused by exit-only lanes or on-ramps. She sang along to the pop music of the seventies and eighties, reveling in the simple fact that she knew the words and everything was in English.

From: JWLongworth
To: DavidP
Date: December 14, 2003
Subject: Safe Landing

The plane came in half an hour late, but all is well. Driving is a little tricky, but I can use my right hand at five o'clock on the wheel so long as I keep my upper arm braced against my body.

And now, to make your day, I FORGOT SOMETHING. In my closet, on the far right side, there should be a black belt with a silver clasp. Could you please bring it with you? *Merci.*

Love, Jenny

De: David
A: Jenny
Envoyé: 15 décembre, 2003
Subject: Re: Safe Landing

Oh, JEEEEzus, you forgot something!!! I may have to cancel my trip and stay here.

Kisses, Me

From: JWLongworth
To: DavidP
Date: December 16, 2003
Subject: Wild Turkeys

Please do not cancel your trip. There is a flock of wild turkeys – two toms and ten hens – gobbling up the birdseed beneath the mountain laurels. They're worth crossing the ocean to see! Wish you were here right now to share this!!

Love, J.

David telephoned the next evening, catching Jenny just as she was heading out to meet Rachel Aronson for lunch. "How's the flock doing?" he asked after they exchanged greetings.

"They're still wandering around, scratching up the snow and hoping I'll put out some more birdseed," Jenny answered.

"Can you encourage one to sacrifice itself for humanity?"

"Very funny," she retorted.

"How's Boston?"

"All's well. Except for my cranky shoulder, it's been fun driving where I know the roads, know the rules, and know which back routes to use when the traffic gets heavy. I do love Boston, and I miss it, but

I love and miss you more, so I'm looking forward to your arrival on Saturday."

They chatted for a few more minutes, then David closed the conversation. "Don't want to make you late for your lunch with Rachel. Give her a big hug from me," he instructed Jenny.

From: JWLongworth
To: DavidP
Date: December 18, 2003
Subject: Thursday

Lunch with Rachel was fun. She sends her love. She seems to be in good shape, but she's feeling stretched thin with holiday preparations.

I asked if maybe she was trying to be two people at once, tackling the holidays as always, but then adding on top whatever Josh used to do. I told her how you felt a need to fill the mother role as well as the father role after Sandie's death.

It was a good discussion. We both wished you'd been there to share in it. Rachel also wanted to know how you and I were doing. I reassured her that despite our strong cultural differences, our conflicts have usually been minor, focused on the merits of melted butter vs. vinaigrette with asparagus, and how to conduct Thanksgiving dinner.

I'll call Graham to confirm the arrangements for Sunday.

Much love, J.

In fact, aided by a second glass of wine, Rachel and Jenny had discussed several conflicts stronger than the question of what to serve with asparagus.

"You'd think by now I'd be comfortable in Geneva," Jenny lamented, "but I still lack an intuitive grasp of the social mores – when to kiss cheeks and when not to, when to use the formal '*vous*' and when to revert to the familiar '*tu*' form of address. It is emphatically *not* the same criteria English speakers use to choose between 'Mrs.

Aronson' and 'Rachel.' Hardest of all, I'm still struggling with the language. I feel like a bumbling idiot in social gatherings."

"But you've been taking lessons, haven't you? I'll bet your French is better than you think it is," Rachel offered supportively.

"I've been taking French classes for over a year. I'm in an 'Intermediate' group, but I think they call us that to make us feel good. I have a good accent – a holdover from my high school training – and that gives me some self-confidence. But most of what I learned in high school is gone. I took German in college, and that pretty well squashed my accumulated French."

"Do you practice your French with David? He's completely bilingual, isn't he?"

"Yes, he's bilingual, but no, I don't practice with him. We've known each other for decades, but in some ways, we're still learning to live with each other. There's too much going on in our relationship to complicate it with communication errors. And besides, we learn differently. I have more of a visually-based memory than he does. I don't remember names, for example, unless I see them written down first. When I began my French lessons, I told David I wanted to find some flash cards so I could build my vocabulary and test myself over and over until new words actually stuck. David just shook his head. 'You're going about it all wrong, Jenny. That's not the way to learn a language. You need to absorb it the way most other people do. Go to the grocery store. Talk to the people around you. Go to the hairdresser's. Go shopping.'

"I understood what he was saying, but I have a phobia about going out alone in a strange city, and my upbringing included strict rules about not talking to strangers. On top of that, I don't like shopping, and I cut my own hair."

"Are you serious?" Rachel asked.

"About what?" Jenny replied.

"About cutting your own hair? It looks great! How do you do it?"

Jenny had to laugh. Rachel wore her hair in a perfectly shaped pageboy. It was expertly and professionally dyed with soft striations ranging from blond to sandy, and a touch of frosting at the edge of her face. Jenny's was its original dark brown mixed with very authentic gray.

"I do it with a good pair of scissors and a three-way mirror. It's naturally curly so that hides any amateur errors in front, but if you check out the back, you can tell it's a do-it-yourself job. I have trouble reaching my arm around to get the neckline even," she pointed out.

"Anyway, enough complaining. My fellow French students were competent, capable women in their previous lives, but, like me, they feel like dummies in Geneva, so I know I'm not alone. There's one woman who has a degree in management and used to consult on cultural differences in the workplace. Then she married a Frenchman and moved to a small village not far outside Geneva. While we were waiting for class to start, we got to talking. 'It took me a couple of years living here,' she confessed, 'before I realized I had no real understanding of cultural differences when I taught it. There is a huge difference between experiencing something versus witnessing it, and I was brought to my knees. I'm still struggling. All the wonder, charm, love, and glorious European cuisine have yet to make up for the challenges.'"

Rachel scrutinized Jenny's face. "So what are you saying? Are you beginning to regret your choice?"

"I love being back in my world as it was before I left. I haven't lost the knack for contented solitude. But watching David enjoying life again makes my discomfort with Geneva seem a small price to pay. I regret that he's so committed to Europe, but I don't regret my decision to live there with him, even if my existence is somewhat circumscribed. If anything happened to David, I'd come back to Boston in a heartbeat, but I'd rather see him outlive me even if means being stuck in Geneva till the end of my days."

Rachel nodded. "You're preaching to the choir," she said softly.

From: JWLongworth
To: DavidP
Date: December 19, 2003
Subject: School's out

If you are home to read this, it means school is *out!* I know you're not looking forward to spending tomorrow on airplanes and in airports, but the wild turkeys await, so it should be worth the effort. May the flight be safe, the meals palatable, the wines potable, and the delays non-existent.

Love, J.

Only the first three of Jenny's wishes were granted. David called from London to say that the plane was facing major delays. "At this point, there's no way to predict when I'll arrive, and it could be late, so I'll take a taxi from Logan. I'll see you in Shawmut."

Jenny didn't argue, but she followed the flight on the airline's website and was standing outside the customs exit when the monitor confirmed that the plane had finally touched down. After an hour of waiting, however, there was still no sign of David. *Did he switch to a different flight?* she fretted. *Has he run afoul of customs with his French cheese or his Gauloises cigarettes?*

"The goddamn luggage conveyer belts aren't working," he fumed when he finally appeared. "My bags were the last ones off the bloody plane!" He had been in transit for over twenty-four hours and was desperate for a cigarette.

David was so exhausted by the time they got home that he slept straight through to sunrise, getting a good jump on the time adjustment. As he sipped his morning coffee, the flock of wild turkeys began to pick their way down the hill toward the lawn. There were fourteen of them this time. "Goddamn!" he exclaimed. "They look almost prehistoric!"

Late morning they headed to Cambridge for brunch with Graham and Barbara Wells. "We're so glad you folks are in town!" Jenny exclaimed. "With your crazy bi-coastal commuting, we weren't sure you'd be in Boston during our Christmas pass-through. We were really sorry to have to cancel the July visit to you in Monterey."

"Well, we were sorry too," Graham replied. "But when David alerted us that you'd be stopping here before going to Chattanooga, we made sure our California obligations were wrapped up in time to cross paths. This has also worked for me because I wanted to see my oncologist while we're here."

A colon cancer survivor, Graham had just gotten a report that his most recent follow-up scans had come out clean. Given Jenny's summer diagnosis and hysterectomy, cancer occupied much of their conversation as Graham prepared omelets and Barbara set out oversized cranberry muffins.

"Actually, my first cancer – the thyroid problem – had a far stronger emotional impact than the uterine cancer, because the prognosis wasn't good," Jenny shared. "I had to ask myself, *If you have only twelve months to live, what do you want to do?* The most radical change I could think of was declining to serve another term on my condo's Managing Board. I was happy with my work; I relished my volunteer activities; I enjoyed my friends; and I loved playing in my garden. I was already living a very nice life. It was something of an astonishing discovery!"

"A part of that speaks to me pretty directly," Graham acknowledged. "I've been thinking a lot about what I might want to change in my life, with this uncertain reprieve I've been given. And it is uncertain. Plus, we know the end of life's story, right? Like you, I take pleasure in seeing, both around and in me, a life that contains so much of what I value. But it also needs a few adjustments."

Barbara broke into a broad smile but kept her own counsel.

"At this point, the kids are out of the nest. Parenting goes on forever, but the hands-on residential care gives way to another chapter. When I stand back and look at it, I wonder where I found time to have a teaching and writing and clinical career at all. I've been blessed, but more than a bit frenetic at times. I'd like to find a way to live with all the same elements but with more serenity and graciousness."

"Wells, the only way you're gonna have more serenity is if you retire from at least one of your three full-time jobs," David cracked.

"We're actually looking at that," Graham answered. "Not retiring per se, but cutting back, maybe working half-time."

"Problem with half-time," Jenny interjected, "is that you usually end up working full time at half pay. I'd love to see David retire," she added, "but I don't think it would work if he tried to stay on as a half-time teacher. I'd rather see him retire altogether and play golf."

David looked at her in amazement. "You want me to retire and play golf?"

"If we could afford it, absolutely," she replied. "You love golf, and it's good for you. You smoke less when you're playing; you relax, and you get some healthy exercise."

Jenny could see him absorbing the thought. "We'll have to talk about it," he said, not a hundred percent sure that Jenny was serious.

As they said their goodbyes, Graham and Jenny had a private moment. "I'm still waiting for your thoughts about the kids," he said, referring to the lengthy e-mails they had exchanged during the past year, partly about cancer but also about the ups and downs of Jenny's life in Geneva. "You've entered into a demanding and emotionally charged situation. Step-parenting is challenging enough, and when it follows close on a death, all that is heightened."

"That's for sure," Jenny concurred. "Things have settled out fairly well with Dellie, but Marc still seems unfocused and unhappy with his life. He's full of confusion and negativity. David worries about him a lot. Both the kids will be with us for Christmas in Chattanooga, so we'll see how things stand. We're hoping that Marc's San Francisco experience is helping him find some stability."

"Well, when you feel like it," Graham offered, "tell me whatever you'd like to share. I'm not sure how I can help, but I'm always ready to listen. Meanwhile, have a great Christmas with the Tennessee clan!"

The next day was given over to jet lag, but that evening they squeezed in a light supper in Shawmut with Ross Barrett and his companion, Kevin McGarry. "That was fun," David remarked after the pair left. "I've always enjoyed Ross's company, but he's definitely a happier person now that Kevin's part of the picture."

"He was alone for a long time after Ramon died. Until Kevin came along, no one could fill the void Ramon left."

"Except you," David said. "At least, up to a point."

"Oh, we were best buddies, no question. We hung out together all the time, but we couldn't help each in the romance department. I don't think either of us expected to find love again, yet lo and behold, here we are, Ross with Kevin and me with you, all living happily ever after."

David gave her a cautioning look.

"Okay, okay, I know," she amended. "Don't jinx it. *Insh'allah,* as Mehrak would say."

They flew to Atlanta the next day, where they met Delphine's flight from Paris and Marc's from San Francisco. Jenny's shoulder protested against the airport hugs, but she was pleased to see the look of excitement on Delphine's face, and while Marc looked thin to her, his color was good. *Of course, that may just be California's year-round sunshine,* she realized.

Delphine napped as they drove north. Marc's cross-country journey had been tiring as well, but he was talkative and seemed eager to get to Chattanooga.

"How are things at school?" David asked.

"Astronomy is fun," Marc shrugged, "as long as I ignore the professor, who's kind of obnoxious. But the news-writing class I'm doing is cheap writing for morons."

"Is the class optional, or is news-writing a requirement for your photojournalism major?" Jenny asked.

"Yeah, it's a requirement, but it makes no sense because what's important concerning photojournalism is that you print from day to day, accumulate negatives, get experience. I wonder sometimes why am I at school. If I want to pass my time in a constructive manner, it's not by taking the news-writing course, which seems mostly useless. Maybe it's stupid, I don't know, but I sometimes think that I should change my major."

"Changing majors is what college is all about," David offered reassuringly. "There's no reason why the ideas you come in with are the ones that should stay with you throughout. The whole point is to open your mind to new possibilities."

"Yeah, but if I change," Marc argued, "I'll be wasting all the classes I already took."

"When Delphine first went to Paris," Jenny remarked, "she ended up changing not only her major, but her school. In the process, she found her way to a very rewarding college experience."

"That's true," David confirmed. "You might want to talk to your sister about it. When you discover your intellect, it seems reasonable to use it investigating different universes. It's not a mistake; it's a winding road. That doesn't mean you won't return to photo-journalism later on, but perhaps it would be better to experiment more today. This is the best time in your life to explore new worlds."

"Well, I obviously made a bad choice, but I thought photo-journalism was the best way to stand witness – to give back a vision to the people who have lost it, to show them the way it should be."

"Standing witness is a good thing," David cautioned, "but you want to be careful about showing people 'the way it should be.' Just remember that this mind-set also exists in people whose values we find repugnant. There are other ways of having influence, without asking the whole world to accept your viewpoint. Beautiful pictures – poignant photographs, for example."

Jenny noted Marc's willingness to question his previously unshakeable decisions. *It suggests at least some progress toward maturity. I also take it as a good sign that he wants to be with the family for Christmas.*

"How's your love life?" David asked after he had exhausted inquiries about Marc's classes.

Marc offered a blunt brush-off in response. "American girls are all air-heads. It's gonna be hard to find someone like Mom."

Jenny considered Marc's comment. *It's not unusual for men to seek attributes of their mothers in the women they date and marry, but if Marc wants to attract a woman like Sandie, he would do well to emulate his father,* she thought. *As it stands now, they're as different as night and day.*

To Jenny, Marc seemed guarded and defensive, whereas David was generous, inclusive, and not afraid to reveal his vulnerabilities. There wasn't even a discernable physical resemblance. Marc was a masculine version of his mother, dark-haired and slight. David, in contrast, had sandy hair and was several inches taller than his son, at least when he stood up straight. *Good posture has never been David's strong suit,* Jenny conceded.

Marc's face was narrow, with an aquiline nose. The eyes were different. The ears were different. The mouth was different. Had Jenny encountered Marc unknowingly, she would not have guessed he was David's son. *Still, he'd be a good-looking boy if he just smiled more often,* she acknowledged.

"Almost there," David pointed out as they crossed the border into Tennessee.

"Hurray!" Delphine piped up, rubbing her eyes and suppressing a yawn.

Marc and Delphine had often spent time with their Chattanooga cousins as they were growing up. The connection became even more important after Sandie's death, and David made an effort to promote frequent communication. Now the family patriarch, David stood at odds with much of what the South represented to him politically and socially, but he relished being with his two younger brothers and their families.

Nate, the middle brother, was a successful real estate agent. He and his wife Margaret lived on Signal Mountain with their children, Gil and LeeLee, in a rambling house that served as the center of holiday activities as well as guest quarters for the youngsters. Within minutes of their arrival, Delphine and her cousin immediately picked up where they left off, disappearing into LeeLee's room to share girl-talk. Marc and his cousin Gil quickly resumed their past camaraderie as well, and seemed to enjoy being together.

Isham, David's youngest brother, lived with his wife Sue Ellen and son Bert in North Chattanooga. He and his family joined the clan for dinner that night. With all three brothers together, there was much boisterous merriment well into the evening.

The traditional holiday social whirl quickly took over the calendar. There were parties around the clock, and on Christmas itself, "all is calm, all is bright," was true only for the latter half of the phrase. Presents at Nate and Margaret's house were opened in a frenzy of flying bits of paper that Jojo, their mixed-breed terrier, leapt up to catch. Cheered on by his humans, Jojo shredded ribbons and ripped wrappings to death in the center of the living room.

"It's just so great to have you-all here for Christmas," Margaret gushed. "You've helped the Perry brothers stay real tight, Jenny, and that's what they like!"

Jenny did her best to keep up with her high-energy in-laws, but, slowed by her painful shoulder and her more reserved nature, she was grateful when David offered her a breather. "We can't leave town without having lunch at my favorite restaurant – just the two of us!" Settling Jenny into a booth at a local diner, David brought her a plate piled high with barbecued ribs and a mound of coleslaw. "And there's bourbon pecan pie for dessert," he grinned, raising his glass of beer in toast. "To us," he said.

"To us," she replied.

At the end of the visit, they said their goodbyes and drove back to Atlanta, putting Marc and Delphine on their respective planes. They originally considered coordinating their return to Europe with Delphine's, but Jenny had lobbied successfully for additional time stateside to recover from the holiday hoopla. They flew to Florida and settled into the Naples apartment that the Longworth siblings kept as a vacation rental and family time-share – a legacy from Jenny's mother.

Jenny was limited by her shoulder, but she side-stroked about the pool and walked on the beach, while flocks of sea birds and pods of dolphins worked their way up and down the coast. They dined on stone crab, hush puppies, and Key lime pie – all treats impossible to find in Geneva – and David gifted Jenny with a New Year's poem celebrating their Florida visit.

"My parents really loved this apartment," Jenny commented as they sat on the balcony and watched the sun melt into the Gulf of Mexico.

"I can certainly see the attraction," David commented. "I've always felt lucky to have teacher-length vacations, allowing for this kind of travel, but given all the recent medical shit you and Graham have gone through, it's hard to ignore the reality that life is short. I've been thinking about what you said, and I'm definitely open to exploring early retirement. It might feel strange at first to be on vacation all the time, but I expect I could adapt pretty quickly," he grinned.

"It would be wonderful if we can pull it off. You know I don't feel morbid about this, but it's only practical to presume my future will be measured in years, not in decades. I dodged a bullet with this last round, but the heavy radiation I had for my thyroid cancer is bound to come back and haunt me some day. I want to use the time well, and to me, that means enjoying as much of your company as possible."

"I hear you, Ducks. I hear you."

One night, long after they had gone to bed, David woke Jenny up to report a full moon setting over the Gulf. Neither of them had ever seen a moonset over water. It was eerie and quite beautiful.

"If you decide to retire early, we could watch the moon setting in any number of places."

"Not a bad idea," he answered. "I want to understand the parameters before we take the plunge, but it's not a bad idea at all."

Jenny heard David's answer as an almost certain "yes." She smiled at him through the moon shadows. "I'm game if you are."

Le Temps - *Pour Sandie*

Il a neigé toute la nuit, mon amour -
Une neige douce à gros flocons pour
Envelopper cette terre qui fut la tienne.
La neige ne tombe plus ce soir.
Le ciel est clair, mon amour.
Il annonce une nuit étoilée à la pleine lune
Pour célébrer le vingt-quatre, ton anniversaire,
et le vingt-cinq, ma deuxième année
De mariage avec ton âme sœur.*

D.P. - January, 2004

**It snowed all last night, my love –*
A soft snow with large flakes
To cover this earth which used to be yours.
The snow no longer falls this evening.
The sky is clear, my love.
We will have a starry night and full moon
To celebrate the twenty-fourth, your birthday,
And the twenty-fifth, the second anniversary
Of my marriage with your soul sister.

Chapter 4

The phone was ringing as they negotiated their suitcases through the front door of the house in Morion. David took the call and within seconds his face crumpled.

Jenny's mind raced. *Is it the kids?*

"Shit, shit, shit!" David repeated after he hung up.

"What is it, David? What's happened?"

"Madame Lamont died last night, apparently in her sleep. That was her daughter calling from Paris. The family found her this morning. She was a surrogate mother to Sandie, and she's the closest thing to a grandmother that Marc and Delphine have ever known. They'll be devastated," he lamented.

"I'm so sorry, David," Jenny said, offering a hug.

"In a lot of ways, Madame Lamont served as a surrogate mother for me too," David added. "I met Sandie just as my own mother's mind was being destroyed by Alzheimer's. Momma lived another ten years with the disease, but as an empty shell. There was a body, but no mind. She was effectively dead to me – and to her grandchildren. Madame Lamont filled the void in dozens of ways."

"I know how much you'll miss her, but look at it from Madame Lamont's point of view," said Jenny, hoping to provide solace. "Her life was rich with family and friends, and she kept her independence to the end. She was a remarkable woman, but she was ninety years old. To die peacefully in her own home and her own bed is surely exactly what she prayed for. It's a passing to be envied."

"I agree that her death was gentle and dignified, but that doesn't assuage my sense of loss."

As David waited for details about the funeral arrangements, he started calling friends who had known Madame Lamont. "Losing her means the end of an era," he told them sadly. Listening to David talk about her, it was clear that the woman had been part and parcel of his life with Sandie in Paris. *He's losing that reflection of Sandie on top of losing Madame Lamont,* Jenny realized.

David put on the Bach cello suites that had accompanied Sandie's cremation service, and the mood remained somber throughout the afternoon.

Word came that the funeral would take place in Paris on Friday, the same day that Jenny's first physical therapy session was scheduled.

"You have to go to the funeral regardless, David. I'm sure Dellie both wants and needs you there. I'll stay in Geneva. I don't know any of Madame Lamont's family, and the service and visiting will all be in French. I've waited a month for this appointment, and I think I should keep it.

"Are you sure you can deal with it on your own?" David asked.

"Not my favorite thing to do, but I can handle it," Jenny replied.

To make it easier, David drove Jenny along the bus route and pointed out which stop she should use. Although the car would be free in David's absence, Jenny couldn't operate a stick-shift with a bad arm. David also prepared a summary of Jenny's shoulder problems in French, along with questions for the physiotherapist.

"I'll be fine," Jenny assured him as he left for the funeral.

When she arrived at the therapist's office, Jenny discovered, to her relief, that she was able to understand almost everything the woman said. *She's Swiss-German!* Jenny realized.

"I cannot repair the damage," the therapist explained briskly, pronouncing her consonants with German precision, rather than slipping over them as the French did. "What I will do is help you strengthen other muscles so they can compensate." She gave Jenny a series of home exercises, and booked her for twelve office sessions, as Dr. Payot had prescribed.

David came home the following day. "The burial was very French," he summarized. "We gathered at the cemetery gates and walked behind the hearse. There was no ceremony per se. Delphine and I joined the family for coffee afterwards. Everyone was sad that Madame Lamont was no longer present but, like you, grateful that her passing was so peaceful."

David sent a quick report to Marc about the funeral. By evening, he had a reply:

> *From: Marc*
> *To: Dad*
> *Date: January 10, 2004*
> *Subject: Re: Mme Lamont*
> i am glad you and delphine were able to go to mme lamont's ceremony, i wish i could of given my respect to this strong and adorable lady that was part of mom's family from my perspective. i considered her as my grandmother and was impatient of seeing her again and chat, life had other plans for her. *vive mme lamont!* marc

David showed Marc's note to Jenny. "He seems to be handling Madame Lamont's passing with relative equanimity," David observed.

"I hope so," Jenny said.

She read Marc's response a second time. "It's really striking how different Marc's English is compared to Dellie's. The contrast is particularly dramatic in their writing."

"Marc refused to speak English until he was nearly ten," David explained. "Sandie spoke to Marc in French, and I spoke to him in English, but just as he was becoming verbal, I was busy at school most of the time. Probably ninety-five percent of his communication was in French. Delphine, coming two years later, got a more even split. Both children attended the bilingual program at l'Académie Internationale, but Delphine's English was aided by having so many British and American friends. Marc didn't have much truck with anglophones once he reached middle school. He also, quite frankly, put a less than heroic effort into his English classes, which is evident in his grammar, syntax and punctuation."

"Well, ungrammatical communication is better than none. It does sound as if he's doing okay about Madame Lamont," Jenny concluded. "She really did have a remarkable life. I hope we have as much wit and energy at seventy as she did at ninety. Assuming we even live that long," Jenny corrected. "Is it indelicate to suggest that this is perhaps a reminder," she added, "that we should tackle the retirement research we've talked about?"

"I've been meaning to find out about my options. I'll make an appointment with Olga."

As Human Resources Director, Olga Gerasimova was the school's chief expert on retirement. "Let us meet in the administrative staff room," Olga suggested. "There we will have a table to spread out all the forms, and we can talk over coffee and tea."

When they arrived, Jenny went to the sink to fill the kettle and was startled to find herself looking at Sandie. There, on the wall, was a large photomontage, with Sandie smiling out through twenty years worth of snapshots. *"Toujours en vie dans nos coeurs!"* was handwritten across the bottom – "Still alive in our hearts!"

Jenny quickly collected herself. *I shouldn't be so surprised. Every time I've met people from the school, David has prefaced the introduction with, "So-and-so loved Sandie."* She set the kettle on a hotplate and joined the others.

Olga listened carefully to David's comments, then suggested a possibility they hadn't considered. "One of your choices is to take an unpaid sabbatical leave. It would protect your benefits, allow you to see what retired life is like, yet maintain the option of returning to your post if you want to resume teaching."

David viewed the concept positively. "It sounds like a good way to test the waters," Jenny agreed, "though I'll need to take a hard look at the finances."

"It might be possible for him to take a leave of only one semester, if you are worried about the loss of salary," Olga mentioned when David ducked out for a cigarette.

"No, I'm pretty sure I can carry us for a year. And frankly, at this stage, time is more important than money."

The next day, Jenny crunched numbers and calculated that they could, indeed, manage for a year on her investment income. Beyond that, David would have to either return to teaching or retire officially, allowing him to access his pension. When David came home from school, Jenny asked cheerfully about his day and was poised to share her financial research until she saw the expression on his face.

"It was fine," he replied quietly, "until the last period. That's when I learned that Liesel Schueler died yesterday. She was a teacher in the science department. She was only 49."

Oh no, Jenny recoiled. *Not another death.*

"That's so sad," she commiserated. "What happened?"

"Pneumonia. She came down with flu over Christmas vacation, and it went from bad to worse. They sedated her at the hospital to make her more comfortable, and she never recovered. She died last night. Olga called an emergency meeting to tell the staff. She's asked me to conduct an assembly tomorrow for the students to talk about Liesel's death."

There was a pause, and then David added, "I did something similar when Sandie was dying. The kids were wonderful."

"The assembly went well," he reported when he returned from school the next day. "The students were respectful and thoughtful. The hardest thing for me is my identification with what Liesel's husband is going through – the disarray, the disbelief, the sadness. Words can't touch it."

The spate of losses created a pall that surfaced in odd ways. David made a braised rabbit for dinner that night, and Jenny, looking to emphasize the positive in their lives, heaped it with praise. "Can you write out the recipe? I'd love to be able to tell friends how to make it."

"It's an easy recipe to follow," David commented, "and probably a good one for folks cooking rabbit for the first time. My favorite rabbit dish is a bit more complicated – a mustard rabbit that Sandie fixed."

"Do you still have Sandie's recipe?" Jenny asked.

"Yes," was the reply.

"So you could recreate it. That might be fun! Why don't you make it next time we get rabbit at the market?"

"I'll make it," he said carefully, "when the time is right. I have some emotional work to do before I can approach that recipe."

Oops, Jenny thought. *I hit a nerve. Small wonder, with all these funerals of late. And it's the eve of Sandie's birthday. I should have thought of that.* "Well, perhaps you can do it on some date that was special to Sandie," she suggested gently.

"Perhaps," David agreed and, turning away from her, started to clear the table.

That night, as per tradition, David composed a birthday poem in memory of Sandie and sent it to Marc and Delphine. To Jenny's copy, he appended a note: "For you, Ms. Boston, with all my love here and now."

The poem celebrated both Sandie's birthday and the second anniversary of David's marriage to Jenny. To her surprise, David referred to Jenny as Sandie's *âme soeur* – her soul sister.

Complete with the occasional sibling rivalry, Jenny smiled to herself.

To celebrate that second anniversary, David promised Jenny luncheon at a three-star restaurant in Mégève, a popular skiing area about an hour away. "It's time to get the hell out of gloomy Geneva and go up into the mountains where there's some serious sunshine," he declared.

It was gray and rainy when they left Morion, but the weather cleared as they drove the winding roads up through the mountain villages. Although Mégève was in France, the great roof overhangs and gingerbread decorations on the lodges made Jenny think of *Heidi.* There had been nearly a foot of fresh snow the night before, the trees were blanketed in white, and there were picture-postcard views at every turn.

The restaurant occupied a converted barn, open from the main floor to the roof, with massive beams, a huge central fireplace, antique country furnishings and folk art decorations.

"This is really beautiful, David," Jenny said as she took in the interior. An old wooden cradle on wheels was used as a bread server. Antique apothecary drawers and carved armoires were set into the walls to hold cutlery and linens. The level beneath the main floor was still a working barn, with stalls and pens for livestock. Large sections of thick glass were set into the planked floor as windows into the space below, allowing them to watch the animals feeding and sleeping.

"Agreed," David answered. "It's a remarkable setting. But it gets better."

The chef specialized in the use of local mountain herbs, spices and plants, and was known for his unusual taste combinations. David and Jenny were given a complimentary aperatif and hors d'oeuvres, handed two set menus, and asked to choose which they would prefer. They picked the more modest of the two, consisting of only twenty servings – each plate presenting two or three dainty items that were consumed in as many bites. Tiny slices of sautéed foie gras, a pumpkin soup served in a miniature pumpkin shell, and a tall flute of bouillon exuding a fizzing vapor were among the offerings.

There was a taste of lobster bisque covered with a froth of whipped cucumber and pistachio. There were two fat scallops drizzled with a syrup made from eucalyptus, sesame and quince. There was a single crayfish dusted with powdered lichen. There was an oyster simmered in a sweet-and-sour wine sauce.

"I wouldn't go back for seconds on some of these concoctions," Jenny allowed, "but it's splendid fun."

All this came before the main course, where they had a choice of duck with peanut sauce or a small medallion of veal with vegetables *en papillote*. The only predictable tastes came from the desserts, and even then, there were surprises. "I would never have thought of swirling black current jam through tapioca pudding," Jenny admitted.

David raised his glass and toasted, "To our continuing adventure."

Jenny reached her hand across to his. "Just in case fate cuts our continuing adventure short, I want you to know, despite all the ups and downs, that being married to you is the most wonderful thing that has ever happened to me."

David squeezed hard, and Jenny squeezed back, as the server stood patiently by with yet another plate of food.

Unfortunately, their celebratory mood was soon cut short by an e-mail from Marc.

> *From: Marc*
> *To: Dad*
> *Date: February 3, 2004*
> *Subject: it hurts*
>
> that was sad about mme schueler. here life goes on, and people joke at problems, but i have no time to laugh. i have a big ball in my stomach, everyday i think of death, and death gets clearer. i am wasting my time and not honoring the life both mom and yourself provided me with. i have to go to class now.
>
> love u, miss u marc

"What on earth has set this off?" Jenny asked after David shared it with her. "Was Marc close to Liesel Schueler?"

"She was one of his science teachers, but I don't know that he had any special bond with her. It may be the cumulative impact of Madame Lamont's death, Liesel's unexpected demise, and Sandie's birthday."

"I sent both the kids an e-mail about our lunch in Mégève. Do you think it bothered Marc that we were having such a wonderful time despite the recent losses?" Jenny speculated. "I remember, during my first year here, how Marc got so upset when he saw us laughing together, as if you didn't care about Sandie any more."

"Marc's mind is a mystery to me," David answered sadly.

"Well, either he's genuinely depressed," she said, frowning, "or he's looking for attention, or both. He may need medical intervention, something pharmacological, or just a good counselor who can work with him on whatever it is that makes him so negative."

Somewhat to Jenny's surprise, David quietly said, "I hear you."

De: David
A: Marc
Envoyé: 3 février
Objet: Re: it hurts

I called this afternoon and left a message. It is 9 p.m. now. There is no word from you, and I'm worried, so I'll try e-mail.

Stop talking about this death thing. It's an insult to your mother's love and care for you, and offensive to me. You have your life to live as an adult just as you had it to live as a child and a teenager. So live it, and do it well! To do otherwise would be a cop-out, cowardice. I don't think that's your way. I hope not.

If you are deeply unhappy, you have to recognize that the way you have lived and the things you have tried thus far have not worked. You have to decide that you want to try a different approach. If you want outside help, medical or otherwise, I would be happy and relieved to make suggestions. I love you very much. I will comfort you, but you have to do the work.

Believe me, it's worth it. Life is a marvelous place to spend a couple of years.

Love, Dad

David showed it to Jenny before sending it. "It's clear, strong and reasonable," she commented, kissing his bald spot as she read the e-mail over his shoulder.

From: Marc
To: Dad
Date: February 4, 2004
Subject: Re: Re: it hurts

salut. i feel kind of down, but i wanted to say that things here are not as bad as i made them sound. i think everything is kinda clogged in me and i have to take it easy. i'm still trying to find my place in this world right now.

love u, marc

"What do you think?" David asked, seeking Jenny's reaction to Marc's reply.

"I don't know, but it has to be a good thing that you're both being honest about your feelings."

David started to give Jenny a hug, but she stopped him mid-squeeze. "Shoulder!" she gasped.

Despite home exercises and regular visits to the physiotherapist, Jenny felt no measurable improvement in her damaged shoulder. She couldn't put dishes up into the cupboards and couldn't make the bed.

"Woman, you sure you didn't rip your shoulder apart just to avoid housework?" David teased, but he well understood her frustration at being reduced to one-handedness. She found it challenging to wash her hair and had trouble getting dressed by herself. David had to do up the hooks on her bra in the morning and undo them at night.

"The night part is more fun," he observed wryly.

Looking for distraction, Jenny busied herself with tax preparation. Although she was a certified accountant, they used a CPA in Geneva to handle their filings. *No way am I going to struggle with tax forms and filing instructions in French,* she had decided early on. To expedite the process, Jenny organized the bank records, totaled deductible expenses and composed explanatory cover sheets. David shook his head in disbelief when he found her with papers spread all over the office floor. "I'd rather go to jail than have to deal with that stuff," he remarked.

"Well, that's proof that opposites attract," she countered. "Unfortunately, I've encountered a problem. Marc never told the Swiss permit office that he's in the US as a student. It will be obvious on the Swiss return that he's living in San Francisco."

Marc had French and American citizenship, but not Swiss. His being out of the country for more than six straight months without permission placed his Swiss residency authorization at risk.

"I mentioned this to Marc over Christmas, but it appears he hasn't done anything about it."

David shrugged. "I expect we can correct the oversight by alerting the permit office and filing a form with a note of apology."

That evening, David had a lengthy telephone exchange with Marc. At the outset, he applied reason. "Your ability to come back and live in Switzerland after you graduate may depend on explaining your current situation to the permit authorities and following whatever protocols they recommend. Failure to turn in the required paperwork could be a blot on your record – and believe me, the Swiss keep very careful records."

Jenny couldn't follow the ensuing conversation because they switched to French, but she could see that David was becoming exasperated. After they hung up, David shook his head. "Marc's view is that the Swiss permit system is a joke, but he acknowledges that some action is required. Hopefully, he'll follow through."

"I hope so too, because I can't list him as domiciled here when in truth he's living in California. I don't fudge facts on tax filings," she added firmly.

The next day, Marc reported that he had gone on-line for the needed permit forms, but felt so depressed about his life that he "couldn't be bothered to deal with a piece of paper. It sucks having to deal with this bureaucratic shit. Being international takes too many f***ing skills."

De: David
A: Marc
Envoyé: 25 mars, 2004
Objet: Re: didn't do it

Dear Marc, I realize you have a lot on your plate: school obligations, losing Mme Lamont, personal confusion. Having gone through times of similar unhappiness, I can identify with the self-pity you express. At the same time, the social world – the world outside you, including the Swiss Office of Population – will not accept it as an excuse. "It didn't prevent you from eating dinner or going to class. Why did it prevent you from sending us a letter? Too bad! You lose your Residency Permit!"

I can help you with the forms if you wish. I believe it is in your long-term interest to do it. However, you have to live your own life. It doesn't change my love for you. Dad

"What happens next?" Jenny asked when she read it.

"I expect he'll relent, and the permit problem will ultimately get settled, but Marc obviously has not found a way yet to make peace with his environment or himself. I wish I knew how to help, but the solution lies with him, not with me."

Marc's subsequent apology was almost as bitter as the call had been.

From: Marc
To: Dad
Date: March 26, 2004
Subject: hya

hi dad, sorry about the permit shit, i have been having a hard time dealing with my frustration caused by these classes where i find myself repeating things done already. i was aware that this might happen but the worse is the class itself. students are all the same, how sad. people think they are so f***ing smart and a bunch of intellectual monkeys because there ass are in college. every time i come back from school i am full of anger. every time i see a friend he asks me what the hell is wrong with me, because i don't laugh, i don't move, i don't live. *so*, i am in a great mood to start my exam session.

love marc

When David showed it to her, Jenny's felt a prickling of resentment. *This keeps happening over and over again!* Marc's unhappiness caused David acute pain, and Jenny's sensitivities were far more attuned to David's anguish than to Marc's. Jenny was always careful to keep her tone civil with Marc, but with David, she was blunt.

"He goes from pillar to post, David, and the pattern keeps repeating. One minute he's pleasant and fun – look at Chattanooga at Christmas. The next minute, he hates the world and wants to shoot himself. I can't help but think there are some mental health issues – a chemical imbalance of some kind. Or maybe it's drugs. You yourself said he was obviously stoned while he was here last August. He really needs to see a doctor or a psychiatrist. Or both."

"Marc isn't exactly receptive to suggestions that he seek help," David replied dryly.

David stayed up late mulling over the problem and finally sent a simple but thoughtful memo to Marc, putting Jenny in blind copy.

De: David
A: Marc
Envoyé: 27 mars, 2004
Objet: Re: hya

I wish I could be there to listen to you talk about the situation – just be together for a time. I have been teaching kids for 24 years, and they teach me new things every day even though we're working on the same "things" I was working on 24 years ago. As we change by living and learning, the "things" we teach and talk about also change because we understand them differently.

Life is worth living even when it hurts. You learn things about yourself at that particular moment. An interesting experience.

I wish you were here.

Love, Dad

David got a note from Marc a few days later, sounding calmer and more positive, but neither he nor Jenny was convinced the equilibrium would last for long. Jenny pressed for direct communication. "If he's doing drugs, they can deepen depression and exacerbate mental health issues. Is this a subject you can confront him about?"

"I've discussed drugs with Marc over and over. I've exhausted my repertoire. I place my hope on the fact that Marc has the solid foundation of two loving parents. Living in San Francisco, building a new life in a new city, may ultimately alter Marc's sense of the world and his place in it. Beyond keeping my fingers crossed that he'll somehow survive this stage and emerge a gentler and wiser person, I don't know what else to do. I think it was Will Rogers who said that good judgment comes from experience, and a lot of that comes from bad judgment."

Jenny wasn't in a strong position to argue. She didn't know what to do either.

A day later, David shifted gears and called Marc. Jenny could only hear one side of the conversation, but she inferred that Marc had finally sent notice of his residential situation to the Swiss permit office. David then urged Marc to come home as soon as the spring semester ended in mid-May, and to spend as much of the summer as possible in Geneva.

"He's planning to take some classes during the summer semester, starting in mid-July, but he'll have eight weeks between semesters," David reported. "I've asked him to spend it with us. It might give me a chance to help him confront his disaffection with the world."

Jenny could see how much David wanted Marc to come home. *But eight weeks? Marc can ruin a day in a matter of seconds,* she fretted. *Still, I don't have a lot of choice here. Go for attitude adjustment, Jenny. Don't spin your wheels in anticipation. Deal with Marc's visit when it happens.*

"So, we'll keep the beginning of the summer open," she confirmed. "But after that? We haven't settled your work status yet. Are you still okay with exploring early retirement?"

"Absolutely. There just have been a lot of distractions of late. I think the notion of experimenting is a good one," David reassured her. "The fact that I can return to my job makes it a no-risk proposition. I'll submit a formal leave-of-absence request next week. I'll finish the spring term and start the unpaid leave in the fall. Then we can do some traveling. The big question is, where do we go first?"

"We missed our California trip last summer because of my hysterectomy. Why not check out the Pacific coast?" Jenny suggested. "We have lots friends there, and you'd be able to spend some time with Marc on his turf."

"Why not indeed? If you can contact everyone we know from Vancouver down to San Diego, that will help us plan the itinerary."

"Great!" Jenny replied. "I need a project to take my mind off my shoulder!"

Jenny e-mailed west coast friends about a possible trip and got a swift reply from Graham's wife Barbara.

> *From: Barbara Wells*
> *To: Jenny*
> *cc: David Perry*
> *Date: April 2, 2004*
> *Subject: Re: Possible retirement travel*
>
> That's so exciting that David is going to retire! And we're thrilled that you're contemplating a visit in late summer. I hope you'll consider an advance scouting trip as well, because I want to do a surprise party for Graham's sixtieth birthday. Is there any chance you two could come to Monterey the second week in May? Also, I'm compiling an album of photos and letters. Would you compose something and send it to me ASAP?
>
> Love, Barbara

"Can't make it because of David's class schedule," Jenny replied, "but we'll definitely contribute to Graham's birthday album." When she told David about Barbara's request, he immediately drafted a letter:

May 10, 2004

(It's a goddamn lie, I tell ya! I'm writing this in April!)

Dearest G,

What's so special about 60? Well, let's see. It was the speed limit we desperately tried to exceed going down hill in your VW Beetle, especially when pursued by some Wrath-of-God Mack truck. It set our pace, fixed our strategy for the years ahead: slow on the uphill, gun it on the downhill.

In the plural, it names the decade that brought us together for the first time. The 60's were special: college; discovering the North; civil rights; Vietnam; Ware Street; learning to cook; Jenny; Paris....

It may also be my age for retirement, which means that if one of us doesn't get hit by a bus, we may see each other more often either here or there.

Amen. David

David's enthusiasm for Barbara's surprise project planted a seed in Jenny's mind. *David turns sixty in July. Should I follow suit and do a surprise party for him?* She felt an instinctive reluctance, and then realized it had to do with French and large gatherings. *What if it's just his brothers and sisters-in-law? I could bring them over as his big present, and it would all be in English.*

Jenny quietly contacted the Chattanooga Perrys to see what might be possible. Both families were game to participate, and Jenny began crafting a detailed plan. High on her agenda was finding a ruse to secure the days around David's birthday so he wouldn't make a conflicting commitment.

If you have to lie, it's best to stick as close to the truth as you can, Jenny reminded herself, recalling the old adage. Jenny's sister Caroline and her husband had promised David that they would someday come to Geneva. Unlike Jenny, Caroline was not one to worry about details until she was right on top of an event, and David knew this about her. Caroline could be vague without arousing suspicion. "Will you serve as my Red Herring?" Jenny asked her.

Caroline agreed and, following Jenny's suggested text, she wrote proposing a visit "sometime around the first week of July. It would be nice to spend most of our time in Geneva, but we may go off on a side excursion or two."

David was delighted by Caroline's proposal. Jenny was delighted as well, because it provided cover for all her planning questions – rental cars, day trips, etc. They blocked out July 1–10 on the calendar as CAROLINE'S VISIT.

Jenny alerted Marc and Delphine and swore them to secrecy. She was pleased when they committed to the enterprise, but recognized that their presence at home meant their bedrooms wouldn't be available for the Chattanooga clan. *Not a problem,* she decided. *I'll put our visitors up in a nearby tourist hotel. That will be simpler, and give them more privacy and independence.* Then a new thought dawned. *I was trying to squeeze everyone into the house, but if I use outside accommodation, I don't need to restrict the number of invitees. Graham and Barbara might be able to come, and there are others who ought to be considered.*

Jenny surreptitiously contacted David's oldest and dearest American friends. "Barbara can't do it," Graham apologized, "and I'll be finishing up a conference in Amsterdam on that date, but as long as you don't mind my arriving a day late, I'll be there."

Within two weeks, she had three additional acceptances – Linda Scharf and Bridget O'Connor, from New York and Connecticut respectively, and Jeff Stone from Los Angeles. Jenny was tempted to invite a few of her own special friends, but decided that eight people – twelve if she included herself, David, Marc and Delphine – were more than enough for a good surprise party. *I have to keep this manageable,* she reminded herself.

A week later, a second carefully staged e-mail from Caroline clarified that her preferred arrival date was Saturday, July 3.

"Fine," said David, making no reference to the third being his birthday. "I'll do a welcome barbecue."

Uh oh. If David does a barbecue, he'll want to invite the neighbors, Jenny realized. "It would be fun to do a barbecue, but can we keep it to just family?" Jenny pleaded. "They will have been on a plane all night, and they're going to be zonked. I don't want to hit them with too much their first few days here."

David acquiesced, but Jenny realized that excluding David's European friends from his birthday celebration would be a serious faux pas. *I need to organize something involving them, but how? My French is still so inadequate. I can barely understand it on the phone, and even face-to-face, a new voice or a sentence spoken without a context can throw me.* With chagrin, Jenny recalled a recent dinner party at the DuPonts. Amid the mix of music and multiple conversations, Jenny was struggling to follow the different speakers when Josette turned and asked her, directly, what she thought about an opinion Josette had just offered.

In front of so many of David's friends, Jenny was loath to admit that she hadn't understood anything Josette had just said. In her embarrassment, she shrugged slightly, and replied that, for the most part, she was "*d'accord.*" She "agreed." *That got me through an awkward moment, but I don't feel good about it,* she admitted to herself.

French or no French, you can't avoid it, Longworth, she scolded. *You're going to have to find a way to include the francophones in David's birthday surprise.*

Perched on a kitchen stool, Jenny mulled over the problem as David prepared a batch of pastry dough. Her eyes wandered to a collage David had created from photographs of Sandie's fiftieth birthday dinner, featuring the Perrys and DuPonts feasting on shellfish. Sandie had sent Jenny a long letter about that birthday, detailing the string of surprises with which she was feted:

> Thank you for your birthday card, Jenny! I had a great 50 celebration! It was for many days, from the day before my birthday, at the office with my desk covered with gifts, and also to the Monday after, when they have given a surprise play and songs about me. All the

> school staff have participated, and I was really touched. Saturday, David has made a surprise breakfast in bed. Then a dinner with the DuPonts, where we pigged ourselves with oysters.
>
> The next day, I was not expecting something. I was doing my accounting, and David told me we were going somewhere, and we had a Chinese lunch with Marc and Delphine. It is not over yet because three friends are giving me a weekend at the Hotel Royal in Evian to have a beauty-and-keep-fit treat. So as you can see, I have been very *gatée*, and I will always think of the big turn as a happy time!
>
> *Bises*, Sandie

Remembering Sandie's birthday report, the mental tumblers clicked into place. *I can plan it like a French meal, with multiple courses and breathing space in between. I'll use Sandie's fiftieth birthday as a model and create layers of surprises, spread over several days, with an ever-shifting cast of characters. And I don't have to do it all alone. I'm sure the DuPonts will be willing to help me.*

Armed with this newfound flexibility, Jenny revised her original plan. *Day One will be the arrival of the Americans. Day Two, Graham's delayed appearance can be the second day's surprise. Day Three, I'll give a restaurant luncheon to include David's special European friends. Day Four could be a barbecue for neighbors and colleagues.*

Jenny e-mailed Josette to ask if she could stop by while David was at school. Jenny looked up the essential vocabulary in her French dictionary, and when Josette arrived, she laid out her vision of a four-day event.

"The third day, I want to do a luncheon at l'Ancienne Auberge – the restaurant where David hosted Sandie's friends not long after her funeral," Jenny explained. "But I have such trouble with French by telephone! Could you help me make the reservation and menu arrangements?"

Josette was pleased to be asked for assistance. "Of course. And also," she insisted, "you must let Michel and me host the final barbecue. We have a yard much bigger than yours, and it is natural that we will give David a birthday party in any case. You must allow him to think we want to do this just for his visitors. The other guests will be a surprise."

"That would be wonderful, Josette. I'll ask Dellie to help me contact David's Parisian friends about the luncheon, and, for the barbecue, I'll give you a list of our neighbors. You have the best judgment about which colleagues and local friends to invite in addition. You must only remember, when you talk with David, to say it is *my* family who comes, not *his*. And it is best not to tell this to anyone except Michel, so no one makes a *faux pas*."

So far, so good, she thought when Josette left. *The next step is to get my shoulder working again!*

"Swear to god, I'm ready to call for amputation," Jenny complained to David the next day. "If I could negotiate directly with Dr. Payot in English, I'd have gotten a referral to a shoulder surgeon ages ago. You're way too deferential to him. I have half a mind to go back to Boston for this."

"The Swiss health insurance folks would probably love that. Then they wouldn't have to pay for it. Hang in there, Kid," David said gently. "Payot is very conservative medically, but he's a conscientious doctor. If therapy truly doesn't work, you'll get your referral."

Jenny scowled at him. Dr. Payot was strongly averse to surgery unless every other option had been exhausted. He kept insisting that her shoulder was "progressing," despite her discomfort.

"No, David, you have to call him," she insisted. "I can't take much more of this. Even the therapist agrees we're getting nowhere. I'm not joking about Boston."

David made the call, and with great reluctance, Dr. Payot finally referred Jenny to an orthopedic surgeon. She was enormously relieved. *I need my shoulder back in action*!

Jenny was given an early morning appointment with Dr. Miescher, a surgeon specializing in shoulder repair. David took time off from school to accompany her. "I do not speak French well," Jenny apologized. "My husband will explain everything on my behalf."

"Ah! You are an American, Madame," the doctor observed, switching seamlessly into English. Jenny gave him the relevant history, and he looked at the MRI scans. "The operation cannot guarantee full restoration of function, of course, but it will eliminate the source of the pain," he explained.

With David's birthday surprise in mind, Jenny asked about timing.

"If all goes well, five or six days in the hospital, six weeks immobilized in a sling, and then physical therapy – an overall convalescence of six months," Dr. Miescher advised her.

"I'd like to do this as soon as possible," Jenny said.

"I will check the surgical schedule and see what is available. Do not worry, Madame. We will take care of this at the first free moment."

"I like Dr. Miescher," Jenny told David as they left the office. "You have no idea how much it means to be able to conduct a medical visit in English!"

"Oh, I know," he replied neutrally.

"No, truly, David. I can't ask questions in French in the way that I can in English, and I can't connect with the doctors in a natural manner. I know the medical care here is excellent, but when the time comes, I want to die in English."

He looked at her, his face very still, and softly repeated, "I know."

When they returned to the house, David offered some stern advice. "I think you should cancel Caroline's July visit. It will be tiring to have your sister and her family here," he argued, "and you'll end up over-exercising your shoulder against orders."

"No, Dearheart. Dr. Miescher said 'six weeks immobilized.' As long as I have the operation soon, it won't be a problem. You're remembering Sandie's experience. Mine will be quite different, I promise!"

David denied making a connection with Sandie's final summer, but Jenny recalled his description of an incident two months before her death, when a group of American friends were in town. Initially Sandie had napped while the visitors were outside chatting, but finally she came downstairs in her robe, intent on joining the group. David had tried to shoo her back to bed, saying she shouldn't over-exert herself, but she was bored and frustrated. "I'm not dead yet!" she had snapped at him.

David yielded on the question of Caroline's visit, but conditionally. "I want you to promise that you will advise Caroline and Charlie of your limitations, and encourage them to be as self-sufficient as possible during their stay."

"I promise," she said, mustering an ingenuous look.

David left to cover his afternoon classes, and Jenny treated herself to a walk. The farm paths were full of peaty earth scent, and the woodland borders were crowded with sturdy dutchman's britches and delicate wood anemones. She was in a good mood, encouraged by their morning conversation with Dr. Miescher, and buoyed, as always, by the bursting energy of April.

David, however, was withdrawn and low when he returned late afternoon. Jenny gave him space. *If I've learned anything, it's that David will find his own way and his own time to share whatever is bothering him.*

It came out at dinner. David had agreed to participate in a student performance of *Le Petit Prince*. "The play won't be presented until the end of June, but people are already working on it. Do you know the story?" David asked.

"I know *of* the story, but I've never read it. My childhood reading was heavy on Wind in the Willows, Mary Poppins, and Old Mother Westwind stories."

"*Le Petit Prince* doesn't have many characters," he explained. "During today's try-outs, there were too many students vying for the available parts. The director asked if anyone would be willing to serve on the stage crew instead. *Le Petit Prince* is a favorite story, however, and the acting roles are coveted. Most of these students are about to graduate from the middle school. There won't be another chance for them. End result, no one volunteered to be left out of the actor pool. The director therefore proposed a lottery, and the students drew straws.

"Armanse, one of the students who drew a short straw, has been at l'Académie Internationale since kindergarten. She's looked forward to being in this play for years. She's normally cheerful and well centered, but she was so disappointed that she couldn't stop the tears. I took her into a separate room and sat with her. 'In September of 2000,' I said, 'the doctor told me that my wife Sandie was going to die of cancer, and there was nothing I could do about it.'

"Armanse remembered Sandie. I wanted to let her know that I understood her feelings of unfairness and helplessness – and at the same time give her some perspective on the relative importance – or lack thereof – of participating in this particular performance."

"That's a pretty heavy conversation. How old is she? How did it turn out?" Jenny asked.

"Thirteen. And yes, it was heavy, but apparently it worked. She dried her tears and rejoined the others. She's a good kid."

Jenny digested this tale. *I think David handled it well, but from now on, every time he sees Armanse, his conversation with her, and his conversation with Sandie's oncologist, will come back to him.*

Dr. Miescher called with an admission date for Jenny's surgery. He had booked her for April 26.

"At least it won't interfere with our spring vacation plans," David commented, "assuming you still feel up to spending some time in Paris."

"Paris is fine," Jenny reassured him. "Distraction helps me cope with the shoulder problem."

This is all working out perfectly, she thought. *I can follow up on luncheon RSVPs with Dellie while we're in Paris. Then, after the operation, I'll be recuperating at home, so I can devote the whole month of May to nailing down the details.*

Their first evening in Paris was just for family. David reserved a table at the Lipp, and they were directed to the upstairs dining area.

"That's because I asked for *non-fumeur.* Non-smoking. The chic crowd is always downstairs, and non-smokers are considered un-chic," David explained. "It matters not one whit to me, because my interest is solely in the food. And I don't mind stepping outdoors to get my nicotine fix."

Unfortunately, despite David's efforts to protect Jenny's respiratory system, sensitized years before by her radiation treatments, *non-fumeur* was a fiction. She was halfway through a steak *béarnaise* when a woman two tables away lit a cigarette. Jenny watched the direction of the smoke and figured she would be okay, but a minute later, another smoker lit up in a different corner. By the time Jenny finished her steak, people were lighting up all over the room. There was still another course to come, plus dessert. She turned to catch David's eye, but he was already aware of the problem.

"We're going somewhere else for coffee and dessert," he announced, signaling the waiter. "Bloody patrons don't know how to read a *non-fumeur* sign." He cancelled the remainder of their order in protest, lodged a complaint with the management, then escorted his wife and daughter to a café with a functioning non-smoking section.

As soon as they were comfortably seated, David stepped outside to have a cigarette. The irony was not lost on either Jenny or Delphine, but throwing words at David's nicotine addiction was neither productive nor a good use of time. Delphine quickly summarized the luncheon RSVPs from French friends, and Jenny brought her up to date on the American and Swiss side of the plan. Delphine was the picture of innocence when her father returned to the table.

"I'm really sorry I put a damper on the evening," Jenny apologized as they returned to the hotel. David pooh-poohed the whole thing, but Jenny found herself somewhat discouraged. "It makes me wonder how we're going to enjoy retirement traveling around Europe without always running into the smoking problem," she sighed.

"Europe will enforce non-smoking rules eventually," David insisted. "The issues are the same, but the Europeans aren't as litigious as the Americans. Still, it will come. Meanwhile, lucky for you, the US has banned restaurant smoking even in the Wild West, so at least we'll begin our retirement travels in an allegedly clean-air environment."

Their final evening in Paris, they were joined by Percy and Joanne Whittington, who were on their way back to England after a visit to the Loire valley. "I'm so pleased that we're crossing paths again so soon," Joanne smiled as they exchanged greetings. "We'd really like to get you over to our side of the Channel one of these days."

"Once David retires, we'll definitely pay you a visit," Jenny responded.

Percy gave David a startled look. "Is it true?" he demanded. "Are you really going to retire?"

"Frankly, I thought I'd go on teaching until I dropped, but Jenny has shown me the error of my ways," David teased. "She wants to watch moonsets around the globe."

"Where will you live?" Joanne asked. "You still have your Boston house, don't you, Jenny? How will you balance your time?"

Joanne's question was not one of idle curiosity. The Whittingtons had a large Victorian house in England, passed down through Percy's family. Percy loved it, but Joanne considered it a gothic horror, in need of constant maintenance and cleaning. She hoped someday to be free of it altogether.

Jenny suspected that Joanne wanted to hear a strong argument for downsizing, but that was a subject she shied away from. *Retirement and travel are one thing. Asking David to give up the house that Sandie so wanted and loved is quite another.*

"I still have my condo in Shawmut," Jenny confirmed, "but it's tiny, and we see that mostly as a *pied-à-terre*. Our first big trip is the Pacific Coast. We have lots of good friends there, and we'll mix social visits with touring. We plan to stop in Boston coming and going, but for the most part, we'll be working our way from Canada down to Los Angeles."

"As far as balancing our time," David chimed in, "we're not locked into anything. The west coast trip will run about two months, and after that, we'll be back and forth, maybe half here and half there."

Jenny could scarcely believe what she was hearing. *Half here and half there?* It was the first time David suggested that they might divide their time equally between Europe and the States. She was quietly thrilled at the prospect.

It was a fun evening. The food was delicious, and *non-fumeur* actually meant *non-fumeur,* so Jenny enjoyed the meal, except for one heart-stopping moment when Percy almost blew the birthday surprise. Jenny had alerted the Whittingtons some weeks back and signed them up for the luncheon. Percy, however, forgot that the whole undertaking was a secret.

"So," he boomed grandly to David as they waited for their dessert, "I understand you're having the whole family over for your birthday!"

While Joanne was giving Percy a savage kick under the table, Jenny jumped in, all smiles. "Yes!" she exclaimed. "It's not my whole family, just my sister and brother-in-law and their brood. But both their girls are teenagers, so that's enough to keep us busy." Percy got the message, Joanne had a good poker face, and David didn't notice anything out of order. The surprise remained a secret.

Circles

I stroked her arm, caressed her cheeks,
Listened to her labored breath,
Followed every move her fingers
Made upon the sheets,
Her whispers, whimpers, sighs
And seldom moments of lucidity
To talk of coming separation,
Her trip alone, my staying here.
I travelled on in sadness,
Being with what seemed an end
But sensing then an awesome start,
Not lethal foe though hardly friend,
A solitary leap imposed
By fate to make me start again.

D.P.- June, 2004

Chapter 5

The phone rang as Jenny was making a list of things to take care of before her surgery.

"Hello?" Jenny answered.

"Bonjour Madame surprise party planner!"

"Hey, Bibi! How are you doing?"

"Good. How was Paris? And how are the secret plans coming?"

"Paris was fun. I feel as if I gained five pounds. And the secret plans have an added wrinkle. David has signed up for a test-run on early retirement, to begin this summer. Some of the birthday events will now be doubling as a retirement kick-off."

"Wow! I thought the only way he'd leave that school is in a pine box. How did you manage to get him to retire?"

"The palm reader said our life lines are really short, so we decided to blow our retirement savings and not worry about reserving anything for long term care."

"Could we have a serious answer, please?"

"The serious answer isn't too far from that. David's addiction to smoking is absolute, and I'm a two-time cancer patient. We don't need a palm reader to tell us that time's a wastin'."

"Is there something more to this shoulder problem than you're telling me?"

"No, it's just another in a series of wake-up calls. Gather ye rosebuds and all that."

"The birthday party is beginning to sound like a major production," Bibi commented, shifting the focus back to the surprise. "I know you're the organization queen, Longworth, but it's going to be a real challenge coordinating that many people. You've got to keep them housed, fed, hidden and quiet until it's time for them all to jump out of the cake."

"I've solved that problem by having a cake too small to jump out of. Rather than fight the inevitable chaos, I'm attempting to stagger it. The key to this whole thing is the smoke screen provided by my sister Caroline. If Day One goes well, everything else will fall into place. David is already planning a barbecue for "Caroline's" arrival on Saturday, so we'll be well prepared for an informal meal at the house. Sunday will be low-key because most folks will be dealing with jet lag, but that's when Graham will appear. Monday is the luncheon where old European friends will join us. Tuesday, we'll probably do a day trip, and in the evening, the DuPonts are hosting a barbecue at their house. That one's for the locals, David's colleagues, and all the neighbors."

"Are the kids involved in all this?"

"They're both coming, which is the most important thing. Dellie has been a big help lining up David's friends in France. Marc seems genuinely up for the party as well. He's pulling together a scrapbook with old pictures, letters and mementos."

"Are things settling down with him?"

"There was a bit of a set-to over his failure to keep his residency permit current, but the past several weeks have been quiet."

"And where does your shoulder surgery fit into all this? When do you go into the hospital? I've heard it takes months to get back into shape."

"I won't have much use of my arm for the first six weeks post-op, but it can't be any worse than what I'm dealing with right now."

"Well, if I can do anything from here, let me know. Does Marc need extra stuff for the scrapbook? I could write a short blurb, maybe something about the first time I met David."

"Good idea. I'm sure he would appreciate it," Jenny replied, giving Bibi Marc's address.

"And you take care of yourself," Bibi ordered.

The day of her shoulder surgery, David helped Jenny check in, gave her a kiss and a hug, and left her in the waiting room. When he returned after his last class, she was in recovery, groggy from the anesthesia. Her shoulder throbbed with pain, and her right hand was completely numb, hanging out of her arm-sling like a cold dead fish.

"Your wife can be released on Saturday if all goes well," Dr. Miescher reassured David.

Saturday? Five more days in here? As with her hysterectomy, Jenny was determined to get out ahead of schedule.

David came by the next morning to see how she was doing. Grouchy from the pain, Jenny hit him with her litany of complaints. "My left wrist is stinging from the IV drip. My right hand is swollen and itchy. There's a wire in my neck for the auto-feed morphine and a drainage tube in my shoulder. Adding insult to injury, the toilet paper dispenser is on the wrong side for my good arm!"

"Would you like me to look for a free roll of tissue you could put somewhere more convenient?" David asked.

Jenny suddenly looked sheepish. "I already found one," she admitted.

David grinned but said nothing. He had to leave for class, but he returned late afternoon with roses and Jenny's wedding ring, which she had left at home the day of the surgery in accordance with clinic policy.

"Gyahhhh. You women and your rings!" David teased when she teared up as she put it back on.

David visited Jenny as often as possible and kept her supplied with distractions, including *The Little Prince* in English, and the International Herald-Tribune, whose crossword Jenny tackled left-handed.

"I had a Sandie dream last night," she announced during a morning visit. "Sandie and I were in a high-end trendy food store.

It had a little café where we were waiting until a clerk became free. Sandie went over to a counter where they had bottled drinks. She came back with an armload of bottles, all different color liquids, plus one large bottle of clear sparkling water. We were having fun shopping together. We agreed that the prices were outrageous, but it didn't really matter. And that was it. The dream made absolutely no sense, but I've decided it bodes well for my early escape from here. After all, we were out shopping."

David smiled. "I'm glad Sandie paid you a visit," he said, avoiding comment on the advisability of an early release. "It's always nice to see my two ladies enjoying each other's company."

The following morning, Jenny impressed the nurse with her ability to shower and apply deodorant on her own. It was not a comfortable process, but Jenny smiled like the Cheshire cat throughout. *"Vous êtes incroyable, Madame!"* said the nurse. "You are incredible!" Jenny's performance was rewarded by a promise that, unless something unforeseen happened, she would be released on Friday – a day ahead of schedule.

"The hospital has had enough," David advised family members. "They're giving her back to me tomorrow." He had a school concert that evening, but withdrew at intermission and arrived for a hospital visit shortly after eight. He kicked off his shoes, sat in the room's only chair, and propped his feet on the bed. He and Jenny were playing toesies when Dr. Miescher walked in. The doctor considered their entwined feet and smiled. "Perhaps, since you are already here, Monsieur, you would like to take Madame home tonight?" he suggested.

Jenny nearly leapt off the bed in her excitement. She hadn't expected this bonus. The doctor changed her shoulder bandage and showed David how to replace it. She dressed with David's help, gathered her flowers, and they walked out into evening air that was mild and soft.

"Oh god, it's so wonderful to be free!" she sighed.

De: David
A: Perry Family, Longworth Family
Envoyé: 2 mai, 2004
Objet: Recovery

Jenny is clearly fine. She's already figured out how to weed with her left hand, how to do her lists for me and her crossword puzzles for herself, and how to type with her upper right arm strapped to her side like a furled flag. Need I say more?

I think the Doc let her out of the hospital early because she was attempting to reorganize the food service, general accounting, customer parking, medical records, cleaning service and reception décor, all from her hospital bed.

Love to all, David

The next day, David had school. The azaleas were in full glory, and the garden was so inviting that Jenny put off dealing with paperwork and spent the morning outdoors. It was not until after lunch that she turned her attention to the surprise.

Before her surgery, Jenny had spotted an ad posted at the International Women's Center by a woman who operated a small catering service. Her specialty was desserts and wedding cakes.

Jenny retrieved the name and number she had written down, and called.

"Lindsey Wilson? Hi, this is Jenny Longworth. I saw your ad at the Women's Center, and I need a large birthday cake for the third of July. Is it too soon to place an order?"

The size, flavor and decorations were all settled in less than ten minutes.

"For a small additional charge, I can deliver the cake rather than your having to pick it up," Lindsay noted.

"For a small additional charge, yes, please, deliver the cake. I just had my shoulder operated on, and I'll still be doing physical therapy come July. No driving and certainly no cake-lifting!"

"Okay. I'll write this all up and send you a confirmation," Lindsey promised.

An hour after the phone order, Jenny realized she had overlooked something.

> *From: JWLongworth*
> *To: Lindsey Wilson*
> *Date: May 3, 2004*
> *Subject: Memorial Rose*
>
> Lindsey, I have one addition to the flowers on the cake. David's first wife, Sandie, died of cancer not quite four years ago. We can do other flowers as discussed, but I'd like to represent Sandie on the cake with a single rose, very elegant, as was my predecessor. Her favorite color combination was yellow and red. Can you do a yellow rose with blush-red on the tips of the petals? This would work well with a lemon cake, *n'est-ce pas?*
>
> Many thanks, Jenny

> *From: Lindsey*
> *To: Jenny*
> *Date: May 3, 2004*
> *Subject: Re: Memorial Rose*
>
> Jenny, no problem. That is a beautiful idea. I was quite touched by it. Lindsey

Jenny accepted the compliment, but was aware that there was a selfish side to her instructions. *I don't want David – or anyone else – feeling that his going forward can only happen by leaving Sandie behind. This event is a milestone. I want something symbolic suggesting that Sandie would have been glad to see David survive and find happiness in a new phase of life.*

The pieces were falling into place. Jenny engaged in some carefully crafted e-mail conversations to further cement the deception. Caroline helped sustain the illusion and aided Jenny's research by posing questions that Jenny needed David's help answering.

From: Caroline
To: Jenny
cc: David Perry
Date: May 7, 2004
Subject: Details

We're thinking of renting a car. Which side of the road do you drive on? Can we use our American licenses?

We're off to New Orleans for a jazz weekend and as many po' boys as I can eat. Crayfish. Crabs. Andouille sausage. Rice and beans. You'll ask yourselves, "Who's that fat woman coming off the plane. Surely, that can't be Caroline?" Stay tuned.

xo, Caroline

From: JWLongworth
To: Caroline
cc: DavidP
Date: May 8, 2004
Subject: Re: Details

Only the British and their recent colonies drive on the left. All continental Europe drives on the right. Your American license should do just fine, but I'll confirm that. Have fun in New Orleans!

Love, Jenny

Jenny had difficulty getting Marc to focus on his travel dates, but when David mentioned to him that he had the supporting lead in the school's production of *Le Petit Prince,* Marc was galvanized into action.

From: Marc
To: Jenny
Date: May 13, 2004
Subject: Re: Update

hi, jenny. i am able to get the plane ticket for around early june, since dad is acting in the play and i cannot miss it. i am highly impressed by the organization of your plan, it will be incredible for dad and all of us.

love marc

From: JWLongworth
To: Marc
Date: May 14, 2004
Subject: Re: Re: Update

Hi, Marc. Thanks for the information. I got a little worried when David said you might go to Spain in early July, but then I realized that was probably a ruse to throw him off track. It will be a big help to have you here for the birthday surprise!

Love, Jenny

In the weeks that followed, Jenny began to nag David about household projects she hoped would be completed before "Caroline's" arrival. Marc worked on the scrapbook project and continued to mention a possible trip to Spain. "I don't want to miss your birthday," he told his father, "but with Jenny's relatives in town, that might be the best time for me to be out of Geneva. That way they can use my room."

Delphine laid similarly deceptive groundwork. "The timing is really bad," she told her father. "My big final is on July 5. Getting to Geneva for your birthday could be a real stretch. Jenny's family will be there the whole next week, won't they? I'll leave the minute my last exam is over, and we can have a late birthday celebration. That way you'll get to do it twice!"

While David was at school, Jenny paid a visit to the small hotel she wanted to use. In careful French, she told the desk clerk the dates she wished to reserve and handed her the guest list. The clerk looked at it and shook her head. "*Ah, non, Madame*. We don't have that many rooms available."

Jenny had a moment of near panic until she realized the clerk thought she wanted seven individual rooms. Jenny pulled out a pen and began bracketing the names of those who would double up. "These are married, and these also. These two friends can share. This one is alone."

The desk clerk issued a tiny sigh and, without missing a beat, switched to English. "This is a very small hotel, Madame. It is difficult to make so many bookings for only one group without a guarantee," she said. "What if they will cancel?"

"If they cancel," Jenny replied, "I will murder each and every one of them."

The woman looked startled. Jenny laughed. "They are all coming for a surprise party for my husband's sixtieth birthday. They already have their plane tickets," she added. "Believe me, they'll be here. And here is my credit card for the guarantee."

When Marc arrived from San Francisco, Jenny enlisted his aid in various projects requiring French, and Marc made arrangements with Michel and Josette to borrow the DuPonts' second car for the week of the surprise.

Mea culpa. I was wrong to think that having Marc here would raise problems. In fact, he's being a big help, Jenny admitted, mentally retracting her earlier resistance. *Marc can be a good kid when he lets down his defenses.*

David, meanwhile, was caught up with the student play and end-of-year events at school, and was oblivious to the secret activity that swirled around him.

Le Petit Prince ran for five performances. David got tickets for Jenny, Marc and Delphine to attend the final night, and Delphine trained in from Paris just for the occasion. The weather was uncomfortably hot. The auditorium was packed and lacking in ventilation, but the play went well despite the steamy conditions. David was a natural actor, freely incorporating his classroom personality and technique into his role.

Having just read the book in English, Jenny was able to understand elements she would never have gotten had she relied on the French dialog. There was one thing, however, that Jenny completely missed when reading the original text. At the end of the story, after the Little Prince returns to his planet, Saint-Exupéry speaks longingly of a star he cannot see, with a rose on it. Sadly, he knows the rose is doomed. David spoke the lines with anguish, his eyes filled with tears. Delphine and Marc, seated beside Jenny, were weeping along with him. Then it hit her. *It's Sandie! For them, the doomed rose is synonymous with Sandie!*

After the play, David received encore after encore, hugs and kisses from the cast, and three huge bouquets. The play's director spoke of David's incredible contribution to the school over twenty-some-odd years, and also the contribution of "his lovely Sandie." As the participants filed off the stage, David came over to Jenny and kissed her lips, not her cheeks, despite the surrounding public.

"Do you want me to take care of these?" she asked, reaching for the flowers bundled against his chest. He barely heard her, because he was quickly engulfed by students and parents. Jenny could feel her discomfort mounting with the crush of people. She finally turned to Marc. "Would you mind running me home? I don't think the star of the show can skip out just now."

"You don't want to stay for the cast party?" Marc asked.

"No, too many people," she answered honestly. "Plus I can't understand a word of French when there's a noisy crowd. It's best I focus on getting these flowers into some water."

Marc delivered Jenny to the house, then returned to join his father and sister for the cast reception.

Jenny tried to sleep, but it was hot, and her shoulder hurt. David didn't get home until after midnight. She heard him in the kitchen, pouring a glass of wine. She put on her robe and tiptoed downstairs. She found him sitting out on the terrace.

"What the hell are you doing up, Woman? You should be asleep!"

Jenny shushed him. He was speaking in full voice, and neighbors had windows open.

"I'm visiting Geneva's newest theatre star," she replied softly, plopping into a chair.

"Goddamn busybody, if you ask me!" he snorted, trying to hide a smile. "Wanna glass of wine?" Jenny passed on wine but opted for a small Grand Marnier. It was cooling down. The sky was filled with stars. The Big Dipper twinkled just above them.

David began to share incidents that had occurred during the play's rehearsals. "My biggest difficulty was with the final segment," he recalled. "I committed to the part before I realized the parallel between the end dialog and my emotions about Sandie's death. The first time I tried it, I cried," he confessed.

My god, she thought. *Is there still that much raw grief?*

"I told the director that I didn't think I could do it. She urged me to keep working with it and promised to develop devices to help me get through. If need be, she was prepared to shift pieces of dialog to the students. As the lines became more familiar," he continued, "I was able to direct the emotion – to run the dialog and the emotion in two different streams, so it heightened rather than interfered with the power of the words."

"I'm glad you're telling me this," Jenny said. *However belatedly,* she added silently. It was disturbing to learn David had been struggling with this since rehearsals began in the early spring. *He never once said a word about it. He often put on those somber Bach cello suites, but I never made the connection.* At that point, Jenny hadn't known the story of *Le Petit Prince* and had no idea David was processing the revived grief that the ending aroused.

"It wasn't a picnic," David commented, "but I'm grateful for the experience. It's a memory I'll cherish," he concluded. "Now let's get you to bed, Ducks. You're still convalescing, and it's the middle of the night."

David left after breakfast for the Sunday farmers' market. Jenny put the plates into the dishwasher, then tidied the newspapers scattered on the dining room table. As she gathered them up, she noticed a theatre program from the previous night's performance. Jenny had converted hers into a fan to combat the heat in the auditorium and had left it behind. She picked up the program, thinking it might contain cast photos that David would want as a souvenir. What she found instead was a full-page dedication to Sandie. She took it downstairs to her office, got out her dictionary, and translated:

To Sandrine Caillet Perry

I dedicate my role to the parisienne who for thirty-one years was my best friend. I also do it because she would have found the idea of a Chattanooga boy playing Saint-Exupéry to be both amusing and ludicrous.

I dedicate my participation in Le Petit Prince to her, knowing that l'Académie Internationale was her planet, and that she had no desire to leave it.

Finally, I dedicate my swan song to her, wondering if we were too distracted by happiness, for the sheep did finish by eating the rose. For me, the five hundred million tiny bells were thus transformed into tears.

David Perry

Jenny sat down heavily in the chair. David had not told her he was going to do this. *Although in a way, it's good that he didn't,* she realized. *Otherwise I would have looked for the dedication and, having read it, I would have been a basket case throughout the evening.*

The dedication gave Jenny more perspective on the children's tears during the performance, and prompted a release of her own. She gave in to them until her runny nose necessitated a search for a box of tissues.

Thank god this didn't happen last night, with all those people around. At least my own tears are private. But will this mourning never end? she lamented.

Delphine returned to Paris to finish the semester, and David moved into the final weeks of school. Marc was increasingly off on his own, taking the car when available and otherwise heading out on his bike. The first week of his visit had gone smoothly, and he had been helpful to Jenny in planning the surprise. Following the play, however, Marc's troublesome behavior patterns began to reappear – parking tickets, lateness or no-shows for meals, and an increasing truculence. One afternoon, as David arrived home with an armload of groceries, Marc stopped him in the doorway with no offer of help.

"I need the car," he announced without preamble.

David set the bags down and fished in his pocket. "Will you be here for dinner?" he asked as he handed over the keys.

"No," was the answer.

As the front door closed without an *au revoir* or goodbye, David shrugged and looked at Jenny. "Maybe we'll just do leftovers tonight. I bought lamb shanks, but I can cook those tomorrow."

"I wouldn't spend a lot of time planning menus around him," Jenny commented. David heard the edge in her voice and gave her a wry look.

"Shoulder giving you trouble?" he grinned.

"I don't have your patience, David, or your tolerance. He seemed in a positive space when he first arrived, but now, poof! I don't understand where his manners have disappeared to. Even if there's a resurgence of grief due to the play, that's no excuse for incivility."

David chose not to argue and busied himself putting the food away. "Drinks on the terrace?" he queried.

"Fine," she said. *So much for a discussion about Marc, at least for the moment.*

"How was your day?" she asked as they settled with their wine.

"Just the usual chaos associated with the final weeks of school. All the students are thinking of vacation, and the teachers aren't far behind. And how was *your* day?" he inquired, returning her question.

Jenny was silent for a moment, then decided to unload. "Not great," she replied. "Half of me is getting anxious about your end-of-school parties this weekend, and the other half is trying to process some issues arising from *Le Petit Prince*."

He looked at her quizzically. "*Le Petit Prince?*"

"The dedication."

He said nothing, but lit a cigarette, took a deep drag, and blew out a stream of smoke. He was ready to listen.

"You have to understand that for most of the play, I had no idea there was any connection," she began. "Until I watched the final scene and saw your tears, as well as Marc and Dellie's, it didn't dawn on me that you identified the rose with Sandie. Then, the next morning, I finally read the program. I never looked at it during the play. It was so hot in that auditorium that I used mine as a fan. When I opened the one on the table, there was the dedication.

"I don't have a problem with your dedicating the play and your role in it to Sandie. It was appropriate and truly lovely. What upset me was that I was unprepared. You didn't warn me, and you didn't share it with me. All those months of rehearsals, all those painful feelings, and you never said anything to me."

He was silent.

"While I was sorting out my reaction, I realized another thing. I know you love me, David Perry. You show it in a hundred little ways. But you so rarely say it. It's hard for me to watch you say it to Sandie, but not to me. Although the really sad thing is, Sandie had to die before you could say it to her. I don't want you to wait until I'm dead. I have visions of your third wife having to suffer through all your laudatory commentary about Sandie and me, while you say nothing about how wonderful Number Three is."

"I say it in my head," he said quietly. "I know that doesn't help you much. When I finished drafting that dedication, I tried writing a poem for you, but it morphed into an intellectual analysis of the process of starting over. I described it as a 'solitary leap imposed by fate,' but the truth is, you jumped right along with me."

"Maybe you could rewrite it? Change the ending to give me all due credit?" She tried to joke but her voice faltered. "We need to hear it, David. We need to hear the words."

By this time David had taken Jenny's hand. She was in tears, and he was emotional as well. "I've had this exact conversation before," he allowed, swallowing hard.

"With Sandie," she said. It was not a question.

"Yes."

"This is part of why she felt the need to go outside the marriage, David."

"I know," he said quietly.

"She did love you, but she needed to hear the words."

"I know," he repeated in a whisper.

They sat in silence for a moment. Then he said, almost sheepishly, "Adelaide told me that I'm the only genuine bigamist she knows – that I truly love two women at the same time."

Jenny had to smile. *He's trying to do what I asked, telling me out loud that he loves me, but he still can't look me in the eye and say it straight out. He has to do it Perry-fashion, quoting one of his colleagues instead. Still, this isn't about making him do things my way. It's about making our marriage work.*

Jenny steered the conversation to the weekend faculty parties, reminding David of her need to stick close to him. The gatherings would be crowded and noisy, with lots of people she didn't know. "Yes, Ma'am," he promised. He gave her a hug and an affectionate pat on the shoulder. She let out a little gasp, and he jumped back in utter chagrin. Jenny laughed and went to him, holding him close. The pain was minor and subsided quickly. For the rest of the evening, David fussed over her convalescing shoulder, hovering like a mother hen.

Once the end-of-school events were over, Jenny expected clear sailing to the birthday surprise, but Marc's behavior increasingly raised concern. On more than one occasion, he appeared vague, glassy-eyed and remote. "I expect he's found a source of weed," David commented when Jenny pointed this out.

"And is this okay with you?"

"Jenny, he's over twenty-one. I smoke Gauloises and drink wine. He smokes pot. I don't exactly have a bully pulpit to preach from."

"Even it it's only pot – and I'm not convinced of that – can we at least make sure we don't hand him the car keys when he's high?"

"Yas'm," David replied.

When Marc announced that he planned to camp out with Delphine in Paris for the last few days of June, Jenny was initially relieved. *Maybe going to Paris will lighten Marc's moodiness.* Within a day, however, Marc reversed course and said he was canceling his plans. "The tickets are way too expensive," Marc told his father. "I can't afford it unless I can borrow some money."

Suspecting David would offer to pay for the tickets, Jenny immediately interceded. "Has the price gone up?" she inquired in an innocent voice. "What does round trip train fare to Paris cost these days?"

Jenny already knew the answer, having researched the amount of money Delphine would need to attend the birthday surprise.

Marc fudged. "Now that the tourists are here, the price is gonna go up a lot. It'll be way over my limit."

"Why don't you let me do a little research," Jenny offered. "There may be a milk run that's far less expensive than the high-speed TGV."

Marc scowled. "Whatever," he shrugged.

Jenny gave David a "time-out" signal, which he acknowledged with a puzzled look. "Before you even think of giving Marc money, you and I need to have a conversation," she insisted once Marc was out of hearing range.

Years before, when Sandie was still alive and none of them knew what the future held, Sandie had mentioned to Jenny how much the children enjoyed their visits to the States. "They talk of going to America for college," she confided, "but I don't think that can be possible. In Europe, university is free. In America, David says it is very expensive."

"Maybe I can help," was Jenny's response.

After much discussion, Sandie had accepted Jenny's offer to contribute to an Education Trust designed to cover Marc and Delphine's college expenses, plus living costs "within reason" while they were students. That Trust had since paid for Delphine's Paris apartment and enabled Marc's attendance at San Francisco State.

"I don't know what's going on," Jenny told David, "but something is up for sure, or Marc wouldn't be so broke that he can't afford a train ticket from Geneva to Paris – if that's even true. Did you notice that he couldn't tell us the price of the ticket? I think he's using this as a blind to pick up some extra funds. And if he really has empty pockets, we're owed an explanation. The Education Trust is there to cover

Marc's basic expenses and his school costs. It's not there to keep him supplied with pot and god knows what else."

David was clearly troubled by the incident. "I hear you, and I agree that I should talk with Marc, but I don't want this blowing up in the middle of Caroline's visit. I suggest that we try to keep a lid on things until after your sister has come and gone."

Caroline's visit! Jenny thought. *He doesn't know the half of it!*

Jenny reluctantly agreed to postpone a confrontation. *Marc is the one loose cannon,* she worried. *Everything else is all set.*

Wanting time to get over jet lag, Nate and Margaret Perry arrived two days in advance of the surprise and were spirited into hiding by the DuPonts. When David saw a news report about storms and flooding in southern Tennessee, he called Nate and left a message asking for a callback. Jenny didn't dare telephone the DuPonts lest David hear her, but she immediately fired off an e-mail:

> *From: JWLongworth*
> *To: Josette*
> *Date: July 1, 2004*
> *Subject: Urgent – For Nate & Margaret*
>
> Hi, Nate & Margaret! David just tried calling you in Chattanooga. He heard news of storms and floods, with some areas being under water. Please "return" his call, but remember to figure out what time it is in Chattanooga and what the weather's like before you dial our number.
>
> So glad you're here. Give my thanks again to the DuPonts for hiding you until the hotel rooms are available!
>
> Love, Jenny

Nate handled his callback with aplomb. David had no idea his brother was only forty minutes away. The following evening, the DuPonts delivered Nate and Margaret to the hotel. Jeff Stone had already arrived from Los Angeles and checked in. The East Coast guests, Bridget and Linda, were in Paris, poised to catch a morning train, and David's youngest brother Isham and wife Sue Ellen were in the air. The stage was set.

Then, in the very first hour of July 3, Jack Pogue called from San Francisco to offer birthday greetings and an apology for his inability to attend. Confused by the time difference, he thought David's surprise party was well underway. Luckily, Marc hadn't gone to bed yet and intercepted the call. David slept through it, but the ringing phone woke Jenny up. She had trouble getting back to sleep. Her mind kept going over the planned sequence of events, looking for flaws.

Jenny wished David "Happy Birthday" as soon as he opened his eyes. Over breakfast, she presented him with a bound collection of their youthful correspondence. While he shaved and dressed, she confirmed via computer that Isham's flight was on time.

Marc was charged with calling the hotel to issue an "all-clear," but Jenny realized, despite her clever planning, that she had no way of being sure Marc was awake when they left. *If I knock on Marc's bedroom door, David might hear it and note that it's a very strange thing for me to do.*

Marc had overslept for important appointments in the past. Jenny dared not take any chances. Complaining loudly to David that there were some dead flies littering the floor, she ran the noisy hand vacuum right outside Marc's door.

Isham and Sue Ellen's plane landed ten minutes early. David was focused on his newspaper when Jenny spotted them coming out of customs. David realized Jenny was in motion and started over to join her. Isham saw him and yelled out, "Hey, Old Man, Happy Birthday!"

David stopped in his tracks. There was a look of confusion on his face. Jenny could see him mouthing, in his usual genteel manner, "What the bloody hell are you doing here?" In happy consternation, there was hugging all around. Then David looked at Jenny, clearly puzzled. "But where's Caroline?"

"I'm sorry, Love. Caroline had to cancel – last minute glitch – so I organized a substitution. I'll explain the whole thing, but first, let's get these people home. They've had a long flight."

When they pulled into the garage, Jenny hopped out and went to open the front door while the others lifted suitcases out of the trunk. Marc, Nate, Margaret, and Jeff Stone were assembled in the living room, with cameras ready. Jenny beckoned to Isham and Sue Ellen, then intercepted David to slow his entrance. "Let me help with those bags," she said, reaching for one of the suitcases David had in hand.

"Woman, you can't lift these with your shoulder! Goddamn busybody!" Jenny yielded to his protest and preceded him to the door. David followed her into the room and froze. His jaw dropped. "Holy shit!" Cameras clicked, and Jenny clapped her hands with glee.

After emotional greetings and excited interchange, David turned toward Jenny, mind obviously whirling, "Is Delphine coming?"

"I'm not going to tell you who's coming and who's not coming," she replied airily.

"Then she's coming," he grinned, satisfied that the answer would have been "no" if Delphine were not scheduled. He was a happy man.

As lunch was being laid out, Michel and Josette walked in. A family wedding precluded their participation in the weekend, but they managed a brief visit. David gave them a colorful account of his first glimpse of Isham and his reaction to finding Jeff and the rest of the family waiting for him in the living room. The DuPonts came in two cars and, as arranged, left the second car behind for use throughout the surprise events.

As people were filling their plates, a cab pulled up. David went to see what it was about, and out popped the East Coast contingent, Bridget and Linda. "Jeezus Christ!" he sputtered. "You too?!!" The three of them hugged effusively, and David led them back to the garden to meet and greet the family.

Surveying the scene, David gave Jenny a hard look. "Are Graham and Barbara coming? Huh? Huh? Are they?"

"I've already told you, David, I'm not going to say who is or isn't coming," she answered. Later, as people arranged themselves in chairs, Jenny outlined the schedule of events, including an optional trip to the farmers' market in the morning for the food lovers in the group.

At two o'clock, Lindsey delivered an enormous pound cake with layers of lemon curd filling, and a single yellow rose with blush-red tips in remembrance of Sandie. All around the top of the cake were the names of the attendees, and around the side, those who couldn't come but sent their best wishes. Graham and Barbara's names were among the latter. Jenny pointed them out. "They really wanted to be here today," she explained apologetically, "but Barbara is in the middle of a course, and Graham couldn't reorganize his conference commitment to make it in time."

The ebb and flow of the afternoon was excellent. Marc was pleasant and social, and seemed in a good mood. Some of the weary travelers stole catnaps in the bedrooms, while others sat under the trees, drinking wine and iced tea, and exchanging news and stories.

Delphine called from Paris. "Happy Birthday, Dad! I'm really bummed that I'm not there. I was hoping to figure out a way to come home for the surprise," she told her father in a teary voice, "but with this exam schedule, there's just no way I can do it."

David was visibly upset. It was a serious disappointment that Delphine couldn't share in the gathering. "Can I say hello to the Chattanooga Perrys?" she asked as he prepared to end the call.

David handed her over to her Aunt Margaret. "Keep a straight face," Delphine told Margaret. "I'm about to get on the train. I'll take a cab from the station. Jenny already sent me cab fare. Please tell her everything's on schedule. See ya in a couple of hours!"

She completely fooled her father. David was so convinced that when he told Jenny that Delphine had cancelled, Jenny almost believed it herself. When Delphine walked in at 6:30 and calmly said, "Hi, Dad," David was astonished.

For all of three seconds, he pretended annoyance at the deception. "You little witch!" he yelled, then grabbed her and gave her a big kiss. He was thrilled.

That evening, David grilled ribs and chicken and opened endless bottles of champagne and wine. Jenny found herself grateful for David's insistence on keeping a well-stocked *Cave*. Things got rowdy after dinner when the Chattanooga guests put on the country music CDs they brought as presents. Fortunately, the neighbors on both sides were away for the weekend.

Jenny joined the revelers briefly, but mostly to say goodnight. She was exhausted. Before she could withdraw, everyone insisted that she and David take a dance turn around the garden. Jenny felt suddenly shy, and from the look on David's face, so did he. As he took her in his arms, she said quietly, "You know, in all the years we've known each other, I don't think we've ever danced together."

"You know," he replied softly, "I think you're right." It was a sweetly charged moment, but since they were not alone, they just danced among the flowerbeds, holding one another tight.

Sunday morning, David and Jenny were up at six. All their guests were at the hotel, and Marc and Delphine were sound asleep. David thanked Jenny again for yesterday's surprise. *He has no idea how much is yet to come,* she thought gleefully. Taking advantage of the calm, they laid out a breakfast spread and restored order to the house. They also sent e-mails, separate but equal, to Caroline.

From: JWLongworth
To: Caroline
cc: DavidP
Date: July 4, 2004
Subject: Success!

The surprise was superb. As David was trying to absorb his brother's arrival at the airport, he kept saying, "But where's Caroline? What happened to Caroline?" I'll give you a full write-up once the week is over. Thanks for playing the red herring!

Love, Jenny

De: David
A: Caroline
cc: Jenny
Envoyé: 4 juillet, 2004
Objet: Scam!

> A goddamn scam that worked all the way! I was totally blindsided. Loved every minute of it except for not seeing you folks. You and Charlie missed a great party! David

Margaret, Linda and Bridget quickly mastered the transit system and arrived at the house via bus. They all wanted to go with David to the farmers' market. Jenny excused herself. "There are more than enough of you to carry the shopping bags, and I have things to do here." In truth, she needed to be home for Graham's arrival.

Graham's plane came in at 11:10. Marc at that moment was taking Delphine to the train station for her return to Paris and her exams, so, as instructed, Graham took a cab from the airport. David was still at the market when Graham arrived. Jenny quickly installed him in Delphine's newly vacated room.

"David kept thinking you might come yesterday, but he finally gave up," Jenny told him. "He's going to be completely flummoxed by your appearance!"

Graham gratefully accepted the offer of some breakfast and settled down at the table with the newspaper. David and company arrived home not ten minutes later. When David spotted Graham calmly sipping his coffee, his delight was palpable. "You're late, Wells," he said in mock indignation. They embraced and chatted while David unloaded groceries.

"Woman, you are downright sneaky!" David told Jenny.

Sunday was an open day. Some of the guests explored downtown Geneva. Others relaxed in the back yard. The evening was capped by a Fourth of July fireworks display sponsored by the local American Club. Half the gathering went off to see the show. The rest were too sated and too comfortable to move from their lawn chairs.

Day Three, everyone assembled at the house so they could drive in caravan to *l'Ancienne Auberge* in France. In her effort to maximize the social compatibility of each carload, Jenny missed one important factor. As a result, Isham, a staunch Republican, ended up driving David's Volkswagen, which prominently featured the "Kerry for

President" sticker he had received months earlier from the States. Earning Jenny's eternal gratitude, Isham diplomatically refrained from comment.

It wasn't until David pulled into the restaurant parking lot that he realized something was afoot. Friends from all over Europe were emerging from cars or gathered in small clusters. Percy and Joanne Whittington stood at the entrance with wide smiles. There was applause as a bewildered David joined the group. The guest list, which he thought would number barely a dozen people, had mushroomed to over thirty.

Once everyone was seated and champagne was poured, David raised his glass in welcome. Nate was about to jump up for a toast, but Jenny quietly signaled that she wanted to precede him. There was something that needed saying at the outset. She rose and tapped her glass with a spoon. The room stilled.

Jenny knew that most of the guests would at some point find themselves thinking, *It's so sad that Sandie isn't here to see this and be part of it.* Jenny wanted to acknowledge Sandie, but she also wanted to underscore that life goes on in a way that can be surprising, rewarding, even joyous – and in a way that everyone present could feel pleased about, and even take some credit for.

"The last time David was here," Jenny began, "was in the autumn of 2000." She repeated it in French. No explanation was needed. Half the people in the room had attended the memorial luncheon David had hosted. The other half had read his account of the day. "It was a very dark and very sad year," she continued. "David had no idea where or how he would find the will to keep going." Then French, then back to English. "But thanks to each and every person in this room … and thanks to his own extraordinary courage … *Le Voilà!* Here he is, celebrating his sixtieth birthday! He seems to be enjoying the occasion, enjoying the ambience, and especially enjoying the company. So I suggest we raise our glasses To Life … *A La Vie!*" Everyone rose and toasted.

With great relief that her responsibilities were over, Jenny sat down, picked up her fork, and the feast began. Their first course was a layered slice of paté followed by *grenouilles sautées* – frogs' legs sautéed in butter and garlic. Jenny thought this might be challenging for the Tennessee guests, but the Chattanooga contingent did themselves proud. The men compared French frogs with southern bullfrogs and told frog-catching stories from their youth.

As the main dish, chicken poached in cream, was being served, David rose and gave a short speech. "The first time I came here," he recounted, "I came with Jenny, back in 1969. The second time, I came with Sandie, in 1970. *L'Ancienne Auberge* has been the site of many important rites of passage for me," he said. He didn't need to cite the celebration of his engagement to Sandie in 1973, or the luncheon for Sandie's caregivers in 2000, or the many occasions in between. He was among friends and family who had lived these occasions with him.

"It is very fitting, therefore, that this should be the place where I formally celebrate my sixtieth birthday and my retirement. Thank you all so much for being here with me," he concluded.

During dessert, Marc presented his father with the album he had compiled, spilling over with letters, photos and memorabilia. Marc then invited those who hadn't already signed it to do so, and chatted with the guests who came forward.

The album project is a success, and it's obvious that Marc's very proud of it, Jenny observed. *Maybe that's something we can build on.*

Finally the afternoon wound down. The rest of the day was devoted to recovering from the four-hour repast. Jack Pogue called again from San Francisco to offer birthday greetings. "Hey, Man," David complained, "you missed one helluva show. The lunch was fabulous, and I almost felt as if I were attending my own funeral, but in the happiest possible way – sipping champagne and listening to the eulogies. Not too much bullshit. Love and lots of sincerity. A most enjoyable experience, and there I was, alive to appreciate it. It *has* been a good life, my life."

The next morning, Jeff and the Perry males went off early to join Michel for a game of golf. Graham stayed behind because he had friends in the city whom he planned to meet for lunch.

"I need you to put on your psychologist hat," Jenny said as she and Graham sat in the kitchen. "I could use some advice about Marc. Dellie seems to be doing well, but Marc has us worried. He has some nice moments, but for the most part he's difficult to be around," she summarized. "He seems out there on the edge – depressed, angry. There is certainly drug use, though he denies it. Frankly, I'm concerned that there might be some mental imbalance. David and I go back and forth on this, and I don't know how to handle it."

"'It' being David, or 'it' being Marc?"

"Both, I guess. David recognizes that there are problems, but he prefers to see this as a phase, as youthful angst exacerbated by Sandie's death. He's not indifferent to it, but it bothers him in a different way than it does me. And I sometimes worry that Marc may drive a wedge between us."

"How so?"

"David loves Marc unconditionally. There's an instinctive, biological bond. I don't have that. I want Marc to meet a minimum standard of behavior. If he were mine, I'd insist on it. And that's completely contrary to the way David handles him. I agreed when we got married that I would bow to David's judgment regarding the children, but it's not easy to sit on my hands."

Graham watched her silently, his head slightly tilted to one side.

"More coffee?" she asked.

"No, thanks. There are, of course, no easy answers, but I've gotten to know David and his brothers pretty well over the years," Graham said. "There's clearly an intense nervous energy that runs through all the Perry males. The older generation tends to rely on legal drugs – alcohol and nicotine – to calm themselves when they feel restless and edgy. All three brothers smoke, and they're not exactly teetotalers."

"You're saying like father like son? I'll grant, David's a committed smoker and loves his wine. And he certainly relied on alcohol to anesthetize himself after Sandie died. But through the worst of it, he remained a kind and thoughtful person," Jenny argued, "considerate and aware of others. Marc, as far as I can see, has shut himself off. It's hard to imagine two more loving parents than David and Sandie, but according to David, Marc withdrew from them in his early teens and cut ties with his school peers."

"Was there substance abuse involved back then?" Graham asked.

"Marc had an arrest for possession of marijuana with intent to sell while he was in high school. Sandie dealt with the police and shielded Marc by telling no one – including David. I unearthed the cover-up when I came across the police report in Sandie's files. David was unaware of it until I told him.

"Most of what I know comes from Marc's former girlfriend, Valerie. According to her, when Marc went to San Francisco the first time, after his high school graduation, he aborted his college plans and once again got involved with drugs. He was living in homeless shelters, dealing on the street. Again, David knew only part of the story until I filled in the details Valerie shared. Following his return to Geneva, and in the face of Sandie's illness, Marc apparently 'dropped out and turned on' at every opportunity. His view was that life was unfair, and the world was a shitty place."

"Life *is* unfair," Graham opined, "but it's also what you make of it. How serious was his drug involvement at the time?"

"I can only speculate. I didn't move over here until a year after Sandie's death. There was apparently a partial turn-around when Marc met Valerie, but that relationship fell apart before he left for college."

"What's David's take on the situation?" Graham asked.

"David chooses to believe that Marc limits himself to marijuana. David is convinced that Marc would never lie to him."

"But you're not."

"No, I'm not. I accept that love and support are powerful tools, but a forgiving posture might be 'enabling' – might actually reinforce Marc's drug use. Still, David isn't ready to cut him off, and I'm not ready to force David's hand. I often feel Marc should be confronted on issues his father is disinclined to deal with, but my marriage is my top priority. I'm not prepared to jeopardize my relationship with David even though Marc may end up paying the price for my looking the other way. So here I am, going around in circles."

"If Marc does have a drug problem," Graham offered, "David would surely agree to avoid giving him cash or anything that can readily be converted into cash. If he has an addiction, he will almost certainly use the money to buy drugs, and you will effectively be enabling him. If Marc is really in need of money, you could always give it in such a way that you know where it's going. You could send a rent check directly to his landlord, or set up a billing account with the campus book store."

"These are good management strategies," Jenny agreed, "but I can't implement strict controls without David's backing, and he's not prepared to go to war with Marc because he believes what Marc tells him. Since you're Marc's godfather, and you're in California much of the year, I'm hoping that Marc might be cajoled into paying you a social visit on occasion. I doubt he would turn to you as a therapist, but he might consider your advice about programs aimed managing anger or finding inner peace – anything that starts him on a road to accepting professional help."

"I'll give it some thought," Graham promised, "and see what I can do."

After Graham left to meet his friends, Jenny attempted a quick nap, but made little headway. The house was the central communication exchange, and people kept calling to check-in. Mercifully, the next act on the schedule was in Michel and Josette's hands. As with the luncheon at *l'Ancienne Auberge*, the number of participants at the DuPonts' barbecue was a complete surprise for David. "God damn, you fooled me again, Jenny!" he marveled as he greeted scores of friends, neighbors and faculty colleagues.

Wednesday, the process began to reverse itself, and Thursday, Delphine arrived home from Paris, just in time to share the Perry clan's last evening in Geneva. Despite Isham's recent diplomatic forbearance on the political front, Marc appeared at the dinner table wearing a particularly crude anti-US T-shirt. Jenny was tempted to draw him aside and point out how his father and his uncles wisely subordinated their political differences to their familial affection and respect. In addition to his inappropriate attire, Marc was clearly high. He was ostensibly pleasant and social, but he spoke to his sister in French throughout, thereby excluding most of the other guests.

As David and Jenny carried plates into the kitchen, she offered a *sotto voco* warning. "Better not let Marc drive anywhere tonight. He's got red circles around his pupils. Not a good sign."

David looked slightly startled by this information, but nodded in acknowledgment.

If I hadn't told him, I don't think David would have noticed, Jenny complained to her mirror that night. *And if I were Marc's mother,* she added, *he would never have been allowed near the table dressed as he was, with such obvious intention to give offense.* She turned away from her image and shook her head. *Patience, Jenny, Patience. Grant me the serenity to accept the things I cannot change.*

After the last of the birthday guests had departed, David cornered Marc and the two of them had a lengthy talk.

"Marc admits to regular use of marijuana, but nothing stronger," David said when he recapped the conversation for Jenny. "His problems aren't drug related, he asserts. He said he made some errors with his budget projections. He blames his financial difficulties on the fact that San Francisco is such an expensive city. I told him we'd help him out, but he needs to find a part time job for spending money."

Jenny took a deep breath. *There's no way to do this without sounding like a complete witch, but here goes anyway.* "For starters, it would be a less expensive city if he stopped spending money on marijuana," Jenny replied. "But there's got to be more to it than that. When Marc went to San Francisco last fall, his bank statements came here so I could make sure he was on track in terms of the Trust budget. During the winter, he switched the mailing address to San Francisco. Do you remember that? At the time, he claimed he wanted to analyze the statements himself and become 'more responsible' with his bank account. Yet his account data was already available to him on line. Now he's telling you that he's short of money because he didn't budget correctly? This, from someone who rerouted his statements so he could be 'more responsible' with his bank account? I don't believe him, David. I think Marc doesn't want us to see where his money is going.

Jenny's words made David uneasy. "I told Marc he has to sit down with you after dinner and figure out what he needs through the end of the year."

"I think you should be the one to do that, David."

"Jenny, I react to finance the way you react to French. I don't understand it, and I'm not comfortable with it. I need you to 'translate' for me."

"Well, at least sit in with us," she insisted.

When the three of them spoke that evening, Jenny carefully avoided accusations. *Given David's parental blinders, they'd probably backfire anyway.* She worked with Marc's current balance, which was next to nothing, and a new set of budget projections. Once Jenny calculated the shortfall, she told Marc she would arrange for an additional transfer from the Education Trust. "That should bring everything back into balance. We're counting on you to keep it that way." Marc seemed subdued and mumbled a thank you.

"That went pretty well," David said as they climbed into bed.

"He's solvent again," Jenny sighed, "but did you understand that nearly three thousand dollars was unaccounted for?"

"Three thousand dollars!" David was shocked. "But where did it go?"

"Remember his reference to all those 'lost' books, the 'stolen' laptop, and the phone bills racked up by roommates? That's his official explanation, but to me, it doesn't compute."

David shook his head. "I can't call my son a liar," he said.

And if I did, Jenny thought to herself, *David might well want to shoot the messenger.*

Early the next morning, David dropped Marc at the airport. "Any further discussion about our talk last night?" Jenny asked when he returned.

"No. Marc was half asleep. We talked a little about the west coast trip you and I are planning, but that was it. Anyway, we'll see him again before too long. Hopefully things will have settled out by then."

David composed a colorful account of the surprise for all the participants. "Now that the comedy is played out," he concluded, "I thank you for the marvelous experience – your connivance, your gifts, your thoughts, your participation, your love. Only the last was not a surprise. Just a renewed pleasure."

Jenny also churned out thank-yous, then sent a description of the birthday events to her friends.

"Mazeltov, Jenny! You really pulled it off," chimed Bibi when she called the next day. "You must be on top of the world!"

"Truth be told, I *am* pretty pleased with myself. But there's a lot more to it than just a well-organized party. When I came to Geneva for Sandie's funeral, I vowed I would make David glad he was still alive. Watching his face through the four days of the surprise, I feel that goal has been achieved. The whole affair was glorious, and he loved every minute of it."

"As well he should have! All credit to the lady of the house!"

"Credit goes way beyond me. It's due to David himself, for his courage, and it's due to the friends and family who love him and have supported him throughout. There were fond remembrances of Sandie, of course, but mostly it was a celebration of here and now, and the fact that he's happy again. For that, I'm definitely feeling a deep and very personal satisfaction. Mission accomplished!!!"

"And all this with only one working arm," Bibi teased.

"Actually, my shoulder's doing really well. The therapist says I'm way ahead of schedule. The doctor even suggested that I should downplay my recovery lest I mislead prospective patients into expecting similar results."

"You lead a charmed life, Longworth. Now give me the details of this west coast trip you're planning."

At the end of the conversation, Bibi returned to the birthday surprise. "Be sure to tell David," she insisted, "that if he does the same thing for you on your sixtieth, I want to be invited!"

"I've got to get flowers for the secretaries at school," David announced, stopping the car at a florist shop after collecting Jenny from her physical therapy session. "It won't take a minute."

Although the teachers were on vacation, the administrative personnel toiled on at l'Académie Internationale until the end of July. *How nice of David,* thought Jenny, *to think of them.*

He emerged with a huge bouquet of roses. "Here," he said, turning the bouquet upside down, then sideways, to get it through the car door.

"Sweetie, this is a little awkward with my right arm," she cautioned. "Lay them on the back seat, and they should be okay." He did so, and got behind the wheel again.

"That's a magnificent bouquet," she said.

"It was a magnificent production," he replied. Jenny thought he meant the final school assembly where he was honored, hence his wish to give something to the staff who helped organize it.

When they got back to the house, David started to take the roses out of the car. "You should run those straight over to the school," Jenny advised. "They won't look so fresh if you wait until tomorrow."

"They're for you!" he said, with mild exasperation.

"But you said they were for the school staff!" Jenny was confused.

"You're not the only one who can pull off a surprise," he hmpffed.

"Well, they're beautiful," she said teasingly, "but when you want to surprise a lady with flowers, you don't just hand her the bouquet upside down and say 'Here.'"

"Oh, yeah? What am I supposed to say?"

"You're supposed to say, 'I love you very much, my dear, and I've brought you these flowers to give expression to my heart.'"

With perfect mimicry, he repeated Jenny's words. She had to laugh. *What can I do but give him a big hug?* She split the bouquet into separate groupings and put flowers all around the house.

"There!" she said. "Now life should settle down a bit. We have lots of time before we leave for the States. It might be fun to do a day trip with Dellie."

"A day trip sounds good," David concurred. "I'll ask her."

"And can we minimize the social events? I still have some holes to plug in our US itinerary, and I could use a little quiet time as well."

"I'm with you on that one," David answered. "I know my retirement has started, but when does vacation begin?"

Commemorative photos glowing with friendship and delight began to arrive from participants in the birthday events. When Jenny had a sufficient quantity, she assembled them in an album. *That was fun,* she concluded as she pasted in the last of the pictures. *Maybe it's time to tackle my long-deferred wedding album as well.*

Unearthing a box from her bottom desk drawer, she brought it into the dining room and started to spread the contents out on the table.

"What are you working on?" Delphine asked as she walked in.

"I just finished putting the birthday photos into an album, and I figured I'd do one for my wedding pictures as well."

"You don't have one already?" Delphine puzzled. "You and Dad got married over two years ago. Mom always did photo albums right away after each trip or holiday."

"I didn't do one right away because there were so few photos to work with. I wanted to wait until I had notes from my friends to add in, but that took a while, and I got distracted by other things."

"Can I see?" Delphine asked, approaching the table.

Jenny lined up the photographs. It was quickly obvious that they had captured the conflicting feelings of the day. There was a formal group portrait, shot in the courtyard after the ceremony, with everyone posed and smiling. In the candids, however, the complicated emotional mix was unmistakable.

"Quite a range," Jenny said, smiling ruefully at Delphine. "I look happy; David looks philosophical; the guests have somber faces; and you and Marc are frankly grim. It wasn't a happy day for you. That's why I wanted to intersperse cards from my family and friends, with their enthusiastic wishes and congratulations. I figured that would cheer everything up a bit."

Delphine frowned, and then twisted her mouth to the side. "Oh well," she shrugged. "Not to worry, Jenny. You've come a long way, Baby!"

"So has your father," Jenny said. *And so have you, Dellie,* she added mentally.

Delphine's choice for a day trip was Gruyère. "I remember going there on a school trip when I was little, and it was cool," she explained. "I think Jenny would like it."

In addition to the huge dairy that processed its famous cheese, Gruyère featured a medieval village set high on a hill with a castle, a commanding view of the surrounding countryside, and several rustic restaurants.

"Has Dellie ever heard the story of your first encounter with a serious French meal?" Jenny asked as they settled at a table.

"Was it Mom's cooking?" Delphine asked, half joking.

"No," David answered. "It was way before that, at L'Escargot in Paris in the 1960's. I took a semester off before junior year and spent most of that time in Paris working odd jobs and just scraping by. A friend of my parents had a niece who planned a Paris visit. The friend asked if I would connect with the niece and take her to lunch at L'Escargot. She sent me $40 and a set of very specific instructions as to what we should order. My first reaction was that I was going to make a tidy profit. I couldn't imagine that lunch could possibly cost $40, which in those days was a lot of money. I was quite happy to comply and was forever grateful that I did so. I don't remember the niece's name, but I never forgot the meal. The bill came to exactly $40, and it was worth every penny. It was fabulous. I had never tasted food like that before."

After lunch, they walked the narrow footpaths beneath Gruyère's castle and could hear the cowbells clanging in the valley below. "I keep expecting to come across Heidi and Peter, driving a herd of goats to a mountain pasture," Jenny commented as David held out a hand to help her down a steep stretch.

A week before their departure for the States, Marikit stood in the doorway of Jenny's office. "I must tell you a story, Madame." A compact bundle of bustling energy from the Philippines, Marikit came every Tuesday morning to help with cleaning and ironing. Jenny had been glued to her computer, finalizing details of their trip, but she turned and gave Marikit her full attention.

"Last week, when Mr. David has taken me to the bus stop, I was asking about his retirement. Was he tired of teaching? 'No,' he answered me, 'I love teaching, but I want to spend more time with Jenny.' He gave me goose bumps from his voice, Madame. From his tone. It was so very sweet and tender. So," she commanded, "you must not be all the time at the computer!"

"Don't worry, Marikit. I'm not ignoring David. The time I'm spending on my computer is all about making arrangements for our second honeymoon."

At the end of August, David and Jenny put Delphine on a train to Paris, and boarded a US-bound flight, leaving the house and cats in the care of Marikit and a roster of neighbors. When they arrived, they ran a marathon of local visits, spent two nights with Jenny's siblings at their summer outposts in Maine, and then flew across the country to Vancouver Island to begin their west coast travels.

They explored Victoria for a day, wandering past the parliament buildings and strolling the inner harbor. David spotted a sunny café on the wharf, where they treated themselves to seared oysters and scallops wrapped in bacon. As they ate, Jenny watched the seagulls do battle for spilled French fries while David paid sharp attention to a shapely female crew hosing down a large yacht.

"I trust you are now reassured that our travels in America will not be devoid of comely maidens," Jenny teased, observing his close interest in the activities on the yacht.

"We're in Canada, Ducks, and I doubt that they're maidens," he quipped.

The next day, they took a ferry to Lasqueti where friends had offered them the hospitality of their island farm. Jenny could happily have stayed a full week, but in no time they were saying adieu and boarding the ferry to return to the mainland.

Crossing back into the United States, they spent time in Seattle, then made their way east to visit Abby Travis, a high school classmate of Jenny's who operated a riding school near the Idaho border. The lush mountain country of the coast gradually gave way to dry hills, and the hills led into rolling prairie that stretched as far as the eye could see. When they arrived at Abby's farmhouse, two large mutts tumbled off the front porch to greet them.

"How does a high school classmate of Jenny's from Boston end up in the hinterlands of eastern Washington?" David asked as they ate the fat salmon from Seattle's Pike Street fish market that they had brought for Abby and her husband Joe.

"I got swept up in the 'back to the land' ethic after college and got hooked," Abby explained. "I've never regretted being out from under urban living. Joe teaches at the University of Idaho, and that gives us access to cultural and academic opportunities, but for the most part, I'm fully occupied with my horses, and the never-ending barnyard chores that fill each day."

"You don't miss Boston at all?" Jenny asked.

"No," Abby replied. "I rarely even think of it. I get east once in a blue moon to see my brother, but I'm always glad to get back to the farm. Living on the land is so real. You're constantly in touch with the earth and nature. There's no pretense."

"And what about you?" Abby said, turning the question. "Do *you* miss Boston? Though I imagine it's hard to beat living in Switzerland!"

"Actually, I do miss it," Jenny replied honestly. "But there are a lot of good things about living in Geneva, and David knows how to take full advantage of the area. There are challenges, but David's heard all this a dozen times, so I'll save the detail for tomorrow."

"Where did you start your trip, and what's on your itinerary?" Joe asked.

"Jenny always has to get her Boston fix, so we got over the worst of our jetlag there." David went on to describe their visit to Lasqueti Island, and their brief stay in Victoria. "You folks are our one inland trip," David explained. "From here we'll be wending our way south along the coast and down the adjacent valleys so we can get in some wine tasting."

In the morning, Abby and Joe gave them a tour of the countryside. "This is some of the best lentil and onion-growing land in America," Joe told them as they drove by massive harvesters kicking up great clouds of dust. "The topsoil goes down twenty to thirty feet. Most of it was blown in as dust during the ice age, which is why we have all these dunes."

Later, Jenny helped Abby feed her colorful collection of exotic chickens. As they visited the horse barn, Abby brought Jenny up to date on her son and grandchildren, and then steered the conversation back to Jenny's comments of the evening before. "What are these challenges you didn't want to discuss in front of David?"

"It's not that they're a secret. He's heard it all before. I just don't want to sound like a broken record. Usually I can pick at a problem and solve it, but in some ways, I feel more unsettled now than I did when I first arrived in Geneva. My progress in French is glacial, the agoraphobia still rears its head, and I don't have much of a network. I get to know people most easily by working side by side, doing projects with them. In Geneva, I rarely have that option. Most of the women I know there work during the day. I need more connection than just chitchat, especially French chitchat, which I barely understand. On top of that, socializing as part of a couple is different from socializing as an individual. David is totally outgoing. He naturally manages the lion's share of the conversation on our side of the table."

"Which means you've had trouble making new friends?"

"Yup. The one English speaker I spend time with is really nice, but she's connected to l'Académie Internationale where everyone knew Sandie, loved Sandie and misses Sandie. It puts a limit on what I can talk about."

"I've noticed Sandie shows up a lot in your e-mail stories. I take it she's still – how shall I say it – a presence in the house?"

"In spades. And it goes well beyond being surrounded by her furniture and her china. Sandie's favorite jacket is still hanging in the coat closet. Her blond wig, which David removed from our bedroom when I moved in, is still sitting on its manikin, atop one of the bookshelves in the atelier. Sandie would have destroyed that wig in two seconds had she recovered. She hated losing her hair to the chemo treatments. Still, David keeps it. He spoke once of donating it to the school theatre department, but Sandie's been dead almost four years now, and there it sits."

Abby looked at her aghast. "Whoa! How on earth do you deal with that?"

"The only thing that works is patience – and pragmatism. I want this marriage to work, and if that means ignoring a wig gathering dust in the attic, so be it."

"You always were the class logician," Abby acknowledged, "and I'm sure pragmatism helps, but there's got to be an emotional toll."

"Maybe I should say 'patience, pragmatism and love.' David's need for me sustained me at the outset, and his love, once I finally learned to trust it, gets me through the rest. It's been a bumpy road, but it was the right one for me to take."

"Despite the fact that it's landed you in Geneva, which I infer is not your first choice of places to live?" Abby had always been an astute listener.

"I have to be careful here, lest I give the wrong impression. We live in a nice suburban house. I have a garden to play in. The markets are fun. The food is wonderful. I'm surrounded by centuries of culture and history, and we're within easy range of every major capital in Europe. By any reasonable standard, I'm a very lucky woman. My malaise is simply homesickness. I can't shake my sense of isolation and my lack of confidence functioning in a different culture. If I were younger, it might be easier to adjust, but when you're in your late fifties, radical change isn't always appealing."

"Now that he's retiring, can you spend more time here?"

"He seems open to the possibility of splitting our time half and half. That's why I want this trip to be five-star in every respect. I want him to be so pleased he'll start planning our next US visit before we even get back to Switzerland. Meanwhile, I'm doing my best to count my blessings, whatever the downsides. Bottom line, he's the love of my life."

"That much is clear. Your experience makes me wonder about the power of these early relationships," Abby mused. "You're not the first person I know who has reconnected with the grand passion of her youth and discovered the passion is still there or easily rekindled. Does that suggest there's some legitimacy to this idea of pheromones? That some people really set off a biologically-based attraction in a way that others don't?"

"Pheromones may have something to do with it," Jenny replied. "The man can make my knees go weak. Still, if David and I had married young, it probably wouldn't have lasted. He wanted to live in Paris. I wanted to live in Boston. He loved chaos. I needed order. If we had married back then, it could have become grim, and it might have been a bitter parting. Fortunately, we went our separate ways without doing damage to each other and somehow sustained our mutual affection. It's something of a Lost Horse story."

"Lost horse?"

Jenny quickly summarized the Chinese tale.

"Ah," Abby smiled. "That makes more sense. As an equestrian trainer, I can tell you that I've never yet met a horse that doesn't know where it is. So now, after these earlier disasters in each of your lives, you're back together, and all is well. But do you ever feel as if your earlier life was a waste of time?"

"A waste? No," Jenny answered. "You know the saying 'past is prologue?' I feel as if my whole life has been preparation for this reconnection – as if everything I did and experienced, including the negatives, helped me to be there for David when he needed me and to merge my life with his. Of course," Jenny paused, "if I had known then what I know now, I would have worked a lot harder on my high school French and stuck with it through college instead of taking German."

Their final chore was gathering the last of the cherry tomatoes from the garden. When they brought their harvest back to the house, David was happily puttering in the kitchen, making an onion pie for their dinner, and preparing a plum cobbler for dessert. Abby was delighted to have guests who took over kitchen duties. "You are a first!" she declared.

David slept soundly that night, but Jenny was awakened by coyotes howling an eerie but melodious concert. She had once heard yipping from the small band of coyotes living in the nature preserve near her Shawmut condo, but she had never before encountered such a stirring and primal sound as the song of the coyotes echoing in the hills of eastern Washington.

Their last morning, they were up at 5:30. After a hearty country breakfast, they said their farewells and headed southwest. Their only company on the road was an occasional massive grain truck barreling along the highway. They passed a packing plant where the smell of onions reached half a mile in either direction. There were long trains with freight cars loaded with lumber and grain. As they traveled along the Snake and Columbia Rivers, great barges moved majestically along with the current.

They chose a route that allowed for extensive wine tasting all the way to Eugene, Oregon, where they settled into an inn for a four-day stay. They were awakened at dawn by the sharp blast of a train whistle as a freight train made its way through a nearby crossing. "Holy shit!"

David exclaimed. "I feel as if I should look both ways before getting out of bed!"

Their suite had a garden patio, but it was unswept and neglected. "I know it's late in the season," Jenny remarked, "but the temperature is still really mild. I'm amazed that they haven't kept it clean!"

To quiet Jenny's fussing, David borrowed a broom from the maintenance staff.

"Once this is clear of leaves, I'm going to tackle those weeds!" Jenny announced.

"Busybody!" David teased as he wiped off the table and chairs.

As Jenny swept, David cleaned debris out of the three stone birdbaths that edged the garden and filled each basin with fresh water. The local sparrows watched with interest and took full advantage of the facilities once David stepped away.

Jenny was reluctant to leave this idyllic retreat, but they still had an ambitious itinerary ahead of them. Heading southwest, they picked up the coastal route and wound their way down to Mendocino.

Once there, they strolled through the town, marveling at the cottage gardens and enjoying the quirky architecture. They peeked inside the old hotel with its carefully preserved mix of Edwardian and frontier aura. "Next time we come," David commented, "That's where I want to stay."

Jenny was pleased that David was already contemplating a return, and each day that followed strengthened his commitment to future west coast visits. They walked in deeply shaded silence among ancient, towering redwood groves. Brushing aside bows heavy with fuchsia blossoms, they strolled down hidden pathways that led to dramatic sea cliffs. Crossing into the Anderson Valley, they worked their way down through Napa and Sonoma.

When they finally arrived in San Francisco, Jack and Janet Pogue warmly welcomed them to their stately Victorian perched high on Pacific Heights, and put them in the same guest room they had occupied during their week's stay nearly four years earlier, not long after Sandie's death

"Jenny, you shouldn't be living in Europe," Jack proclaimed once they were comfortably settled. "You should be in Washington, DC, running the Pentagon! David's Birthday Bash sounds like it was only a tad less complicated than the landing at Normandy, but with more drinking. I love how people kept popping up every time Monsieur Perry turned around. It sounds like it was an absolutely glorious party. Janet and I are unimaginably sorry we couldn't be there."

"We were sorry too," Jenny replied. "You would have made a great addition to the mix!"

"And you, Perry! I envy you this retirement scam you're pulling, traveling all over the place while they keep a seat warm for you at your school. I'm giving some serious thought as to how I could pull off something similar. I have visions of sitting on the stoop, playing my harmonica while everyone else goes to work."

"So far, it's not a bad gig!" David grinned.

"What do you folks want to do while you're here?" Janet asked.

"We have lots of friends to see, but first and foremost, I want to spend some time with Marc. We're meeting him at his school tomorrow. After that, I'll have a better idea as to how our schedule will play out."

"Well, you've got a key, so come and go as you wish," Jack advised. "And meanwhile, lets open some of that wine you brought!"

Bother – *For Sandie*

The tiny garden terrace outside their room
Abounded in shade plants of varying height
Which, rustling in a lazy breeze,
Splashed late summer light
On three birdbaths – two big, one small –
That surveyed the site in triangulation.
He refilled them, and quite by chance –
Though something must have moved him thus –
Brought the garden back to life
And thought of Sandie –
Four years dead that month – his first wife.

He hadn't done it knowingly for her
But was rather bothered by the dryness of it,
The stone deadness of the shallow basin.
Filling it, Sandie moved through his mind
In summer shorts and short-sleeved shirt.
Others might have seen life
Without the water, and felt fulfilled.
He had simply yielded
To his sense of bother
And discovered once again that
Sandie was with him still.

D.P. – September, 2004

Chapter 6

Marc's previous rants against the school's bureaucracy reverberated in Jenny's mind as she and David went out to meet him. Her tension built as they walked to the rendezvous point, but to her surprise, Marc demonstrated genuine enthusiasm as he led them on visits to his classes and introduced them to his favorite ethnic eateries.

"That's where I work weekends," Marc said, pointing to a rounded storefront with a psychedelic sign proclaiming *The Yoghurt Yurt*. "It's minimum wage, but I get free yoghurt."

Marc was totally in charge of the tour, and it was a role he seemed to enjoy.

"I'm gonna do a class on glass blowing," Marc told his father as they walked. "At first I thought I should only do the required stuff so I can get finished with school, but then I had a really strange impression, like everything was suddenly clear in my head. My first reaction was, it's not possible that my brain is capable of seeing everything so clear, but I kept remembering how you're always saying 'Follow your bliss.' I figure it can't hurt to do something fun even if it can't be a career."

"Whoever is teaching the course has made a career of it," Jenny suggested.

"Yeah, but there's a lot of special training and stuff before you're allowed to teach. That's, like, entrance exams and graduate school, and it's hard enough for me to just do college."

"One day at a time, Marc," his father interjected. "Some things get easier with familiarity and practice. Don't sell yourself short."

"I guess. Anyway, San Francisco's kinda crazy, so I'm bound to fit in somewhere."

That's quite an attitude shift, Jenny noted.

"He clearly takes pride in his familiarity with the city and seemed very confident squiring us around," David said as he and Jenny returned to the Pogues after a day with Marc. "He's a little casual in the way he expresses it, but it strikes me that Marc really likes living in the States."

"I'm glad for him and for us too," Jenny said. "Based on Marc's frequent negative remarks about Americans, I half expected that he might give up on school and return to Geneva."

Jenny made her comment lightly, but she had long harbored a fear that if Marc came back to Geneva, he might ask to live with them while he sorted out his plans. *David would never refuse him, despite the tension that his presence creates. If his stay stretched into months and beyond, the stress would surely weigh on our marriage.*

"What intrigues me," she continued, "is Marc's comment about realizing he wanted to do something 'fun' and being so surprised that his brain was 'capable of seeing everything so clear.' It suggests that up until now, everything in his life as been not-fun and very foggy."

"That's probably close to the truth. Maybe the clouds are lifting," David suggested. "Maybe he's finally growing up, and his grief over his mother is shifting into a gentler remembrance. I certainly hope that's the case."

"Amen," Jenny echoed.

Organizing the calendar between Marc and their friends in San Francisco was a juggling act, but Jack and Janet were consummate hosts and made their home and kitchen available for whatever entertaining David and Jenny wished to do.

"Guests again this evening?" Janet asked hopefully, since David always took charge of the cooking when he was responsible for the invitees.

"Not tonight," Jenny answered. "We're off to Sausalito to have dinner on Bibi Birnbaum's houseboat."

"Is this another college friend?" Janet inquired.

"Not college, but the friendship goes way back. Bibi and I have known each other since before my first marriage. Bibi left Boston almost two decades ago and moved to California. She has kids in San Francisco and Piedmont, and grandchildren on both sides of the Bay."

David and Jenny had visited Bibi the first winter after Sandie's death, but David had been so preoccupied with his loss that he retained only the dimmest memory of the occasion. This time, he was eager to see what houseboat living was all about. Bibi offered them wine "below decks" and gave them a tour of her compact domicile.

"The use of space is really creative and efficient, but oddly, now that we're inside, it doesn't feel like a boat at all," Jenny admitted.

"Maybe that's because we're up on pilings. There's no rocking," Bibi said.

First on the agenda was an update on Bibi's grandchildren who were, unquestionably, the brightest, cutest and most precocious grandchildren on the west coast, if not in the entire country. "Caleb is ten months old now, and I regularly escort him to infant massage and Kindermusik. He absolutely melts my heart," she explained. "He makes beautiful gurgles, and we have long meaningful conversations."

Bibi had read Jenny's account of the birthday surprise and wanted detail on the more complicated deceptions. "I've always regarded Jenny as one of the most truthful people I know," David chuckled. "Now I will never trust her again. She had me absolutely convinced that Caroline was coming, and then she fooled me again and again with Delphine, Graham, the restaurant luncheon, and the DuPonts' barbecue."

After an hour of conversation, David wanted a cigarette. "You ladies chew the fat," he said. "I'm going to go out and heat the atmosphere." Taking his wine glass, he headed up the stairs to the dock.

As soon as David was out of earshot, Bibi looked Jenny in the eye. "So how's love everlasting?" she asked.

"It's pretty amazing," Jenny answered. "I feel we somehow turned a corner with the surprise party and David's retirement. He seems genuinely happy, and I have a lot more confidence now about my place in his life. We still have our ups and downs, but I have not a single regret."

"Well, it's a miracle of miracles, Jenny. I have three other friends who got married the year you did, and you're the only one who made it. You work hard to honor David's past while living in his present, but your story is still remarkable. I mean, think of it – all those years with you in Boston and him in Europe. It's not that you were unhappy, but there you were, steady-state, being a good citizen, good neighbor, good colleague and good friend, and all the while unknowingly tilling the ground for the unseen life ahead."

"I'm the only one who made it? That's disturbing, Bibi! What happened to the other three? Why did the marriages fail? We're talking grown-ups here, yes? Women in their thirties and up?"

"More like forties and fifties. Libby, a fellow editor, had recently been widowed. She married a younger guy, an attorney, his first time. They met playing tennis. Not much else in common. Divorced in six months. Julie, my long-ago neighbor, married a wealthy banker. His kids and ex-wife hated her though she had no part in the marital split. He hated his ex-wife and mother – a bad sign. Divorced in a year. Erika, my college roommate, once divorced, married an artist with a complicated past, an ex-wife who kept showing up and a kid who thought Erika was trying to poison him. The artist took up with the next-door neighbor. End of story.

"It goes without saying, they didn't have what you have. I see two things about you and David that make you a success. One, a long history of friendship and communication, past and current. You guys really trust each other. Two, your relationship with Sandie, which seems pivotal to me. You can be annoyed, even angry with her – there's her affair, for example – but basically you respect her. You can see all the good things she contributed to David's life. And then there's grace and fate and a little bit of grit.

"Just being in the same room with you two, I can feel the affection and compatibility. I'm really happy for you, and it gives me hope too. Of course," she paused, "If I ever get married again, he'll have to understand that my grandchildren come first. And everything else is okay? The French is coming along?"

"I've pretty much given up on the French, Bibi. David's friends laugh because I look as if I'm watching a ping-pong match, jerking my head back and forth so I can focus on the person who is speaking. If I don't see people's lips and facial expressions along with their words, I get lost."

"That must make your phone conversations interesting," Bibi teased.

"I avoid French telephone conversations like the plague. I secretly harbor the wish never to hear another word of French. What others consider the most romantic language in the world grates on my ears as nasal and whiney. On top of which, the francophones are getting impatient with me. They hold a definite disdain for Americans who are tongue-tied in French. They assume it's a matter of hubris on our part, as if we can't be bothered learning someone else's language. Oh, Lordy, don't get me started. It's one drawback to living in Geneva that I don't think I'll ever overcome."

"And what's with the stepkids?"

"Dellie has started her senior year, is majoring in art history, and loves living in Paris. She's fun and interesting and very grown up. As for Marc, we've spent a lot of time with him since we hit San Francisco, and he seems to be doing better. I'm not convinced that he's out of the woods, but that's a whole day's worth of conversation, and I hear David coming, so let me take a rain check on that one."

David poked his head in the door.

"That was quick," Jenny said as David deposited his empty wine glass on the table.

"That's because I haven't had a smoke yet. I forgot I left my ciggies in the car. I'm going to the parking lot to get them. You ladies doing okay?"

"I missed you terribly," Jenny sighed, "but I can hang on for as long as it takes you to get your nicotine fix." She blew him a kiss and returned her attention to Bibi.

"Anyway, one good thing that has come out of my isolation is I've been writing a memoir. I've excerpted four years of journal entries and e-mails, starting with Sandie's illness and ending with David's surprise birthday party. David said his birthday tributes reminded him that he has lived a truly wonderful life, despite the painful episodes. So the memoir starts with despair and ends up with hope and happiness. You can tell I'm a Disney fan at heart, but *this* happy ending is a true one – at least for the moment. The memoir is pretty much finished, and I'm going to give it to David as a present when we get back to Boston."'

Jenny meant this news to be on a par with the announcement of an upcoming trip or the description of a special restaurant they had recently patronized. She had overlooked the fact that Bibi was in the publishing business. Bibi was as serious about her work as she was about her grandchildren, and her face went very still.

"There might be a market for it," Bibi said thoughtfully. "Successful middle-aged divorcee gives up home, business and friends. And cat, yes? Helps to have some animal interest. Goes off to marry old flame who is newly widowed and still grieving. Struggles with new culture, new language. Has to cope with friends of deceased first wife. Has to cope with stepchildren. *Ménage-à-trois* with a ghost. Hmmmm."

"What, publish it? No, Bibi. It's very amateur, and it's also awfully revealing. The principal characters, myself included, all have flaws that I hesitate to shine a public spotlight on."

"Everybody has flaws. They make a good story. Who wants to read about a bunch of goody-goodies?"

"No, there are people who could be hurt by some of what's in there. And besides, *nihil nisi bonum*."

Bibi narrowed her eyes. "*Nihil nisi bonum?* Just 'cause you guys went to Harvard, you have to speak in Latin? Translation?"

"It's not obscure, Bibi. *De mortuis, nihil nisi bonum*. Of the dead, speak nothing but good."

"Of the dead? What, you're talking about Sandie's affair? But you've told me her behavior, while not kosher, was understandable, and that David forgave her absolutely. So why is it a problem? Sex helps sell books, you know."

"David and I have settled the affair in our minds, but very few people know about it, and the children don't have a clue. I think they should be told once they're older and have experienced the complexity of marriage, but for now, David wants to keep a lid on it."

"What else are you hiding?"

"Well, to give you an example, most of David's friends were nice to me when I first moved to Geneva, but there were exceptions. One woman in particular went out of her way to make me feel unwelcome and unwanted. I filled many a page of my journal venting about her vindictiveness, and some of those stories are in the memoir. If I call her out in public, there will be repercussions."

"And what's wrong with that? Sounds like that's one friendship David could do without. Does he know about this?"

"He will when he reads the memoir."

"So once he knows, why hide it?"

"You forget. We still live in Geneva. Even if I get my six months here, I'll have to go back and socialize with these people the other six months. David will keep mum about the story once he knows it, but publishing it could generate toxic fallout."

"There are such things as *noms de plume*," Bibi argued. "You could write under a fake name and fictionalize the story. Change a few genders, a few ages, a few nationalities. Put the story in Rome. Or maybe Florence. I like Florence better. Make David the Bostonian and you the southern belle. And take this nasty woman who's been mean to you and just alter a few superficial facts. Change her hair color. Make her a Jezebel who hates you because she secretly covets David, and you snatched him up before she could make a move on him."

Jenny's eyes flew wide.

Bibi took one look at her face and clapped her hands. "Oh my god! That's it, isn't it? She's jealous! She wanted David for herself! Jenny, you've got to expose her, even if it's only via fiction! It will make your story a lot juicier, and surely you deserve a little revenge."

"Bibi, no. Revenge just breeds more revenge."

"Longworth, you are too proper even for a Bostonian. We'll let this rest for the minute, but once David has read the memoir, ask him if it's okay for me to see it. I promise total confidentiality. If it has the makings of the Great American Novel, we can talk about ways to share the story as fiction, without opening Pandora's box. Deal?"

"Bibi."

"Just ask him. If he says no, then so be it."

They heard the door open. "We'll see," Jenny said, closing the discussion.

On the way back to Jack's house, Jenny told David Bibi's tale about her three friends with recently failed marriages. "So many people seem to encounter difficulties when embarking on a second marriage," she commented. "It makes me aware that I'm incredibly lucky."

"Amend that," he said gently, "to *we're* incredibly lucky."

As they approached the fourth anniversary of Sandie's death, David wrote a memorial poem and sent it to Marc and Delphine. Entitled *Bother,* the poem was set in a "tiny garden terrace" that Jenny recognized instantly as the one off their room at the inn in Oregon.

Of course, she realized. During their first evening at the inn, David had reminisced over dinner about his longstanding love affair with Paris. "The first time I ever encountered the city," he recalled, "I was overwhelmed by the effect of the golden light reflected by the soft colors of the sandstone buildings." Then, without warning, he had choked up, his eyes filling with tears. He took off his glasses and cleaned them with the edge of his napkin to steady himself. Jenny had stretched her hand across the table, and for a few seconds, they touched fingertips.

"Center of the universe," he commented, raising his wine glass.

"To your happy memories of Paris," she replied, raising hers.

Reading *Bother* several weeks later, it did not surprise Jenny to learn that "Sandie was with him still." *Paris is with him still too. I have to remember that Paris and Europe mean as much to David as Boston and the States do to me.* Then Jenny's practical bent kicked in. *But if I can keep things in balance, a fifty-fifty living arrangement – half here and half there – should work for both of us.* Her optimism was high.

Marc phoned when he got the memorial poem, and he and his father had a lengthy conversation. "I'd like to do a trip with Marc," David announced after they hung up.

"Where are you thinking of going? We don't have much time left before we have to leave for Boston, and we still haven't scheduled a run down to Monterey to see Graham and Barbara. There's also the question of a visit to Jeff and Kelly in LA."

"I'd love to see them all, but we did just catch up at the birthday party, and Marc is the priority. He thanked me for the time we've spent together so far, and said he's really looking forward to being in Chattanooga at Christmas. I think Marc is finally waking up to the value of family."

"So, do you want this trip to be just a father-son jaunt?" Jenny asked. "I could stay here with the Pogues or go to Sausalito and camp out with Bibi."

"No, I'd like it to be the three of us. I was thinking of Yosemite. I worked there summers as a teenager. There's also a tie-in to Sandie, which is important to Marc. He won't remember it, but Sandie and I took him there during one of our earliest family visits to the States. I think he was two years old at the time. In fact, that was the trip – 1981? '82? – that ended in Boston. We stayed at your house, remember?"

"I remember," Jenny answered. "That's when I first met Sandie. She was pregnant with Dellie at the time." *Almost a quarter of a century ago. None of us even dreamed what life – and death – would bring.*

David planned the itinerary, driving the gold country route through Angel's camp and Sonora. Once into Yosemite, he treated Marc and Jenny to a personal tour: the parking lot he helped build; the cabins where he lived; and the trash pickup system that was part of his job routine. "Heaving heavy trash cans as if they were beach balls was how we tried to impress the girls who were camping up here."

"Did it work?" Jenny asked.

"Sometimes," David said – and smiled.

Their second day at Yosemite rewarded them with a bear sighting – a half grown cub scampering clumsily down the side of the hill. They took a small tram up through Mariposa, and, like the other tourists, they posed for pictures in front of the famous "Tunnel Tree," a sequoia so large that a road ran through it.

A man behind them, waiting his turn, offered to take a picture of the three of them together and reached out a hand for Marc's camera. Marc gave it to him, but as they assembled for the shot, Marc complained, in a low voice, "I hate it when someone interferes with my art!"

Jenny was startled. She found it difficult to think of tourist snapshots as "art." *Why is Marc suddenly angry?* She shot a glance at David who dealt with the situation by turning to the photographer.

"Thanks so much!" he exclaimed with enthusiasm. "That was really nice of you! Enjoy the rest of your visit!"

Unfortunately, his father's example didn't have the desired impact. When Marc later checked the photo on the camera's tiny screen, he commented harshly, "The guy took a lousy picture too."

David held out a hand for the camera and considered the image. "Better than I could have done," he shrugged.

The minute they were alone, Jenny spoke up. "What happened back there with the photo? Up until that point, this outing seemed to be going well."

"I don't know what sets him off, or why he feels so threatened. I sometimes wonder if Marc is bi-polar," David speculated sadly.

It was a worry Jenny had long shared. "Could we get him tested?" she asked.

"Marc pretty much refuses to seek help at any level. We can't force him, and until he's willing, we can only guess about underlying medical issues. Let's just be thankful that most of the trip has been positive. I still think we're making headway."

Jenny didn't argue, but she questioned David's optimism.

Once back in San Francisco, thank-yous and goodbyes were issued. They touched down in Boston mid-afternoon on Sunday, with almost a full week ahead of them before the scheduled mid-October return to Geneva.

When Jenny stepped out of the car in Shawmut, she drew a long, deep breath. The advent of fall in New England was a tangible event, not just a change in the calendar. The smell of the earth was different. The smell of the air was different. The light shifted, as did the wind. The squirrels were frantic with activity, gathering and storing whatever they could find. Migratory birds were in the air, practicing their flight patterns for the long journeys ahead. Bees and wasps were everywhere, searching for some last drop of sweetness to add to their winter stores. Other places offered other wonderful seasons, but autumn in New England was unique.

Oh, I do miss this place!

Jenny did a final edit and declared her memoir done. It took three ink cartridges and several hours to produce a copy on her little home printer, but finally, there it was – five of the most eventful years of her life reduced to a two-inch stack of paper. She hadn't thought to buy a pre-drilled ream, so she spent nearly an hour wielding her three-hole punch before she could put the tome into a binder.

Jenny handed the memoir to David on October 1, the anniversary of the luncheon Olga hosted at her farmhouse after Sandie's funeral. The events of that day had moved Jenny to tell David how deeply she loved him. The events of that night had moved her to show him. According to David, that was the day he decided he wanted Jenny to move to Geneva.

"It's sort of a love letter," she told David as he took the hefty tome, "but it pulls no punches. I wanted to capture the complexity of our shared life."

"Gotta be the longest and most complex love letter I've ever received," David said as he gauged the weight of the memoir.

He started reading it that night. "You're right about not pulling punches," he commented halfway into chapter two. "I'm gonna have to take this in small doses. Did I really drink that much when Sandie died?"

"Sorry, Love, but yes, you did. You used to sit in the kitchen, no lights on, working on a glass of something to numb your mind as evening closed in. I remember you describing the emptiness of the house as palpable. 'There is so much aloneness in grief,' you said. The kids were really scared for you. We all were. Once I came over to join you, you gradually moderated your alcohol intake, but it took a while. A *long* while."

When David finally doused his bedside lamp, he leaned over to plant a kiss on Jenny's forehead. "You tell a good story," he said softly.

"I have a good story to tell," she replied, kissing him back as he drew her to him.

They returned to Geneva to find the garden in need of serious attention, the mail piled high, and the cats miffed by their long absence. While Jenny tackled weeds, bills and bank statements, David restocked the larder and contacted friends. He was eager to share stories and catch up with everyone, with the result that their calendar quickly sprouted a slew of social commitments.

"David, this is too much," Jenny protested as she saw him jotting down yet another entry. "Please don't add anything more."

"This one will be easy," David reassured her. "It's just dinner tomorrow with the DuPonts."

Jenny felt overwhelmed by the intensity of their social calendar, but countering David's outgoing nature wasn't easy. In an effort to find positive distraction, she composed an account of their west coast travels and sent it off to east coast friends. In her missive to Rachel

Aronson, she included the text of *Bother,* the memorial poem David had composed for the fourth anniversary of Sandie's death.

"David's poems are so lovely," Rachel wrote in swift reply. "I used to bemoan it when something unexpectedly brought Josh's loss back to me, but when I read *Bother,* completely unprepared, I could respond to the beauty and sentiment, and found it comforting. Another milestone for me. Please thank David for that, and continue to enjoy your wonderful retirement together."

Jenny relayed Rachel's appreciative words. "That's nice of her to say," David mumbled. Often shy about compliments, he quickly shifted the focus. "By the way, the DuPonts have invited some of their neighbors to join the dinner party, so I want to bring an extra bottle wine."

"I thought this was going to be just us," Jenny said warily.

"You don't have to feel shy," he teased. "You've met everyone before. They were all at the barbecue Michel and Josette gave during my birthday surprise." David meant well, but it was not a helpful thing to say.

When they arrived at the DuPonts' door, Michel received them with a warm smile. Josette came bustling out of the kitchen, untying her apron en route. Jenny was re-introduced to the two couples who lived on either side of the DuPonts. She had no recollection of meeting them before. She was used to Michel and Josette's speech, but the others' voices were new to her ears. She worked hard to follow the French conversation but missed key words.

Smile, Jenny. This too shall pass, she reminded herself.

"You were awfully quiet tonight," David commented as they drove home.

"Hard to contribute when you aren't even sure what the topic is," she said. "Socializing is a breeze for you, David. Lots of people, lots of chatter – you thrive in that environment. I don't. For me, it's ...." Jenny paused, searching for a diplomatic word.

"For you, it's something of an on-going French lesson," David offered. "Which may not be a lot of fun, but it *is* the best way to learn the language."

"But I'm *not* learning it, David. Combining French lessons with social protocol doesn't work. They're antithetical. No one at the DuPonts' last night came to give me a French lesson. They were there to eat, swap stories, and enjoy themselves. I can't be a good student and a good guest at the same time. If I were there as a student, I'd be constantly raising my hand to ask about words or phrases I didn't understand. As a guest, I can hardly interrupt every other sentence. I also don't want to spoil the party by revealing my frustration and boredom. Social protocol demands that I pretend I'm having a delightful evening. Doing so takes every ounce of concentration I have, because what I really want to do is escape. I end up coming home with knots in my stomach. There's no room for absorbing even one new word of French in those circumstances."

David studied her silently.

"Mostly, I'd like to avoid participating in more than one French-speaking event per week. At the rate we're going, I'll end up with an ulcer. Maybe we could do a little traveling, which would give you a legitimate excuse to turn down some invitations."

"All right, Ducks," he said cautiously. "Why don't you come up with some possible itineraries. We might squeeze in a short trip before we go back to the States for Christmas, and we can certainly do some traveling after the holidays."

Before immersing herself in travel research, Jenny did a quick review of their finances to get a sense of the parameters. In doing so, she was forced to confront the declining value of the American dollar against the Euro and the Swiss Franc. Since David's "experiment" in retirement was, in truth, an unpaid leave of absence, they were totally dependent on Jenny's American investments for income. "Until the dollar comes back up, I need to put a hold on most of my travel fantasies," she reluctantly reported to David. "My monthly transfers from the States are worth 20% less than they were when I first set them up. We'll have to stick to places we can reach by car, and where you have friends who would be pleased to have us stay with them."

Two days later, David called Jenny down to his computer. "I've got a short-term, low-budget escape for you," he announced. "The Genazzinis want to know if we'd like to go down to Tuscany and have Thanksgiving with them."

"Oh, that will be fun!" Jenny was delighted. "You can practice your Italian with Carlo, and I can enjoy non-stop English with Eleanor!"

"It'll definitely be fun, but there's a serious side as well. They have a friend who just lost her husband. Eleanor thinks it might help her to talk with someone who's been through it."

"I expect it will," Jenny concurred. "If anyone can offer helpful counsel, it's you."

When the time came, they loaded the car with French cheese, a ten-liter *cubiton* of *Côte du Rhône,* and an empty container for olive oil. Six hours later, they turned onto the dusty road that led to the Genazzinis' farmhouse with its olive groves and fabulous view. Once David and Jenny had freshened up and enjoyed a welcoming glass of wine, Eleanor and Carlo whisked them away to a tasteful Bed & Breakfast, set in an old vineyard and run by their newly widowed friend, Lucia. Lucia was bravely trying to keep the place going despite the recent loss of her husband, Luigi, to lung cancer. She appeared in work pants, wearing Luigi's parka. They waded through a pack of friendly but undisciplined dogs, and Lucia gave them a blue ribbon tour.

That evening, Lucia came over to the Genazzinis' house for dinner. David fixed fondue, the makings of which he had brought, complete with cooking pot, from Geneva. As they ate, Lucia talked about her husband, with Eleanor translating as she went along. Lucia seemed in control of her emotions, but Jenny could sense the sad undertone.

The next day, with a windy rain beating on the windows, David and Jenny sat in front of the fire in the Genazzinis' living room while Eleanor gave them some backfill. "Luigi developed a bad cough about two years ago, but he refused to see a doctor about it," Eleanor recounted. "He and Lucia were working day and night, setting up the B&B, and Luigi didn't want to take time out over what he dismissed as smoker's cough. When he finally got it checked, it was too late. It's hard for me to even imagine how tough this is on Lucia – the financial struggle on top of the emotional loss."

The topic ultimately prompted David to talk about Sandie. Eleanor and Carlo were familiar with the story, but they listened attentively as David recalled his reaction to Dr. Blanchard's prognosis that the battle was lost.

"I had promised Sandie there would be no lies, but that meant I had to walk into her hospital room and tell her there was no more hope." David's voice caught on the word "hope." He took a moment to steady himself. "It was equally hard telling the children. Delphine was with Jenny in Boston, looking at colleges, so I had some help there, but Marc was backpacking through Eastern Europe. By the time he returned to Geneva, Sandie was too far gone to respond cogently to his presence. I think he still hasn't gotten over that."

Jenny sensed a subtle glance from Eleanor, monitoring Jenny's reaction. "It must be hard for you when David relives those days," Eleanor commented later, when she and Jenny were alone.

"Yes, but I've learned how important it is for survivors to talk openly about their lost spouses. We saw it with Lucia last night," Jenny pointed out. "It's been over four years since Sandie died, but even now, there are moments when David wants to talk about her."

"I can see that," Eleanor replied. "What I don't see is how you manage to handle it so calmly."

"Oh, I'm not always calm about it, but the last thing I want is to drive David underground. He can't help feeling what he feels when he feels it. Besides, I've gotten to know Sandie posthumously far better than I knew her when she was alive. In the beginning, she was a pretty intimidating act to follow. From every side, people described her as the perfect wife and mother, but I've gradually come to see that she was as human as the next person, with strengths and weaknesses.

Plus, I'm a lot more confident about my place in David's life than I was when I first moved to Geneva."

"I inferred that you and Sandie were old and dear friends. What do you mean when you say you got to know her far better after she died?"

Careful, Jenny. You just skated close to the edge. It's up to David to decide whom to tell about Sandie's infidelity.

"Sandie and I first met in the early 1980's. She was gracious at the outset, but initially she was *not* pleased that David and I were still so close. According to one of her confidants, I was the only one of David's former girlfriends who made Sandie nervous. Sandie apparently believed that she had 'caught the train between stations,' and that David might have married me instead, had the timing been different."

"Is that true?" Eleanor asked, intrigued.

"No. At least, I don't think so. Even if David and I had taken a stab at it, his attachment to Paris and mine to Boston would have made for some very rough sledding. But Sandie accurately sensed the continuing emotional intimacy David and I shared. She ultimately decided I wasn't a threat, but it took the better part of a decade for that to happen."

"Seeing now how devoted you are to David, hiding your feelings must have been difficult all those years."

"Oh, I didn't hide them. I just managed them. Of all the building blocks in my friendship with Sandie, the care with which I channeled my love for David was the most important one. My access to him was heavily dependent on Sandie's feelings about me. Had she disliked or distrusted me, our shared time would have been minimal. I worked hard to earn her friendship, and I demonstrated my respect and admiration whenever possible. In the process, I elevated her in my mind to an exaggerated level of perfection, but now that I've spent four years living with her husband and her children, in the midst of her possessions, her friends, and her world, I have a much clearer understanding of who Sandie was."

The conversation shifted to the Thanksgiving menu: wild boar, polenta with local mushrooms, and fig tart – a major departure from American tradition. Lucia joined them for the feast, affording further opportunity for her to talk with David.

At the end of the week's visit, the ballast of French wine, French cheese and Swiss chocolate David had brought was replaced by a similar quantity of fresh parmigiana, Italian sausage, Lucia's olive oil, and a *cubiton* of the neighbor's homegrown wine. "You know," said David after they said their farewells and took the *Autostrada* north, "I love France and *Suisse Romande,* but I have equal affection for Italy. If we ever give up Geneva, maybe we should think about retiring to someplace near the Genazzinis."

Eleanor had talked about local real estate during their visit. The prices in Tuscany were not beyond reach, but David's comment brought close to the surface what had been simmering in Jenny's mind for some time. *I don't want to retire to Italy – or Paris – or Switzerland. I'd like home base to be an English-speaking country. One where people drive on the right-hand side of the road,* she amended. Despite the seditious thoughts that flashed through her head, Jenny's response was carefully non-committal.

"We have a lot of thinking to do about the future. So many lovely places, so little time," she smiled.

"We need to focus on Christmas," Jenny announced once they were home. "We've got to coordinate Marc and Dellie's travel and book their tickets. Given how awful the exchange rate is, I'd like to see if Marc can buy his ticket directly. Then we'll reimburse him in dollars when we get there, and avoid the conversion costs."

From: Marc
To: Dad
Date: November 30, 2004
Subject: Re: Xmas Tickets

i tried getting a credit card, but they said no because i'm not at yoghurt yurt any more, and even though i got another shit job here to make ends meet, it's only for christmas sales. they said apply for some kind of account-limited card but i'll never have enough for a plane ticket anyway and i don't want to waste more time in transaction and deals backed up by facscist capitalistic anglosaxones.

i hope you can get the ticket for me.

love you, marc

David forwarded a copy to Jenny. "Do you think the yoghurt place fired him?" she asked. "And do we know what he's doing now?"

"No, but he's obviously unhappy with it, whatever his job is," David said sadly. He digested Marc's words for a day, then sent a reply.

De: David
A: Marc
Envoyé: 1 décembre, 2004
Objet: Re: Re: Xmas Tickets

We'll take care of the ticket, and Jenny will send you the details.

It sounds as if you're having difficulties with your job. I don't know how I can help from here, but I am always willing to listen.

Bises, Dad

That afternoon, Jenny went after a pesky fly in the kitchen. She misjudged her swing and knocked one of Sandie's little pitchers off the windowsill with the flyswatter. It didn't break, but David was upset. "I don't understand why you find the bloody flies so goddamn offensive!" he snapped.

She was stung by his tone, but held her tongue. *It's Marc who's really upsetting him,* she guessed.

"Sorry about my bad aim," she ventured an hour later.

"Me too, Ducks. Wish you'd gotten the little bastard. And I'm sorry I was short with you. I just don't know how to help Marc learn to live peacefully and lovingly with himself and others."

The Conundrum – *For Rachel*

Death didn't come to us;
It came to them - the other us -
But grief did, as a black hole,
Too massively personal to be shared,
A closed horizon, livid in its color,
No communication possible.

No one can bond in grief.
Yet we bonded instantly, but distantly,
In loss, which operates like gravity,
Permitting two loosed spirits
To orbit a common throbbing center,
Their stories identical but different.

I find the forces of loss increase
With time and distance as though,
Having amassed such grief,
Life's light in me learns
To avoid the dark warp
While drawing on its memorable energy,
Squaring it with my own accelerating life.
The question is, does it ever bring true relief?

D.P. - December, 2004

Chapter 7

"I'm amazed we were under the limit," Jenny commented as she watched their luggage carried off by the conveyor belt behind the check-in counter. "Between the French cheese and the Swiss chocolate, our Christmas gifts must weigh twice as much as the clothing we packed."

Once they were airborne, David pulled out the thick memoir Jenny had given him back in October. "It's a good thing you used your carry-on bag for that," she remarked. "Otherwise there would have been a surcharge."

"Airplane's a good place to finish it," David shrugged. "I've been reading it in small doses, because I find I relive the experiences as I read about them. Makes it a pretty emotional process."

"Where are you in the story?"

"You and I have finally managed to get married, despite Marc and Delphine's opposition, but one of my poems has you all riled up and worried that you made a big mistake."

"Was that the 'Across Your Garden' poem?"

"Yup."

Just months after David and Jenny were married, David had written a poem in memory of Sandie that Jenny came upon by accident. Although David was open about his grief, he had not shared this particular poem with her. At the time, Jenny's insecurities took the upper hand. There was a line that made her fear David regretted their marriage and was just biding his time until he and Sandie were reunited in death. In her journal, Jenny agonized over the poem's meaning. That passage made its way into the memoir.

"It makes me realize that you need to know some things about the way I write poetry," he frowned, shaking his head.

"Like what?"

"Like the fact that I use poems as a kind of steam valve," David pointed out. "I give vent to my feelings of the moment. I expect it's pretty much the same way you use your journal."

Jenny considered this. "Yes," she agreed. "It's true. When I'm happy, I write happy thoughts. When I'm angry, I write angry ones. I don't philosophize about joy or sorrow. I simply express it in writing."

"Well, I do the same," David explained, "but with poetry rather than prose. When I wrote 'Across Your Garden,' you were in Boston, attending your high school reunion. I was alone in Geneva on a gray rainy day, and I wasn't happy about it. It's funny," he added. "You take my poems very seriously, yet Sandie used to regard my poetry as trivial."

"But you wrote very different poetry back when Sandie was alive. Your poems were usually whimsical – devoid of romanticism and focused on light-hearted topics. Only with Sandie's death did you address issues like love and loss. Still, I don't think your poetry is trivial even when it's playful. I see it as your way of revealing feelings that you don't generally express in prose. Maybe that's why I look for meanings behind the words. Anyway, you'll be pleased to know – at least I hope you will – that I'm feeling far more secure these days than I did back in the timeframe you're reading about."

"Me too," he replied simply, and returned to his reading.

Jenny smiled to herself. As she had hoped, her memoir was proving an excellent vehicle for reviewing sensitive subjects and serving as a catalyst for an on-going conversation.

David finished the tome as they were skirting the coast of Nova Scotia. "It's fascinating to read about oneself from someone else's perspective," he commented. "You don't flatter me. Sometimes I read something, and then I have to stop and think, is that me? And yes, it is. So it's interesting. I feel almost cheated that I'm at the end."

"Any closing is arbitrary as long as we're still alive," Jenny said. "Ending the memoir after the birthday party seemed a logical stopping point, but if you want more, I always have the option of writing Memoir II."

The early winter darkness had descended on Boston by the time their plane was on its approach to Logan airport. Some of the boats in the harbor were festooned with brightly colored Christmas lights. *I'm home!* Jenny exulted silently when the wheels hit the tarmac.

When they got to Shawmut, they found orange juice, milk and a pecan pie in the refrigerator, with a note from Ross:

> Kevin and I are off to New York and aren't coming back until after New Year's. We dandy dons in gay apparel wish you a most *Joyeux Noel!*
>
> Sorry to miss you. Ross

Jenny was sorry too. Ross wasn't much on e-mails, so she relied on their infrequent visits to catch up.

Despite jet lag, they arranged to meet Rachel on their second evening for an early dinner in Brookline.

"Shall I gift-wrap some of the chocolate?" Jenny asked. "I'm sure I have ribbons somewhere."

"No. For Rachel, I'm going to do a poem."

A few hours later David handed Jenny a handwritten draft titled, *Conundrum.* "I'd like you to read it," he said, "and see what you think."

Jenny absorbed the poem line by line. Studying the final stanza, she was confused. She read it a second time:

> … I find the forces of loss increase
> With time and distance as though,
> Having amassed such grief,
> Life's light in me learns to avoid the dark warp
> While drawing on its memorable energy,
> Squaring it with my own accelerating life …

She looked at David, puzzled. "How can the forces of loss be increasing at the same time that 'life's light' is improving things?"

"Because the forces of loss are *positive*," he explained. "It's not the *sense* of loss that has increased. It's the *power* of loss – the *energy* that loss creates – that has increased. The power of loss has propelled me, forced me, into this new life, with its challenges, its new direction, and its new friends, of which Rachel is a prime example. That's why I want to give her the poem as a present."

"And what about me? How do I square with your accelerating life?" Jenny asked in a teasing tone.

"You're one of the challenges," he laughed. "Of course, you were a challenge in my old life as well. You're not exactly new."

"Watch it, Perry! You're heading out onto thin ice. Ladies don't like to be classified as 'old.'"

"Yas'm," he replied, giving her a kiss.

That evening, at the end of their dinner date, Rachel mentioned how much she had appreciated *Bother*, the poem David had written for Sandie back in September. "It was really thoughtful of you to send it to me, Jenny. And it was lovely of you to share it, David. It really speaks to where we are in this process," she added.

"I'm glad you liked it," David replied. "I've written another one, and this time it's for you. Don't read it now. Wait until you get home," he said, handing Rachel an envelope containing *Conundrum*.

The next morning, Rachel called as early as she dared, hoping that their disoriented internal clocks would have them up with the first rays of sun. Despite Jenny's concern that the 'forces of loss' might be misunderstood, Rachel had read *Conundrum* exactly as David intended.

"Well, of course," Rachel explained. "I know what he intended because I know exactly how he feels and where he is. I must have read it twenty times," she added.

Jenny handed the phone over to David and watched his face soften as he listened to Rachel's words. There was no joking or joshing, and his voice was very gentle when he said goodbye.

"What did she say?" Jenny asked him later.

"She liked the poem," he said simply. Then he paused. "She also said, 'This must be hard for Jenny.'" After a second pause, he asked, "Is it?"

"Having waded through my memoir, you should have a pretty clear idea by now of what's hard for me and what isn't."

"My sense is that it isn't always consistent."

"Well, that's true. But while there are certainly moments when life with you is hard, this isn't one of them. And Rachel has a lot to do with that. Her tutelage helped me understand your grieving process. The problem I have with *Conundrum* is the very last line: 'Does it ever bring true relief?' Because my goal is precisely that – bringing you true relief. I want everything to be perfect for us. I accept intellectually that it never will be. But in case you missed it, I am crazy about you, David Perry, and I have no intention of abandoning my quest."

"Hmpff," he said, fighting a smile.

The sun delivered a sparklingly bright morning. As she gazed out the window, Jenny spotted the local band of wild turkeys heading in dignified procession through Sandie's memorial garden. *All's right with the world,* she decided.

Because of the time difference, she waited until after lunch, and then dialed California.

"Hi, Bibi. We're in Boston."

"Hey, Jenny. How's the frozen north?"

"Blue skies, crystal clear air. It's nice to get away from those gloomy clouds that hang over Geneva all winter!"

"Complains the woman who just spent a week in Tuscany!"

"Well, yes, it's true, we did escape to Italy for Thanksgiving."

"And had a great time, according to your e-mail. Your description of your friends' place was luscious. I could practically see the ancient town perched on the hill across the valley, smell the olive oil and taste the farmer's wine. You two are giving yourself happy lives, and it's fun to hear about it. Now here's the big question. Has David finished the memoir? Will he give me permission to read it, mouth sealed, scout's honor? Now that we've gotten past Hanukkah, I need a new project."

"We are indeed giving ourselves happy lives, and things might get even happier, at least for me. I told you, didn't I, that David is open to spending a lot more time in the States and has talked about a fifty-fifty split?"

"Yeah, but how would it work? You'd live half a year here and half there?"

"We haven't really figured it out yet. It might be broken up with travel on both sides of the ocean. David wants to see the kids on a regular basis, and there are some financial issues. We also have to make arrangements for the cats. I expect it will be a process of trial and error."

"What's happening on the Marc front?"

"Nothing catastrophic, but he hasn't been happy with his pocket-money jobs. He could still benefit from some attitude adjustment."

"Do you have plans to come back to California any time soon?" Bibi asked.

"Not at present. We'll see Marc in Chattanooga, and we're scheduled to return to Geneva right after Christmas. I doubt we'll get back to the States until the summer."

"So, that's for the future. Meanwhile, you didn't answer my question about the memoir."

"David finished it on the plane coming over. No small task! It's nearly five hundred pages."

"No editor in her right mind is going to let you submit a manuscript that size to a publisher," Bibi advised.

"Bibi, at the moment I have no intention of submitting a manuscript of *any* size, to *any* publisher."

"So, lemme read it, and then I'll tell you what's needed to get it into shape. Whatever you want to expunge, I'm pretty sure the rest of the story won't suffer. And with five hundred pages, you'll need to make some major cuts anyway."

When the conversation ended, Jenny consulted with David. "I don't mind Bibi's reading it," he said. "I told you before that you tell a good story. The only thing I ask is that Bibi not repeat anything concerning Sandie's affair. I need to do some thinking about when, where and whether that information goes public."

Jenny sent Bibi an electronic copy with a cover note. "I have to confess I'm really curious as to what you'll think of it," she admitted.

They celebrated Christmas in Chattanooga. Marc flew in from California, and Delphine made the trip from Paris. Jenny was braced for some surliness on Marc's part, but he seemed in a cheerful mood as they greeted him at the airport. David asked about his job situation, but Marc's response seemed calm and reasonable. "This last one's over 'cause it was just for the Christmas season, but there's a new pizza place opening up near school, and I've signed up for an interview after New Year's."

Later, when Marc opened his suitcase, he pulled out several bubble-wrapped bowls and vases he had made in his glass-blowing class. "These will be my Christmas presents for all the family," he announced. The glass was a rich cobalt blue, and though the objects were a bit off balance, the irregular shapes were interesting and attractive. Listening to Marc talk about them, it was clear he had taken delight in his glass blowing experience.

"It's nice to see Marc excited by something," Jenny said quietly to David. "The art world is one of the few environments where he seems comfortable and productive."

The Christmas celebration followed a familiar pattern, relaxed and chaotic at the same time – non-stop parties, mounds of high-calorie, high-cholesterol food and more wine and eggnog than was sensible. There was also feedback about the surprise party from the friends of Nate and Isham who had lived it vicariously.

"Nate declared it was just the best surprise you could imagine," one of their neighbors told Jenny. "He said you had it organized down to every little detail, and that no General could've done it better. Y'all must have had the most wonderful time!"

Margaret's friend Marian jumped in. "Margaret told me about Sandie's rose on David's cake, and your speech at the restaurant. She said it meant so much to the whole family, because you never make them choose between you and Sandie."

"I owe Sandie a lot," Jenny started to explain, but Marian plowed ahead.

"And you just have to know that all the honor you give to Sandie reflects back on you tenfold. You look so happy when you're with David you might as well be an angel with a halo, and it's because Sandie is blessing you both," she declared firmly.

Any thoughts Jenny might have entertained about meriting a halo were swiftly dashed by an e-mail from Bibi, expressing shock at the revelations found in Jenny's memoir.

From: BIBirnbaum
To: Jenny
Date: December 26, 2004
Subject: Memoir shock!

I just finished Chapter 2. Longworth, you have been holding out on me. I started your manuscript thinking that the Jezebel woman and Sandie's affair would be the main sensitive issues. But those are *bupkis* when stacked up against the Jenny-David sex part. The reader is going to be scandalized. I don't think you appreciate what a shock it was for me to realize you slept with him before he even got Sandie's ashes back from the crematorium.

I know you, and now I feel I know David. I can see that your motives were as pure as they could get under the circumstances, but lemme tell you, the reader's jaw is going to drop. You explain your actions in words, but you've got to help the reader feel at a gut level how afraid you were, how worried you were for David. The reader needs to share your deep distress about his mindset. And the reader needs to understand David's struggle as well, the urgent need to grab the life raft you held out to him, the courage it took to dare to believe in a future.

Call me. Bibi

Jenny didn't want to call from Nate's house, so she sent an e-mail response instead.

From: JWLongworth
To: Bibi
Date: December 27, 2004
Subject: Re: Memoir shock!

Now you understand why I'm not chomping at the bit to adapt the story for public consumption. I expect the project would benefit from some serious aging. If I wait ten years, I'll have the perfect opener: "Once upon a time...." By then, our memories will be fuzzy around the edges, so it'll be easier for family and friends to view it as a fairytale.

Love, Jenny

From: BIBirnbaum
To: Jenny
Date: December 28, 2004
Subject: Re: Re: Memoir shock!

Yeah, but your story has a lot of potential immediate value for people dealing with grief, old loves and second marriages. I'd hate to see you shelve it. That's too puritan – sort of like *Banned in Boston*. I'm sure there are ways to rewrite it so you won't be overly exposed at a personal level.

Happy New Year - Bibi

They made the return to Geneva early in January. David was eager to get back to Europe, but as Jenny boarded the plane, she felt as if she were honoring an appointment with a dentist. Once they got to Morion, however, her spirits revived. Despite their feigned nonchalance, the two cats, Minuit and Carotte, were enthusiastic about their reappearance, and thanks to Marikit, the house was clean and tidy.

Unlike the previous year, David didn't have to go back to school after Christmas vacation, and he quickly immersed himself in cooking, filling the kitchen with delicious aromas. He had no difficulty filling the days with things he enjoyed – reading, writing and painting – and in deference to Jenny's request, he limited francophone social events to one a week.

For her part, Jenny went to work on the logistics of splitting their time between the US and Europe. She pulled together the requisite financial data and set up a meeting with their accountant.

"You don't need me for this discussion do you? You're the money manager, and the guy speaks English," David said, hoping to be excused from the meeting.

"You have to come, David. There are major decisions to be made. If we don't plan this properly, our happy retirement could turn into a financial nightmare."

The CPA had been forewarned about David's aversion to accounting jargon and was careful to use simple language. "Based on the figures you provided," he began, "you cannot afford to travel and still keep the two properties you own solely for your personal use. The extreme choice is selling one of your houses. Alternatively, each dwelling could generate rental income when you are not in residence. Even then, you'll have to be careful. The Geneva house is by far the more expensive because you are carrying a large mortgage. Making your retirement official and collecting your school pension would help, but that alone won't cover it," he said, turning to David, "and the unfavorable exchange rate has upped the dollar amount Jenny has to contribute from her US income. If you're open to rentals, I can do some projections for you."

"Would our tax situation be better if we weren't based in Geneva?" Jenny asked. "David was fantasizing recently about retiring to Italy, and we've talked about France as well. Would that make a difference?"

"Frankly, the simplest and most financially advantageous move would be to change your legal residence back to the US. All your original retirement planning was knocked for a loop when you moved from Boston to Geneva. As you know, your tax burden is extremely high here, Jenny. If you give up Swiss residency, you would no longer be liable for Swiss taxes."

"I thought there was some kind of reciprocity," said David, clearly puzzled. "If you pay taxes here, you don't have to pay them in the States, do you? Isn't it six of one, half dozen of the other?"

"It's not that simple," Jenny interjected. "Swiss taxes are structured differently. Since my retirement investments aren't part of a pension plan the Swiss recognize, they subject them to a hefty annual 'wealth' tax. I have to sell stock each year to pay the Swiss tax, which not only depletes my retirement capital but also makes me subject to US capital gains taxes. It's a vicious circle."

The CPA nodded his agreement.

"Why didn't you tell me this?" David asked. "I didn't realize the Swiss were eating up your retirement money with a wealth tax."

"I didn't see that we had much of an option." *And I couldn't imagine that you would consider moving back to the States,* she added mentally.

"So," David said, turning to the accountant, "you're recommending that we give up our Swiss residency?"

"I'm simply saying that repatriation would have a dramatic impact on your tax burden," he replied. "From a purely economic standpoint, you would benefit substantially if you treated Jenny's Massachusetts condo as your official home, and your Geneva house as your vacation residence."

"And how, exactly, would we go about this?"

Jenny held her breath. David was comfortable splitting time between the old world and the new, but equal-opportunity travel was not the same as legal residency. There were political issues involved. Europe had been home to him all his adult life. When he left for Paris as a young man, it was the Age of Aquarius. Embroiled in the turmoil engendered by the Vietnam War, he turned his back on the American political scene and gave himself emotionally to his new home across the Atlantic. He had once vowed he would never go back except as a tourist. *Repatriation has to be a sensitive subject,* Jenny presumed, *even though the war ended decades ago.*

The accountant focused first on issues unaffected by nostalgia and sentimentality. "You'll have to notify the Office of Population, prepay a year's Swiss taxes, and make some decisions about your health insurance. Once you've decided on your official departure date, we'll do up an estimated tax report. It would be simplest if you chose the close of the year, but we can pro-rate it if you want to do this before December."

By the end of the meeting, to Jenny's astonishment, David concurred that it was a move they should make. On the way home, however, he began to express some reservations.

"I don't have a problem signing a form saying we're moving from Country A to Country B, but I want to be sure that we keep this house," David insisted as they pulled into their driveway.

Jenny was well aware that David was not ready to make irrevocable decisions about a home that carried so many emotional attachments.

"Legally there's no problem. As the accountant said, we simply redefine Geneva as our vacation residence once we move back to Boston. We know we can't maintain two houses for long on our retirement income, but we have time to restructure things. What we should get started on is some cleaning out and cleaning up. That way, this house will be available as a short-term furnished rental the next time we leave. With all the multi-national corporations in Geneva, there must be lots of families moving here who need a place to live while they look for permanent housing. Six-to-eight weeks worth of rental income would pay a whole year's worth of property tax."

David suddenly looked skeptical. "What do you mean by cleaning out and cleaning up?"

"Renters need space for their clothes and personal items. That means a goodly supply of empty closets and empty dressers."

David couldn't argue against Jenny's logic, but he wasn't enthusiastic. David was a packrat in his own right, and he was protective of Sandie's belongings, still present throughout the house.

Jenny didn't press the issue, but began to quietly consider what could be easily shifted to the basement *Cave* for storage. She started with her office. There were sheaves of papers from Sandie's era that Jenny had set aside when she first came to Geneva. *A lot of that material must be outdated by now,* she guessed.

It was a slower process than she anticipated. Almost everything was in French, and from time to time, Jenny stumbled upon items that were emotionally difficult. In a folder with old medical bills, she found a copy of a letter describing the treatment options Sandie was considering for the lesion on her spine. "What everybody seems to agree on," Sandie had concluded, "is that it evolves very slowly. There is no emergency about a surgery." Two years later, Sandie was dead. *If I'm tripping over things like this,* Jenny worried, *what is the clean-out going to be like for David?*

From: BIBirnbaum
To: Jenny
Date: January 17, 2005
Subject: Manuscript

Finished your manuscript today, and I'm sorry it ended. It was a fun read, and I want more. I've gotten over my initial shock at the revelations in the early chapters. Probably everybody reads things through the lens of their own sensitive places.

As a parent of kids who were known to be difficult, I appreciate your stepmother problems. Marc jumps off the page. I think his double is the kid who works in the mailroom at my office. I find myself wondering when or how he was wounded? Do you think he sensed Sandie's affair?

With careful revision, the story could be told, and I think it's worth telling. The last section is the best, because we see the growth in the characters. That's the essence of a good story - or a good life I guess.

I'll write more soon, but right now, I seem to have the flu. I'm envious that you have David to cook such good meals for you.

Love, Bibi

PS - I have anxiety attacks too, though probably not as bad as you. It sucks.

From: JWLongworth
To: Bibi
cc: David
Date: January 18, 2005
Subject: Re: Manuscript

Bibi, I appreciate your enthusiasm for the memoir, but I have far bigger fish to fry. We are poised to shift our legal residence back to the States. I'm not sure how this will all shake out, but David has agreed to short-term rentals of the Geneva house when we're out of town. I have embarked on a major clean-out. David accepts it intellectually, but this process is bound to put us at loggerheads.

Still, I have to tell you, I love it that you think I could turn my Geneva experience into a novel people would want to read. It's a nice antidote to anxiety attacks when a professional editor makes you feel like a future candidate for the Best New Author of the Year award!

Take care of yourself. Lots of orange juice and bed rest!

Love, Jenny

As per tradition, David composed a sentimental poem in honor of Sandie's January 24 birthday and sent it to Marc and Delphine. The following day, a second poem appeared, rolled up and tied with a red ribbon. This one was for Jenny in celebration of their third wedding anniversary. It was a spoof, incorporating a mis-adventure they had with the bank regarding an automatic payment withdrawal. David described their marital adventure as continuing "just fine" despite their cash shortage.

I certainly wouldn't mind if David wrote romantic verses for me, Jenny decided, *but I'm okay with his saying our marriage is "just fine."*

The tone of the poem reminded Jenny of a recent conversation with a neighbor. "What do you do to be so happy?" the woman had asked David and Jenny.

"We get along well," replied David simply.

February ushered in a few rare sunny days. The temperatures were crisp, but there was no wind. Jenny celebrated by bundling up and working outdoors during the afternoon, clearing winter debris until the light began to fade. When she went in, there were rich aromas filling the house. She followed her nose and settled into her customary spectator seat on a stool at the counter that divided the kitchen from the dining room. She perched there in part to be out of the way, but mostly because it gave her a front row seat to watch David playing French Chef.

"Here I sit, a lady of leisure," she said, taking the proffered glass of wine, "while a tasty dinner is being prepared for my enjoyment."

Rather than offering a light-hearted retort, David was suddenly very sweet. "You're no more spoiled than I am," he said, "finding that the garden is restored and the taxes are processed with no effort on my part. You scratch my back...," he concluded.

The following weekend, the *bise*, the icy north wind that periodically swept down the Rhône Valley, was out in force. Knowing Jenny was a hothouse plant, David suggested he go alone to the Sunday farmers' market. "I'm only going to buy a few things. You don't have to come," he insisted.

"David Perry, you, at the farmers' market, are the proverbial kid in a candy store. You always fill way more than two bags, and you'll need help carrying them."

At the end of their shopping run, when they emerged with four bulging sacks, Jenny couldn't resist an I-told-you-so. "See," she said. "I knew you needed me."

"Oh, I need you all right," he replied with a wry grin. He went no further, and Jenny realized she was being blessed with one of his rare romantic comments.

Jenny smiled. *Tomorrow,* she sensed, *it will be safe to start tackling the closets.*

Jenny forced herself to try on every stitch of clothing she owned, knowing that David's good cooking had an unfortunate and cumulative side effect. For every five items of hers that she consigned to the Goodwill pile, she pulled an old item out of David's closet and laid it on the bed. "If it fits, you can keep it," she reassured him, "but if it doesn't, it needs to find a new home."

"Busybody!" he shot back, but he cooperated, as she knew he ultimately would.

David began to inform people casually about the proposed transition, minimizing the significance of the decision. To hear him describe it, their extended travel plans, not their residency status, would be the primary determinant of where they hung their hats at any given moment. When he mentioned the clean-out effort to Delphine, she agreed to make a trip back from Paris that weekend.

Jenny expected some procrastination before Delphine got down to work, but the minute she was home, Delphine threw open her closet doors and started right in. Within an hour she had filled three enormous plastic bags with clothes to be given to charity. "Wow!" Jenny said, wide-eyed. "I'm impressed, Dellie!"

Delphine just shrugged. "I had tons of clothes from my teenage days, and it was time for them to go," she observed sagely, having reached the ripe old age of twenty-two. "And then," she said after a pause, "there were all of Mom's things. None of her clothes fit me. I only saved them because I was so upset. The belts and sweaters and jerseys were like pieces of her, but I don't need to keep them anymore. There are other people who can use them."

Delphine surveyed her old bedroom. "There are two of these I'd like to take back to Paris, but the rest should be tossed," she advised, pointing to the posters on the wall. She proceeded to remove them, revealing tack holes and areas where tape had stripped paint from the surface.

"Delphine's room could do with some patching and a fresh coat of paint," Jenny advised David. When he started to grumble, Delphine defended the upgrade. "It *has* been ten years, Dad. If Mom could see this, she would definitely want it repainted. The rug's in pretty bad shape too," she grinned. "You know what a mess teenagers make!"

Delphine also fixed a critical eye on the kitchen. "I just washed down the kitchen walls in my apartment, and it was really gross how much grease there was," she said, wrinkling her nose. "As long as you've got a painter coming in, maybe you should have him do the kitchen too. If I were some big-shot international executive's wife looking to rent a house, I'd insist on a clean kitchen, even if it's only for a few weeks. Mom would agree with me. You know she would."

"Your daughter has a point," Jenny said, backing Delphine's advice.

It took some strategic lobbying, but David eventually caved in. "Now I'll have to move every bloody thing off the counters and the shelves," he sighed.

"I'll take care of that," Jenny intervened. "I'm the one who wants the kitchen cleaned and repainted. There's no reason you should have to take care of the preparation."

David did a hundred and eighty degree turn. "Of course there is! I have to be responsible for something," he argued. "Besides, if someone else did it, what would I have to bitch about?"

An hour later, David drove Delphine to the local Goodwill drop-off to deposit her bags of clothing. When they returned, he called Jenny out of her office. "The three of us need to talk," he said with a long face. Delphine was settled at the dining room table, her eyes fixed on a placemat. "Delphine didn't realize we were planning to repatriate, and she's very upset by our decision," he told Jenny. "She doesn't want us to move to the States, and feels I should have talked with her and with Marc before we decided."

Jenny looked at him, startled. "I thought you told Dellie and Marc about this weeks ago!"

"Well, I told them about the clean-out, but I don't remember what I said about the whys and wherefores," David mumbled apologetically as Delphine quietly shook her head.

Jenny turned her attention to Delphine. "Dellie, I'm sorry this information is coming as a surprise, but for starters, we're not 'moving to the States' – certainly not in the way you think. We're talking about dividing our time between Europe and America, and we're repatriating for technical reasons having to do with currency exchange rates and Swiss taxes. It means some paperwork, and making sure we don't spend six consecutive months in Geneva, but that's hardly a major change. I don't think we've spent six consecutive months in Geneva since I moved here. Even when David was teaching, we took advantage of school holidays to visit people outside Switzerland."

"So, you're not going to sell the house?" Delphine asked.

"No, we're not going to sell the house," David said firmly.

"Especially not after going to the trouble of painting your room and your father's kitchen!" Jenny teased.

Delphine gave a half smile, but Jenny sensed she still needed some reassurance.

"The big adjustment isn't going to be our residency status. It's going to be the presence of renters during the times we're all out of Geneva – you and Marc at school, David and me in the States or traveling. From where I sit, I expect you and your father will see as much of each other after the legal transition as you do now – and probably more. There is certainly no immediate change. We'll be here well into the summer, off to Boston for eight weeks, and then back in Switzerland for most of the fall. Beyond that, we'll see what fate has in store. You never know. You might end up getting a job in Timbuktu after you graduate."

"Feel better?" David asked his daughter.

"Yeah," Delphine shrugged. "I guess it isn't such a big deal after all."

From: BIBirnbaum
To: Jenny
Date: February 19, 2005
Subject: More on the Manuscript

I've been making editor's notes. When you went off to marry David, I thought he was the one who was lucky. Time shows that the luck is double. I'm touched to see his commitment to you, and the way he takes care of you like a mother hen, with his funny ways and yummy food. If your story were a novel, this would be a wonderful part of the character development process – the change in what the reader can see.

Re Sandie's affair, the tension is powerful, and it really lets us see inside the minds and hearts of the players.

For the fictional version, you need to think about the ménage-à-trois. Is it ever going to end? It's hard for the reader to envision it continuing for the rest of your lives. If it remains a constant, you need to explain and justify it.

Love, Bibi

From: JWLongworth
To: Bibi
Date: February 20, 2005
Subject: Re: More on the Manuscript

Bibi, I can't stop you from making editor's notes, but right now, our ménage-à-trois is essential to the success of my "clean-up and clean-out" project. For example, David initially opposed repainting the kitchen. "I don't want to move the frigging frying pans, and I work perfectly well with the walls I've got," he argued. I was nearly won over by his suave synthesis of southern colloquialism and Harvard alliteration. I mean, how many men do you know who work perfectly well with the walls they've got?

Fortunately, Dellie was visiting, and she invoked her mother's housekeeping standards. Without Sandie in our corner, we might not have won the day. A ménage-à-trois can have its good points.

Love, Jenny

Jenny sometimes teased David about his resistance to change, but she well understood that sorting through old possessions could release difficult memories. In a box sitting on top of an armoire, Jenny found a yellow wallet tucked in with some ski mittens. The wallet was empty except for two small feathers. She recognized them instantly. They were from one of the hawks that hunted the skies over Jenny's condo in Shawmut. She had sent them to Sandie for luck when Sandie was undergoing her final chemotherapy. "Keep those good and lucky feathers coming!! We were able to do the treatment on Wednesday!" Sandie wrote in thanks. She died a month later.

Jenny looked at the feathers and shook her head. *Bibi wonders if the ménage-à-trois will ever disappear. Somehow I don't think so. And maybe that's as it should be.*

When Delphine came home for spring break, she alerted Jenny and her father that she had been invited to serve as a bridesmaid in an August wedding in New York. "They're going to pay for my travel," she said, "but I'm hoping to line up a job for part of June and July so I'll have some spending money in the States."

"There were a couple of summers when you helped your mother with administrative work at school," David recalled. "Why not stop by l'Académie Internationale to see if they have any summer projects available."

Delphine followed up on her father's suggestion, but returned home obviously discouraged and on the edge of tears. "Both the women I talked to were new. They didn't even know who Maman was," she moaned.

In an effort to soothe her, David shifted the focus. "I wouldn't worry too much if you don't line up a job. Since you have to go to the States anyway, why not take advantage of the free plane ticket and come with us to Boston in July? No point in being jet-lagged for all the wedding hoopla. Stay with us, relax, and when you're ready, we'll put you on the train to New York." Delphine's turn-around was swift. By supper she was cheerful and optimistic again.

Jenny, however, was subdued throughout the meal. When she and David retired to their bedroom, she shared her concerns.

"When Dellie graduates, she'll face a major transition. While she's a student, her expenses are paid by the Education Trust, but that money stops with graduation. She will soon be living an independent life, and she needs to find independent means to finance it. You and I can help in small ways, but we can't be her primary source of income. We can't just step in and take on the bills the Trust has covered these past four years. We need our resources for our own living expenses, plus a reserve for the future. Unless Dellie is planning to move back here and live in this house, she needs to find a job, and she needs to find it soon. As of June, her Trust funding ends."

"What are you suggesting?

"First and foremost, we need to spell out the financial issues and help her understand some fiscal realities."

"Can this maybe wait until she's gotten through her exams?" David asked. "In the meantime, you could do a test run, and help *me* understand the fiscal realities of her situation."

This is going to be a challenge, Jenny realized. But all she said was, "Yes, Dear," and then kissed him goodnight.

Graduation – *For Delphine*

College graduation!? Can't get my mind around it,
        Ma fille.
High school seemed to stand on childhood extended
                Really,
But a BA for me belongs to age, adulthood reached,
                        Leaving
Little time for me to linger in your life at
                                Home.
I catch myself imagining your mom, watching you
                                        Here
Near the Champs-Elysées, receiving your *diplôme*
                                In Paris.
Her joy mirrors today's sun, her smile the Seine,
                        Always
Curving through my chosen center of the world - by birth
                Hers -
Yet as our time flows toward new horizons,
        Now yours.
Love, Dad

D.P. – June, 2005

Chapter 8

The American University in Paris held commencement exercises the first week in June. David booked a room for them on the top floor of a small hotel in the sixth *arrondissement*. When they arrived, Jenny opened the curtains to see what their view might be and discovered that the sole window faced an interior airshaft.

With no outside balcony and only a single narrow staircase leading up here, we will clearly be toast if there's a fire, Jenny thought to herself.

Catching her frown, David defended his choice. "It's not exactly a great view, but in this crowded quarter, a window on the street can be very noisy," David said. "Besides, this is Paris. We'll be spending every waking minute outside!"

Jenny made no protest. *It wouldn't make a dent anyway,* she knew. David's enthusiasm for Paris was absolute.

The morning of Delphine's graduation, Jenny dressed in silk slacks with a light beige blouse, a peach-colored jacket and an apricot-hued scarf. The effect was marred only slightly by her practical flat shoes, a compromise necessitated by her arthritic hip. David, whose preferred dress was bluejeans and gaudy shirts, put on gray wool slacks, a discreet buttoned-down shirt, his navy blazer, and rarity of rarities, a tie. "You look very proper and paternal," Jenny concluded. "You're very handsome when you get dressed up." *But then,* she smiled to herself, *I find him very handsome no matter what he's wearing.*

The commencement exercises opened with the traditional "Pomp and Circumstance," and parents craned their necks to see their offspring file in. In the middle of the processional, Jenny felt her throat tightening. *Sandie would have been so thrilled by all of this. David must be thinking about that too.*

As Delphine was handed her diploma, the Dean announced that she was graduating Cum Laude.

"What does it mean?" Delphine asked her father after the ceremony.

"Cum Laude? It's Latin for 'with honor.' The French don't use the term in academic awards, but the Americans do. In essence it means, 'with excellent grades.'"

"Oh." Delphine gave a modest little shrug. "I want you to meet some of my professors," she said, changing the subject. "I'll be right back."

As they waited for Delphine's return, Jenny shared her earlier thoughts. "I couldn't help but think of Sandie during the ceremony. She would have loved this – the pageantry, the procession, the caps and gowns."

"Yes," David responded. "She would have, but you have to realize, Ducks, that had Sandie lived, Delphine would never have gone to the American University of Paris. She would never have had this particular college experience, nor this particular college graduation. We'd probably be in the States right now, celebrating Delphine's graduation from Boston University with a picnic in your garden in Shawmut."

He's right, Jenny realized. *I'm not sitting in Sandie's seat. It would have been a different seat, in a different auditorium.*

Delphine reappeared with one of her Art History professors, who congratulated them on Delphine's performance. "You must be very proud of your daughter," he said, beaming at David and Jenny.

"Actually, she's my stepdaughter," Jenny corrected, "but yes, we're both very proud of her, as her mother would have been."

"We're taking you to lunch at Laserre to celebrate," David advised Delphine.

"I've heard of it, but I've never been there," Delphine commented.

"No, I shouldn't think so. It's not exactly student fare," David laughed.

"Your father and I went there thirty-six years ago, and spent the then shocking sum of $100 on a three-course luncheon consisting of a slice of foie gras, Dover sole, and a dessert. There was some champagne involved, so that surely upped the total, but we were nonetheless astonished that a lunch tab could run to three figures!" Jenny recounted.

David and Jenny smiled at each other. It was a delicious memory for both of them.

The restaurant was only a few blocks away, but Delphine had begun her day with a sunrise celebration at the Eiffel Tower, and walked from there with her classmates to the Graduation site. Her feet were swollen and blistered. The minute the Commencement events were over, Delphine took off her shoes. As she pattered barefoot down the Paris boulevards towards the restaurant, Jenny, walking behind her, couldn't help laughing. In contrast with her white dress, the soles of Delphine's feet were completely black from the soot and street dirt.

The shoes went back on temporarily as a doorman in formal attire greeted them and ushered them into the dining room. The day was warm, and the restaurant was running air conditioning equipment. "That's something they didn't have back when we came here," David noted.

One of Jenny's strongest memories from their original visit was Laserre's ornate ceiling, constructed like a set of giant horizontal sliding doors. When the cigarette smoke became too thick, the ceiling would open, the doors slipping back into a recess. The smoke drifted up and was replaced by a downdraft of more-or-less fresh Parisian air.

"With this modern air conditioning, I'm afraid Delphine might not get to see the ceiling in action," Jenny whispered to David as they were led to their table. Once they were seated, however, two diners across the room lit up cigars. Jenny directed an alarmed look at the offending smokers. The waiters reacted immediately and within seconds, the ceiling, subtly painted with misty clouds, rolled back majestically to reveal the Paris sky and several pots of bright geraniums hanging from a lattice work over the opening. The smoke rose to the heavens. Delphine was duly impressed.

"Ladies, would you like champagne as an aperatif?" David asked. He chose a bottle, and they stayed with it throughout the meal. As many as five waiters hovered within range to take care of their every need and desire. Everything was beautifully presented, with Jenny's sautéed morelles set amidst vegetables sliced wafer-thin and arranged in an artful pattern. Delphine's sole *meunière* had an edging of carrots and greens, layered to give the appearance of a flower border.

For dessert, David ordered a *timbale,* and Jenny had *crêpes Suzettes,* prepared from scratch at a side table. Delphine was sensible and had a single bite from David and Jenny's respective desserts.

"Oof. Now that we've had a spoonful of sugar, maybe it's time for a dose of medicine," David said, trying to set a light tone. "Jenny wants us to talk about finances," he added, passing the buck.

"Oh, thanks!" Jenny shot back. "Nice way to end the meal! Besides, Dellie's never going to believe our resources are finite after what we just spent on this lunch!"

David looked uncertain. "Uh, do you want to do this later?"

"No, now is as good a time as any. Your daughter has a good head on her shoulders, and I doubt anything I say will come as a surprise."

Delphine watched this exchange with interest. "So what's not a surprise?" she ventured.

Jenny turned her attention to Delphine. "All your school expenses – including your apartment and most of your travel – have been paid out of an Education Trust that was set up many years ago. You know this, yes?"

"Yes."

"Your apartment lease is up, so rent isn't an immediate issue, and you'll be staying with us into August. We'll carry you through the summer, but you'll need to find employment right after the New York wedding if you're planning to come back and live in Paris. I can help you pull together a budget. Any job you get will presumably be at a starting salary, so you should look for a roommate to help with rent."

Delphine twisted a strand of her hair. "I have a friend from school who's interested in sharing her apartment in the fall. Her current roommate is moving out end of August."

"See!" Jenny said, throwing a teasing glance at David. "I told you Dellie had a good head on her shoulders!"

"The thing is, I've applied for a three month winter internship with Sotheby's in London. I should hear from them any day now. It would be a really good experience, and would look great on my resume, but it doesn't pay anything. They don't even cover travel."

"Do they provide housing?"

"Nope."

"When is the internship?"

"It starts beginning of January."

"Okay, this is getting complicated. Maybe we *do* want to talk about this later. If you get an acceptance from Sotheby's, we need to do a lot of creative thinking."

"Financial meeting adjourned," David smiled. "Would anyone like a brandy with the espresso?"

They spent two more days in Paris, then caught the train back to Geneva. "You're looking very pensive," Jenny noted as they sped through the Burgundy countryside.

"It was hard to watch my daughter demonstrate, at each instant, that she has added universes of experience to her life that are hers alone – universes of which I will never be part. That's one thing life does to surprise us parents. Time passes and passes us by. That's just the way it is."

"Even so," Jenny protested, "I find it gratifying to see young people, especially young women, gaining their independence and expanding their 'universes of experience' as you call it."

David nodded in acknowledgement, but made no further comment.

Jenny had hoped for time to decompress after their return from Paris, but everyone wanted to welcome Delphine home and hear about the graduation, so David committed them to hosting a barbecue at the first opportunity.

On the appointed day Jenny put out extra chairs while David fetched wine glasses and bowls of nuts. As the neighbors gathered and the French conversation swirled about her, Jenny set her face in a smile, cut her food in small pieces, and chewed each bite a long time. If someone posed a question, a mouthful of food gave her time to construct an answer or an excuse to pass if she couldn't discern the subject matter. *Look cheerful, Longworth,* she chided herself. *You only have four more weeks before we fly to Boston.*

David, of course, was quite content to be in Geneva. "Back from a great visit in Paris," he wrote Graham. "Delphine is home now, and we're here in Geneva until mid-July – hallelujah! I'm looking forward to doing as little as possible."

Marc called to announce that he had found a bargain flight and was coming home. "He's arriving next Wednesday," David advised Jenny.

"That's a change. I thought he was going stay in San Francisco to do another summer semester," Jenny remarked.

"I think the fact that Delphine is here has something to do with it, but he said he'd rather do a normal academic year and graduate next May rather than try to push things."

"Is he planning to stay in Geneva until September?"

"I didn't get his return date, but I assume so."

"If yes, that rules out a short-term rental for August."

"That's okay," David said. "I haven't talked with any rental agencies yet, and this way, Marc can go through all his books and records and help with the clean-out, so there's no problem"

Unless you consider our income. "Well, this may be fortuitous," Jenny said out loud. "We can hold a family conference about our rental calendar. And since Dellie just got a 'yes' from Sotheby's, maybe we can do a financial overview for both the kids. One thing seems clear. We need to have a tenant lined up for whenever we take off for Christmas."

Jenny paused and frowned. "Actually, let me amend that. Now that I think about it, we may need to do Christmas here in Geneva. Since we're shifting our legal residence effective December 31, there could be any number of unanticipated loose ends at the last minute. So, correction: we need to have a tenant lined up for the first of January."

In addition to returning children, June brought out-of-town visitors. Freja Dehmel, a friend from Hamburg, traveled to Geneva to spend three days with them. Though they didn't see one another often, Jenny counted Freja as very special among her European friends. It helped that she spoke such fluent English, but equally important was the fact that Freja hadn't entered their lives until after Sandie's death. All the women Jenny knew in Geneva had known Sandie first. It was inevitable that they would make comparisons, but for Freja, "David and Sandie" existed only as an historical reference. With Freja, Jenny walked in no one's shadow.

The afternoon of her arrival, they whiled away the time on the patio, looking out over the flowerbeds.

"Jenny's tamed the place," David commented. "When Sandie and I first moved here, I was so excited about having a real garden that I planted things without understanding how big they would get. I spent our moving-in day digging holes in the back yard. Needless to say, Sandie wasn't too pleased with me, given that the house was full of boxes to be unpacked."

"So you, too, have done good things for the garden," Freja said with a smile for David.

"Yes, but the best thing I did for the garden was bring in Jenny," he replied.

While David started dinner preparations, Freja and Jenny went out for a walk, strolling past fields of young sunflowers bordered by brilliant orange poppies.

"I must tell you, Jenny, how I enjoyed your description about Dellie's graduation," Freja commented. "I can imagine David in his jacket and tie. Surely he was dashing in such an outfit! And I can see Dellie with her uncomfortable and dirty feet!"

"They were absolutely black," Jenny recalled, shaking her head at the image.

"What I love most is this," Freja continued. "Always are you aware of Sandie and sensitive to those she has left behind. I think it is not so common in most people. You have had an impact on Dellie and her choices in life. I see no reason why you must apologize and say, 'Oh, but I'm her stepmother.' That fact does not make it that you do not deserve praise or that you must feel less pride in what she accomplishes."

"I feel a lot of pride in Dellie's accomplishments, but I can't take much credit for them. I arrived very late in the game," Jenny demurred.

"I understand how you feel and how you stand back, but I am very moved by your sensitivity. You and David and Sandie are interwoven in a strong net of love and humanity. I have a friend," Freja went on, "who is making a marriage with a widower. She feels she must eliminate all traces of the first wife, but I think she is so very wrong. When I try to explain how well it serves your marriage that you always honor Sandie, she cannot imagine that it would be so. I still remember when I first came to Geneva. You shared for me some of your story then, and I felt the angels so near."

Jenny was sorry Freja's stay was so short. "You are always welcome here, and some day, you must come see us when we're in Boston," Jenny insisted.

"And you and David must come some day to Hamburg," Freja rejoined. "I will take you for smoked eels to the Island of Sylt!"

After Freja's departure, the limitation on francophone events crumbled under the weight of the children's presence and the spreading news that the Perrys were officially repatriating to the US. With long summer evenings, David was in his element, hosting barbecues and dinners al fresco at every opportunity. Friends and neighbors reciprocated, and there was a constant barrage of social gatherings. David's July birthday was celebrated with a cookout at the DuPonts' house. In contrast to the previous year's surprise event, it was billed as a small, no-frills affair, but to Jenny's dismay, "just family" turned out to include Josette's siblings, their spouses, their offspring and in-laws, and several grandchildren. There were at least two-dozen people on the patio when they walked in. The cigarette smoke was ubiquitous.

"Ah, you are here! Come, we must show David his birthday present!" Michel pressed glasses into their hands, and Josette led them around the side of the house where a sapling had just been planted.

"It is for David, a Laburnum tree dedicated to Sandie's memory," Josette explained. "It has long yellow blossoms in the spring, and it grows wild in the Vercors region, where we have shared our last golf outing with David and Sandie."

"That is very kind, Josette. I will like to see it when the yellow flowers come," Jenny said, hoping her French was correct. She stepped back as others admired the tree. *It's a nice gesture to Sandie, but an odd birthday present for David,* she felt. *I wonder if this is intended as a reminder that David's life is deeply rooted here.*

Summoning her usual defenses, Jenny stayed close to David when possible. She took a slow stroll through the vegetable patch when the cigarette smoke became too thick, and did her best to grin and bear it until they could politely take their leave.

"I get the sense that the DuPonts are baffled by our decision to repatriate," Jenny commented as they drove home.

"The tax issue is complicated. I'm hopeless at explaining high finance, and you don't have enough French to take them through the technicalities."

"I don't think it's the tax issue that baffles them. I sense a not-so-subtle disappointment that I have failed to fall head over heels in love with living in Europe."

David was silent for a moment, then ventured a comment. "Everyone at that party grew up around here. This is their home, and they love it. Imagine if a man from Geneva married your closest friend in Boston. You introduce her new husband to everything you love about the area – the history, the architecture, the lobster fests, the different ethnic neighborhoods, and the beaches. You introduce him to your friends and colleagues, you entertain him, and you do everything in your power to make him feel welcome. Then, after four years, the Genevan convinces your dear friend, ostensibly on technical grounds, that they should decamp and spend at least half the year, preferably more, in Switzerland, rather than in the States. How would you feel?"

"Touché," Jenny conceded. After another moment of silence she asked, "Is that how you feel?"

"No, Ducks. I know there's a lot more to this decision than resolving a tax problem, but I also know you've been a real trooper. You didn't come to Geneva for Geneva's sake. You came because I was here, needy as hell, but in an unmovable state. If you could have figured out a way to ship me back to Boston and take care of me there, I expect I would have found myself installed in Beantown right after Sandie's funeral. You've spent four years struggling to adjust to a new world, and it's clearly not something that comes easily to you. You've earned the right to call the shots for a while, Jewel. Besides, I don't give a shit where I am so long as there's good food, good wine and good company."

"I love you, David Perry."

"Hmpff," he grunted.

Once home, she presented David with a handwritten gift certificate for the cactus of his choice. "That way you can get something that is guaranteed to survive our absences," she smiled.

In fact, Jenny had hoped to present David with an actual plant. Since Marc had the car in constant use during the previous week, Jenny had requested that Marc pick up a small cactus for her at the garden center. When she asked him about it on the eve of David's birthday, he looked confused for a second, then shrugged. "Sorry, I didn't find any opportunity to go to that part of town."

Marc's unreliability was hard for Jenny to deal with. His anger at the world seemed to have diminished, but in its stead there was a vagueness – a disconnection that she found troubling. Since his arrival in Geneva, Marc let them know his dinner plans more often than not, but he hadn't been home much, and when he was, he usually left a trail of litter in his wake. Jenny had tried three times to schedule a family meeting to talk about renting the house, but Marc either "forgot" or called home at the last minute saying something had come up.

A discussion about rentals isn't critical at the moment, Jenny finally concluded. *An August rental is now moot, and David and I will be here from September through December, finalizing the paperwork for repatriation. The Education Trust will see Marc through to his graduation next summer. Dellie's the one I have to think about.*

The week of hot weather following David's birthday was broken by a severe thunderstorm that rolled in over the Jura Mountains. Jenny discovered too late that Marc had left the skylight in the TV room wide open.

"David, we need to talk about this," Jenny insisted. "I really think we should put Marikit in charge while we're away. She's willing to stay here for the duration."

"Marc isn't the tidiest human being on the planet, but he's going to be here until September," David argued. "I see no reason why he can't take care of the house and the cats while we're in Boston."

"I don't think Marc is capable of being a responsible house-sitter," Jenny countered as she enlisted David's help with the sopping rug. "He doesn't think things through or plan ahead. We're lucky this rug absorbed the rainwater before it got to the wiring in the corner. This could have led to some serious damage."

"Maybe the open skylight is a blessing in disguise," David offered. "It may serve to help him pay better attention in the future."

"He needs to do more than pay attention. I asked him this weekend to be sure all his things were picked up so Marikit could clean unimpeded. But when she arrived, there were papers strewn all over the living room, clothes piled in the TV room, and boxes blocking the laundry. His room was a mess, and so was his bathroom. He had two days notice and still, nothing got done."

"Well, I'm sure he and Marikit will work it out. Everything will be fine," David said, closing the discussion.

Jenny didn't share David's confidence. *Is this worth fighting over? I'm not emotionally invested in this house or this furniture, but I'd like to be sure the cats won't suffer in our absence.* She didn't press the issue, but she made a mental note to talk with Marikit about keeping an eye on the felines.

David planned a special family dinner for their last evening in Geneva. He told Marc that he wanted to eat between 7:00 and 7:30. At 7:45, Marc walked in with an apology, a vague excuse, unfocused eyes and a vacant smile. He traded jokes with Delphine and was cheerful throughout the dinner, but it was obvious to Jenny that he wasn't all there. When the meal was over, David wanted to instruct Marc regarding the garden's watering needs. Jenny suggested he wait. "He's stoned, David," she said quietly.

David didn't disagree, but he seemed not to register the full extent of Marc's fog. "It's not complicated; he'll remember what I tell him."

I doubt it, Jenny said to herself.

She dealt with the problem by repeating the directions to Marc in the morning. As soon as she, David and Delphine boarded the plane, Jenny closed her mind to the fate of the house in Morion. *Lord, help me to accept the things I cannot change. Concentrate on Boston,* she told herself. *Soon you'll be home.*

Their first full day in Shawmut, David peered into cupboards and sorted through the kitchen drawers. "Ducks," he called out, "your kitchen lacks some pretty basic items. We gotta get us a good chopping block, a decent food mill and some kind of blender, or we're gonna starve to death." He tacked a piece of paper up on the refrigerator and started a list.

Jenny watched with secret delight. *If this is going to work, he has to be totally comfortable in my world. It has to become* our *world. And it looks as if he's really settling in, putting his stamp on my condo as I did on his house in Geneva.*

Jenny gave Delphine a tour of the garden dedicated to Sandie, showing her the memorial marker at the beginning of the path, and the little bridge that arched over the stone-filled streambed. "It's great," Delphine said, voicing her approval. "Mom would have really liked it."

With that, Jenny pulled a small plastic bag from her front pocket.

"What's that?" Delphine asked.

"Several months back," Jenny explained, "I came across some old French centime pieces. 'Might as well toss them into a fountain,' your father told me. 'The French won't exchange them for Euros any more.' But I had a better idea," she said, rattling the bag. "Given your mother's past financial acumen, I thought we should entrust this French money to her perpetual care. If you go collect your father, we can toss it in now."

Minutes later, Delphine reappeared with David, and the three of them walked to the edge of Sandie's Garden. In unison, each hurled a small handful of coins across the expanse of flowers and shrubs. David and Delphine were grinning happily at each other as they returned to the house.

C'était bon, Jenny thought. *This was good.*

Jenny expected to devote substantial energy to repatriation issues, but her discussions with the Social Security Administration and the health insurance agents were surprisingly simple, leaving her more room for family activities.

David and Jenny drove Delphine in town to walk Boston's historic Freedom Trail, and David set aside some father-daughter time, taking her to the Museum of Fine Arts and introducing her to the Isabella Stuart Gardner Museum.

"I'd love to have Ross and Kevin down before Dellie leaves for New York," Jenny remarked. "How about a picnic on Saturday? Do you mind being surrounded by the senior set?" she asked, turning to Delphine.

"Nah," Delphine replied.

"Ooops – I'm going to need some more peaches for the cobbler," David discovered the morning of the picnic.

"I can zip over to the market," Jenny offered.

When Delphine volunteered to go with her, Jenny promised to take the scenic route, driving past historic homes and through the old town center with its shady Common and white clapboard churches. As she pointed out landmarks and offered recollections, Delphine interjected a very adult observation.

"It must have been hard for you to leave your home and all your friends," Delphine said.

"Yes, it was," Jenny answered frankly. "Home, friends, work – everything. But from where I sat, it was imperative to go to Geneva and be with David. He was in such despair that I was really afraid for him."

"Well," Delphine said softly, "you did the right thing because you've really done a lot for Dad. I was afraid he would drive off a cliff or something. He seems really happy now. He would never have come this far without you." If Jenny hadn't been belted in behind the wheel, she would have given Delphine a big hug on the spot.

"Dellie, thank you. That's the absolute top of the list of what I hoped you and Marc would someday feel. I know it wasn't easy for either of you to cope with the changes."

Delphine downplayed the issue. "Yeah, but you and Mom think a lot alike, so I sort of figured out finally that she would have agreed with most of what you did."

Ross and Kevin arrived at three for the picnic. Kevin's normally pale Irish complexion was exceptionally pink from an overdose of Cape Cod sunshine. Even Ross's rich chocolate skin had darkened to a color closer to burnt sugar.

"Look at you sun bunnies!" Jenny exclaimed as she greeted them. Kevin was a new face for Delphine, so there were introductions and backfill as David opened a bottle of champagne.

"The last time I saw you was five years ago I think," Ross told Delphine. "You and Jenny were running around Boston looking at college campuses."

"And now she's a Cum Laude graduate," Jenny said proudly.

"Impressive," Ross said, and meant it. "What are your plans now that you have a degree?"

"I love art history," Delphine replied, "but most good jobs in the field require at least a Masters. At some point, I'll have to go to graduate school, but meanwhile I've got a three-month internship at Sotheby's in London starting in January. Until then, I'll be sharing an apartment with two friends in Paris and trying to find a temp job through December."

"Sounds like an exciting time in your life," Ross commented.

"And what have the three of you been up to since you arrived in Boston?" Kevin asked.

"Well," David replied, "I could tell you that we've been busy as popcorn on a skillet, but in truth, Delphine's been hanging out at the condo's pool, I've been practicing golf shots on the lawn, and Jenny's been puttering in the garden. Beyond that, I cook, we sample the local ice cream, and we drink wine."

"A man after my own heart," Kevin laughed, "though I've been known to choose a Guinness over a glass of wine."

The picnic was in fact a lobster fest. David took lots of pictures including a close-up of Delphine eating an ear of corn dripping with butter. "*This* you don't get in Geneva," he declared.

They paused before attempting dessert. "Give me a garden tour," Ross suggested to Jenny. The two of them strolled across the lawn, leaving David and Delphine to soak up Kevin's advice about the best places to visit in Ireland, should they ever make it to the Emerald Isle.

"I take it that the shift to American residency is on track?" Ross asked.

"Legally everything is in place. Emotionally, David seems fine with it thus far. In *his* mind, it boils down to minor adjustments in our travel schedule. The biggest problem will come when finances force us to do something with the house in Geneva."

"I thought your finances were going to improve substantially with this move."

"Well, at first glance, yes. My next year's tax obligation will drop by quite a bit. And David is retiring for real effective September 1. His pension and Swiss social security will kick in then, so we'll be back to two incomes."

"Then where's the problem?"

"The problem, or perhaps I should say the challenge, is the kids. We've been heavily dependent on the Education Trust to cover their tuition and cost-of-living expenses. That's over for Delphine, and will end for Marc when he graduates. They haven't been raised with that American focus on early independence. The realities of being a self-supporting adult will doubtlessly come as a shock to them. We'll do our best to help them with the transition, but we don't have the means to support both them and ourselves. You heard Dellie mention graduate school. The Trust will be exhausted by then, so she'll need to find scholarships and work-study programs.

"How do you and David plan to deal with it?"

"That hasn't been addressed yet. David is protective; I take the view that a little struggle builds character. The reality is that we can't continue to support his children in the manner to which they have become accustomed, so I see some highly charged debates on the horizon. There are a lot of things I'll have to play by ear."

"Jewel, you're a CPA and a good one. When it comes to finances, I've never seen you play things by ear. Somewhere in that shrewd Yankee head of yours, there's a plan."

"Can I plead the fifth?"

"Have you done something incriminating?"

"No, but I've come up with ideas that the Master of the House may not be ready for."

"Such as?"

"Sandie willed her share of the house in Morion to Marc and Dellie. They each now own a quarter of the property. David has the usufruct and can occupy it for the rest of his life. So long as he's alive, he has control, even if he doesn't actually live there. We could rent out the house, for example, and give Dellie a quarter of the net rental income to help her during her London internship."

"Hasn't David already agreed to the idea of rentals?"

"Yes, but short term rentals only. To generate the kind of income Dellie needs, we'd have to do something closer to a year's rental, maybe even more, which is a horse of a very different color. And down the road, Marc may need similar help."

"Wouldn't it be simpler just to sell the house?" Ross asked. "You've said it's way bigger than you need. If Marc and Dellie got half the net proceeds, they could invest their share and use the income to supplement their basic living expenses until they get on their feet."

"I can't imagine David selling that house. That was his chief concern when we talked about shifting our legal residence to Boston. He's pretty adamant about it."

"You two could use his share to get a little pied-a-terre in France – something less expensive and more manageable that would meet David's need for a home in Europe."

"Sounds logical, but this decision will be based on emotion, not reason. And in some ways, I understand how he feels. I was adamant about keeping this condo when I moved to Geneva. It was my safety net - my Linus blanket."

They arrived back at the terrace just as Delphine disappeared into the house with her father to put together a tray of coffee cups and brandy snifters.

"You're looking conspiratorial," Kevin remarked as Ross and Jenny joined him. "What are you two up to?"

"Kevin, I'd tell you if I could, but Ross is so careful about attorney-client privilege that I don't dare even offer a hint."

The following week, David and Jenny put Delphine on the New York train for her week of wedding festivities. "Alone at last!" Jenny teased as they walked from the garage back to the house. David started joshing her in return, and suddenly they were holding hands. It was easy, spontaneous, and surprising. David was not a hand-holder. Jenny saw no point in calling attention to the rarity of the event. She simply enjoyed his touch. She had to let go as they entered the kitchen, however, because the phone was ringing.

"That was Graham," David reported afterwards. "He arrives this weekend, and he'll be here until September."

"Will Barbara be with him?" Jenny asked.

"No. Graham said she's stuck in California. He's lonesome and looking for company. He wants us to come up for brunch on Sunday. I told him yes."

Traffic in the city was relatively quiet when they drove to Cambridge to see Graham.

"What's with the 'For Sale' sign?" David demanded as they walked in the door of Graham's duplex.

"Well, like you guys, Barbara and I are adjusting our living patterns in anticipation of retirement. I'm giving up most of my east coast responsibilities, keeping only the things I can handle with telecommuting. We're not going to be in Boston often enough to justify keeping this place, and we're looking to get a condo in Santa Cruz. I'm becoming a certified Californian!"

Jenny smiled to herself. Graham was indeed becoming a Californian, with a tucked-in fitted shirt left unbuttoned to the waist to reveal his tanned and yoga-trained torso. It was a harmless vanity, noticeable primarily because it was so un-Boston. Jenny felt a wave of affection for David, who was seditiously indifferent to fashion and whose only vanity – at least the only one she knew of – was having his face feel baby smooth after his morning shave.

"Got something for you," Graham said when David went outside to smoke. "Sorry it took so long," he apologized as he handed Jenny a large envelope.

Graham had contributed a copy of a 1970's photo to David's surprise birthday album the year before. It featured David, grinning from ear to ear, with a laughing Sandie slung over his shoulder in a fireman's carry. After the event, Jenny had asked to borrow the original so she could make enlargements for the children.

Jenny drew out the photograph, regarded it in silence and then frowned.

"When you do digital copies, they can repair those creases and that damage along the edge," Graham offered reassuringly.

"No, no," Jenny explained. "That's not what I was reacting to. I just got hit with a memory out of left field."

"Good or bad?" Graham asked, ever the psychologist.

"Half and half. As you surely recall, David and I went around in circles back in our Cambridge days – sometimes friends, sometimes lovers."

"I do, though I could never figure out how your respective psyches supported that elasticity with such resilience."

"I'm not sure we figured it out either, but we both recognized the dynamic as curious. David once told me that the woman of his dreams would be French. Since that wasn't a possibility for me, I asked what other qualities appealed to him. His physical ideal, he revealed, was someone petite and slender – a girl he could throw over his shoulder. Literally. That's what he said."

"And what was your reaction?"

"What do you think? At five-foot-five, I might have vied for a petite label, but my genes handed me a sturdy athletic structure. Slender was never a possibility. Anyway, that's the memory that surfaced when I looked at this photograph of Sandie slung over his shoulder."

"Does it bother you now?"

Jenny shook her head. "No. Sandie was the right fit for David's youthful passions, and this doesn't need to be a competition. Hands down, I make a terrific second wife!" she laughed, lightening the mood.

"You two certainly look contented," Graham agreed.

"And I, for one, certainly feel that way! Anyhow, thanks for the photo. I should be able to send the original back before we leave."

On the drive home, David detoured through the back streets of Cambridge and did a nostalgic pass by the apartment building where he, Graham, and Jenny once lived – the place where he and she first met.

"Being back here stirs a lot of warm memories," he said as they crossed the bridge into Boston and headed back to Shawmut. "It feels good to be here."

"I'm glad," said Jenny. "It feels good to me too."

August flew by, filled with side trips to Maine, Gloucester and Provincetown. Labor Day arrived long before Jenny was ready for it. The maple trees displayed their first hint of color, and Jenny would happily have extended their stay in Shawmut, but there was work to be done in Geneva.

"We're off tomorrow," Jenny told BiBi, as she made her final round of phone calls.

"It seems like you just got there. Did you have time to do everything you wanted to do?"

"Too short to do *everything*, but we covered a lot of ground. I thought the repatriation paperwork was going to occupy a lot of our visit, but it was a breeze. We managed to have time to ourselves and still see all the usual suspects – at least the east coast ones. I'm just sorry we couldn't get you to come to Boston."

"Me too, but summer is my busiest season with the grandkids out of school. If you guys would just stay put for another month or so, it would be easier to plan a trip."

"Why don't you come to Geneva? You've never been, and if you want to see the scene of the crime in its original state, you need to come over before the year ends."

"Before the year ends? Why?" Bibi demanded. "You're changing something major?"

"The target date for shifting our legal residence is January 1, so we need to be out of the Geneva house by December 31. It will stay furnished, but with the streamlining it needs, I expect it'll feel more like a hotel suite than a home. If you want to see it the way we live it, best to come sooner rather than later."

The following afternoon, they checked in at Logan's international terminal, bought four lobsters packed for travel at the airport Lobster Pound, and boarded their plane. The house in Morion was silent when they arrived the next morning. Marc had left for school in San Francisco two days before.

Their neighbor Mehrak had dispatched his gardener to their yard, so the grass was nicely mowed, but the house was a mess. Jenny let fly in the only safe direction available. "David, there is no excuse for this! The compost and trash bins are overflowing. The cat box hasn't been cleaned. The dryer vents are full of lint. Marc's room looks as if a tornado hit it, and he's left us an unpaid parking ticket to deal with!"

David was patient with Jenny despite the fact that he, too, was jet-lagged and disappointed by Marc's lack of responsibility.

"I'm sorry I'm being so crotchety," Jenny finally apologized, blaming travel fatigue for amplifying her discontent and unleashing her tongue. Her short-term solution was to go to bed and get some sleep. David wasn't far behind.

When Marikit arrived in the morning, Jenny got an earful. "I am sorry, Madame Jenny, but I cannot do this again. Every week when I have come, the house is always filthy. Marc was always giving parties and each time the kitchen and the terrace are left a mess that he expects me to clean. There are dirty glasses and dirty plates and cigarette butts everywhere. He also does not take care of the cat box. When one of the cats was sick on the rug, he has just covered the sickness with a paper towel and left it."

Jenny commiserated and repeated Marikit's tale of woe to David. "It was so bad that Marikit nearly walked out," she reported. "We could have lost her altogether."

David sighed and shook his head. "I'll talk to Marikit and give her something extra for everything she had to put up with."

"Marc's the one you need to talk to," Jenny insisted.

"I hear you, Jenny, and I will, but right now we have a lobster supper to put together for the neighbors. We've got to eat those critters tonight."

The last thing Jenny wanted was a social evening, but David was right. The lobsters had been boiled on arrival, and although they now sat in the refrigerator, they wouldn't keep long. While David prepared the meal, Jenny tackled the logistics of serving a twelve-person buffet indoors.

An hour later, David surveyed her arrangements with approval. "You're being a good sport," he said.

"The only reason I'm being a good sport," she replied, narrowing her eyes at him, "is because I love you – and boy, are you lucky that I do!"

When David called Marc about the housesitting problems, he found his son rudderless and in a funk. "Marc wants to take a break from school," David told Jenny when he got off the phone. "He doesn't like any of his classes. He wants to do more glassblowing, and he wants to learn about ceramics and sculpture. Art obviously has a lot more appeal for him than academics."

"Why does he need to take a break from school? Surely they offer courses in manual and applied arts."

"I don't know. Maybe he's up against a set of required courses that don't leave room for art-related classes. He said he might go back after New Year's for the spring semester. He thinks he can squeeze in enough credits next term to graduate in June."

"I suggest he reverse his thinking," Jenny said firmly. "This semester is already paid for. If he squeezes in enough credits *this* term, then he can get his diploma in December and be free to do what he likes afterwards. The Trust money goes on hold if he's not in school. How does he plan on paying his living expenses if he drops out?"

"He asked me for a loan."

Jenny pursed her lips and slowly shook her head. "And what did you tell him?"

"I told him I'd talk it over with you."

"He's twenty-five years old, David. It's way past time for him to own up to the consequences of his actions. The Trust will cover him so long as he stays in school, but if he opts out, he's on his own. He's an adult, and he's free to do what he wants, but he has to take responsibility for it."

"I'm really not sure he can handle it," David worried. "Marc's not much of a problem solver."

"Maybe you're not giving him enough of a chance to become one," Jenny criticized. Then her voice softened. "Do you remember," she asked, "the time you visited a classroom where the teacher pre-empted the children's learning process by giving answers or directions before his students had a chance to puzzle things out? Do you remember how disappointed you were in his teaching method? How you felt it really set the children back and discouraged their natural curiosity and exploration? Well, you remind me of that teacher when it comes to your own children. I think they should figure things out and find their own solutions. Yes, we should offer guidance and be a resource, but you want to jump in and bail them out. It may be instinctive for you, because you're their father, and you still see them as children. But I view them as adults, and I expect them to behave and react as adults."

David acquiesced and urged Marc to stick with school. "The school fee has been paid already, and we're not in a position to give you a loan at this time," he told him. Marc said he would think about it, but he advised his father a week later that he was dropping out anyway.

From: Marc
To: Dad
Date: September 19, 2005
Subject: new job

i hope you won't be pissed, but school has to wait until i can sit still in a classroom again. i found a job. i began today with greenworld. i'm trying to get people subscribed in the street, direct dialogue. i guess it's ok, but i'm continuing to look for something else because the pay is only 12$, so i'm kind of like asking myself what should i do. anyhow, these guys at greenworld think their such hotshots, actually their not. they don't know much except think their cool for working there. they talk more than they listen, a dangerous specie. they think everybody is stupid and unaware of what is going on environmentally wise...i guess they took me for a true american citizen.

love, marc

David shared the e-mail with Jenny. "It's a good thing that he's lined up a job, but given his attitude, it's not likely to last long," she commented.

Auburn Hair – *For Sandie*

The midday light on her auburn hair
As she walked toward the tramway
And the distance separating us
Made me think of you yesterday
As I drove home.
I cried alone softly but not for long.
The hurt doesn't last as long today,
Suddenly five years on.
Great god! Where have they gone?

This morning Minuit knocked
A bowl off the shelf
And broke the pottery vessel
You made yourself
And signed with an S so long ago.
I was angry, chagrinned.
I gathered up the pieces
And washed them gently,
Hoping, as all the King's men,
To put you back together again.

D.P. – September, 2005

Chapter 9

As if to recognize the fifth anniversary of Sandie's death, gloomy weather settled over Geneva on September 25. After David lit a memorial candle, Jenny handed him the reprinted photo of Sandie in a fireman's carry over David's shoulder.

"This is really nice," he said, giving Jenny a kiss. "This is the one Graham took, yes? We should duplicate it for Marc and Delphine."

"I already have. I ordered extras. There are enough for the kids and for Sandie's dearest friends."

Good, Jenny thought. *He's happy with the photograph, and the memory doesn't make him feel sad.* But Jenny saw only what she wanted to see. Reality was brought home to her that afternoon when she read the memorial poem David sent to Marc and Delphine. In it, he described being reduced to tears by the sight of a woman who reminded him of Sandie.

The poem went on to lament a ceramic bowl that one of the cats had knocked off a shelf, shattering it on the tile floor. It was a bowl Sandie had made during a school pottery class. Jenny had been about to toss the pieces in the trash when David intervened. "No," he insisted. "I want to try to fix it."

Rachel had warned Jenny more than once that there would always be moments when David was blindsided, but she was still taken aback. *Is the prospect of renting out Sandie's house adding to the strain? Or is it maybe worry about Marc?* David had recently called Marc to ask how the Greenworld canvassing was going. Marc's response was not reassuring.

"Marc says he's going to quit at the end of the week if his success rate doesn't improve," David had reported glumly. "According to Marc, no one at the shopping center wants to sign up. 'They're too busy spending money on themselves,' he says."

Jenny could think no helpful advice to offer. Delphine was due in from Paris for a weekend visit, and Jenny hoped that would cheer David up. Fortunately, when Delphine arrived, she had lots of positive news to share. "I'm getting along really well with my roommate," she announced, "and I've landed a fun temp job helping a Parisian artist set up exhibitions."

It wasn't until the end of her stay that she alerted her father that she was in trouble financially. David immediately opened his wallet and handed over a hundred Euros. "We'll go by the bank tomorrow before I take you to the train station, and I'll get whatever you need," he said.

"Before you do that," Jenny intervened, "let's take a look at where the holes are in Dellie's budget." Jenny shifted her gaze to her stepdaughter. "Your mother had some simple systems to make sure there was money for the bills before anything was spent on non-essentials. I can fill you in on her trade secrets."

"I already sort of know what the problem is," Delphine admitted sheepishly. "My friends assume I can afford to go out anywhere, anytime. Everyone thinks the Swiss are rich. I didn't want to spoil everyone's plans by saying I didn't have enough to buy a glass of wine or go see a movie. I kept hoping a second job would come through to replenish the coffers, only it hasn't," she lamented.

"It's time to be honest with your friends," Jenny advised. "Tell them you'd love to come along and enjoy their company, but you're on such a tight budget that if you go out to a bar, you won't be able to pay the phone bill," she counseled. "You can blame us for being so stingy!"

"David, we need a summit meeting," Jenny declared the minute Delphine was beyond hearing. "We've given Marc and Dellie a great deal of leeway during their college years. They've had a lot of freedom, but not much responsibility. They have to start assuming some of the burdens of adulthood."

David was taken aback. "What, are you suggesting we just cut Dellie off? She's not going to become an independent adult overnight. She's likely to flounder through the process, and she'll need help staying afloat."

"I agree that she's likely to flounder. Her brother is already doing so. But we've been firm with Marc, and we should be consistent."

"Actually, Marc has raised the question of a loan again, so maybe a little help to each child would keep things in balance. And with a loan, we'd eventually get it back so our retirement accounts won't suffer."

Jenny shook her head. "Every loan you've given them ends up being discharged as a Christmas present or a birthday gift. Every repayment schedule has been a sham. There have never been any consequences when they defaulted. They don't take it seriously, and why should they? Frankly, I don't think parents do their adult children any favors by bankrolling them without a clear set of expectations and some meaningful accountability. You and I both worked our way through school and were self-supporting once we graduated. Marc and Dellie need to learn to stand on their own two feet. They need a good solid push."

"Mixed metaphor," David commented.

"Oh, stop!" Jenny protested. "David, this is serious."

"So, what's your solution? I'm not going to let them starve."

"Nor am I, but they have to learn to live within a set income. If that means no movies and no bar hopping with friends, so be it."

"Jenny, we've got to give them a basic amount to live on."

"What's your definition of basic? Does that include Marc's marijuana? And which pocket do you intend to take it from? Maybe I'm being super selfish, but time is short, and I'd like us to be able to do the things we've talked about. We're living on our retirement income now, and that's finite."

"Would it be possible to rent out your Shawmut condo for the next few months? That could cover Delphine's London expenses and help get Marc through until he goes back to school," David suggested hopefully.

"For starters, I'd have to fly to Boston, move anything antique up into the attic, and pack away fragile items in the garage. People who rent part-time furnished housing in Boston usually want it for the full academic season – September through May. I love my unit, but it's ten miles out of town, nowhere near public transportation, and it's a bear to heat in the winter. We may need it as early as Christmas, and for tax reasons, we have to be able to prove that we legally reside there, effective January 1."

"Well," David retreated, "what if we rent out this house for longer than just the few months we talked about?"

Jenny was momentarily startled. *David just pre-empted my ace in the hole. He's handed me a critical opening. Should I take it?* "This house? You're talking what? Six months? A year?"

"It wouldn't hurt to look at the issue, would it?" David queried.

"No," Jenny agreed, "It wouldn't hurt at all, but we'd need to do a lot more than just clean out a few drawers."

"What do you want me to do about Delphine? She's leaving tomorrow."

You're shoveling against the tide, Jenny, she realized. *You have to yield on this for David's sake, even though it may not be the best thing long-term for the kids.*

"Ask her how much she needs. Let Dellie be the one to figure out what sort of gap she's looking at. Don't give her more than five hundred Euros. And don't give her more than she requests. If she's accurate, she can be proud of her judgment. If her estimate is wrong, that will give us a talking point for our budget discussions."

"Okay, Scrooge," David said with a grin. "And then maybe we can talk about Marc?"

"You may laugh, but my first responsibility is to make sure that *you* don't starve. Besides, wrong character. I'm not Scrooge. I'm the wicked stepmother."

Once Delphine was safely on her way back to Paris with three hundred Euros in her pocket, Jenny pulled together an agenda. That evening, as David poured the wine, she carefully laid out the issues concerning their financial status and a long-term rental for their Geneva house.

"First and foremost, I continue to believe that we should let Marc lie in the bed he's made. He had a viable option to remain in school for the fall semester, and he chose not to. So I still say no. But if you insist on overriding my vote, you should give him the same amount you gave Dellie."

David nodded. Jenny knew he would send the money.

"Now, about the house, we need to find a professional service that can advise us on rental rates, help us find a tenant, and manage the property in our absence. Then we have to remove our personal belongings and store them in the *Cave*. I'd like to shoot for a rental as of January 1. We'll be on our way to the States, Dellie will be in London, and Marc will be in San Francisco. The house will be vacant. It's the logical date."

David looked at her, slightly shell-shocked. "Do you really think we could do it that fast?" he asked.

"I know *I* could," she answered. "You're the one who's the packrat. The kids may need time to get used to it, but if they're direct beneficiaries, I'm pretty sure they'll accept the idea."

"Jeezus!" David said, shaking his head.

"I can handle the cleanup and the packing, but finding a management company requires French. Can you take care of that? I could put together a list of questions if that would help."

"Sandie and I lived in an apartment complex until we bought this house," David said, "and we always got quick service when there was a problem. I'll contact the company that handled it – *Varet & cie.* Maybe they also manage home rentals."

David's discussion with *Varet & cie* produced unexpected advice. "For a house of your size, there are not Swiss who will rent and then move on. The Swiss already have housing and will stay where they are until they have reason to move. Your market is the international clients – diplomats who are assigned to the United Nations, and executives who work at the multinational corporations headquartered here in Geneva. They will one day go back to their home country. They want to rent, but for a much longer time than six months. The normal contract for such a house as yours is three to five years. And it must be unfurnished. The corporations pay for families to bring their belongings with them."

"Unfurnished? Three to five years?" Jenny was startled by the recommendations David brought back from his meeting.

"Should we give up on the rental idea and go back to the drawing board?" David asked.

She shook her head. "This is going to take some serious thinking. From everything you've said about Varet & Company, we should trust their advice. But oh my god, David! This is major."

After a nearly sleepless night, Jenny announced her conclusions over breakfast. "I think it's doable. I've got almost everything figured out – except the cats."

David refilled his coffee cup. "Go," he said.

"This could be like your Lost Horse story – a blessing in disguise. If we rent the house out for three years and share the income, the kids would have a safety net while they're figuring out how to support themselves, and it would let us test a range of options without doing anything irrevocable. This is extra income, and with our share of it, we could rent European vacation properties in different countries and different settings. We could choose rentals with sufficient room for the kids to come visit, and our friends as well. After all this "sampling," we'll know where we want our European *pied-à-terre* to be, and Marc and Dellie will have a clearer sense of whether or not they ever want to live in Geneva again. Then and only then do you have to make decisions about handing the house over to the kids, keeping it as a rental property, or selling it outright."

"I need to discuss this with Marc and Delphine before we commit to this."

"Let's put together an e-mail and get it off to them today."

"No, I have to do this in person."

"How can you do it in person?" Jenny asked. "Dellie's not coming home until Thanksgiving, and we won't see Marc until Christmas. We've already floated the idea of renting and clean-out. You can wait to discuss the duration of the rental in person, but in the meantime, I need to get started. I promise I'll keep the house livable until the last minute. The first step is selling or giving away everything we don't need or want. Next, we move the lesser-used 'keepers' into the *Cave*. Our final month, the remaining items go into Marc's basement room, which we can close off and lock."

"Is there room to store everything down there?"

"There is if we keep only what we really want. Think of that room as a moving van. There's plenty of room if we organize the space properly."

David issued a deep sigh and called *Varet & cie*. A formal but pleasant young man came out to assess the house and recommend a rental rate.

"You sure you can do all this in less than three months?" David asked.

"I can if you don't get in the way too much," Jenny replied. Her tone was joking, but she didn't underestimate the challenge ahead. *We are about to embark on nothing short of a triage of David's worldly goods. It is absolutely inevitable that we're going to get on one another's nerves in the process. At best!*

"*Eh bien*, Monsieur, Madame, may I understand that the earliest occupancy date will be 1 January, 2006?" the agent asked.

David and Jenny looked at each other. "Yes, 1 January, 2006," David confirmed.

A few days later, as Jenny carried out cartons of items to go to Goodwill, she noted that the roofing was starting to go up on the new housing project behind their house. The last remnant of what had been an open field had disappeared from view. It gave Jenny an uneasy sensation of being walled in.

"It's really sad to lose that lovely sheep pasture," she complained to David. "And the poured-concrete construction in the new houses is really unattractive," she added in a pained tone.

"Don't worry, Jenny," David snapped. "I'll get you out of here soon enough!" She was stung by his tone and tried to backtrack, but he turned abruptly and went into the house.

David later apologized, but he clearly had no enthusiasm for the clean-out. "Goddamn it, Jenny, even Lucifer took a certain amount of time to get the hell out of heaven! And he was an angel, which I most assuredly am not!"

David's resistance to the dismantling of his home surfaced in a variety of ways. He was an innately generous person, but he had trouble with the anonymous nature of Goodwill collection boxes. He wanted each item to go to a known and trusted new home, and he wanted to oversee the relocation in person.

To help him focus, Jenny suggested that David tag books for l'Académie Internationale's fundraising flea market. He started pulling volumes off the shelves, but none of them were for the school. He had in mind individual recipients, and he started laying books out on the floor with post-its on them. By the end of the day, the living room looked like a cross between a checkerboard and a miniature slalom course.

He was also adamant that Marc and Delphine be involved in each decision, down to surplus school supplies and duplicate garden tools. Since neither child was present, this presented a roadblock until Jenny realized she could e-mail them photos. As they signed off on surplus flower vases and old board games, Jenny packed the released items in boxes marked FLEA MARKET. To her dismay, David was not above rooting through them and overruling his children's decisions. "I don't care if he said no! Some day Marc is going to want this!"

Despite these hurdles, they made progress, even though they were sailing against the wind.

From: JWLongworth
To: Bibi
cc: DavidP
Date: November 3, 2005
Subject: One step forward

Sorry to be such a spotty correspondent. I have been triaging and packing up household goods ever since we got back. David helps by reading each book before deciding its fate. It slows the packing process, but we're getting there. I'm pushing to donate as much as possible to the school's flea market fundraiser. After a week of screening, David has approved for the fundraiser one trowel (I have two others,) three teacups missing their saucers, and a toaster that only takes thin-sliced American sandwich bread.

I'm so glad you've decided to come over for Thanksgiving! I can use the moral support!!! I can also use some Pepperidge Farm Herb Seasoned Bread Stuffing. Can you squeeze a few packages into your suitcase?

Love, J.

From: BIBirnbaum
To: Jenny
Date: November 3, 2005
Subject: Re: One step forward

What a crack-up! This is when you should send David off on some critical errand while you get a high-sided dumpster brought to the house.

Good luck with your packing. I know you will do it with your trademark efficiency even with a male millstone around your neck.

I'll definitely make room for lots of stuffing mix in my bag. Lemme know if you think of anything else you need for Thanksgiving.

Love, Bibi

As Jenny worked her way through the house, David holed up in his atelier with its crammed bookcases and mounds of school papers. Jenny's remark that he had to read each book before deciding its fate was exaggerated, but not by much. He could evaluate a book by its title, but each scrap of loose paper carried memories that had to be processed before David could consign it to the recycling bin.

> *De: David*
> *A: Graham*
> *cc: Jenny*
> *Envoyé: 11 novembre, 2005*
> *Objet: Holidays*
>
> Things here are mildly chaotic, primarily due to our decision to rent the Geneva house while we're stateside. Jenny is doing financial gymnastics figuring out our future, trying to reduce our domestic clutter, and at the same time working her way towards Thanksgiving with her friend Bibi who's coming over from San Francisco.
>
> We're doing Christmas here this year. Too much on our plate to attempt a trip to Chattanooga. Fortunately, winter is having a hard time getting started, which means I can still smoke on the terrace when I'm not wading through decades of history.
>
> Delphine currently has a temp job in Paris and a three-month internship in London lined up for January. Marc is AWOL from school, semi-employed, and into glass blowing. The cats are growing old and rotund. So am I.
>
> Hope all is well with you and Barbara.
>
> Love, David

Bibi arrived in Geneva the Monday before Thanksgiving. They met her at the airport and welcomed her to the house with a champagne toast. Bibi lasted through dinner, then collapsed into bed.

David offered a tempting brunch in the morning, and they spent a little time catching up. "I was expecting your house to be nearly vacant," Bibi observed, "with all the clean-out you described. But it looks nice – comfortable but uncluttered."

"You should have seen it a month ago," Jenny replied. "The drawers and cupboards were full to bursting, and there was scarcely an inch of surface without something sitting on top of it. We have a long way to go, but it's a lot better than it was."

David lowered the newspaper and looked at Jenny over his glasses, but made no comment.

After Bibi's second cup of coffee, Jenny gave her a docent's tour of the photographs gracing the walls and tables. She started with the memorial collage Josette had created, which hung in the hallway outside their bedroom. "This collage covers roughly two decades and captures Sandie from her arrival in Geneva until just prior to her death." As they descended the stairs, Jenny pointed out the montage from Sandie's fiftieth birthday dinner, and then the portrait David had painted. With it came the story of how both Sandie and Graham saw the painting as an inadvertent blending of Jenny's face and Sandie's, with Jenny's eyes and Sandie's nose and mouth.

When Bibi looked at the picture Jenny had recently given David – the early one of David with Sandie in a fireman's carry – she shook her head. "That's Sandie?" she said. "How can that be Sandie? It looks just like you," Bibi puzzled.

"No, truly, that's Sandie," Jenny assured her.

"Well, you look like you could be sisters," she concluded. "Or maybe even twins."

David walked in as Bibi made her comment and laughed. "You're not the first one to say that. I'm off to the recycling center," he advised. "See you ladies in a bit."

"I do accept that the identity is unclear," Jenny conceded after David left. "Sandie is upside down, after all, and both she and I wore our hair in pixie cuts when we were in our twenties. I gave a copy of that photo to the DuPonts as well. I later learned that Josette was very upset that I was offering them what seemed to be a happy photo of David and *me* on the anniversary of Sandie's death. Michel had to call David for clarification because Josette didn't want to thank me until she was reassured that it was Sandie."

"There are so many layers to your story," Bibi observed. "Situations like that offer honest glimpses about the conflicting emotions everyone is dealing with. Reading the memoir, I felt sad reliving the last days of Sandie's illness. Being here, seeing the setting for real – her house, her furniture, her photographs – I almost want to cry. I know she wasn't always an angel, but who is? At the same time, seeing you and David being so obviously happy together, I want to cheer. It's wonderful to be in the same room with you two – there is so much love it makes me smile. Your memoir captures that conflict and explores the grief process well. I really get how David could begin a new life with you while still mourning Sandie so strongly."

"If I explore the grief process well, the real credit goes to Rachel Aronson. One of these days, you two will have to meet each other. Rachel helped me understand how David could plunge from engaged and cheerful to withdrawn and sad in a matter of seconds. 'Memories come and go with the tiniest trigger,' she warned me, and she was right. David teared up only a few weeks ago after spotting a woman whose hairstyle and hair color were just like Sandie's."

"You guys have such a complex relationship. You really should share it. I know you keep balking about rewriting the memoir as fiction," Bibi said, "but there are lots of ways to shield the identities of the real players. Your themes are universal and don't need a rigid cast of characters to get them across."

"Maybe some faraway day, but right now there's too much going on."

"What's the big deal? Isn't your repatriation just a matter of checking a different box on your tax forms and making sure you don't hang out in Switzerland for more than half the year?"

"The bureaucratic part is tedious, but it's not difficult. It's the social process that's burning up time and energy. Packing up the contents of this house requires a thousand little decisions, and most of them have emotional riders. If I were the only one involved, I'd have this all organized by now. But for David, the prospect of sorting through years' worth of accumulated possessions is a daunting task.

Still, since it's David's life that I'm turning upside down, he gets to have some say in the matter. So do the kids."

"Sounds like Memoir II to me," Bibi quipped.

That evening, as they sipped their wine in front of the fire, David and Bibi spoke of their experiences watching their children go through dark and dangerous passages. Bibi's son had been semi-delinquent as a teenager, and her daughter had suffered from depression in her early twenties.

"I have to tell you that when I read the memoir, I felt sympathy for Marc right along with you two. He sometimes makes a wicked mess of things, that's for sure. I wonder where this rage of his comes from, and whether there's a way to validate some anger while helping him change his self-destructive behavior."

David shook his head. "I wish I knew how to help him, but I'm at a loss. Marc can be very loving one minute and despicable the next. Sometimes the only thing that gives me hope is the Joseph Campbell story about young people who 'take the left-hand path,' going at life the 'wrong' way – the way that is unconventional and doesn't have cultural approval – yet somehow emerging from their journey with maturity and wisdom. Marc definitely seems to be on the left-hand path."

"Who is Joseph Campbell?" Bibi asked.

"Campbell was an American professor and lecturer on religion and mythology. Jenny's the one who introduced me to him," he said, turning to her with a nod. "We lost a classmate, Ramon Delgado, to AIDS back in 1988."

"Yeah, I know about Ramon," Bibi interrupted. "He was Ross's first love. That's how you met Ross, right?" she said, turning to Jenny.

Jenny nodded, and David continued. "Jenny came to visit Sandie and me in Geneva not long after Ramon died. We talked at length about life and death and how we deal with it. Jenny mentioned a recent TV interview with Campbell called 'The Power of Myth,' and she later gave me an audiotape as a present. I began reading everything of Campbell's I could find. Years later, when Sandie was dying, Campbell's stories and commentary helped me put Sandie's life, and her place in my life, in perspective. It didn't eliminate the hurt, but gave me a way to deal with it. I owe Campbell – and Jenny – a great debt for allowing me that passage." Nothing was resolved in terms of Marc, but the conversation with Bibi helped remind David he was not alone in his parenting frustrations.

Thanksgiving dinner was planned for Saturday, allowing Delphine to take a Friday morning train and join them. She remembered Bibi from her first trip to San Francisco and immediately inquired about Sausalito and the houseboat community where Bibi lived. David set out paté, cheese and salad for lunch, and the four of them sat down to eat. He had intended to find a quiet moment to talk with Delphine about the question of a long-term rental, but Bibi unwittingly set the cat among the pigeons at the start of the meal. "I'll bet it's going to be hard for you, not having this house to come home to," she said, turning to Delphine.

Delphine gave a start. "What do you mean?"

David took a deep breath. "The management company handling the rental has advised us that we have to offer a much longer lease than just 3-6 months."

Delphine's jaw dropped.

Jenny immediately attempted damage control. "They're talking a couple of years, Dellie. We were sort of shocked at first, but after thinking about it, we realized it might solve several problems at once." She turned to Bibi as if the explanation were for her benefit. "Since half the house belongs to the kids, they could benefit from the net proceeds while they learn how to be financially independent. Marc and Dellie could draw on their share of the rent to help with things like graduate school, basic living expenses, and some travel. That's assuming," Jenny said, turning back to Delphine, "that you would be interested in doing so. We can always put the money into a savings account if you prefer. We haven't yet calculated exactly how much this will generate," she continued, switching back to Bibi, "but it should provide a basic cushion."

"So, after the lease is up, would you reclaim the house and use it for vacations?" Bibi asked.

"The long-term future of this house is still wide open," Jenny replied. "If Dellie or Marc wants to return to Geneva and live in it, that's certainly a possibility. But it doesn't make sense for David and me to move back in. We need to downsize and find something a lot smaller – preferably with no stairs."

Ever direct, Bibi asked Delphine how she felt about living in Paris versus Geneva.

"I love this house, but I definitely prefer Paris," Delphine replied. "I like coming home to Geneva where I have a cook in the kitchen and flowers in my room. It's always nice to have parents taking care of you, even if you're officially on your own! Still, I'll be sad if we ever sell it."

It was the first time Jenny had heard Delphine comment on the "welcome home" bouquet she always placed on Delphine's bedside table. *It's nice to know that Dellie appreciates it. Nice too that I'm considered a "parent."*

Jenny also registered that Delphine was reacting primarily to the question of an eventual sale, not the proposal of an immediate rental, however long-term.

"And what about you?" Bibi asked, turning to David. "If you let go of this house, would you buy a place in Paris to be near Dellie?"

"In Paris? No," said David. "Jenny's a die-hard country girl, and I've discovered that cities no longer hold the same appeal for me. Paris is a city for the young."

Jenny was intrigued by his response, and relieved. *If David wanted to exchange the house in Geneva for a small apartment in Paris, I would accept his doing so, but he's right. I have no desire to live in a city.*

When David stepped outside for a cigarette, Jenny offered Delphine a further explanation of her wish to downsize. "Apart from the obvious need for fewer stairs and less maintenance, I've had cancer twice now, and who knows what the future holds. If something happens to me, David will probably return to Europe full time, but he shouldn't come back to this house. It's too isolated. Yes, we have neighbors, but everyone is separated by tall hedges and high walls. You have to drive to get to the stores. When your mother died, David just sat alone in the kitchen and drank. Do you remember that?"

Delphine nodded silently.

"What if your father had decided to go buy cigarettes after downing a half-pint of scotch, and taken the car out? And what's to stop him from running that risk if I die, and he comes back here alone? I want him someplace where he can easily see people who know him and care about him, and they can see him – someplace where he can walk to the *tabac* for cigarettes, and to a neighborhood café for a glass of wine.

"As far as Europe goes, I'm hoping we can replace this house with a small village bungalow, with room for guests, lots of social activity out front and a little private garden in back. I don't really care what country it's in. I've seen a charming little farm town not five miles from here, with modest houses clustered in the center, a café, a bakery, a post office and a bus stop. That's the kind of place that would be perfect for the two of us, and good for him if he is alone."

"I hadn't thought about it that way," Delphine admitted.

By the time David came back in, Jenny, Bibi and Delphine were busily debating the merits of a retirement cottage in France versus Italy or Switzerland. Delphine later told her father that she felt much better about their plans. That helped David feel better too, though he still had little enthusiasm for the notion of a three-year rental. He understood why they needed to do it, but sentiment was in the way. Sandie had loved the house.

That evening, the four of them were about to sit down to dinner when the phone rang. David took the call. It was Marc. After a moment's chatter, his face stilled, and he shut his eyes, a sure sign of bad news. They spoke for another minute, then David hung up.

"He sends kisses to everyone," David reported with a sigh. Jenny waited. After a pause, David added, "When he dropped out in September, he had to move out of college-owned housing and put a large security deposit down on an apartment. It screwed up his budget, and he's running out of money." Given Delphine's presence, Jenny refrained from comment.

As they lifted their forks, Delphine took a deep breath and reported that she, too, was having money problems. "I love working for an artist, but his exhibition schedule is kind of weird, so it's not really full time. That's why I was able to come here on a Friday. I'll be working part time at Galeries Lafayette to help with Christmas sales, but that job doesn't start until December. So, I'm really glad you're going to rent the house to help us out," she ended, giving her father a hopeful smile. "Thanks, Dad."

"What now?" David asked as he and Jenny prepared for bed. "Do we give her more money? The rental income won't be available until January."

"I'll talk with Dellie," Jenny said wearily. "And you should find out from Marc exactly what his situation is and what he thinks he needs. Just please let me get through Thanksgiving before we have to make major decisions. With Bibi here and everything, I really can't deal with this right now."

The house was bright with sunshine for their Saturday Thanksgiving celebration. Their guests included Mehrak and Manuela, the DuPonts, Adelaide Swanton, and Olga and her husband Jacques. Jenny served a classic menu, although she forgot to put out the cranberry-orange relish she had made the day before. The meal was a success regardless, and they definitely did better than the pilgrims in the wine department.

To facilitate communication, there was an anglophone end of the table and a francophone one, but on both sides, the Perry's repatriation and house rental plans were the major topics of conversation. David's explanation was positive and even enthusiastic, but despite it's being in French, Jenny could tell that Josette's reaction was not-so-subtly negative. *I wonder if she worries that I may eventually steal David away from Geneva altogether.*

Just before she and Jacques left, Olga took Jenny aside. "Jenny, you must give me the recipe for your bread stuffing. It is delicious and so light!"

For a brief instant, Jenny considered taking credit for it, but then she relented.

"Wait just a second. I'll get it for you." She went into the kitchen and returned with one of the extra stuffing packages Bibi had brought over. "The recipe's easy," she said. "It's right on the back. You just add water, butter and stir."

Olga's face always displayed a certain gravity, but her eyes twinkled as she tucked the bread stuffing into her bag. "I won't tell a soul," she promised.

Then she fixed Jenny with the piercing look that was her trademark. "You are truly glad to go back to the States, *n'est-ce pas?* I know that Geneva has not always suited you."

"Yes, I am truly glad. David seems okay with it too," Jenny added, "but this house was enormously important to Sandie, so I want to be sure we handle the move in a way that gives her all due respect."

Olga's reaction was the opposite of what Jenny expected. With a frown, Olga leaned toward her, her voice low but strong. "You must forget Sandie. You must stop thinking about Sandie. You must be selfish and do things for you. I loved Sandie. Sandie was very special to me. I prayed, when she was sick, that I would be taken instead. I will never get over losing her. But Sandie is dead," she said firmly. "And that's that. I don't believe in anything else. You must go forward and live your life for *you*," she urged. "And for David," she added. "He deserves that."

Jenny stood speechless, watching Olga disappear out the door. *She's not one for superficial conversations,* Jenny acknowledged as she slowly recovered her composure.

Sunday morning, they awoke to an inch of snow on the ground. It was unusual for Geneva and fun for Bibi, who hadn't seen snow in two decades. As they chatted over mugs of coffee and tea, Bibi again encouraged Jenny to turn her memoir into fiction. "But you need to be more descriptive," she advised. "None of these people look the way I thought they did!"

"To be honest," Jenny admitted, "I've lost the impetus. A lot of what drove me to write was my angst and my isolation. Writing was my way of coping. At this stage of the game, David has embraced his new life, and I feel the marriage is on solid footing. My journal used to be full of neurotic outpourings, but now it's filled with garden notes, dinner menus, and sentimental observations. When David went out to cut back the rosebushes for the winter, he wore a totally ridiculous hat, clearly cultivating his 'old codger' image. He looked so much like a big scruffy teddy bear that I had to go give him a hug – and that was my journal entry for the day. It's hard to imagine such domestic tranquility being fodder for a riveting best-seller."

While Jenny and Bibi chatted, Delphine started through her things in search of treasures for l'Académie Internationale's fundraising flea market. Once she finished triaging her own possessions, she lent a hand ferrying cartons and bags into the garage, to be taken over to the school later.

"Dellie deserves credit for being a willing player in this whole rental scheme," Bibi remarked. "Perhaps that's due in part to the long friendship that preceded your stepmother role in her life, but it seems also due to her inner strength and her sense that her mother trusted you."

"The prospect of a steady income may have something to do with it as well," Jenny noted wryly, "but I agree, she has a lot of inner strength. It's fun watching her discover that about herself."

Delphine left for Paris late Sunday with her finances somewhat improved. Bibi's flight to California was scheduled for the following day. David dropped Bibi and Jenny off at the departures entrance and went to park the car while they stood in line for Bibi's check-in. "I'm glad I came," Bibi said. "It was great to meet some of your characters in real life, and I'm especially pleased that I got to see David in his home environment. You've made a good choice," she remarked. "An excellent choice. I really like him."

"Well, that's good," Jenny laughed. "He likes you too."

"Even better," Bibi smiled.

That evening, David placed a call to Marc to get a handle on his situation. "Hey there," he said, opening on a positive note when Marc answered. "We had a crowd over for Thanksgiving, and Jenny used that loopy blue glass vase you gave us last Christmas as a centerpiece. Everyone loved it!"

David's cheerful demeanor quickly dissolved into a deep frown. He listened intently, with only an occasional monosyllabic interjection.

"All right. Let me know what happens. Jenny has the wiring instructions for your bank. We'll figure something out." David put down the phone and shook his head. "I need a cigarette," he said, flipping on the stove exhaust in the kitchen.

"Marc is pretty much out on the street at the moment," David announced after taking a deep drag on his Gauloise.

"Out on the *street?*" Jenny echoed.

"The story is really jumbled. When Marc moved into his apartment, he had some friends living with him who weren't supposed to be there, and apparently there was a party and some damage. Marc says it was minor and claims the landlord saw it as an excuse to kick him out and keep the security deposit."

"Wait. Has he already vacated the apartment? Didn't he have a lease? Surely there must be some kind of notice requirement!"

"It turns out this is old news. The first apartment is history. Apparently the eviction happened back in October. Marc and his friends then decided to 'squat' a vacant house. When the house's owner discovered the illegal occupancy, he sent an eviction notice. Marc ignored the order, assuming that it would take a while before there was serious enforcement. Two days ago, the owner put all Marc's possessions out on the sidewalk and boarded up the cellar door he had used as an access. Marc lost camera equipment and other valuables in the process. He says he's sleeping on a friend's couch and trying to find places to store his remaining possessions until he finds another apartment."

"David, I am totally confused. This makes no sense. Why would he think the eviction notice would take 'a while' when he'd just been successfully kicked out of his previous apartment in record time?"

"I don't know, Jenny. I don't have any answers. I just know he's in trouble and needs help."

Jenny had to go upstairs and take a steaming bath to calm down. When she felt she had her temper under control, she returned to the kitchen and sat down with David to assess the situation.

"The most practical solution is to get Marc back into classes. He's clearly ill equipped to handle independence. If he re-enrolls, he'll be eligible for school-owned housing. That's his absolute best option – and ours – for his staying in California. If he gives up on San Francisco and moves back to Geneva and this house, life could get pretty tense. Dellie's internship financing and all our retirement plans are riding on our being out of here by January 1. Marc could throw a spanner into the works that would do massive damage."

"Even if he doesn't go back to school, I can't imagine him wanting to come home and live in Geneva."

"I hope you're right. I don't want to force you to choose, but if Marc moves back here, it will surely drive a wedge between us."

"I've already made my choice," David replied grimly. "If something happens to Marc, I'll cry, I'll hurt, but I can't lead his life for him."

From: Marc
To: Dad
Date: November 30, 2005
Subject: fiscal shit

hi there, got your message about signing up for school again, but i've got stuff to do before i can deal with it.

i lost my check book and my computer with the shit that happened, haven't had the chance to do anything about it... will have to see what else is missing ... it's a mess.

i'm still coming home for christmas, but both my passports were lost too, spent $300 for an expdited u.s. passport, will have it next monday...can you get me a ticket? i have a meeting set with the consulat francais when i am in geneva, can't wait to spend my time doing bureaucratic crap on my christmas stay.

j'tembrasse. m

David booked a roundtrip ticket for Marc, and focused his communications on getting Marc to re-enroll. By the weekend, there was some progress.

From: Marc
To: Jenny
Date: December 3, 2005
Subject: winter semester

hi jenny, i have taken the decision to take classes again during this coming january. i hope the education trust can again pay for school. the california budget cut has sent the fees in inflation. i cant clearly remember the amount i last gave you as a budget but things have gone up, i hope it is feasible.

thanks this helps me tremendously.

love and kisses, marc

Jenny immediately went to find David. "I don't know why he didn't copy you on this, but Marc just sent me an e-mail saying he's re-enrolling. I hope he hasn't missed a critical deadline. He also says he needs a bigger budget."

"How much?"

"No specific amount. 'Things have gone up,' he says. Fortunately, this can come out of the Trust, but I am really concerned about what Marc's doing with his money. I'm going to ask that the Trust pay bills directly wherever possible rather than funneling the money through Marc. We need to lay out a plan of action before Marc arrives."

"He gets in on Saturday, December 19. He flies back the Tuesday after Christmas."

"That gives us two weeks to get ready and just over a week to settle things out with him."

"Yup. But in the meantime, I'm going to need a few days in Paris. I've been in Geneva so long that I've apparently dropped below the radar of the French Social Security folks. I have to get the paperwork straightened out before I can collect my French pension."

"I'll miss you, but at least it leaves me free to start boxing up the kitchen unimpeded. When do you want to go?"

"As soon as you can spare me. But for god's sake, leave me enough pots and pans to handle Christmas!"

Piles – *For Jenny*

Like moles, he leaves dusty piles behind
As he tunnels through time –
Books, notes, papers, paintings –
Most simply posed on floors and tables
For unwary walkers to trip over.
Like garden worms,
He has ingested and digested much –
The memories stored in mounded age –
The current piles
Now meant to serve some vital,
Unknown, future growth.
It drives his gardener crazy
To find literary hillocks
In the middle of her orderly plot –
Lots of which mean nothing
To her and should, she feels,
Be turned into compost
For someone else's spiritual
Or intellectual lot.
He, however, never knows
When he might find a time
To tunnel further
Looking for missed morsels of memory.

D.P. – December, 2005

Chapter 10

De: David
A: Jenny
Envoyé: 7 décembre, 2005
Objet: Wednesday progress
Att: Piles

Got started with the *Service aux Retraités*. Should be able to come home on the Friday train. Don't throw anything out while I'm away.

Love you, David

Jenny laughed aloud when she read the poem David attached to his e-mail.

From: JWLongworth
To: DavidP
Date: December 7, 2005
Subject: Re: Wednesday progress

Missed morsels of memory indeed! Honey Chile, when you get home, go take pictures of your piles, and I'll put them in a photo album you can peruse to your heart's content.

Today I'm tackling the TV room. Sorry you're not here to join in the fun.

Love, me

De: David
A: Jenny
Envoyé: 7 décembre, 2005
Objet: Re: Re: Wednesday progress
Boy, oh boy, me TOO! Am I sorry!

The afternoon of David's return from Paris, they got a call from the rental agency saying they had found an ideal tenant – a young Swedish couple with two small children. The agent brought them by for an interview, and there was instant rapport. To Jenny's relief, they didn't want to move in until January 10. "This means the cleaning crew can wait until after New Year's to do the windows and floors!" she told David excitedly. "This buys us some extra days. We can be in residence right up to the witching hour."

The next morning, Jenny tackled the top shelves of the living room cabinets. She wrapped Sandie's collection of little porcelain figurines, then took down some plated-silver bowls and salt servers. Tucked behind them was a rounded silver box. She recognized it before she even drew it down. The box had graced the table during the private marriage ceremony she and David held at the house, weeks before their official *Mairie* wedding. She took it carefully in hand and went in search of David. She found him sorting through school notebooks.

"We still have a small cache of Sandie's ashes left," she said, holding up the silver box.

He looked at it and nodded. "Yup," he said.

Jenny paused, but when David added no further comment, she raised the obvious question. "What do you want to do with them?"

"I've considered taking them to the US," he said, "but I think Sandie would rather stay in Geneva. I doubt, however, that she'd be thrilled sitting in the *Cave* while a bunch of strangers occupy her house. I think she'll be more comfortable hanging out with her roses."

That evening, they took the silver box into the garden. Lifting the lid, David scattered the powdery remains around the Abbaye de

Cluny roses they had planted several years before in Sandie's memory. When they returned to the house, he handed the box over to Jenny. There was no further discussion. She rinsed it, dried it, packed it with Sandie's porcelain figurines, and taped the carton shut.

Not surprisingly, Jenny had a Sandie dream that night: Sandie was wan after her illness, and very weak, but she came and sat down with David and Jenny as they waited somewhere on a curb. They kissed cheeks, and Sandie seemed totally understanding that David had married Jenny. Now that she was back, Sandie would simply proceed independently, as a single woman. Lots of other people arrived and began milling about, and suddenly there was an explosion. When the dust settled, Sandie was nowhere to be seen. There was more to the dream, but though it was vivid when Jenny first woke up, the ending quickly evaporated.

Dust? Ashes? I've just dealt with both in the waking world. It's the explosion that's the puzzling piece. Am I blowing up Sandie's world by dismantling her house? Jenny gave this some serious thought, then exonerated herself. *No. I'm doing my best to keep her family safe and well. David's happy. Dellie's internship expenses are being covered. And Marc – Marc I don't know, but we're trying.*

High on the countdown list was the challenge of finding new homes for the cats. Happily, Marikit agreed to take charge of Carotte, who was aging and something of a couch potato. "Carotte was Madame Sandie's favorite," Marikit confided. "The last time I saw Madame Sandie, she was sitting in the garden with Carotte on her lap. 'Marikit,' she said to me, 'When I am gone, will you look after Carotte?' 'I always look after Carotte,' I promised, 'and Mister David also.'"

The difficult placement was Minuit, their highly territorial black cat. They finally prevailed on Olga and Jacques to take him, hoping their farm would provide sufficient room and entertainment to compensate for the loss of his familiar domain.

They accomplished Minuit's transition with multiple visits. "He seems increasingly comfortable in his new environment," David reported, "but Jacques says that Minuit often sits in front of the barn and stares at the driveway. Jacques is convinced that he's waiting for our car to appear."

Jenny felt tears start in her eyes when David told her this. It pushed an ancient button of childhood grief tied to the loss of her first dog. Her parents had to put the dog to sleep, but, thinking it was kinder, they told Jenny and her siblings that they had given him away to a farmer. For months afterwards, Jenny cried herself to sleep believing that her dog was sitting forlornly in some barnyard, not understanding why he had been sent away, just waiting, sadly but patiently, for Jenny to come find him.

The stress affected them in different ways and at different times. Whenever David hit a bump, he found a reason to absent himself from the house, running an errand or taking some give-away item to a neighbor. He also devoted substantial time to the Internet:

> *De: David*
> *A: Graham*
> *Envoye: 12 décembre, 2005*
> *Objet: Dissolution*
>
> My computer desk is one of the few remaining islands of permanence here at home. I have forbidden Jenny to so much as look at it. She has packed up the entire rest of the house in the time it's taken me to empty one bookshelf. I accept that all this is necessary, but I'm not made for programmed changes.
>
> Marc is flying in for Christmas. Delphine will join us at the last minute. We're out of this house at the stroke of midnight on New Year's Eve. If the boat don't sink and the train don't turn around, we'll be in Boston the following afternoon.
>
> I'll call when we get in. David

As Jenny struggled to coordinate packing, storing and housecleaning, she began having weird and complicated dreams involving window washing and lost lampshades and blinds that wouldn't work. The surest indicator of her stress level was that she started craving comfort food. At breakfast one morning she cut two fat slices of wholegrain bread, put them in the toaster, and got out the last of her American extra crunchy peanut butter. David poured himself a second cup of coffee as Jenny stood by the toaster, trying to organize her thoughts for the day ahead. The toast popped up with a loud noise and gave her a serious start. David looked at her quizzically. "When you jump at the toast popping up, despite the fact that you've been standing there waiting for it, you know your nerves are in bad shape!"

Marc arrived a week before Christmas. His room was filled with boxes and furniture, so he was assigned to Jenny's office, where the fold-out couch was still in place. Marc slept through his first day but joined his father and Jenny for dinner.

David reviewed the process that had led them to opt for a three-year rental and described the family that was coming in. To Jenny's surprise, Marc seemed almost indifferent to the decision to rent the house. Rather than debating the decision, Marc wanted to know how much money the rental would generate.

Jenny had calculated a conservative minimum net and gave Marc a figure. "We're depositing your share and Dellie's into your respective Geneva accounts. Dellie will be drawing on hers immediately while she's in London, but with your return to school, your expenses will be covered by the Trust. Before you go back, you and I can sit down and go over the details. Meanwhile, I put a couple of boxes in the basement hallway for you to go through. There are some items you may want to take to San Francisco with you."

"What will happen when the three-year lease is up?" Marc asked.

"That will depend on how everyone feels about the house at that point," David answered. "I want to give you and your sister a few more years to decide where you want to make your life, and whether or not you want to move back to Geneva. The rent should generate enough income to give you and Delphine a cushion, and let us stay in different parts of Europe for two months at a stretch. Wherever we are, we'll make sure there is room enough so that you, Delphine and our friends can join us."

"I thought you were talking about buying something smaller."

"We initially looked at downsizing," David explained, "and in the long run, we probably will, but we can't afford to buy another property unless we first sell this house. And that, I'm not ready to do," David said firmly.

Marc seemed genuinely curious about the locations they wanted to explore. The conversation was primarily geographical rather than financial, and it made for a pleasant evening until David brought up the subject of Marc's lost computer. "We were thinking of getting you a replacement for Christmas," he said, "but I'm hesitant to buy it here. Not only are the prices better in the States, but you'd also have an American keyboard and a warranty you could take to the computer store if you needed a repair."

"Nah. I don't need one. I've got my phone, and the only e-mail I get is the jokes you send," he told his father. "I can't be bothered with reading that stuff. I don't wanna waste my time on such foolishness."

Jenny was disturbed by Marc's thoughtless remark, but David let it pass without comment.

"Can I have the car?" Marc asked the next day. "I need to do some Christmas shopping." He was out all afternoon and came home late for dinner. To Jenny's eyes, he was obviously high.

"Did you give him any money?" Jenny asked David quietly.

"We're not getting him a computer, so I gave him a hundred Swiss francs. He arrived here flat broke."

"Well, he's stoned, so he's obviously spending it on something other than Christmas presents. David, this isn't helping him."

"Are you sure he's stoned? I figured it was just fogginess from jet lag."

There were two similar incidents as the week progressed, and the mood was tense until Delphine arrived from Paris. Because of her holiday job, she couldn't come home until Christmas Eve, but once there, she overlapped with Marc for two full days. Jenny could feel a change in the household dynamic when Delphine was present. She and Marc were as different as siblings could be, but there was a deep affection between them, and Marc always seemed happier when Delphine was around.

Christmas morning, David turned his attention to cooking. They had a mid-day dinner with roast goose, baked rice and a custard tart for dessert. "Delicious!" Jenny declared. "And now I can pack the roasting pan!"

Afterwards they adjourned to their nearly vacant living room to open presents. Marc had brought more blown glass from San Francisco. Delphine presented everyone with scarves from Galeries Lafayette. David and Jenny gave the children sturdy canvas tote bags monogrammed with their initials. "All-purpose," Jenny beamed. "Good for travel, and good for storage."

The next day, Jenny reworked Marc's budget, but in fact made few changes. "Your share of the rent money will be deposited regularly into your Swiss account, but I urge you to draw on it very sparingly, if at all. The exchange rate will work against you. The Trust money should see you through if you use it wisely," she counseled. *Unfortunately, that's a big "if,"* she knew.

David took Marc to the airport on the twenty-seventh. Delphine was off two days later on the train to Paris where she would pick up some clothing and then head on to London.

Their final three days in the house, David insisted on paying personal visits to all his Genevan friends and colleagues. Jenny knew it was an emotional time for him, but she was itching to be done with the goodbyes. She reviewed the final countdown list, confirmed the January cleaning appointment, and gave an emergency key to Marikit. The last day of December, they locked the door to the storage room, handed over multiple key sets to the rental agent, and went next door to Mehrak and Manuela's house with their suitcases to spend the night. Manuela dropped them at the airport on the first morning of the New Year, and Jenny nearly skipped to the check-in counter, feeling light-hearted for the first time in months.

David, in contrast, was tense and irritable as they boarded. "I am not ready for this trip," he grumbled repeatedly. Fortunately, his mood brightened with a glass of wine and a good book – salvaged from one of his piles.

They began their descent into Boston with the last of the sunlight. A southern approach into Logan had them winging over Cohasset and Hull. To David's amusement, Jenny got excited as she identified the beaches and coves beneath her.

"You are definitely a Bostonian," he commented wryly.

Thick flakes of snow started to fall as they pulled into Jenny's driveway in Shawmut. They awoke the next morning to a white world with deep drifts softening the contours of the yard. Jenny's condo, surrounded as it was by woods and fields, was always beautiful in the snow.

David made Jenny's tea, then settled himself at the computer with a cup of coffee. He composed an e-mail to their neighbors in Geneva, thanking them for all the memories. "Please rest assured that we are not deserting Europe," he closed. "I can't walk away from thirty-plus years of my life. We expect to return often, but the fact of leaving Morion for such a long time makes me sad and very nostalgic." Reading the words over his shoulder, Jenny was reminded of how much David was giving up to come live on her side of the world.

He sent a quick note to Marc and Delphine reporting their safe arrival in Boston, then stepped outside to have a cigarette. He lasted all of thirty seconds.

"God damn!" he shuddered. "It's colder than a witch's tit out there!"

"Well, yes," Jenny laughed. "It's January, and this is New England. But there's no wind and not a cloud in the sky, so it'll probably warm up ten degrees or so during the day."

"What's the temperature right now?"

Jenny peered through the kitchen window at the thermometer just outside.

"It's eight degrees."

"Centigrade?"

"No. Fahrenheit."

"Holy shit!"

"Why don't you make a grocery list," Jenny suggested. "We'll venture out late morning. It should be in the double digits by then."

Jenny called Ross and invited him and Kevin to dinner on Saturday. "Sorry, Jewel, Kevin is flitting about the Emerald Isle visiting family, but I would be delighted to come."

"Maybe we could invite Rachel down at the same time," David suggested. "Do she and Ross know each other?"

"They've met, but their circles are very different. Anyway, it's moot because Rachel is out of town. Her family has a tradition of going someplace warm and sunny at the end of December – far away from the incessant ringing of jingle bells. But we can definitely do something when she gets back."

The sunshine was strong enough to melt the snow from the trees, but with nightfall, the temperatures dipped into the single digits again. "I hope you have one helluva supply of firewood," David said, pulling on a second sweater.

"Wimp!" Jenny teased. "This weather never bothered you when we were in college."

A slow smile spread over David's face. "That's because we had some really fun ways to keep warm."

On Saturday, David started cooking early in anticipation of their dinner with Ross. "I have a question for you," Jenny said as she watched him roll out dough for a savory *galette*. "I'd like to talk with Ross about Marc. Is that okay with you?"

"You're free to talk with your friends about anything. But why Marc?"

"The drug issue. I think Ross may have some useful insights and maybe some advice. When he's not being a lawyer, he volunteers at the Martin Luther King Community Center, working with at-risk kids. These kids live in a world occupied by addicts and dealers, and it's a world Ross knows well. He's told me some amazing stories from his long-ago days as a teenage junkie. He was a full-fledged heroin addict at fourteen. It's nothing short of a miracle that he survived a ghetto childhood in one piece, but here he is, decades later, a successful attorney and respected community advocate."

David was obviously uncomfortable with the implications. "It seems like overkill. Marc isn't very judicious about his marijuana use, but that doesn't make him an addict."

"He's using more than marijuana, David, and he's less than honest about what he does with his money."

"What do you mean?" David demanded, startled.

"Remember how he kept borrowing the car over Christmas, saying he needed to go buy Christmas presents?"

"So?"

"What did he give each of us for Christmas?"

"Blown glass."

"Right. Things that he made himself."

"Maybe he was getting presents for friends in San Francisco."

"I helped him pack, David. He wanted to take back some of his old LP records to sell, and he had trouble getting them in. I reorganized his suitcase so they would fit. There were no Christmas presents."

Once Ross arrived and was served a glass of wine, Jenny shared her concerns. "We have a problem, Ross, and we need your advice and counsel, not as a lawyer, but as someone familiar with the drug culture."

Jenny gave Ross a summary of Marc's history, citing erratic behavior, irresponsibility, and uncontrolled outbursts. David interjected his hope that Marc was only using marijuana, but when

Jenny described the times she had seen Marc with glassy eyes and red rings around his pupils, Ross shook his head.

"Red eyes are normally associated with Cocaine, Heroin and Quaaludes, not marijuana," he advised matter-of-factly. David winced at his words.

"Marc felt very close to his mother, and her death may be a factor in all this. There's also a possibility that he suffers from depression and maybe something more serious," David explained.

"Whatever the contributing factors, Marc denies there's a problem," Jenny pointed out. "He refuses to seek or accept any help, which leaves us not knowing where to turn."

"Your first step is to educate and protect yourselves. There's a lot of good information on the Internet, but you're going to encounter philosophical extremes," Ross explained. "Some people will recommend an Intervention. Others will argue that Marc won't accept help until he hits bottom, and that you may diminish hope of his recovery if you postpone that event by cushioning his descent. Personally, I suggest that you consult a therapist who specializes in addiction, and I recommend you get in touch with groups like Al-Anon. That said, it's especially important to give Marc as much emotional support as possible. Patience, love and hope are incredibly important in beating this thing."

There wasn't much more Ross could do beyond wishing them luck and the strength to persevere. The rest of their evening sounded a lighter note and was devoted to a tasty *galette provençale*, a hearty boeuf bourguignon, and catching up on each other's activities,

"David, Ross is right," Jenny said as they climbed into bed. "I think it's time we got some professional guidance about Marc. Would you be willing for us to see a counselor?"

"I don't know what it's going to accomplish, but if you think it would be helpful, sure, let's see a counselor," David said with a shrug.

The next morning, Jenny contacted a friend who recommended two private clinicians. Jenny drafted a briefing document and gave it to David to look over. After an introductory paragraph explaining who they were, the summary concentrated on Marc:

> Since his early teenage years, Marc Perry, now in his mid-twenties, has expressed hostility toward all forms of authority, displayed contempt for most educational and social institutions, exhibited angry and violent behavior, isolated himself from friends and family, been secretive, irresponsible and has caused his family a great deal of anxiety.
>
> He has also, at times, been charming, amusing, affectionate, helpful and contrite. He has innate artistic talent, and has shown interest and enthusiasm for painting, photography and glass blowing. David remembers his own youthful rebellion and has generally tolerated Marc's foibles with the thought that if we could see Marc through this 'phase,' he would become more mature and responsible with time.
>
> We are seeking professional guidance because, rather than improving, Marc's behavior seems increasingly erratic. David has accepted Marc's past protestations that his drug involvement is limited to smoking pot, but we no longer trust Marc's representations. There is also a possibility of an underlying biological issue. Marc denies that there is a problem and refuses to seek professional help.

"Is there anything you want to add or edit?" Jenny asked.

"No, it's just that I'm really uneasy about accusing Marc of lying when I'm not absolutely sure."

"That's something you should tell the therapist when we see her. She may have some helpful ideas."

"You already have an appointment?"

"No, but I have two names. I'll call them Monday morning and sign up with whichever one can give us an appointment first."

Offsetting worries about Marc, David received a cheerful report from Delphine, who was settling happily into her internship at Sotheby's.

From: Delphine
To: Dad
Date: January 15, 2006
Subject: London

Hiya! I'm pretty well settled. Yesterday I worked with a restorer to make condition reports on several paintings that will eventually be auctioned. So that was interesting, looking at these works under UV lights. The other interns are all fun, and it's nice to be surrounded by people whose hopes, dreams and blunders are similar to mine. The house I live in is adorable, despite the fact that the kitchen was flooded yesterday ... and my roommates are very cool.

Bises, Delphine

The outdoor temperature dropped into single digits again that night, and again they drew their chairs close to the fireplace.

"I know you love this place, Ducks, but we might do better to schedule our Boston stays sometime other than the dead of winter."

The conversation started in a joking tone, but it gradually morphed into a serious discussion about whether they should choose someplace with a milder climate as their primary base in the US. Jenny had grown up in Boston and was inured to the harsh winters. She loved the seasons. She had lifelong friends in the area, and Boston was an important connecting point for her family, since Maine was a traditional summer gathering place for her siblings.

"I have to admit," she said, "that I forgot how cold this house can get. When I lived here, I used to spend the really bitter days in town, in my office, which was always toasty warm. And since I lived alone, I could just crank up the electric blanket on a frigid Sunday and snuggle in bed with a book or a movie."

Of immediate concern, Jenny's unit had no place where David could comfortably smoke. He had to stand outside on the open porch or use the tiny guest lavatory, with the door closed and the little exhaust fan running on high. Had there been any hope that such inconvenience might motivate him to quit, Jenny would have dug in her heels, but that was not the case. David was already making a major change in his life to accommodate her wishes.

"Do you have someplace specific in mind?" she asked. "Like your home base, Chattanooga?"

"No, not Chattanooga, but it might be fun to visit different parts of the country."

"Why don't you make a list of places you'd like to check out, and what sort of environment you're looking for."

"You're the List Lady. Why don't you start? I'll add ideas as they come to me."

"Well, there's no rush. I'd have to sell this place before we could buy a place somewhere else."

"Why couldn't you rent it the way we've done in Geneva?"

"The house is full of antiques. Most renters don't want to have to worry about the furniture."

"You've got a decent-sized attic. You could stick your furniture up there and offer this place unfurnished. There's no reason to sell unless you're absolutely sure that's what you want to do."

Jenny didn't want to give up Boston any more than David wanted to give up Geneva, but she had urged him to rent out his house while they considered their European options. *It's not unreasonable to do the same thing here, and consider our American options. But I need to give it some careful thought first.*

Carla Klein, the first therapist Jenny called, gave them a Wednesday appointment. The drive up to Brookline was surprisingly traffic-free. They arrived early, poked their heads into a bookstore to pass the extra time, and then walked over to Carla's office.

"I've read the report you sent," she said. "It was very helpful. Let's start with your telling me what you hope to achieve in talking with me."

Each in a different way, David and Jenny expressed the frustration of knowing there were serious problems but not knowing what to do about them.

"We need professional guidance not only about Marc, but also about ways to protect our own relationship and our sanity as we move forward," Jenny added.

Like Ross, Carla urged them to explore Al-Anon. "I think you've done a really good job keeping the lines of communication open," she reassured David. "Your dilemma is finding a hook with which to get Marc connected to some acceptable form of help. I can suggest some resources in San Francisco," she concluded, "and I can certainly be available to you by phone whenever you're not in Boston."

"What did you think?" Jenny asked as they walked back to the car.

"I think it was useful to talk, if only as an aid to sorting things out in my own head," he replied.

The frigid temperatures they encountered in January gave way to a February thaw. Jenny found an Al-Anon group that met in Quincy. She and David attended three weekly sessions, but he had difficulty identifying with the situations different participants spoke about.

"Now that he's back in school, Marc seems okay these days. I'm not really getting anything out of these meetings," David confessed.

Jenny didn't argue, and their attention was soon drawn away from Marc by Delphine. She had applied for a Masters of Art program with a British institute, but a document in her submission was somehow misplaced, invalidating her application for the fall term. She learned of the setback too late to remedy the omission, making a shambles of her plans for the year ahead. In words brimming with disappointment and distress, she reported the setback, leaving David in a deep funk and very touchy. Jenny saw Delphine as a capable young woman who would quickly overcome this disappointment. David saw her as his baby girl in distress. "We have to go to London," he announced. "Maybe we can straighten this out."

My words aren't going to calm him down, Jenny knew, *but maybe Delphine can reassure him that it's not the end of the world.*

From: JWLongworth
To: Delphine
cc: DavidP
Date: February 27, 2006
Subject: Bummer

Hi, Dellie – David told me about the snafu with the MA program. What a disappointment! He's ready to fly over to London and give that Institute a piece of his mind, which we would certainly consider doing if it would really make a difference.

Realistically, I think we'll just have to hope this is a Lost Horse story, and that something better awaits you around the corner. Maybe you're meant to spend next year in gay paree rather than foggy London town!

Love, Jenny

De: Delphine
A: Jenny
cc: Dad
Envoyé: 28 février, 2006
Objet: Re: Bummer

That's exactly what I think: the horse story! We'll just have to see what happens. But I'd love to have you visit anyway. Come while I'm still at Sotheby's so I can give you a tour!

Love, Dellie

Delphine, as Jenny expected, was handling the situation in a pragmatic and no-nonsense manner. By the end of the day, everything was under control – or so Jenny thought until she received a note from Marc saying he was again short of funds.

From: Marc
To: Jenny
Date: February 28, 2006
Subject: budget

hello jenny,

i apparently did not do a great job at evaluating my budget when we talked at christmas and so am now in a situation where i am a little short. as you said, i don't

> want to use the money in geneva if the trust can help. I will try to find another part time job to keep afloat on my own. i am sorry for writting you so late, in hopes that it is not a problem.
>
> thanks. love marc

Jenny showed the missive to David.

"Can the Trust up his allowance?" David asked.

"The Trust is paying all academic bills directly now – housing, fees, cafeteria, books, the works. Marc receives an additional fifty dollars a week in discretionary funds. He can only be short if he doesn't accept that operating on a 'budget' means keeping your spending within your income."

"Maybe he needs it for dates."

"Fifty dollars should more than cover two movie tickets and a pizza. He doesn't have to treat someone to champagne and caviar."

"If the Trust doesn't cover it, he'll take the rental money out of his Swiss account."

"So be it, but I don't think that's the important question here. I'd like to know why he needs more than fifty dollars a week spending money. That's more than a lot of his fellow students are working with."

David just shook his head.

"Can you handle this?" Jenny asked. "I don't have your patience. If I try to talk with him about this, there will not be a happy resolution."

David nodded wearily. "I'll give him a call," he said quietly. "And you know what? I've been thinking about Delphine's asking us to visit. She sounds okay, but I think maybe a trip to London isn't a bad idea."

He's obviously anxious about both kids, Jenny observed. *He may also be a little homesick for Europe. It can't hurt to try a quick hop across the Atlantic.*

"You're on," Jenny announced after checking the off-season rates. "We can come close to paying for the flight just by lowering the thermostat to fifty degrees for the time that we're gone!"

A week later, they landed at Heathrow, checked into their hotel, then took a bus to Trafalgar Square only to find Admiral Nelson wrapped in scaffolding for cleaning. They got another bus up to Bond Street, where a helpful London Bobby with a strong Russian accent told them how to get from Old Bond Street to New Bond Street, and thence to Sotheby's. They walked into a posh and somewhat hushed reception hall. David spoke to a receptionist, and Delphine was called down to give them a brief tour. She couldn't take much time out of her day's schedule, so they left her after half an hour and rejoined her that evening for dinner.

As they ate, Delphine talked about her Sotheby's experience. She also mentioned casually that she had broken up with the young man she had been dating in Paris. David and Jenny had met him once, briefly, but at the time there was no indication that the relationship was serious.

"You got lotsa time, Kid, lotsa time," David commented in an attempt to reassure Delphine. It wasn't clear how painful the breakup was, but Jenny sensed that Delphine was putting up a brave front. There must have been at least some hurt involved. Jenny offered up her own experience of breaking up with her first husband, Seth, after fifteen years of marriage.

"At the time, it was incredibly painful and humiliating. In retrospect, it left me free to go to your father when he needed me. In that sense, it was the best thing that could possibly have happened to me."

David frowned. "But if Seth had changed his behavior – if you had worked it out and stayed together, you might still have had a happy life," David countered.

"David Perry, there is no way in the world I could ever have been as happy with anyone else as I am with you."

"Get outta heah!" was his response.

Jenny reached over and touched David's cheek. He made a face. "I need a cigarette," he announced as he rose from the table.

"Don't get lost," Jenny teased.

Delphine pursed her lips exactly as her mother used to do. "You're so cute with Dad," she said. "The way you kiss the top of his head or give him a squeeze when he's standing at the stove." She seemed to study Jenny. "I don't think Mom was very physical."

Jenny was surprised. "I remember Sandie as being very affectionate, always touching and hugging you and Marc. The same with her friends. She and Josette were often arm in arm when they walked together."

"Oh, she was affectionate with us. I mean with Dad. We never saw them hugging and kissing," she said matter-of-factly.

Does she suspect? Jenny wondered. *Is there some kind of subconscious awareness about Sandie's affair?* Jenny shied away from potentially dangerous territory and commented, quite truthfully, that David didn't have a huggy-kissy sort of personality.

Changing the subject, Jenny asked about Delphine's plans.

"Now that I don't have to be here in the fall, I'm going to go back to Paris as soon as the internship is over. I have a couple of roommate possibilities. I'll get a job and maybe do some classes at the Louvre to build up my resume."

"Sounds very sensible to me," Jenny smiled.

In the days that followed, they filled their calendar with museums, visits with British friends, and a surfeit of pub meals. As Jenny had hoped, the visit seemed to reassure David that Delphine was in good shape, and that Europe was still standing. This time, David was neither tense nor irritable as they boarded the flight back to Boston. When they reached home, David called Marc to let him know they had arrived safely.

Jenny expected David to report on their visit with Delphine, but he was strangely silent, listening intently to whatever Marc was saying on the other end. When he hung up, David looked at Jenny and shook his head.

"There's some kind of snafu about Marc's course credits. He's been told that he won't have enough credit requirements to graduate in June. He's going to have to take some additional courses this summer in order to get his degree."

"Did he fail some courses, or has he just not taken the ones he needs?" Jenny asked with concern.

"I don't know the details," David answered. "At this point, I'm just hoping that he'll continue rather than dropping out. Perseverance hasn't been one of Marc's strong points."

"Do you think he'll do it? Take another semester? The Education Trust is getting near the bottom of the barrel, but I absolutely agree that continuing is the best course of action. Ross stressed the importance of emotional support. We went to London to give Dellie a boost. I wonder if we should pay Marc a visit."

"When would we go?"

"Does he have some kind of spring break? We don't have to make it sound like a crisis response. The crocuses are up, but the rest of the yard is slush and mud. It's not unreasonable for us to crave some balmy California weather, and we're in good shape regarding frequent flier miles."

"I'll sound him out on it. I'm not excited about getting back on an airplane so soon, but I think we need to see what's going on."

David sent Marc an e-mail, asking about the timing of his spring break. When twenty-four hours passed with no reply, he sent a second note, and followed up in the morning with a phone message.

Marc's silence weighed heavily on David, and Jenny was sufficiently tense by late afternoon that she joined him for a glass of wine, even though it was only 4:30. He looked at her in surprise. Jenny usually insisted that the clock strike five before she had a drink.

"Blood pressure," she said by way of explanation. He understood without further clarification. "It's a lucky thing that you and I are such good friends," she told him. He reached for her hand and gave it a squeeze. It almost made it worth the stress they were enduring.

From: Marc
To: Dad
Date: March 16, 2006
Subject: Re: Spring break

come if you want, but here things are as cold as the weather and as dumb as a soap opera. Everything is so f***ed up. i had to step out for a long walk by the coast. even if i get a degree, graduation means some minimum wage job, why bother? i'm tired of bull shit, to much on tv already, i have things to do, no matter what I will finish my days alone in a coffin, so where'z the point of putting all that energy in something that is not going to finish well.

peace and love (been living in s.f. loo long!!!!) marc

p.s. don't share this mail with anybody, i have enough troubles

"Considering the PS, I don't think Marc wants me reading this," Jenny commented after David called her to the computer. "It seems the world hasn't arranged itself to suit him. He sounds like a sulky teenager. It's all 'me, me, me.'"

David remained silent. Jenny's caustic remarks obviously weren't helping to ease his paternal distress, so she downshifted.

"Clearly, Marc's reactions to adversity go way beyond the norm. Think back over the last few years. Marc must have been more than rude to get himself permanently banned from British Air flights. You've seen him pull railings out of walls and break chairs. He's smashed more than one telephone that we know about. That level of aggression and rage must have biological components. He needs real help, professional help."

David didn't argue, but he made no comment.

"Perhaps you could call Jack Pogue and see if he's game to have us occupy a guestroom for a week or three. I'll take a look at flight schedules and see what's possible. It may not do any good, but we've got nothing to lose by going."

David let a deep sigh escape. "Carla Klein said she knew of resources in San Francisco, didn't she? At this point, I'm willing to talk with anybody. Can you get the contact information from her? There has to be a way to get Marc to see someone."

That evening, after supper, David turned on his computer and sat staring at the screen. Jenny got into bed with her book, but the desk where David was sitting was only a few feet away, and it was obvious that he was frustrated at being far away and having no magic bullet.

De: David
A: Marc
cc: Jenny
Envoyé: 16 mars, 2006
Objet: You!

Marc, I do not accept your telling me what I may or may not share with other people, and I will not put up with your bullshit. I have lived long enough to write this letter in great part because I have shared my feelings when I was lost, and others have helped me, thanks to that sharing. That is my way of living, and it is certainly not you who is going to change it.

You have reached an age when the adult world asks you to assume responsibility for your life. Get your degree, then choose what you want to be – gardener, pilot, glassblower, painter, garbage man, programmer, day care assistant, teacher – and do it. You have to go out into the world, and prove to yourself and others that you can finish what you start. Your first job may be minimum wage, and you may not like it. But do it anyway until you find another one that you like better.

You are angry. I hear it in your letters. I hear it on the phone. You sound like a dumb-ass eighth grader. If you don't know why you're angry, go get professional help. Get off your ass. You are an adult. Act like one. Only you can do it and only if you want to. It is your responsibility.

I love you. Dad

Yessss! Jenny exulted when she read her copy. *The love is still apparent, but there's a new firmness.* Jenny was convinced it was good for all of them, and she felt a great sense of relief.

Throughout the next day, David was edgy, waiting for an answer from Marc to his "dumb-ass" e-mail. When it finally came, Marc avoided a direct response to his father's remarks, but the tone suggested that some of what David said had gotten through. Most importantly, Marc indicated that he would welcome a visit.

"Now that I know Marc's okay with our coming, I'll call Jack to see if he's up for guests," David told Jenny. "We can get our tickets once we know what dates work best for him."

The Glowing April Moon

The glowing April moon
Reflects a light
The high scattered
Problem clouds
Not only fail to hide
But actually illuminate
In the bright, blue
Darkness of the night.
Their broad, billowing
Outlines suggest to me
Mindful curves
And glowing paths to take.

D.P. – April, 2006

Chapter 11

As they winged their way to San Francisco, David settled in quickly with a book. Jenny pulled out the flight magazine and flipped through it. The feature article immediately caught her eye: "America's Ten Best Retirement Cities."

She had no interest in living in a city, but she read the article anyway. Several of the recommendations involved smaller urban centers rather than a large metropolis. Thinking back over their recent discussion about a warmer home base, Jenny skimmed through the article a second time. It stressed logical considerations – scenic area, quality health care, reasonable housing costs, good community resources – but it lacked any reference to what Jenny considered a critical component: proximity to friends and family. David and Jenny knew people at scattered points throughout the country. Hands down, however, the largest concentration of friends, for both of them, was on the west coast.

This adds a whole new dimension to visiting Marc, she considered. *Marc will be our major focus, but hopefully we'll have time to do a little research.*

They took a cab from the airport to the Pogues' house. David called Marc as soon as they had said hello to their hosts, and invited him for dinner the following evening.

Jack and Janet were about to leave for a three-week stay in Mexico. "Can we take you to the airport in the morning?" David asked. "Our biological clocks are on eastern daylight time, so we'll be up before dawn."

"Thanks, but no thanks," Jack answered. "We've already reserved a shuttle. Just enjoy the house, don't forget to water the plants, and feel free to exercise the car while we're away," he instructed them.

The next day, Jenny called area friends to alert them to their presence. She also called Elspeth Warrington, the San Francisco therapist Carla Klein had recommended, and scheduled a meeting for David and herself.

Marc arrived at the Pogues' house shortly after six. He needed a haircut and was dressed in sandals, torn jeans and an old t-shirt. He seemed to be in good spirits, slightly cautious, but cordial with Jenny and cheerful with his father. He had committed to a final summer semester, so that bridge had been crossed.

"Since you're doing another semester, are there any elective classes you want to add on top of the required credit courses – classes that might be fun?" Jenny asked. "Art? Music? Dance?"

"Right now I'm far from knowing exactly where I am heading towards," Marc replied. "All I know is, after I graduate I'm thinking about getting a full time job, so to get a serious and more stable revenue source."

Jenny was about to ask what kind of job he was considering, but she caught a subtle hand signal from David, as if to say, "don't push." She pressed no further and let the subject drop.

The rest of the conversation ranged over safe topics. Marc had a full class schedule, but thought he might take off a little time to meet his father at a few museum exhibits. David promised to find out what was on display and call Marc with some ideas. In the interim, David and Jenny had time for friends.

Bibi invited them over to Sausalito for lunch. When they arrived, she showed them the latest grandchildren pictures, and they brought her up to date on their repatriation. "One of the things we've realized is that maybe we should locate our US base somewhere other than Boston," Jenny advised. "Spring has announced itself, but for the most part, the weather has kept us huddled indoors. We need to be someplace where we can spend more time outside."

"Finally some common sense!" Bibi exclaimed. "I loved Boston when I lived there, but I don't miss those winters one bit. You should give some serious thought to California, and especially Sausalito. You'd have all the advantages of San Francisco right across the bay, but none of the disadvantages of living in the city. Plus we have sunshine and warm temperatures when they have fog and cold wind. And another thing. You'd be close to Marc, but at a safe distance, if you know what I mean."

After lunch, Bibi walked them around the docks where they admired the tiny gardens and quirky decorations in front of the houseboats. They chanced upon a realtor's Open House and ducked inside for a quick tour. It was a well-appointed boat, but the owners wanted over a million dollars for it. When Bibi got her houseboat, nearly twenty years earlier, the area was derelict. Developers were lobbying to have the wharves condemned so they could build a condominium complex at the water's edge.

"You certainly bought at the right time, Bibi. The prices have gone up a wee bit, haven't they," Jenny commented.

"I know," Bibi laughed. "Whoda thunk it? Maybe you should look into buying now, before the prices go up any further!"

"This is out of our league, Bibi. I'd have to sell my condo in Shawmut three or four times over to be able to afford one of these houseboats! Besides," she added, "I need more garden space."

They had an appointment the next day with Elspeth Warrington. She was a tall woman with a no-nonsense demeanor and thick graying hair pulled back in a bun. She came out from behind her desk to welcome David and Jenny, and they settled as a threesome into a grouping of comfortable armchairs.

"Carla Klein has briefed me on your situation," she began, "and forwarded a copy of the client summary you gave her. Your succinct explanation of Marc's history seems to validate what Carla surmised – that Marc could be a substance abuser with a probable psychiatric diagnosis. He also sounds like a bright and talented young man. You two are doing exactly the correct thing in seeking education and advice from professionals."

"Carla talked about the importance of finding a hook to get Marc connected to an effective form of help. Needless to say, we haven't found it yet," David admitted.

"Help for Marc is tricky," Elspeth advised, "because he seems so far from understanding how his behavior impacts himself and others. You might ask Marc if his life is working for him. It's a blunt question, but it may help him examine his feelings a bit. If you see any recognition that he isn't okay with his life, offer to pay for therapy for a year, to work on whatever he sees as the issue."

"What if he denies that there's a problem, or says he's going to solve it himself?"

"Even if Marc isn't ready to accept help, you can certainly plant seeds by saying, 'I'm concerned.' When he starts blaming and denying, keep lobbing the ball back in his court, but gently, not in anger. He will no doubt try to put you on the defensive, but don't fall for it. It may be useful to point out that he may have a contributory medical condition – one he can't treat on his own.

"If you decide to start this conversation," Elspeth continued, "be sure to pepper it with praise about the things you love and are proud of in him. It can be very effective to say, 'Your life sounds so hard now, Marc. I really want to help make it easier.' The life of an addict *is* hard. He may be ready for some relief. I'm sure your intuition will tell you what is best."

"And if this approach goes nowhere?" David asked

"Then we should discuss an Intervention. You know what that is?"

"We've read about it," he replied.

"Good. The more research you do the better. This can be a major undertaking depending on how many times we meet to prepare and how many people are involved, but it's usually well worth the effort. In any event, it sounds like you are totally on the right track here."

Both David and Jenny felt better after the session. "I like her," Jenny said, "and I think that was useful. It's still not totally clear when and how we're going to proceed, but it feels good to know that help is readily available."

David and Marc spent a morning at the Museum of Modern Art, but David was reluctant to initiate a discussion in a public setting, and Marc didn't have time for lunch. "I've got a big paper due," he told his father, "and it's the whole grade so I'm gonna need to work on it for a couple of days."

"Since Marc isn't available, why not do some touring?" Jenny suggested. "Graham and Barbara are still in the middle of their move, but we haven't seen Jeff Stone in nearly two years, and I've never been to Los Angeles. We have a standing invitation to visit, and this seems an ideal time to do so!"

Jeff and his girlfriend Kelly lived in Pasadena. David and Jenny charted a course down I-5 past stock farms and flat fields until they crossed through a steep mountain pass and dropped down to the outskirts of Los Angeles. The trip took over six hours, with only the briefest of stops for lunch and David's cigarette breaks.

"From Shawmut, six hours of driving would have gotten us through Providence, New Haven, New York, Philadelphia and within striking distance of Maryland and Delaware," Jenny marveled. "It's beginning to sink in just how enormous California is."

Jeff and Kelly treated them to a home-cooked dinner followed by Kelly's special nutmeg cake. "I will personally introduce you to my favorite parts of LA," Jeff promised when David revealed that he and Jenny were considering California as a possible retirement setting. David and Jenny found the freeway system overwhelming, but their hosts did all the driving, so they were spared getting trapped in the wrong lane at sixty miles per hour. A day of intense sightseeing was topped by a visit to Jeff's favorite Chinese restaurant where they dined on short ribs wrapped in lotus leaves, fish baked in seaweed and a dessert specialty called eight-surprises rice pudding.

They plotted a different route back, exiting Los Angeles via Santa Monica. They spent a day in Santa Barbara, enjoying the old mission and the streets lined with citrus trees, heavy with oranges and lemons. "Maybe we should pick a few of those oranges and take them back to Marc," David suggested. "Students can always use extra food."

"Actually, that's a great idea. Let's find a nice woven basket. We can get something edible at each place we stop, and give Marc a 'care package' when we get back."

From Santa Barbara, they cut north to Solvang, a quaint mountain village filled with wine bars, and continued on to Paso Robles for some further wine tasting. They spent a night in San Luis Obispo, then drove through Gilroy, the garlic capitol of California. "We'd best roll up the windows," Jenny laughed, "or else Jack is going to wonder why his car smells so strongly of garlic!"

Once back in San Francisco, David checked in with Marc to see if he could take a break and come over for lunch. They settled instead on meeting at a little café near the campus. "Why don't you use it as a father-son opportunity," Jenny suggested. "I'll stay here and catch up on my e-mails."

At the top of her in-box was a note from Graham.

> *From: Graham*
> *To: Jenny; David*
> *Date: April 5, 2006*
> *Subject: Visit*
>
> Barbara and I have finally completed the move into our new townhouse in Santa Cruz, and we're ready and eager for guests. Rumor has it that you're considering a move to California, so you must come down as soon as possible! There's another unit up for sale in our complex. I'm attaching photos and specs. It would be absolutely fantastic if we could be neighbors!
>
> Love to you both – G.

David and Jenny agreed to a weekend visit to Santa Cruz. The evening before their departure, Marc joined them at the Pogues' house for dinner. Jenny added ribbons to a few of the food items they had gathered to make Marc's gift basket more festive and presented it to him as they finished dessert. "A few souvenirs from our trip to LA," Jenny smiled.

Marc seemed pleased at first, but then he held up a packet of macadamia nuts and commented on how expensive such things were. "Some people could eat for a week on what these cost," he said with a hint of disapproval in his tone. "I'll have to make sure none of this goes to waste. I'll get some good food storage containers as soon as I have some extra money."

To Jenny, the notion that Marc didn't have enough money for plastic containers was ludicrous. Jenny was searching for a diplomatic way to point this out when David pulled out his wallet, withdrew several twenties and handed them to Marc. Jenny looked at David in utter astonishment. He realized his error and tried to amend it with a clumsy attempt at humor. "Just make sure you spend that wisely. Don't go buying drugs with it."

Marc immediately went on the defensive. "Why do you think I'll buy drugs with it? I smoke weed, but I never do anything stronger. I've had friends die from that stuff. I don't touch that shit," he told David angrily. David was caught off guard.

"What do I have to do to make you believe me?" Marc insisted.

David had no ready answer. He hesitated, then tried to apply the language Elspeth Warrington had suggested. "It's just that your life seems really hard these days, Marc. We're concerned about whether your life is working for you, and we want to help."

"If you want to help, then stop treating me like a baby and mind your own f***ing business!"

The therapist had counseled that angry words were counterproductive, but Jenny couldn't control her thoughts. She had promised David she wouldn't intervene, but she was sorely tempted to tell Marc it would be easier to believe he wasn't an addict if he stopped behaving like one.

Marc turned heel and walked out, leaving the gift basket behind. David went after him, following him out to the street. Jenny stayed where she was. After about ten minutes, David returned alone.

"What happened?" Jenny asked softly.

"I apologized. I didn't know what else to do. I understand that we should avoid giving Marc cash, but the ban goes totally against my instincts. I find it very hard to think Marc would lie to me." He paused and took a deep breath, then continued in a calmer voice. "I told him we were worried about him, and since we didn't know how to help, we were clumsy sometimes in expressing our thoughts and feelings. I told him that I loved him no matter what he did, but that I hoped he would find a way to be at peace with himself and the world."

"I think we could use a little distance," Jenny suggested. "A few days in Santa Cruz will be good for us."

Before they left Saturday morning, David sent Marc a quick e-mail telling him of their Santa Cruz plans. "I'll leave a key under one of the geranium pots in case you want to come for your food basket," he added as a PS.

They took Route 1 south and enjoyed a spectacular oceanfront drive along the California coast. When they reached the Wells' townhouse, Barbara gave them a quick tour, then served coffee in the kitchen. As David and Jenny described their recent trip to Los Angeles, Barbara excused herself briefly and returned with a sheaf of printouts for available properties she had gotten from the broker who sold them their new home.

Jenny laughed as she glanced through the fliers. "Barbara, we're still processing the very idea of moving, and we're a long way from committing ourselves. Before we do, we need to get a feeling for different areas, check out neighborhoods, and explore the countryside. It doesn't make sense to look at actual houses."

"We have a great realtor," Barbara said, undeterred. "She'll drive us around tomorrow, and she can tell you everything you want to know about Santa Cruz."

"Barbara, no. It's crazy to spend time with realtors. We're just starting our research."

"But I've already booked her," Barbara countered. "She's sort of a personal friend, and she understands that you're at the very beginning of your house-hunting."

"We're at the very beginning of our *region*-hunting, not our *house*-hunting. I would feel badly wasting a realtor's time. You need to cancel the appointment."

Barbara appealed to David, but he shook his head. "Jenny's the boss," he said. Barbara reluctantly called the realtor's number and left a message asking her to call back.

Graham drove them all down to the harbor, about five minutes away. They watched sailboats coming in and out of the marina as they sat on a restaurant deck, eating seafood and chips.

"At the moment we're still working full time and commuting to Monterey," said Graham between bites of fried calamari, "but we hope to downshift soon to a shorter work week. We don't know many people in Santa Cruz, but we love the area, especially the amenities which abound thanks to the University. It's sort of Cambridge West," Graham declared. "Book stores, theatres, lectures, galleries, and restaurants galore."

"Plus tattooed street performers and lots of aging hippies," Barbara added.

After lunch, Graham took them to the opposite end of town for a walk along West Cliff Drive that featured, as the name suggested, cliffs overlooking the bay. The weather was lovely, and everyone they encountered looked healthy and happy, including the canines trotting alongside their owners. Their hosts were doing a good job selling Santa Cruz without having to say a word. The realtor called back as they were nearing the end of their walk. Barbara passed the phone to Jenny. "She wants to talk with you."

Jenny was not happy about the ambush and silently vowed to be absolutely firm. The realtor handled her objections with respect, reason and humor. By the time she hung up, they had confirmed the appointment with the proviso that they wouldn't waste time looking at specific properties.

The conversation over dinner turned to Marc. "I'm familiar with the history," Graham commented, "but it's disturbing to learn that Marc's behavior is becoming more volatile."

David recapped their meeting with Elspeth Warrington and described some of the resources that had been suggested. He also described the awkward confrontation with Marc over the food basket. "Unless Marc is willing to seek or accept professional help, we're at an impasse."

"What about a gift certificate to a workshop at Esalen?" Graham asked. "No one thinks of Esalen as a treatment center. It's a non-threatening environment. It would expose him to people who value openness and sharing, and who respect exploration, dialog and different kinds of therapy."

"He might accept it coming from you," said David, "but at the moment, anything we recommend is resented and rejected." With that, David rose from the dinner table to go out and smoke.

"Is it really as bad as it sounds?" Barbara asked after David left the room. "I don't begin to know Marc, but the few times I've met him he's been polite, even charming."

"He talks a good game," Jenny said, "but his behavior doesn't match his words. I've seen him be charming, too, but he basically views the world in hostile terms and defends himself against it with cunning and anger. He routinely blames others when things go wrong. Given our blowup of a few nights ago, it may take a while for the dust to settle."

"Ouch! That must be really tough on David – and you too."

"The hardest part is not knowing what to do. A gift certificate to Esalen seems like a great idea," Jenny added as David returned, "but I think it will need to be a back door approach. Marc loved a glass-blowing class he once took. If there were some workshop like 'Personal Growth Through Artistic Expression,' he might be willing to participate. If he became more trusting, it would improve his chances of seeking help."

"Do you want me to look into it?" Graham asked, turning to David. "I can get an Esalen catalog, and it would be easy to do a gift certificate. Actually, I think I missed Marc's last birthday. As his godfather, I owe him a present, so this could work out well."

David agreed that it was worth a try. "It certainly can't hurt," he commented later to Jenny as they climbed into bed.

After breakfast, Jenny and Barbara readied themselves for the arrival of the realtor. "Having given it careful thought," David announced, "I believe I can make a better contribution to our retirement research by checking out the local golf facilities than by driving around neighborhoods." Graham immediately suggested a nearby public course, and David happily set off to spend his day on the links. Graham also bowed out, pleading an overload of domestic projects, so the real estate tour was ladies only.

Jillian Rider picked up Jenny and Barbara at ten and drove them through Santa Cruz and several adjacent towns quadrant by quadrant. Given the Perrys' interests, she concentrated on locations near golf courses, farmers' markets and nice walking areas.

It was early afternoon by the time they completed the neighborhood tour. Jillian suggested lunch, "to give you a feel for some of our nice little cafés and coffee shops." They had no objection, so within two minutes Jillian pulled up at a homey bakery café. As they ate, she posed questions about Jenny's past, present and future.

As they debated dessert, Jillian looked at Jenny thoughtfully. "You know," she said, "if you have no other commitments, it might be a good idea to look at some specific properties after all. You've spent most of your life where houses are designed and constructed based on New England weather. You have the same situation in Geneva – a particular kind of architecture, design and materials. California houses are very different from what you guys are used to, and any photos I send aren't going to give you an accurate feel for that difference. I'd like to show you some interiors to get your reaction to light and layout. I know several houses that are empty and don't require an appointment. I've got keys, and we could just run in and out."

Jillian's logic was unassailable. Jenny and Barbara were enjoying the day and each other's company, and they agreed to her proposal. They walked through half a dozen houses. In each case, Jenny noted what she liked and what she didn't like.

"Well, that's been really helpful," the realtor concluded as they exited the last one on her list and climbed into her car. She started to put the key in the ignition, and then stopped, frowning slightly. "Can you handle one more house?" she asked. "I think I have a really good picture now of what you want, but I'd like to do a reality test to make sure I've got it right. There's a three-bedroom single-floor plan for sale the next town over. It's a little outside your price range, so I'm not suggesting it as a house you should seriously consider. I just want to make sure that what I'm picturing in *my* head and what you're picturing in *your* head are the same thing."

Again, the logic was unassailable. They drove to a mountainside community called Allenridge. Just minutes above Route 1, they passed through a wooded hollow and turned into a "no outlet" road that ended in a cul-de-sac with eight houses, set well back. The third on the left was a modest California ranch, painted moss green with black shutters. The entry opened into a living room featuring a wall of windows looking west. The dining area was backed by sliding glass doors and an expansive deck. There was a massive oak tree offering dappled shade from the afternoon sun.

Perfectly situated for observing sunsets, the deck looked out over a sloping back yard which was very private and desperately in need of a gardener. Jillian apologized for the garden's state of neglect, but Jenny considered this a plus. Barbara and Jenny looked at one another. "Do you want me to call Graham?" Barbara asked.

"It can't hurt for them to see it, and it will help Jillian to get David's take," Jenny rationalized.

"The owners put it on the market in February," Jillian told Jenny while Barbara talked to Graham. "They're eager to sell, and they just dropped the price by ten percent."

Within twenty minutes of Barbara's call, David and Graham were on their way. When he walked in, David immediately approved of the layout of the large open kitchen, and was particularly pleased by the deck and the sunset brewing over the far hill. Graham quietly beamed at David's obvious delight, hoping this might pre-empt any further research. Jenny, too, could see that David was happy with it. In a moment of insanity, she agreed to speak further with Jillian over the next two days.

That evening, David debriefed about his golf game. "What's mind-boggling is that this public course is one of the most beautiful and challenging I've ever been on," he declared. "There I was, surrounded by redwoods, with deer peeking out from the forest and no sign of civilization from any vantage point." Equally important, David enjoyed the people he played with. One was a realtor who extolled the virtues of Santa Cruz County. One was a high school teacher who assured David that the school system welcomed tutors and volunteers of all stripes. One was a watercolor enthusiast who gave classes in conjunction with a community artists' association. Though they were drawn together by pure chance, the three golf partners were a perfect fit with David's interests. "And the best thing is, they told me that they play all year round. All you need in January is a good sweater!"

"Would you give me your totally candid assessment of that house?" Jenny asked as she and David prepared for bed.

"Can we even afford it?" he queried.

"Probably not," she answered, "but I don't want to waste time and energy figuring that out unless you love the state, the community *and* the house."

"Well, I certainly like California. I like the energy, the diversity and the terrain. There's a lot that's new for me here, lots of things to explore, but there's also familiarity. Sandie and I were in San Francisco for over a year. Thanks to our recent travels, I now have a sense of both north and south. Plus, the Californians know how to make good wine and good cheese. Can't go wrong with that."

"So, no other state you'd rather have as home base?"

"Nope."

"And what about Santa Cruz? Think of everywhere else we've been: Mendocino, Sonoma, Sausalito, San Francisco, Pasadena, L.A., Santa Barbara, Paso Robles, San Luis Obispo. How does Santa Cruz compare?"

"You left out Gilroy, the garlic capitol," he said with a straight face.

Jenny raised her eyebrows.

"Okay, okay," he resumed. "Santa Cruz. I love that it's a university town. It's funky and independent and freewheeling. I trust everything Graham says about it in terms of amenities. I also like the location. San Francisco is close enough that we can easily see Marc, Jack, Bibi, etc. The airport run to San Jose is thirty-five minutes. That's the same as Shawmut to Logan. And finally, there's a fabulous year-round public golf course where I can play 18 holes for twenty-five bucks. Hard to beat."

"And Allenridge?"

"Nice house. Good kitchen. Great deck. I can almost see us sitting out there in our rocking chairs, sipping wine and watching the sun go down."

"Sweetie, please be serious. I have a mountain or two to move if we really want to consider this."

"I *am* being serious. I like it. It has neighbors close by but lots of privacy. Barbara says the town center has a mom-and-pop grocery, a county library branch and a pottery shop. I've always wanted to live near a pottery shop."

"David."

"And it would be fantastic to hang out with Graham and Barbara. Shades of our college days and the Ware Street apartment." His tone no longer had a joking edge. "And it might help to be near Marc instead of living on the other side of the continent."

"So, is it worth our considering a bid?

"You're the CPA, Good Lookin.' I'm just a poor retired schoolteacher. My earlier question stands: can we afford it?"

"I'm not sure yet, but it's a lot less than that houseboat we saw on Bibi's dock."

Jenny was wide-awake much of the night, her mind spinning. All things were possible, she believed, but pulling off a house purchase would involve, at a minimum, securing an immediate home equity loan on the Shawmut condo, and either finding a Boston renter post haste or taking a second mortgage on the Geneva house. They would be going way out on a limb in a precipitous juggling act. It was a bridge too far.

"I love the house and the neighborhood, but no matter how I look at this, I see it as a risky financial proposition and an extended logistical nightmare," Jenny told David over breakfast. "I'm good at finance, but I'm not a magician. How upset will you be if we pass?" she asked.

David was completely understanding. "We can always come back another time and look at properties then. Maybe we'll find one with a vineyard out back," he added hopefully.

"You wish," she replied.

Jenny called Jillian to relay their conclusion.

"No problem," Jillian responded. "If this were the only house of its kind for fifty miles, I'd argue with you, but now that I know what you want, I'm certain I can find something you'll love just as much when the time is right. Plus," she added, "the sellers' realtor told me that if it doesn't move soon, they may pull the house off the market for a few months, then try again. If you like, I can keep an eye on it for you."

Jenny happily accepted her suggestion. For the next two days, David and Jenny explored the territory they might one day call home. The nearby state parks abounded in ancient redwood groves, breathtaking vistas and hundreds of miles of trails. There were easy walking paths over high ocean cliffs with great spumes of spray rising several stories high as waves crashed upon the rocks below. They drove through the university campus, visited the arboretum with its otherworldly Australian and New Zealand plants, and wandered through downtown Santa Cruz, listening to street musicians, and enjoying sidewalk cafés reminiscent of Europe.

They planned to drive back up to San Francisco Wednesday morning, but Barbara persuaded them to stay for the afternoon farmers' market held in the center of town.

When they got there, Jenny found herself regretting that she hadn't brought a camera. The market was a cornucopia, overflowing with variety, color and abundance. "This is amazing!" David said, shaking his head in disbelief. "This is better than Geneva!"

"It's hard to leave," Jenny told Graham as they readied themselves for a return to San Francisco.

"It was wonderful to be with you two so much!" Graham responded. "And the idea that you might come and live parts of the year in Santa Cruz is just, well, fantastic! I should have some concrete thoughts on Esalen seminars within the next week or so," he added turning to David. "We'll talk then."

David contacted Marc when they got back. The conversation was without rancor, and David arranged a father-son get-together the following afternoon. Marc had not collected the gift basket in their absence. After mulling it over with Jenny, David decided to take it with him to their meeting.

"I think you've made the right decision," Jenny said. "It may help spark a conversation. Even if Marc chooses not to comment, you'll know, assuming he accepts it, that you have a truce of sorts."

"It went well," David reported when he returned. "We checked out a bunch of galleries and had a nice time. He's coming over tomorrow night for dinner. I told him how impressed we were by Santa Cruz, and laid a little groundwork for his visiting Graham. So we'll see. We still have another week here. I think we just have to play this one day at a time."

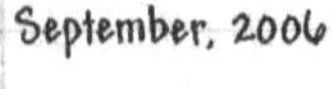
September, 2006

Small Talk

"With young people
Where do you draw the line?"
She asked him, making small talk
While waiting
For the youngsters' dance to end,
But stressing line.

In his mind, accentuating you instead,
He answered, "In the sand at night;
The waves erase all trace
Long before daylight."

Chapter 12

Much as she had enjoyed seeing Bibi and their other California friends, Jenny was delighted to be back in Boston. The yard was filled with daffodils, and the azaleas were in bloom. "I'm going to spend the whole day outdoors playing in the dirt," she announced to David as she pulled on her gardening clothes.

"Would you come look at this first?" David asked, calling her over to his computer in a subdued tone.

Oh god, she thought. *What now?*

> *De: Delphine*
> *A: Dad; Jenny*
> *Envoyé: 28 avril, 2006*
> *Objet: No jobs!!!*
>
> I am totally discouraged!!! I've been to every museum and art institution in Paris since I got back, and I haven't found a job yet. Everyone wants someone who already has experience! I'm living on the Geneva rent money, but after I pay my bills, there isn't even enough for a cup of coffee. This is such a bummer. I hate being a grown-up!
>
> Any ideas?
>
> Love, D.

"Can we wire her some money?" David asked.

"Can we? Yes. But should we? To her credit, she's asked for ideas, not money."

"She's already been to all the museums and galleries. What new ideas can we give her?"

"It seems to me that she's been going at this head-on – which is fine – but since that hasn't worked, she should consider some sideways and back-door approaches. There are a lot of indirect routes to landing a job that she may not have considered. What if I share some simple thoughts on job-hunting? I might even be able to package my suggestions to help Marc as well. If my advice is officially aimed at Dellie, Marc might consider it with a more open mind. This could be a chance to generate some useful exchange between the siblings."

David gave a reluctant assent, and approved Jenny's lengthy reply.

From: JWLongworth
To: Delphine
Cc: DavidP; Marc
Date: April 28, 2006
Subject: Re: No Jobs!!!

Dear Dellie –

I'm about to give you a lot of advice. Think of it as coming from an objective financial professional rather than a busybody stepmother.

The job of your dreams will not simply be handed to you. You may have to take jobs you don't like. You may have to put in a 60-hour workweek. You may have to forego entertainments that you've taken for granted in the past.

Your father was a garbage collector at Yosemite as a teenager, and he cleaned toilets as part of the dorm crew when he was at Harvard. He worked as a bus boy and a hotel night clerk when he first moved to Paris. It was an odd pathway, but ultimately it led him to a life he loved.

You want a career in art history, and your long-range plan of getting an MA and a PhD is a good one. Meanwhile, look at anything and everything that might help you afford that cup of coffee. You take it for granted, but your bilingualism is an incredibly valuable asset. Check out businesses that cater to English-speaking clients: tour guides, hotels, English bookstores. Go see if the American or British embassy needs a receptionist.

Post ads at the American University for personal services like dog-walker or babysitter. And while you're looking for work, accept the fact that you may have to forego café visits for a while.

Being a father and seeing the child within you, David wants you and Marc to have a pair of water wings before entering the pool. I see you as adults and believe that you've had some good swimming lessons already. It's time to jump into the deep end. Learn to live within your means and accept the compromises that may involve.

Most of all, believe in yourself. You'll get there.

Love, Jenny

To their surprise, the first response David and Jenny received was from Marc rather than Delphine.

From: Marc
To: Dad
Cc: Jenny; Delphine
Date: April 29, 2006
Subject: salut

i got you guys e-mail with delphine which i am still digesting. she's having a tuff time, but, i guess we all need to go through it. we both decide to leave geneva, for one thing, because we were given the chance to, but without, perhaps realizing the delicate and difficult task it might be.

i on my side am still struggling, i put myself in a difficult situation in the past 5 years, but i learned, i hope? and soon i try to make it out on my own, like the rest of this planet. work odd jobs and stay focused on what i would really do, don't give up, that's all i'm left with. it might take a long time, but i'll get there, so will delphine. i to would like to attend school again, maybe in a year or so, keep focused and willing to sacrifice.

je vous embrasse tous.

ciao marc

"It looks as if Marc absorbed at least some of the advice directed at Dellie," Jenny commented. "He also admits that his 'difficult situation' is one he put himself into. Maybe there is light at the end of the tunnel after all!"

"It certainly does seem like positive progress," David said hopefully.

There was silence on Delphine's end, which left her father increasingly nervous. After several days with no response to Jenny's memo, David sent Delphine a worried note asking how she was doing.

"*Two* jobs!" Delphine exulted when her father answered the phone the next morning. "I have *two* jobs!"

"You found two jobs in the space of one week?"

Jenny's ears perked up when she heard David's query. "Is that Dellie?" she mouthed.

David nodded. The conversation shifted to French, then David held out the phone to Jenny. "Delphine wants to talk to you."

"Congratulations!" Jenny said.

"Thanks! It worked! It really worked. I never thought of my English as an asset, but you were right. There's a bilingual school just two blocks away that runs a summer kindergarten, and they want me to be a teacher's assistant. And there's a gallery in Montmartre that needs extra help on weekends for all the American tourists. Two jobs! I'm gonna be rich!"

"Excellent," Jenny laughed. "Next time we come over, you can treat *us* to coffee!"

When the call was finished, Jenny gave David a hug. "See?" she smiled. "Dellie's disaster of last week has turned into a blessing!"

May was a glorious month. Jenny's gardens exploded with color. David took advantage of the mild weather to investigate local farmers' markets and wine shops, and they regularly invited friends over to partake of his cooking.

"Who needs to go to France when I have my very own French chef right here in my kitchen," Jenny teased.

"Speaking of which," David replied, "we need to figure out when we're going back to Europe, and where we want to go."

"How long a trip are you considering?"

"Several months, I should think. We need to spend some serious time in the center of the universe," David announced.

"Paris? Several months in Paris seems like overkill. Maybe we should explore a bit."

"We *will* explore," he corrected. "I'm talking about Italy. Paris is the *other* center of the universe. I want to introduce you to the Amalfi peninsula."

"Okay, but before we book anything, we should find out what happens if Marc gets his degree at the end of the summer semester," Jenny advised. "If there is a graduation event, we need to organize our travel around it."

David called to find out how Marc was doing and to pose Jenny's question.

"I don't care about my graduation paper," Marc told him. "It's not worth anything so I might as well burn it right there if they have a ceremony. Once I leave here the Trust money stops, and I'll be out on the street."

David's careful probing revealed that Marc was discouraged by the cost of the glass-blowing programs he looked at. "I don't know what I can do to make money enough to live on and go to class and pay for school at the same time. Delphine sells her English in France, but how do I sell my French here in America, where nobody speaks it and people think they are so much superior to anybody European."

"You have the Geneva rent money to help you with the basics," David reminded him. "Also, most schools have scholarship programs, and you could apply for a student loan."

"But then you owe the government money, and I don't want to pay for their wars and support their super-power ego. Anyway, I'm not very career-oriented. I don't need a fancy degree. I just want to do my art."

They sparred for another minute, and then Marc asked if his father could give him an open-ended loan of a thousand dollars "kind of like a graduation present."

From the next room, Jenny heard David slowly speak the line they had rehearsed months before. "Marc, I need to think about that. I'll consider it and get back to you."

Marc has to be asking for money.

"What happened?" Jenny pressed when David hung up.

"Don't even ask," he said, shaking his head. He sat down at his computer and started typing:

De: David
A: Marc
cc: Jenny; Delphine
Envoyé: 1 juin, 2006
Objet: Your request

Dear Marc –

You told me that you are not very career-oriented. So be it if you can make a living in another way (preferably legal for your own good.) Well, I am not very loan-oriented because I'm not a good-enough banker to get the money back. You have never paid back a loan spontaneously, and I've never felt the time was right to ask for it. This cannot continue because it is wearing me down. I don't think I have ever refused to give you money when you said you needed it, but the time has come.

You have to find ways to make it on your own even if you don't like what you have to do in the beginning. That's one of the major inconveniences of being an adult. There are things I don't like, but I do them because I want to continue doing the things I *do* like to do.

I'm very down. I have a problem I cannot solve: my own failure to help you be independent. You seem unable to take care of yourself, and I don't understand why. I worked every summer starting at age fourteen. I worked part time all through college. I worked fulltime after that, doing odd jobs at first and finally finding my career. I worked non-stop until I retired.

I want to give up and say figure it out yourself. Jenny may have some ideas, but those are my thoughts. That is my decision.

I love you very much. Dad

When Jenny read the e-mail, she was impressed by David's blunt words. *But how do I deal with his closing comment? I've exhausted my store of ideas. I can only say what I've said before. I believe Marc needs a therapist to deal with his negativism. Without professional help, he's going nowhere.*

It took nearly a week before Marc telephoned his reply. The conversation was in French. Jenny couldn't fit the pieces together, but David's tone was calm and sympathetic. When he finally hung up, David looked at Jenny. His eyes were moist, but he was smiling.

"'How beautiful upon the mountains,'" he said quietly.

Jenny wasn't religious, but she knew the bible as literature.

"'Are the footsteps of the bearer of glad tidings,'" she said, continuing the verse. She watched David's face carefully.

"Yes," he nodded. "Marc admits that his life is a mess. He knows he needs to do something to straighten it out, but he isn't sure where to begin."

"He just did," Jenny replied. "He just *did* begin, with that phone call and that admission. This is fantastic, David! We should contact Elspeth Warrington right this minute and see what she recommends."

"Yes, definitely a breakthrough," Elspeth concluded when Jenny described David's e-mail and Marc's call. "My suggestion is that David talk with Marc and arrange for him to come see me. You can tell him that I am already familiar with your family and your situation, and the purpose of the visit is to apprise him of the different resources available. Tell him that you will pay for therapy for a full year, assuming it's indicated. Can you handle that?"

"We'll handle whatever is needed," Jenny answered.

"I'll cover all the options, but the best treatment for Marc in the city right now may be the old tried-and-true Haight Ashbury Clinic. I also have the name of an urban-earthy guy who I think would be an excellent therapist for Marc. He has a lot of experience with recovery and dual-diagnosis – mental health and addiction. I would be perfectly willing to work with Marc myself, and I will offer that possibility, but he might do better with a fellow male."

Following Elspeth's advice, David strove to break down Marc's resistance to professional counselors. "You said you weren't sure where to begin. We think meeting with Elspeth Warrington is the starting point. You might also talk with Graham. You view him as your godfather and family friend, but he's also a professional therapist, and you can be sure he has your best interests at heart."

Marc finally agreed to see Elspeth and said he might contact Graham as well. David quickly sent Graham a heads-up.

> *De: David*
> *A: Graham*
> *Envoyé: 10 juin, 2006*
> *Objet: Miracles*
>
> Marc called yesterday saying he wants to straighten out his life. We have a good contact in San Francisco, Elspeth Warrington, whom Marc has agreed to see, but I also suggested he get in touch with you for ideas about programs. If the Esalen option is still open, this may be the time to go for it.
>
> Thanks in advance for anything you can do. David

"How do you want to play the summer travel plans?" Jenny asked.

"I think we should stay in the States for now, to see how things go. I want to be here for Marc in case he needs us. Italy can wait."

Jenny made a silent wish. *I hope that Marc will someday justify the faith his father has in him.*

Out loud, she offered compensation. "We can always consider local travel. My siblings would love to have us spend time in Maine. Or we could go to the Cape. Ross and Kevin just bought a little condo in Provincetown. And if you're homesick for the sound of French, we could always drive up to Montreal or Quebec."

"All possible, but frankly, I think we've earned some time free of obligations and itineraries. It might be nice to just kick back in Boston and do nothing for a while."

Two days after a stunning display of Fourth of July fireworks over the Charles River, Jenny was out on the patio pulling weeds when David called her into the house.

"Can you pickup the extension? Elspeth's on the phone."

"I'm speaking to you with your son's consent," Elspeth clarified. "We are arranging a psychiatric evaluation to see if Marc is suffering from bipolar disorder. Many of his behavioral issues are consistent with bipolar disorder symptoms – unpredictable periods of aggression and anger, moodiness, inattention, and so on. The evaluation may take a while, and it's difficult to make a confident diagnosis when substance abuse is present, so we'll be working on multiple fronts. Marc has agreed to contact your family physician in Geneva to obtain a full medical history. Meanwhile, I have a question. Did Marc ever have a childhood head injury that might have gone unreported to his doctor? A bad spill from a bike, or falling down stairs? Or maybe a sports injury?"

"Not that I can recall," David replied. "He played the usual school sports, but I don't remember any injury beyond scuffed knees and a sprained ankle. Why do you ask?"

"Since there doesn't seem to be obvious manic behavior, I wondered whether we might be dealing with a TBI – traumatic brain injury."

"Is there any indication that that's the case?"

"My inquiry is speculative at the moment, and frankly, this is a new area for neuroscience. The frontal cortex doesn't reach full development until a person's early-to-mid-twenties. It's a critical part of the brain, where executive functions like planning, self-control and abstract thinking take place. People whose frontal lobe has been damaged can exhibit poor planning and organizational skills, depression, impulsive behavior, frustration, distractibility – in short, problems similar to those experienced by bipolar patients. So we want to take a look at that possibility."

"Jeezus!" was David's only comment.

"Is there anything we can do from here?" Jenny asked.

"Just keep doing what you're doing. Stay in touch with Marc regularly, talk with him about what's happening, and be good listeners. Do some research into bipolar disorder, and also read about TBI. So long as I have Marc's authorization, I'm available to you as well. If you're worried about something, don't hesitate to give me a call."

Elspeth's open invitation proved immediately useful. Jenny was back in touch the following day. "We have a good friend, Ross Barrett, who does volunteer work with at-risk kids here in Boston. When we gave him an update on Marc, I mentioned your question about traumatic brain injury. He said we should also consider the possibility that Marc's early drug use could have impaired his development. 'It's like crack babies or kids with fetal alcohol syndrome,' he said, 'only in those cases, the developmental damage happens during pregnancy. But I see kids at the community center who are poisoning themselves with drugs that can trap them in a state of permanent emotional immaturity, even if they later quit.'"

"We'll certainly explore that," Elspeth reassured Jenny. "Once Marc trusts us enough to share the details of his earlier life, we'll have more to work with."

Marc began regular sessions with a psychiatrist, and also asked to continue meeting with Elspeth.

"I'm glad to hear that," Jenny remarked when David told her. "I like her. Maybe she represents the sympathetic mother figure whom Marc has missed so much," she speculated.

From Paris, Delphine sent word that she had been invited to stay on for the full academic year at the bi-lingual school where she was working. "It's a way to make a living until I can position myself to enter an MA program," she wrote, but she clearly liked her job and was enjoying her independence.

Trusting that Marc was in good hands, David and Jenny dared to relax. For David, that meant hosting picnics and barbecues. The social calendar was reminiscent of a busy summer in Geneva, but all the events were in English so Jenny was able to enjoy them more.

For Jenny, relaxing meant spending as much time in the garden as possible. The goldfinches had arrived and were feeding on the seed heads of the daisies. Hummingbirds worked the array of flowers in the beds near the front porch.

Their summer idyll was enhanced by good news from California.

"Looks like I'm finally going to graduate," Marc reported mid-August. "I passed my exams, and I have enough credits for a BA degree."

"Will there be a graduation ceremony?" David asked.

"Nah, they just mail you the diploma. They do a big ceremony every May, and I could show up for that next year, but I don't see the point. It's just a huge crowd and a whole lot of people shuffling on and off a stage."

"Well, we'd certainly like to do something to celebrate," his father said. "When Delphine graduated, we went to Paris and took her to lunch at Laserre. How about if we fly to San Francisco and take you to Chez Panisse or wherever you want to go? We could invite Jack and Janet Pogue to join us if you'd like. Or maybe drive down to Santa Cruz? I'm sure Graham and Barbara would love to be in on the congratulations."

"Yeah, but it'll depend on my job. Since I'm new, I can't take any time off yet."

The job was news. Marc had used his French to win employment at a specialty food store selling imported French cheese. "I kinda feel like I'm pretending, really hamming it up with my accent, but one of the other guys is French too, and it impresses the customers when they hear us yakking away *en français*."

"We'll check into flights and get back to you," David said. "*Félicitations* on the job! Love ya, Kid."

As soon as the conversation was over, Jenny got out the calendar. "How about right after Labor Day weekend?" she suggested. "Go for ten days, perhaps? Or should we do two whole weeks? We want enough time to do whatever Marc wants to do, plus I'd like to talk with Elspeth again, and maybe meet Marc's psychiatrist."

"Let's keep it under ten days unless Marc needs us to stay longer. I'd love to get to back to Europe before too long, and October would be an ideal time to go to Italy."

They headed for the west coast and again accepted the hospitality of Jack and Janet Pogue. David called Marc while Jenny unpacked, and he arranged a brunch meeting for the three of them the following day.

Marc appeared in blue jeans and an old sweater, sporting a jaunty French beret. They chatted about inconsequential matters until the food arrived. Marc seemed genuinely pleased that his father had come to see him.

When David asked about the therapy sessions, there was no apparent defensiveness in Marc's reply. "It's kinda interesting. I always wanted life to be flowing like a stream, making its way down a gentle slope, but all the times it hasn't worked that way, I used to get angry, and I had to make all kinds of hell-raising and emotion-destructing to get back at it. I was sorta like throwing rocks at the ocean to stop the tide. I can see now that it didn't work, and I threw out my shoulder in the process."

David suddenly looked alarmed.

"No, no, I didn't *really* throw it out," Marc explained. "It's just that I was, like, hurting myself and not getting anywhere."

"How are things with the apartment and your new roommate?" Jenny asked. "Do you like him?"

"Him is actually a her," Marc said shyly. "Her name is Olivia."

The color rising in Marc's cheeks suggested that Olivia was more than just a new roommate.

"How did you meet?" David asked. "What does she do?"

"I met her at school. She was teaching a pottery class for the extension program. She's a ceramic artist, and she has a small studio in Oakland that she shares with two other potters. Thanks to her," he summed up, "I've been able to keep my head on my shoulders."

Their schedule was too tight to include travel to Santa Cruz, but Graham and Barbara came up for lunch in San Francisco. They also made time to spend an afternoon with Bibi in Sausalito. The most important meeting on their calendar, however, was a session with Elspeth Warrington.

"At some point, we'd like to meet with Marc's psychiatrist too," David said as they settled into chairs in Elspeth's office. "Is it okay to call him directly, should Marc set this up, or do we do this through you?"

"I anticipated this and spoke with Dr. Hanford prior to your coming here today. He would be delighted to meet you, but he doesn't feel it's appropriate to discuss the work he's doing with Marc. At this stage, you have to trust and respect his judgment."

"But you share information with us. Can't Dr. Hanford do the same?"

"I'm a family counselor, and I deal with your family as a unit. I also have Marc's consent to discuss his issues and his progress, within the limits he sets. So, with that in mind, let's talk about where we are. The diagnosis that is emerging is that Marc's early drug use has interfered with the normal development of the part of the brain that governs self-monitoring, organizing skills, future planning, and so on. Drugs and alcohol can interrupt the brain's maturation process during adolescence, and cause long-range problems with social, occupational and executive functioning"

David was taken aback, but also skeptical. "You're saying that this happened just because he smoked pot as a teenager?"

"There was a good deal more than marijuana use, but even 'just' pot can be damaging in sufficient quantities. What moved him to substance abuse at a young age is something he's working on with Dr. Hanford. What I want to talk about with you is the nature of the damage."

David slowly shook his head, his eyes directed downward toward tightly clasped hands.

"I can see that you're distressed," Elspeth said gently. "What are you thinking?"

"I can't believe he lied to me," David replied, his voice barely above a whisper.

"You're not alone," Elspeth noted sympathetically. "There are scores if not hundreds of studies indicating that children routinely lie to their parents, yet very few parents find this easy to accept. Childhood mendacity is absolutely normal behavior – a survival tactic if you will – based on instinct. Children are dependent on their parents, and they want to keep in their good graces. They lie to avoid negative consequences. Lying is perceived by a young child as a safe and reasonable response, giving the adults the answer they want to hear. In an older child, lying can also be an indication that he or she is struggling with a stressful situation or environment. It's a sort of coping mechanism, a way to get control of something the child can't otherwise handle. I can refer you to some helpful literature on the subject if you wish."

David said nothing, but Jenny indicated acceptance of the offer.

"The more difficult issue before you," Elspeth continued, "is that Marc will never 'recover' whatever development was blocked or skewed. At one level, he recognizes that many of his peers have a capacity he lacks, or that he possesses only in limited quantities. This recognition will help him address his past tendency to erupt when frustrated that he couldn't handle certain responsibilities or pressures as well as his peers. But the fact remains that in certain behavioral areas, his responses will be adolescent rather than adult. He will find it difficult to break down tasks into logical sequences. He will misjudge the time or materials needed to complete a project. He'll be reactive rather than proactive. To use non-technical language, he's a bright young man, but he will sometimes behave like a scatterbrain.

"At one level, he now understands the neurological basis for this. At another level, because he can't actually perceive the deficit, he remains at risk of repeating the behavior that gets him into trouble. People with brain deficits are often unaware that there's anything wrong with them."

"So now what?" Jenny asked.

"I'd like to schedule a session with all three of you in the same room. How long are you here for?"

"We fly back to Boston on Sunday, the seventeenth," Jenny told her. "After that, we're hoping to go to Italy for a few months."

"When will you return to California?"

"We haven't looked that far ahead," David interjected, "but nothing is written in stone. If you need us to spend some time here, we'll do it."

"Let me consult with Dr. Hanford and with Marc. We're not involved in a ten-meter dash. Therapy is a slow process. Are you going to be back in the US for Christmas?"

"We certainly can be. We can be wherever we need to be if it will help Marc," David replied.

"I don't think you have to turn your lives upside down right this minute, but that's helpful to know. And I don't think I'm out of bounds when I say that Marc seems to really appreciate your support and encouragement."

They returned to Boston with reassurances from Elspeth that the suggested family counseling session could comfortably wait until Christmas, giving Marc more leeway to progress at his own pace. The possibility of a trip to Italy quickly moved to the foreground. They searched the Internet and found a listing for a restored villa in Ravello, nestled into a cliff face overlooking the Mediterranean.

"Ravello will be an ideal base of operations," David promised. "There are dozens of great day trips we can do from there."

Jenny booked the rooms and then tackled the plane tickets. "Do we want to go straight to Rome, or should we fly in and out of Paris and spend a few days with Dellie on either end?"

"In and out of Paris," was the answer.

Jenny made plane reservations and put them on twenty-four hour hold so David could run the timing by Delphine. "I'm sure this'll be fine," he said as he e-mailed the details to his daughter. "This is going to be a great trip!"

The following morning, Jenny was about to head out to the garden when David called her back. "I spoke too soon," he told her. "You'd better come read this."

"Oh god, David, what's happened? Is it Marc? Dellie?"

He shook his head. "Just read it," he said.

> *From: Jillian Rider*
> *To: David Perry; Jenny Longworth*
> *Date: September 20, 2006*
> *Subject: Your House*
>
> The house you liked so much in Allenridge is back on the market. The owner has dropped the price another ten percent. Are you still interested in moving to California?
>
> Best, Jillian

Relief flooded through her, but Jenny was still shaken by the content of the e-mail. "You had me scared to death, David. I thought there'd been a disaster or something. But even so, this is nuts! This is absolutely nuts."

David observed her reaction but made no comment.

"Okay, let's think about this rationally," she said finally.

David poured himself some coffee and fixed Jenny a fresh cup of tea.

She looked at her watch. "If it's ten a.m. here, it's only seven a.m. in California. Jillian obviously sent this last night. No point calling back until at least nine her time. That gives us two hours – but is that time enough to make a decision?"

"I guess we'll find out," David shrugged. "And it's not as if she gave us a deadline."

They went outside and sat in the morning sunshine. The wild turkeys put in an appearance, emerging from the woods and crossing Sandie's memorial garden in a stately procession.

Jenny took a deep breath. "The critical question," she began, "is whether we still feel the same about Allenridge now that we have a little distance – and now that Shawmut is at its most beautiful. You have to admit, there's nothing like fall in New England."

"Granted," he agreed, "but I'd like to be nearer to Marc, and Allenridge seems ideal. How about you?" he countered.

"I'm game to try California. I like the concept of us having a fresh start. I think it's a good idea for us to define together the ideal community and the ideal house – not yours, not mine, but *ours*. Even so, I face the same issues with my condo that you faced with the house in Morion. I don't want to sell. I want the option of returning if circumstances warrant it."

"Can we do both?" David asked.

"We can *own* both, if that's what you mean, but I'll have to rent out the condo full time to keep us in the black."

They talked for another half an hour. "I can't believe how bad the timing is. If we'd known about this while we were in San Francisco, we could have gone down and taken a second look at that house. We've only seen it once, and then we were looking at it more as tourists than as serious buyers."

"If you were to look at it again, what would you focus on?" asked David.

Jenny frowned, summoning up her memory of the house. "I don't remember anything negative, at least nothing that would give me pause. Little things like fixtures and outlets can always be changed. So can appliances. The only thing that would scare me off is a major structural problem. And you?"

"Same," he answered simply.

"I'm still struggling with the timing, though," she reiterated. "This will blow the Italian trip. I should be able to cancel the Ravello booking without penalty, but you've been looking forward to this for so long!"

"The Amalfi Peninsula has been there for thousands of years. It'll wait for us," he replied calmly.

They finally decided to make an offer contingent upon a passing grade from the housing inspector. "We'll leave the rest in the hands of fate," David concluded.

Jenny called her bank to initiate an equity line of credit on the condo. At noon in Boston – nine o'clock in California – she rang

Jillian. A month later, after a steady stream of phone calls and faxed documents, they were the proud owners of a house in California.

David phoned Marc to give him the word, sent an e-mail to Delphine, and then called Graham.

Jenny's first call was to Bibi.

"I'm sending out a general report, but I wanted you to get the news in person. The Allenridge house is now officially ours."

"You did it! Oh, this is fantastic! Mazeltov! I'm so excited that we'll be on the same side of the country. When will you make the move?"

"It depends on how quickly I can organize everything on this end. We're going to rent out the condo in Shawmut, just as we did with the house in Geneva. This will allow us to experience life in California without burning any bridges. I'll keep you updated on the timing. I can't wait to show you the house!"

"And I can't wait to see it. Plus, once you're here, it will be easier for me to convince you to do your book!"

"Bibi, you are relentless. A novel is a fun fantasy, but it was the powerful reality of my experience that inspired me to write the original memoir. There's a lot of good fiction already available. I don't feel it's my life's purpose to add to it. I think learning how to garden in a climate with no winter and very little rain is going to be my major focus. If California's weather is as glorious as everyone insists, why on earth would I stay indoors, typing away on a computer?"

From: JWLongworth
To: Friends & Family
cc: DavidP
Date: October 27, 2006
Subject: California, here we come!

It's done! We have bought a house in Allenridge, CA, about ninety minutes south of San Francisco. We will be next to Santa Cruz and near both the University and Cabrillo Community College, offering all sorts of cultural opportunities. The oceanfront is dramatic and accessible, and the house is on the edge of the

> mountains with lots of wildlife, redwood forests and conservation land. There are vineyards galore, several golf courses in easy range and at least three farmers' markets that we know of. We love Boston, but New England winters aren't great for golf, so we're going to see what West Coast life is like. Will send more details when we get there. Y'all come visit!
>
> Much love, David & Jenny

Drawing on their Geneva experience, Jenny found a Boston management firm to screen tenants and take care of maintenance issues not handled by her condominium association. There were administrative details to address, but there was little clutter to dispose of, since Jenny's plan was to empty her unit and ship the contents to California. When she was sure everything was under control, she contracted for the moving van and committed them to a departure the day after Thanksgiving.

Their last afternoon in Shawmut, Jenny glanced up to track a bird's flight and spotted a high patch of shimmering rainbow hovering below a backdrop of wispy mares' tails. It was directly overhead and was amorphous rather than a classic arc. There was no rain. She called out to David to come look at it.

"I've never seen one before, but I think it's what they call a sundog," he speculated.

That night Jenny had a complex and vivid Sandie dream. When Sandie first appeared, Jenny was standing on a high perch – a ladder or balcony – looking down at David, who in turn was looking up at her. A romantic song was playing, and David and Jenny mouthed the words at each other, being too far apart to hear clearly. David then faded out, and Sandie's presence became more pronounced, in a smattering of scenes bearing no apparent connection. She joined Jenny and a few other women at a table, maybe at a teashop, since they were eating light fare and chatting. She looked great. The image in the dream was almost certainly drawn from a photo Jenny had recently come across featuring a windblown Sandie on Lem's sailboat in Maine.

The women in the dream were amazed that Sandie was alive. "I'm still very weak," she reported, "and I have to take lots of medicine." They all discussed her treatment. Jenny was curious as to why Sandie had chosen to let people believe she was dead. Then, Sandie had to leave to catch a bus. Jenny offered to walk her to the station, in part to help her and in part to talk about David. Sandie had difficulty walking so Jenny gave Sandie her arm. She still had trouble moving.

"Would you like me to carry you?" Jenny asked.

"Yes," Sandie replied. Jenny picked Sandie up and cradled her like a small child. She weighed almost nothing. Jenny knew she would have no trouble carrying her. Then she woke up.

When Jenny told David about the dream, he gave her an odd look. "I guess that means Sandie is coming to California with us after all," he said smiling. He put his arms around Jenny and drew her to him for a long hug.

The moving van came early in the morning. The cleaning contractor stopped by at noon for a set of keys. Jenny did a final walk around her gardens, then got into the car and watched Shawmut disappear from view as they headed for the expressway and the airport.

To her surprise and relief, she felt no qualms. *I can always come back if I need to,* she realized.

They arrived in California well ahead of the van, stopping first in San Francisco to see Marc.

"We're at Jack and Janet Pogues' today and tomorrow," Jenny told Bibi. "Then we head to Santa Cruz where we'll stay with Graham and Barbara until our furniture arrives. You have to come down and see us as soon as we're settled in."

"How long will you stay put? Will you be here through the winter holidays?"

"Definitely. We'll have both the kids with us for our first Christmas in Allenridge. Italy is on hold until next spring."

"So Dellie will come over from Paris?"

"Yes. She has two weeks vacation, and she seems excited by the prospect of sunshine and warm weather. I'm hoping, if she enjoys her California visit, that she'll come to the States for graduate school. She wants an advanced History of Art degree, and there are some great programs on this side of the Atlantic."

"And how's progress with Marc?"

"Things are going well. Elspeth has been enormously helpful. We all like her, including Marc. She doesn't mince words, but she's very supportive. She believes there's a developmental deficit, but she takes a very positive view. 'So long as there is understanding and a good attitude,' she said, 'impulsive behavior can turn into spontaneity, and unstructured thinking can become creativity. Brain development during adolescence is the basis of a person's transition into adulthood. Given the history, Marc isn't likely to become a multi-tasking executive, but he could be a great sci-fi writer, a sculptor, or a painter. You may have a wonderful artist in the making.'"

"And what's with the girlfriend. You've met her?"

"Olivia. Yes"

"Good news? Bad news?"

"Oh, definitely good I think. Olivia shares Marc's interests, so there's a lot of commonality, but she's also very focused – very grounded. She's a good example of a healthy balance of work and play."

"Says the workaholic Yankee!"

"I used to be a workaholic, Bibi, but David has corrupted me. Life is now dominated by French cuisine, fine wine and the pleasures that await us in Allenridge."

The moving van was still three days away when they shifted to Santa Cruz. Graham and Barbara gave them house keys so they could come and go as they wished. They spent the days exploring. David's evening reports sounded like a tourist bureau ad.

"I initially approached California with certain prejudices," he admitted, "but I was completely wrong. This place is amazing. The weather is glorious, the people are friendly and helpful, and I've already found three organizations looking for volunteer language teachers."

His greatest enthusiasm was for the markets, the freshness and flavor of the produce, and the variety of offerings. "I stopped at a stall to see if they had fish collars. Their selection was fabulous, and I came away with the fisherman's phone number. He said to call him whenever I want something special, and he'll reserve it for me right off the boat!"

David's e-mails to Europe spilled over with compliments for their new home. "It's a dream come true," he wrote in French. "*Une ambience superbe*! We are ten minutes from the ocean, five minutes from deep redwood forests, and the markets have an abundance you cannot imagine. I can't even begin to describe the fish. *Incroyable*!"

When their furniture arrived from Boston, they officially took up residence. Graham and Barbara brought over Greek take-out for their first dinner in their new home. They were surrounded by boxes, but their kitchen counter displayed half a dozen different bottles of wine, all from the Santa Cruz Mountains.

"*Some* people unpacked today," Jenny explained to Barbara, "and *some* people went wine tasting."

"*Some* people insist on boxes being unpacked in a particular order," David countered, "and *some* people have the good sense to get out of the way and take care of making sure we have something to drink."

He went on to wax eloquent about the profusion of wineries and showed Graham the brochures he had picked up about local wine tours and tasting events.

"You're like a little kid on Christmas morning," Graham chuckled.

"And what about you?" Barbara asked. "Are you as thrilled as David is?"

"Well, so far, I love the setting – the open space, the ocean, the forests, the clean air – but I've been reading about the water restrictions. Having grass or water-guzzling plants is pretty irresponsible, if not an outright violation of the Water Department rules."

Jenny led Barbara out on the deck to underscore the challenge she faced. The back yard was filled with thistles, poison oak and blackberry brambles. "I'm going to research drought-resistant native plants, but I know nothing about them. If all I can do is a cactus garden, this could be something of a disaster, because I really don't like cactus. I'm trying to keep calm by remembering David's story of *The Lost Horse*."

"The lost horse?"

"It's very Zen," Jenny commented after telling Barbara the cyclical tale of disasters and blessings. "David told it at the conclusion of Sandie's memorial service."

"But doesn't that imply that Sandie's death was possibly a blessing in disguise?" Barbara asked, clearly puzzled.

"No, it's more abstract than that," Jenny corrected. "David recently wrote a poem about the power that loss exerts, forcing us onto new pathways we wouldn't otherwise have explored. Sandie's loss forced David to take up a different life. The different life he chose led him to me. He channeled his grief and chose to move in a hopeful and positive direction."

"So," Barbara recapped, "it's more like, the wheel of life keeps turning? Losing Sandie didn't destroy the possibility that different blessings lay ahead?"

"Right. When I think about it, though, it seems to me that David is the source of his own blessings. He's kept the best of his memories but hasn't lost his appetite for the present and the future. Coming to California is a good example of that. He intertwines past and present into a seamless whole. Look at him laughing with Graham! They're teasing each other like college roommates again. He's happy. California has been a good choice."

"You've been a good choice too" Barbara whispered as they rejoined the men.

David rose as the two women entered the room. "David Perry, do you know how lucky you are?" Barbara asked him, her tone serious but her face in a smile.

David swirled the wine in his glass and held it to his nose to savor the bouquet. He then raised the glass slightly in Jenny's direction. "Oh, yes," he smiled. "I know."

Rainbow in the sky – *For Sandrine & Jennifer*

Signs converge, even if late, as do lives.
Living in California with my two wives
Seems highly improbable,
But is both fate and true.

Sandie,
Coming back without you, but not really,
Recalls our time together long ago
Among the light brown hills,
Waking up to the fog and the clouds,
Surprised by unexpected rain.
Just goes to show that even old,
We can still be young again.

Jenny,
The high flight of a passing bird
Draws my wandering mind
Toward images of our togetherness,
Spurred by memories,
Yet buoyed by lazy presence
As you willfully project our way
Into some planned
But unknown future space,
And weave a tale
To give two aging heroes place.

Actually, Jewel, now that
I'm here, I'm elated.
Thank you.
Love. David - 11/06

Printed in the United States
By Bookmasters